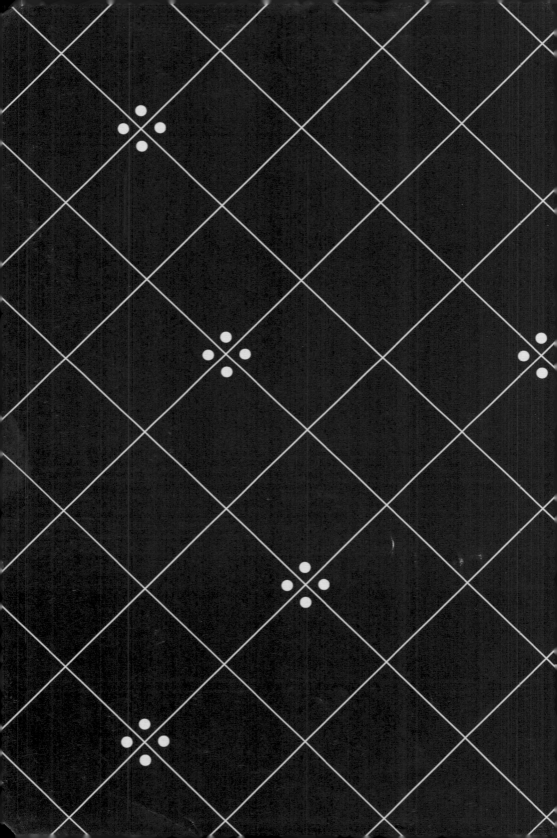

DRAGON KINGDOM
of Wrenly

GHOST ISLAND

By Jordan Quinn
Illustrated by Ornella Greco at Glass House Graphics

LITTLE SIMON

New York   London   Toronto   Sydney   New Delhi

LITTLE SIMON
An imprint of Simon & Schuster Children's Publishing Division
1230 Avenue of the Americas, New York, New York 10020
First Little Simon edition July 2021
Copyright © 2021 by Simon & Schuster, Inc.
All rights reserved, including the right of reproduction in whole or in part in any form.
LITTLE SIMON is a registered trademark of Simon & Schuster, Inc., and associated colophon is a trademark of Simon & Schuster, Inc. For information about special discounts for bulk purchases, please contact Simon & Schuster Special Sales at 1-866-506-1949 or business@simonandschuster.com.
The Simon & Schuster Speakers Bureau can bring authors to your live event. For more information or to book an event, contact the Simon & Schuster Speakers Bureau at 1-866-248-3049 or visit our website at www.simonspeakers.com.
Designed by Kayla Wasil
Text by Matthew J. Gilbert
GLASS HOUSE GRAPHICS Creative Services
Art and cover by ORNELLA GRECO
Colors by ORNELLA GRECO and GABRIELE CRACOLICI
Lettering by GIOVANNI SPATARO/Grafimated Cartoon
Supervision by SALVATORE DI MARCO/Grafimated Cartoon
Manufactured in China 0421 SCP
2 4 6 8 10 9 7 5 3 1
Library of Congress Cataloging-in-Publication Data
Names: Quinn, Jordan, author. | Glass House Graphics, illustrator.
Title: Ghost island / by Jordan Quinn ; illustrated by Glass House Graphics.
Description: First Little Simon edition. | New York : Little Simon, 2021 | Series: Dragon kingdom of Wrenly; 4
| Audience: Ages 5–9 | Audience: Grades K–1 | Summary: "Fresh off the excitement of the Night Hunt, Ruskin, Cinder, Groth, and Roke set out for a camping trip on Ghost Island, which, according to Groth, is definitely not haunted despite its name"–Provided by publisher.
Identifiers: LCCN 2020027675 (print) | LCCN 2020027676 (ebook) | ISBN 9781534478664 (paperback) |
ISBN 9781534478671 (hardcover) | ISBN 9781534478688 (ebook)
Subjects: LCSH: Graphic novels. | Graphic novels. | CYAC: Dragons–Fiction. | Fantasy.
Classification: LCC PZ7.7.Q55 Gh 2021 (print) | LCC PZ7.7.Q55 (ebook) | DDC 741.5/973–dc23
LC record available at https://lccn.loc.gov/2020027675
LC ebook record available at https://lccn.loc.gov/2020027676

Contents

Chapter 1

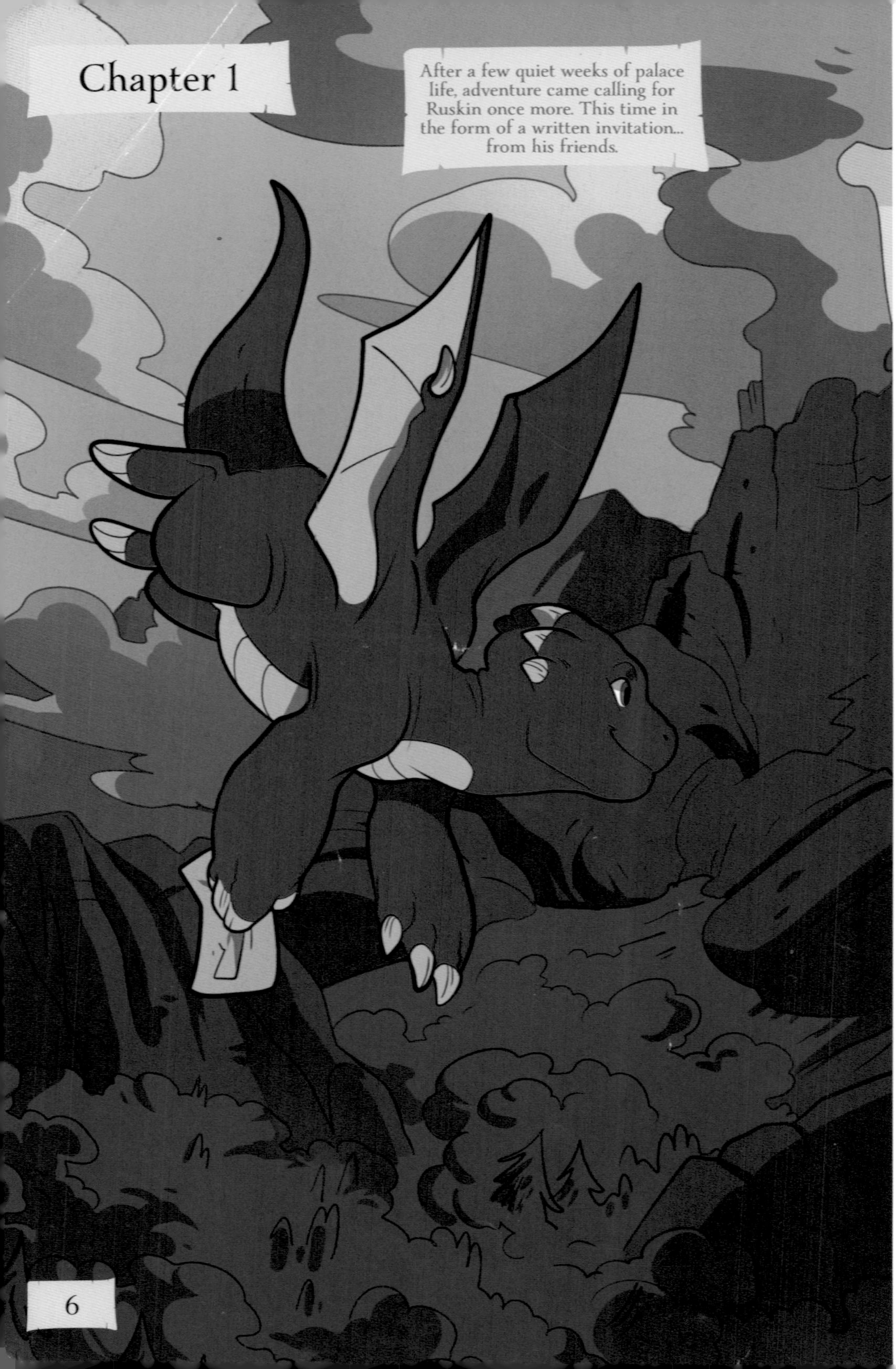
After a few quiet weeks of palace life, adventure came calling for Ruskin once more. This time in the form of a written invitation... from his friends.

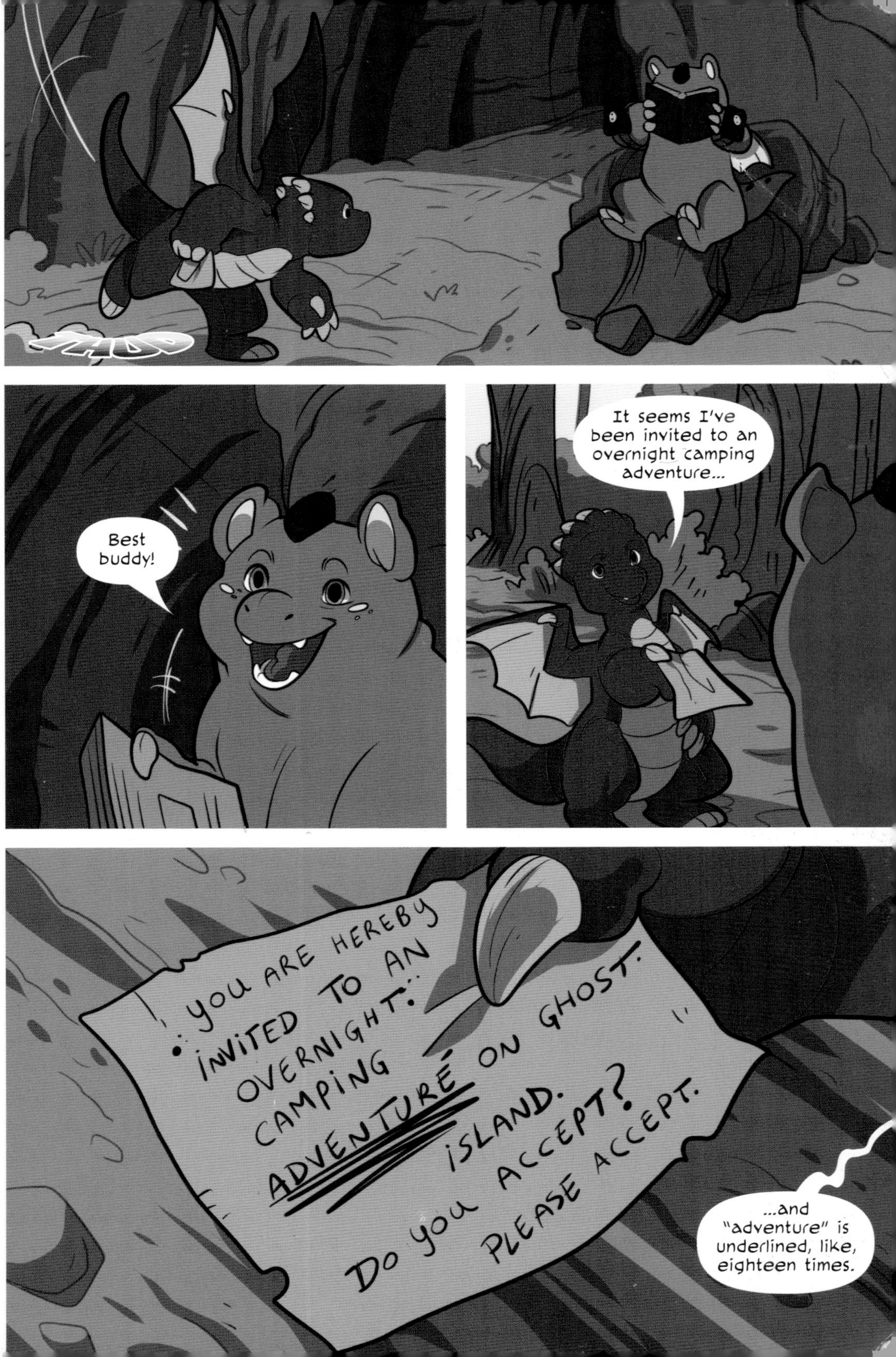
THUD
Best buddy!
It seems I've been invited to an overnight camping adventure...
YOU ARE HEREBY INVITED TO AN OVERNIGHT CAMPING ADVENTURE ON GHOST ISLAND.
DO YOU ACCEPT?
PLEASE ACCEPT.
...and "adventure" is underlined, like, eighteen times.

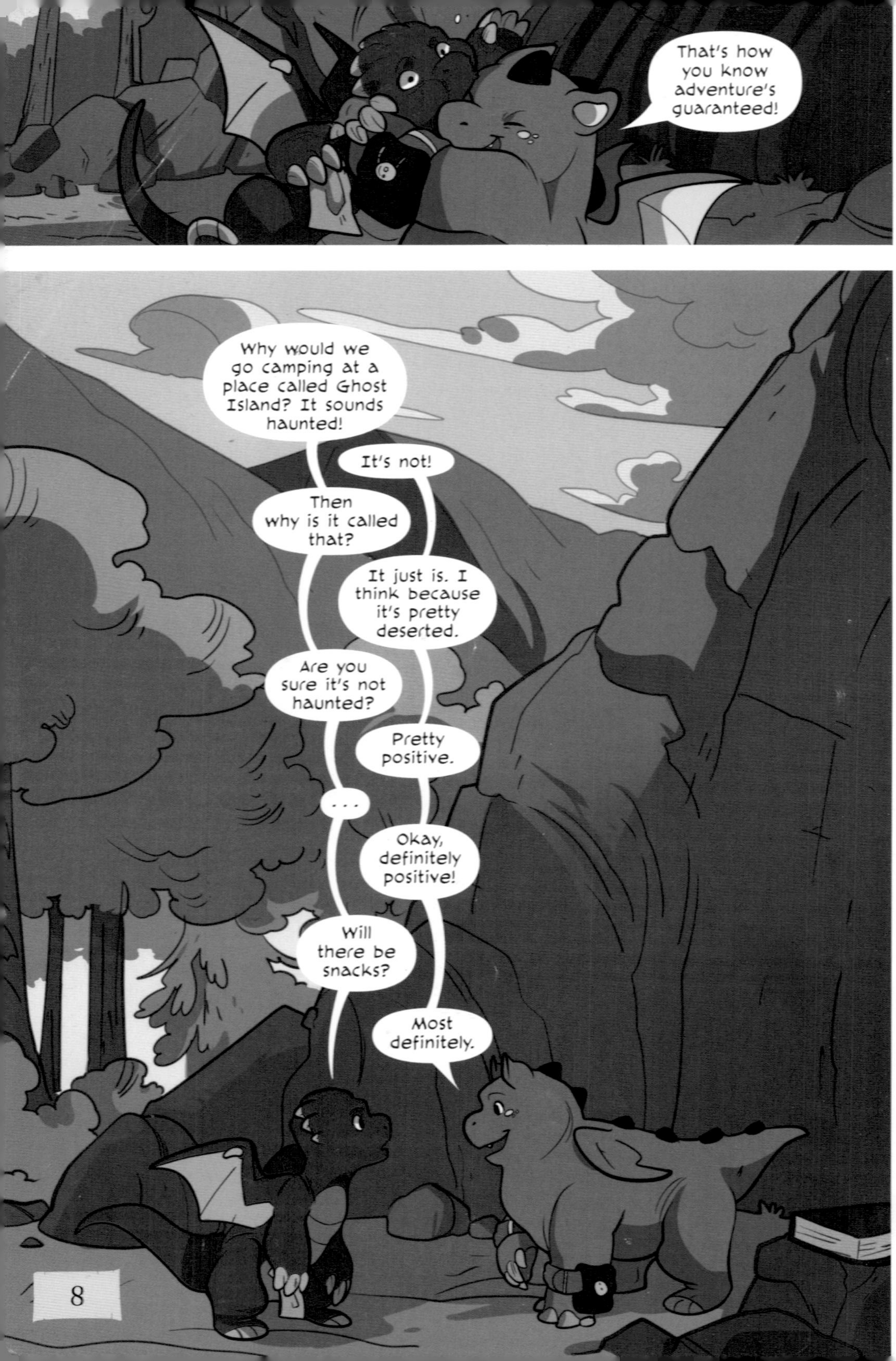
That's how you know adventure's guaranteed!
Why would we go camping at a place called Ghost Island? It sounds haunted!
It's not!
Then why is it called that?
It just is. I think because it's pretty deserted.
Are you sure it's not haunted?
Pretty positive.
. . .
Okay, definitely positive!
Will there be snacks?
Most definitely.

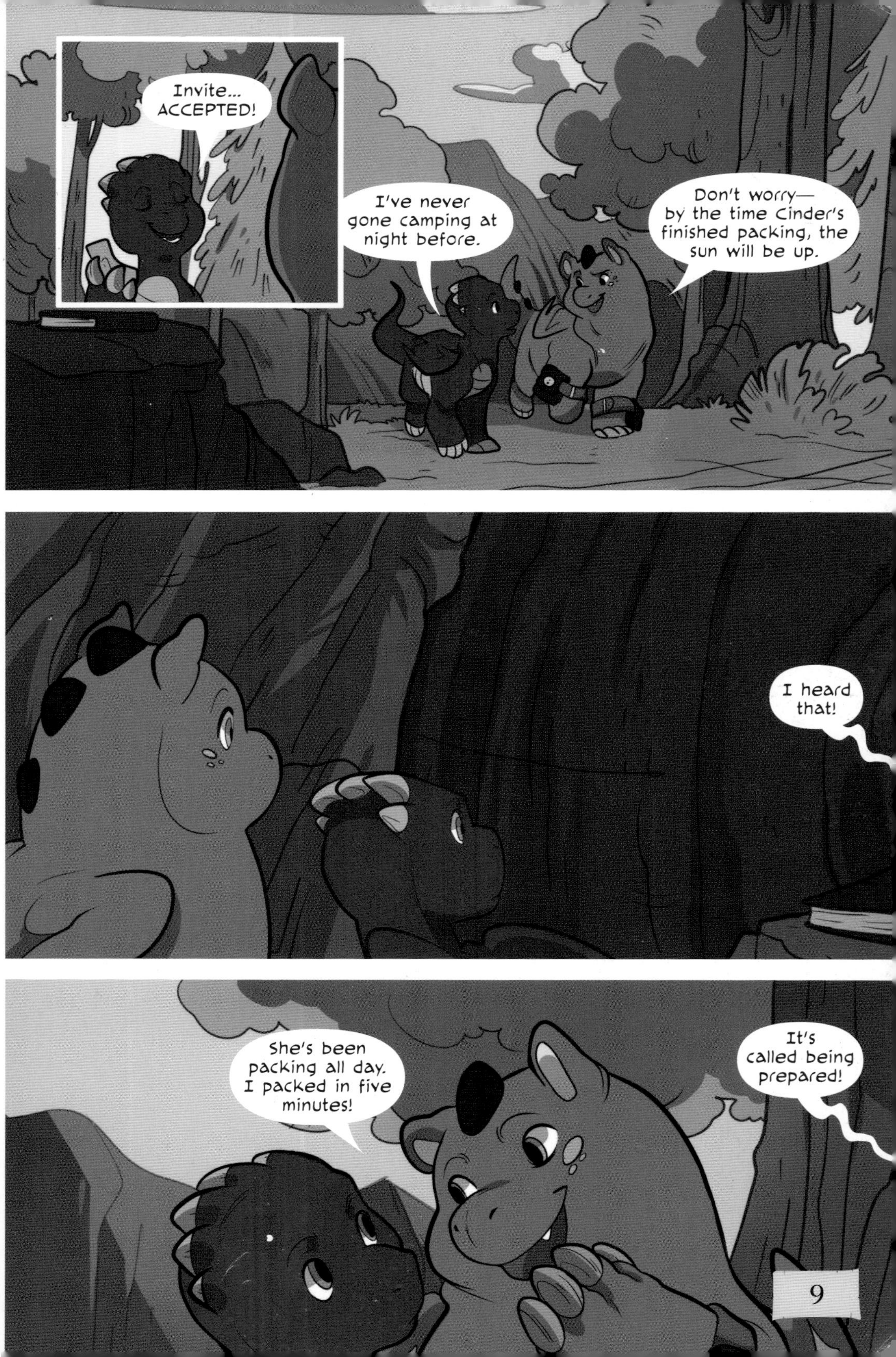
Invite... ACCEPTED!
I've never gone camping at night before.
Don't worry— by the time Cinder's finished packing, the sun will be up.
I heard that!
She's been packing all day. I packed in five minutes!
It's called being prepared!

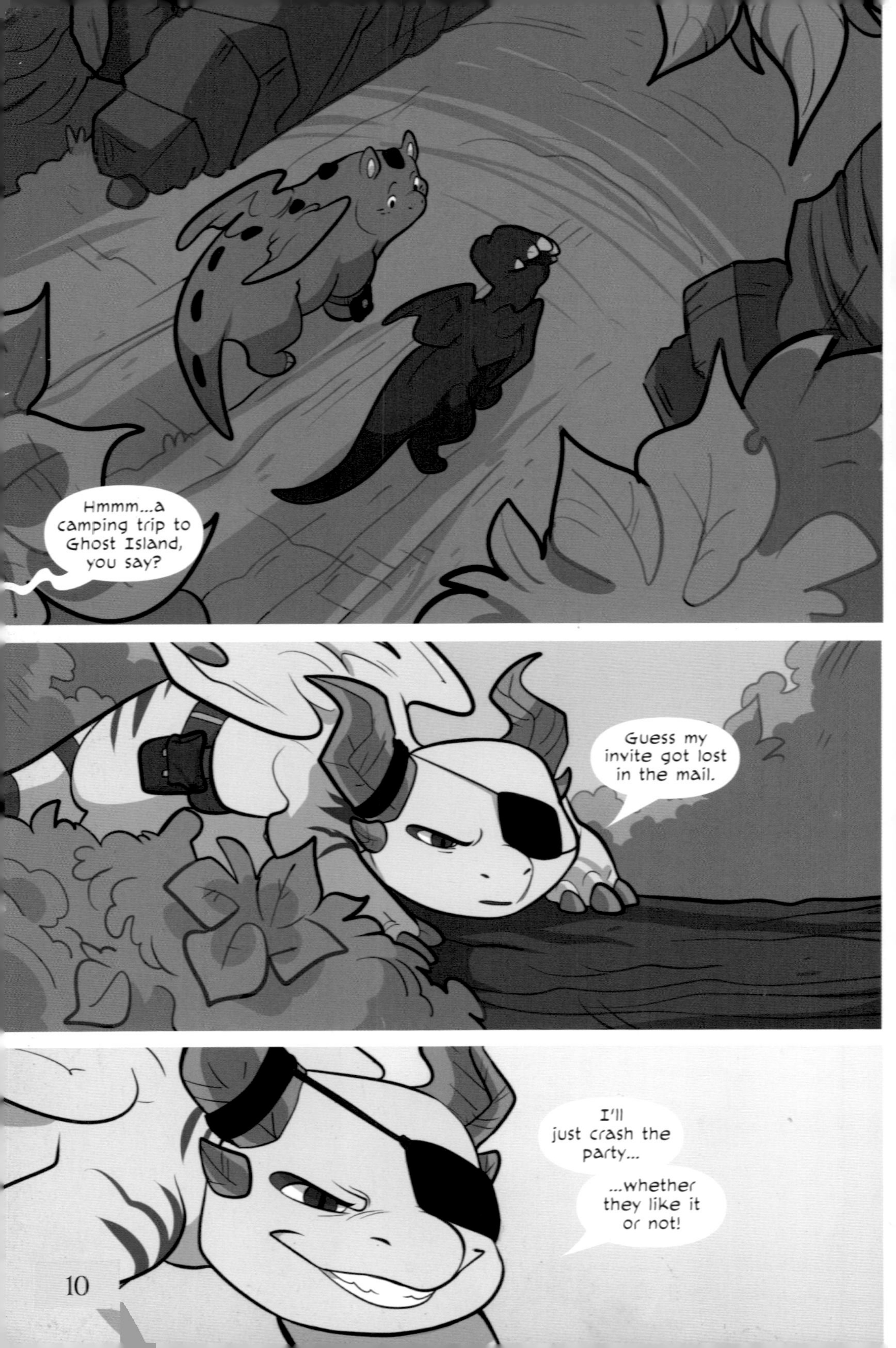
Hmmm...a camping trip to Ghost Island, you say?
Guess my invite got lost in the mail.
I'll just crash the party...
...whether they like it or not!

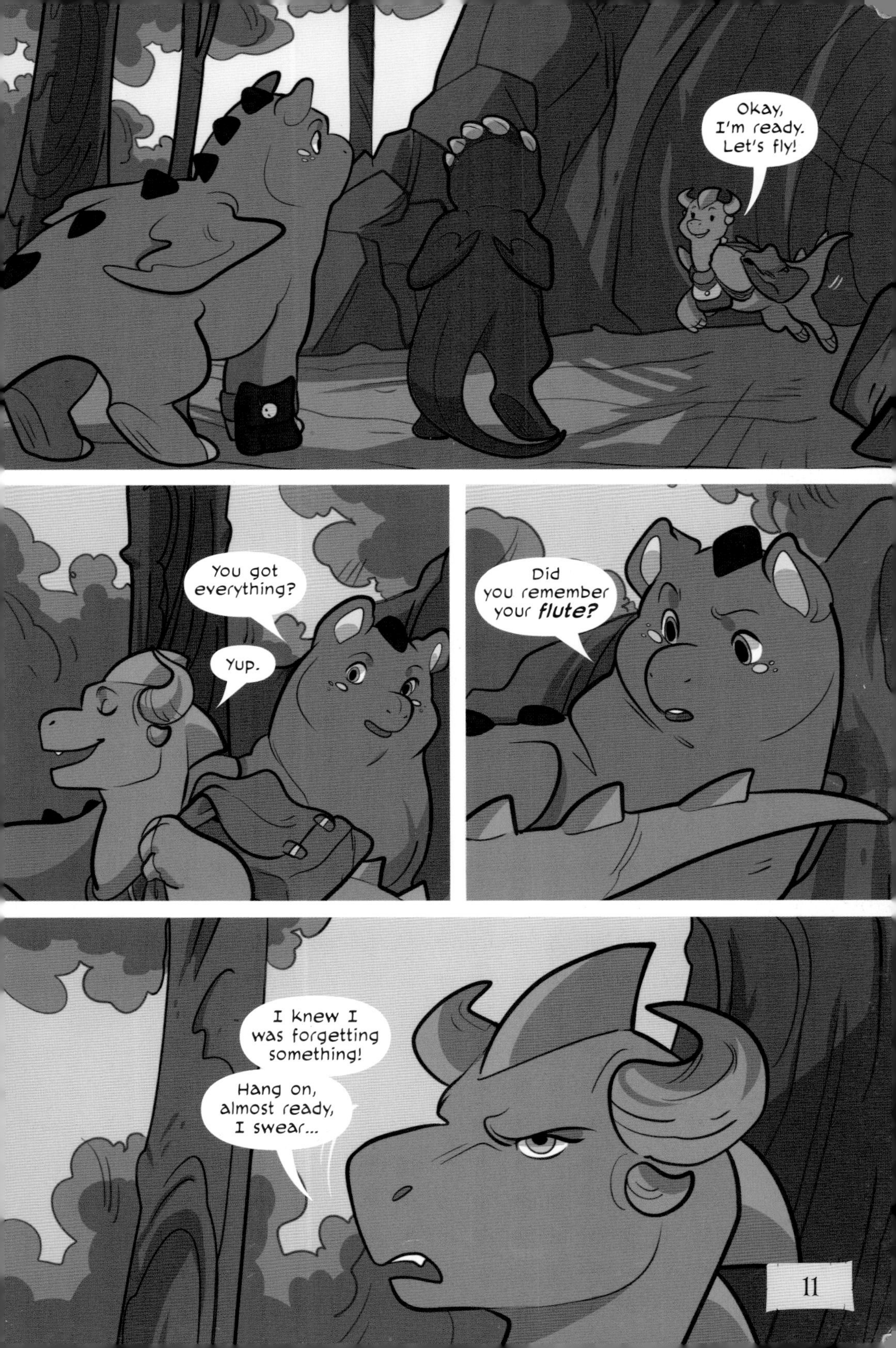
Okay, I'm ready. Let's fly!
You got everything?
Yup.
Did you remember your **flute?**
I knew I was forgetting something!
Hang on, almost ready, I swear...

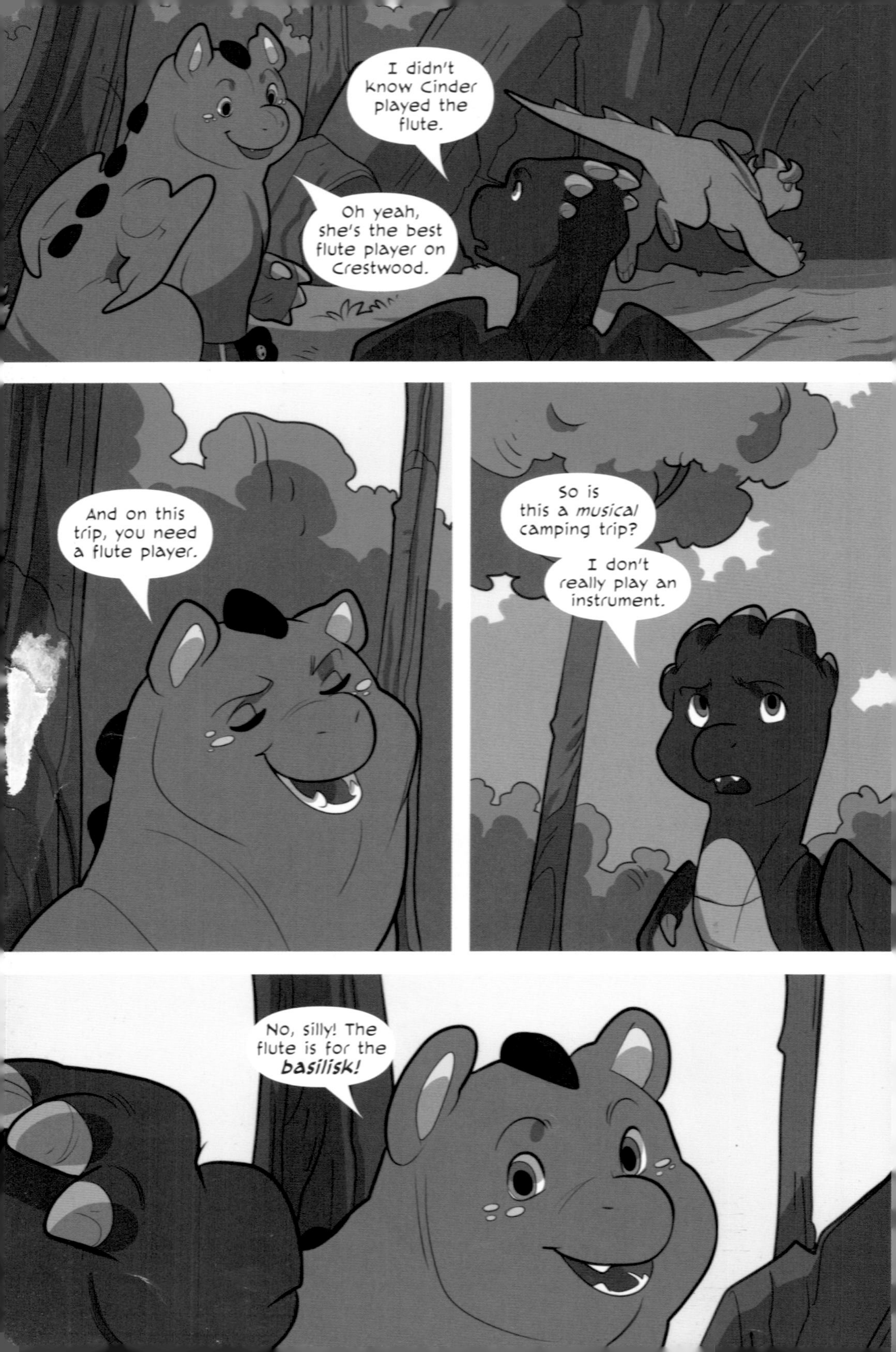
I didn't know Cinder played the flute.
Oh yeah, she's the best flute player on Crestwood.
And on this trip, you need a flute player.
So is this a *musical* camping trip?
I don't really play an instrument.
No, silly! The flute is for the ***basilisk!***

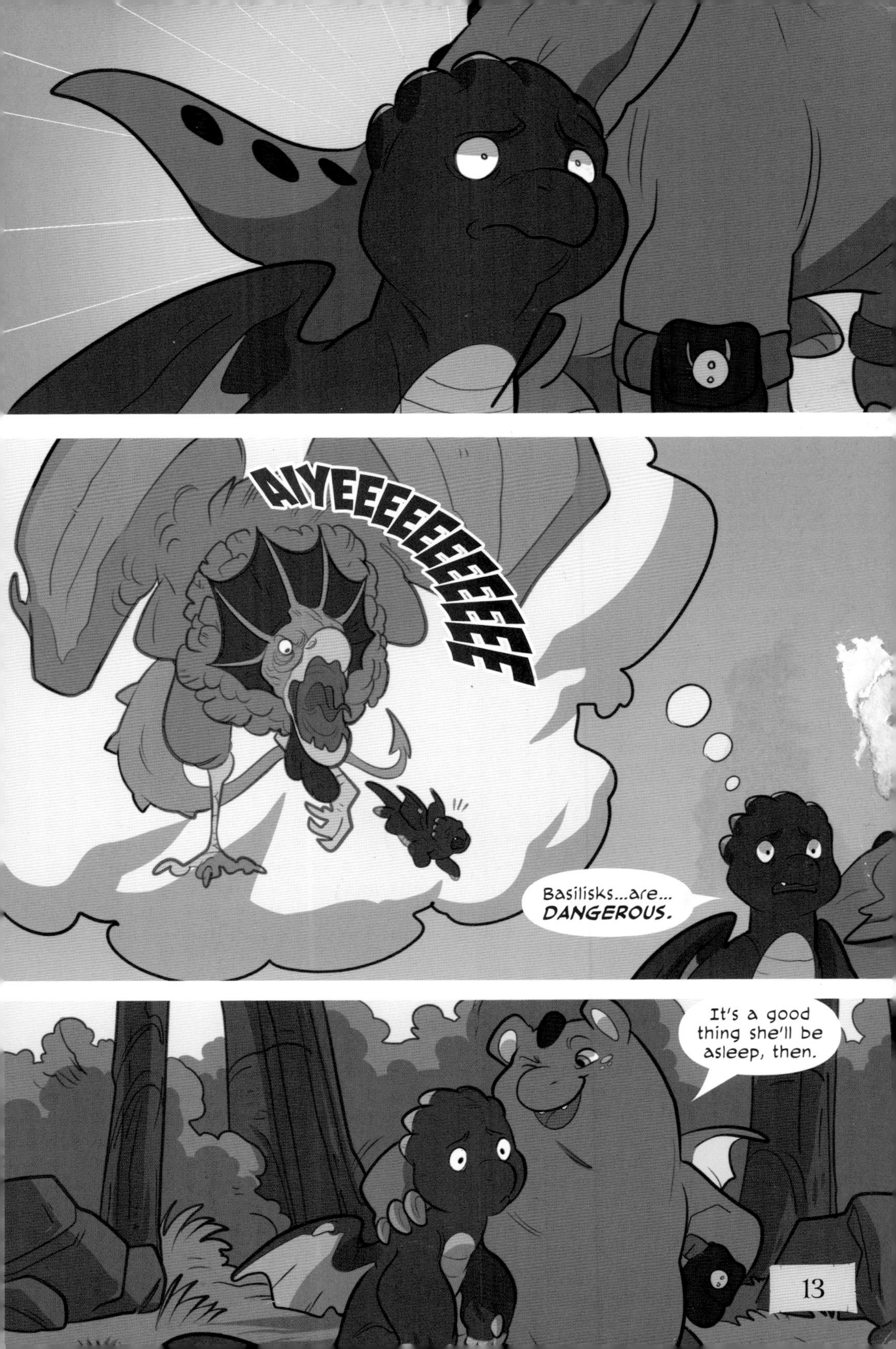

AIYEEEEEEEEEEEEEE
Basilisks...are... DANGEROUS.
It's a good thing she'll be asleep, then.

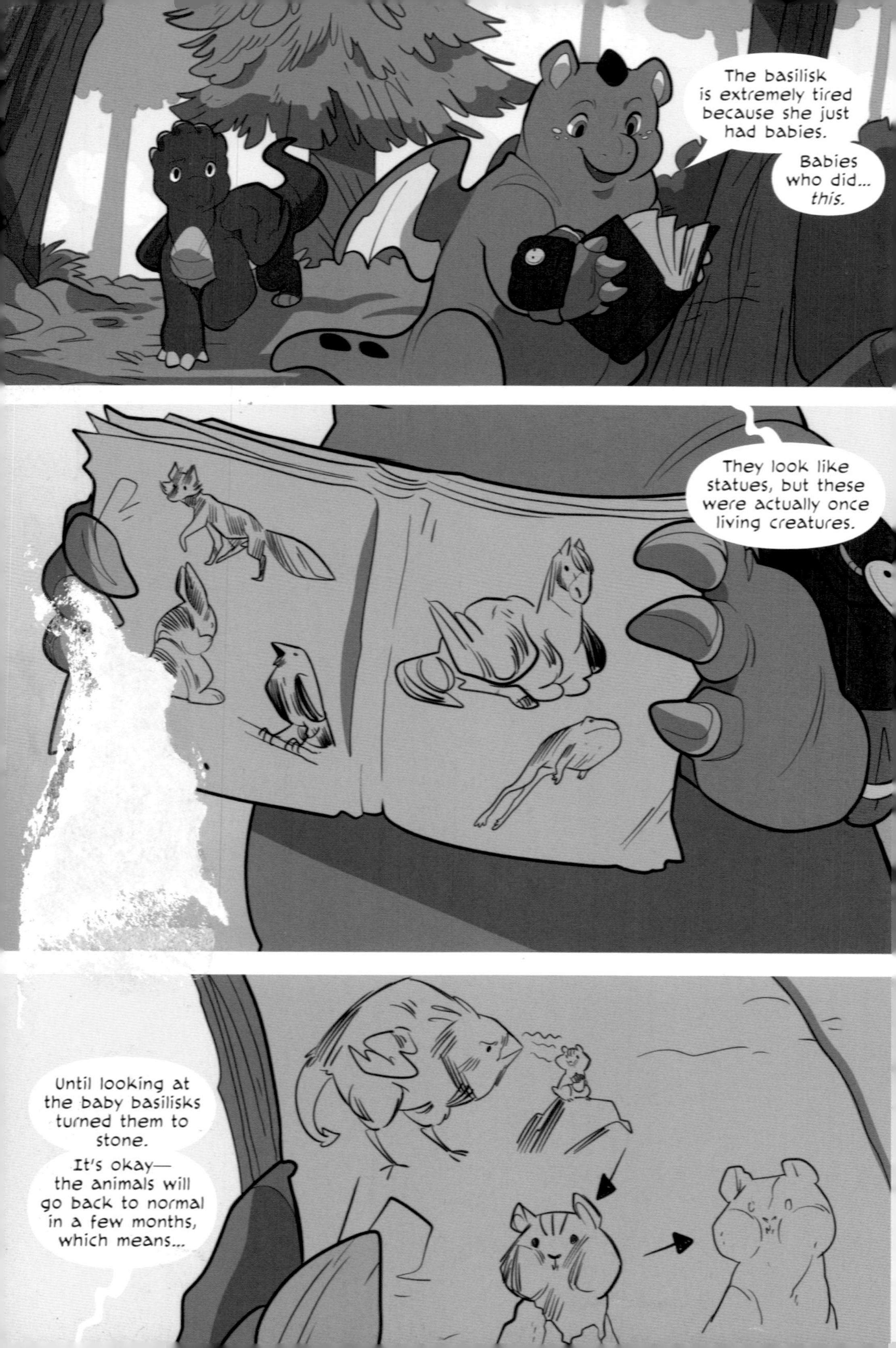

The basilisk is extremely tired because she just had babies.
Babies who did... *this.*
They look like statues, but these were actually once living creatures.
Until looking at the baby basilisks turned them to stone.
It's okay— the animals will go back to normal in a few months, which means...

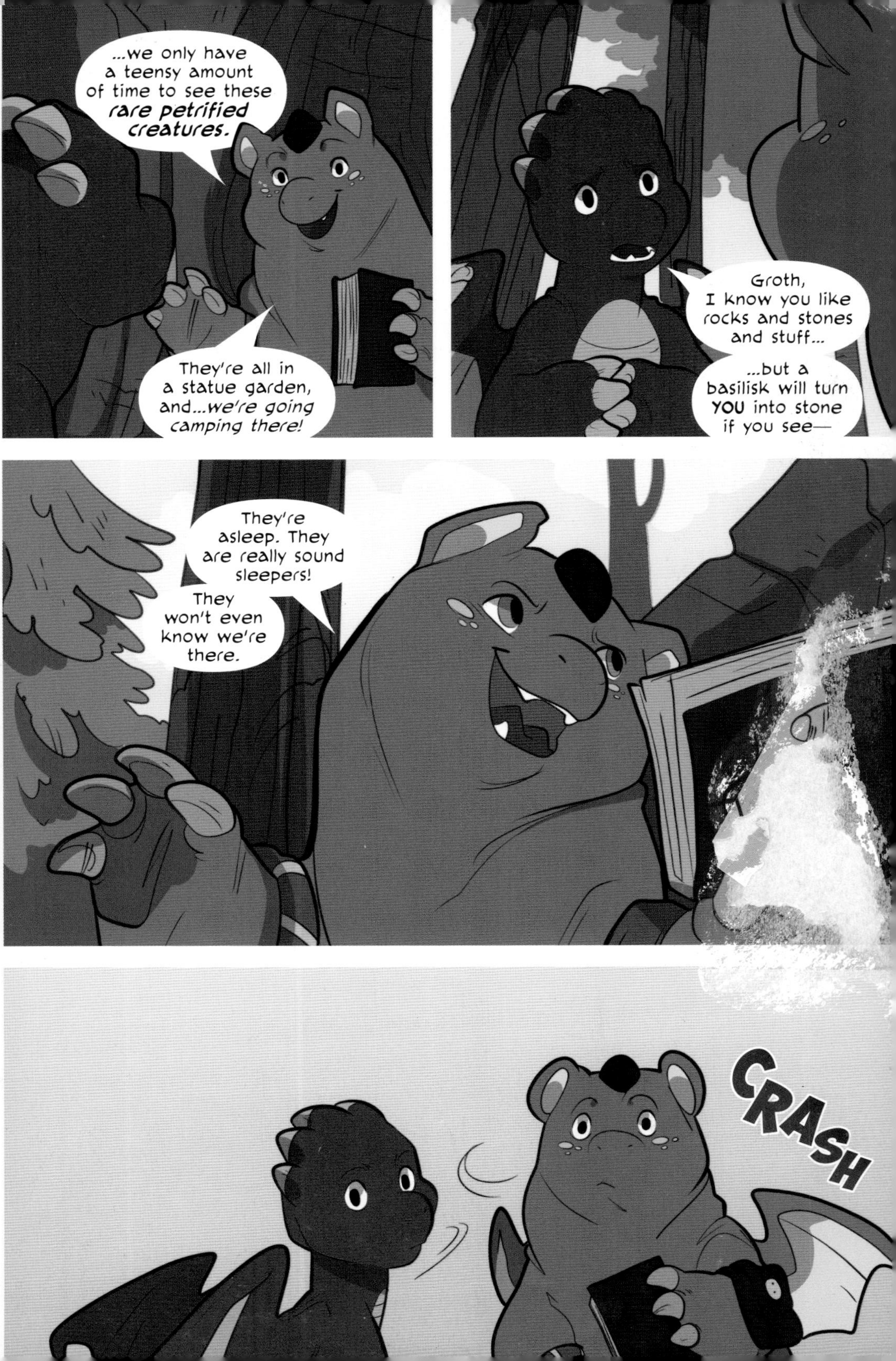

...we only have a teensy amount of time to see these *rare petrified creatures.*
They're all in a statue garden, and...*we're going camping there!*
Groth, I know you like rocks and stones and stuff...
...but a basilisk will turn **YOU** into stone if you see—
They're asleep. They are really sound sleepers!
They won't even know we're there.
CRASH

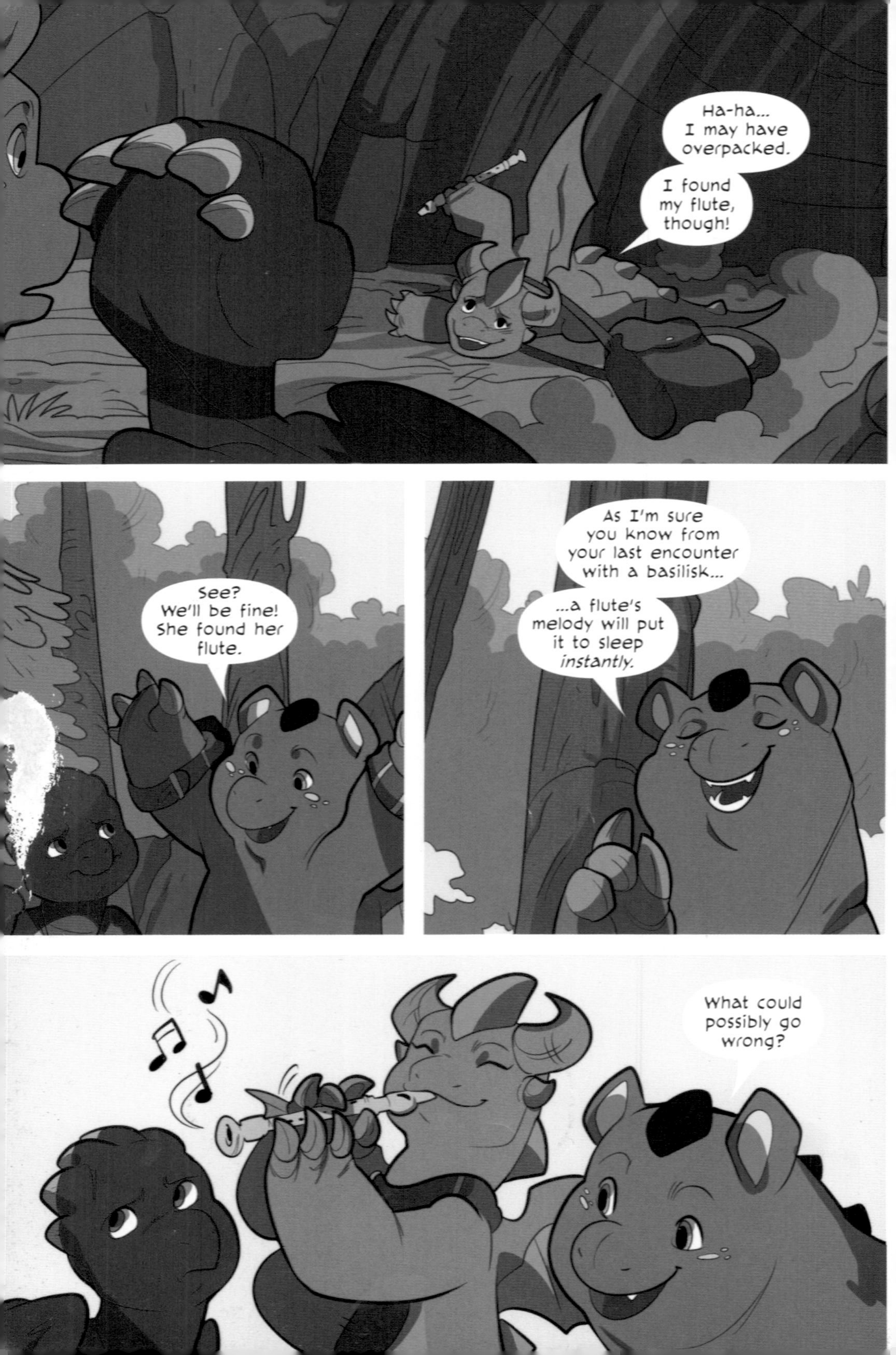
Ha-ha... I may have overpacked.
I found my flute, though!
See? We'll be fine! She found her flute.
As I'm sure you know from your last encounter with a basilisk...
...a flute's melody will put it to sleep *instantly.*
What could possibly go wrong?

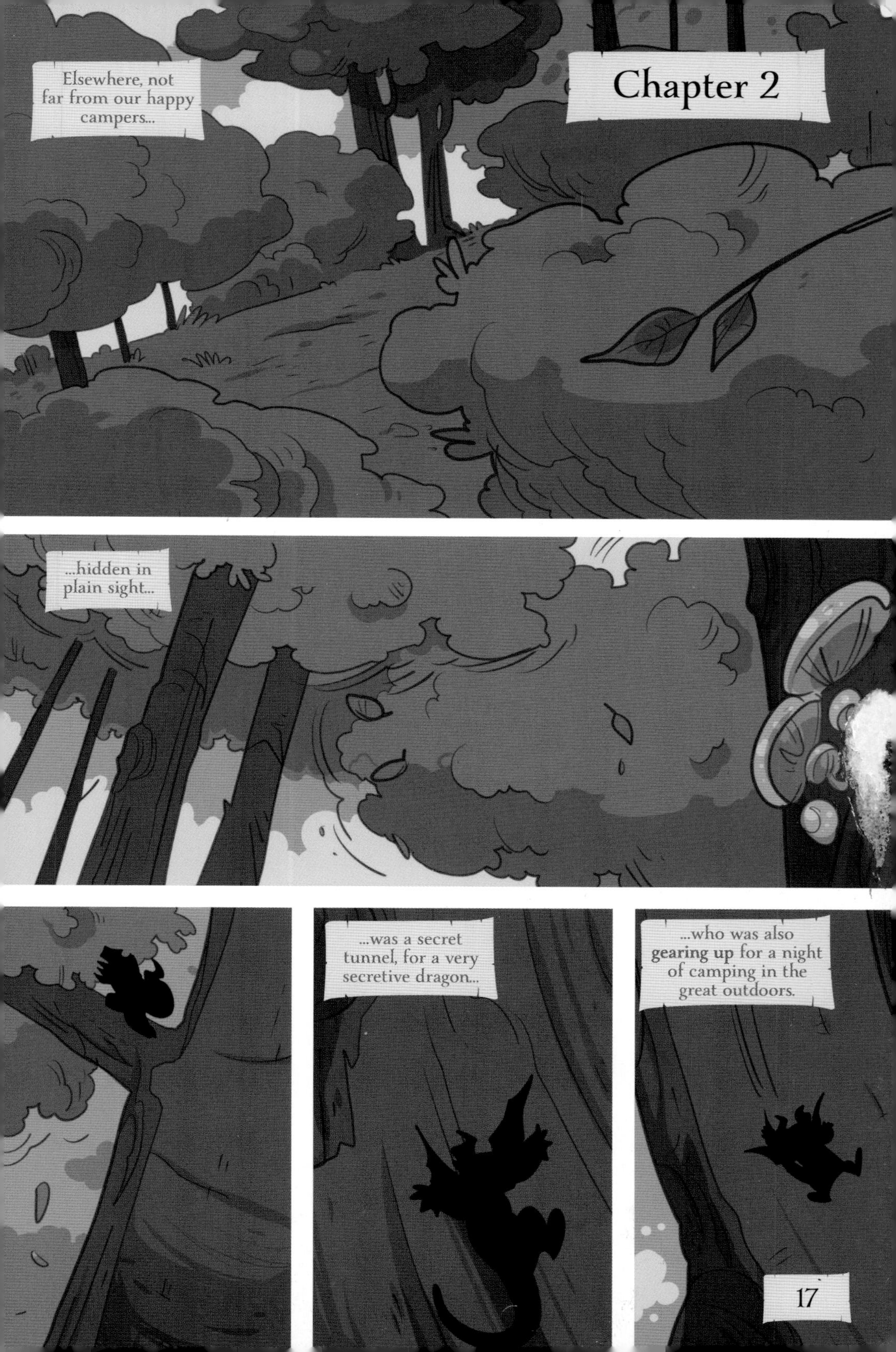
Chapter 2
Elsewhere, not far from our happy campers...
...hidden in plain sight...
...was a secret tunnel, for a very secretive dragon...
...who was also **gearing up** for a night of camping in the great outdoors.

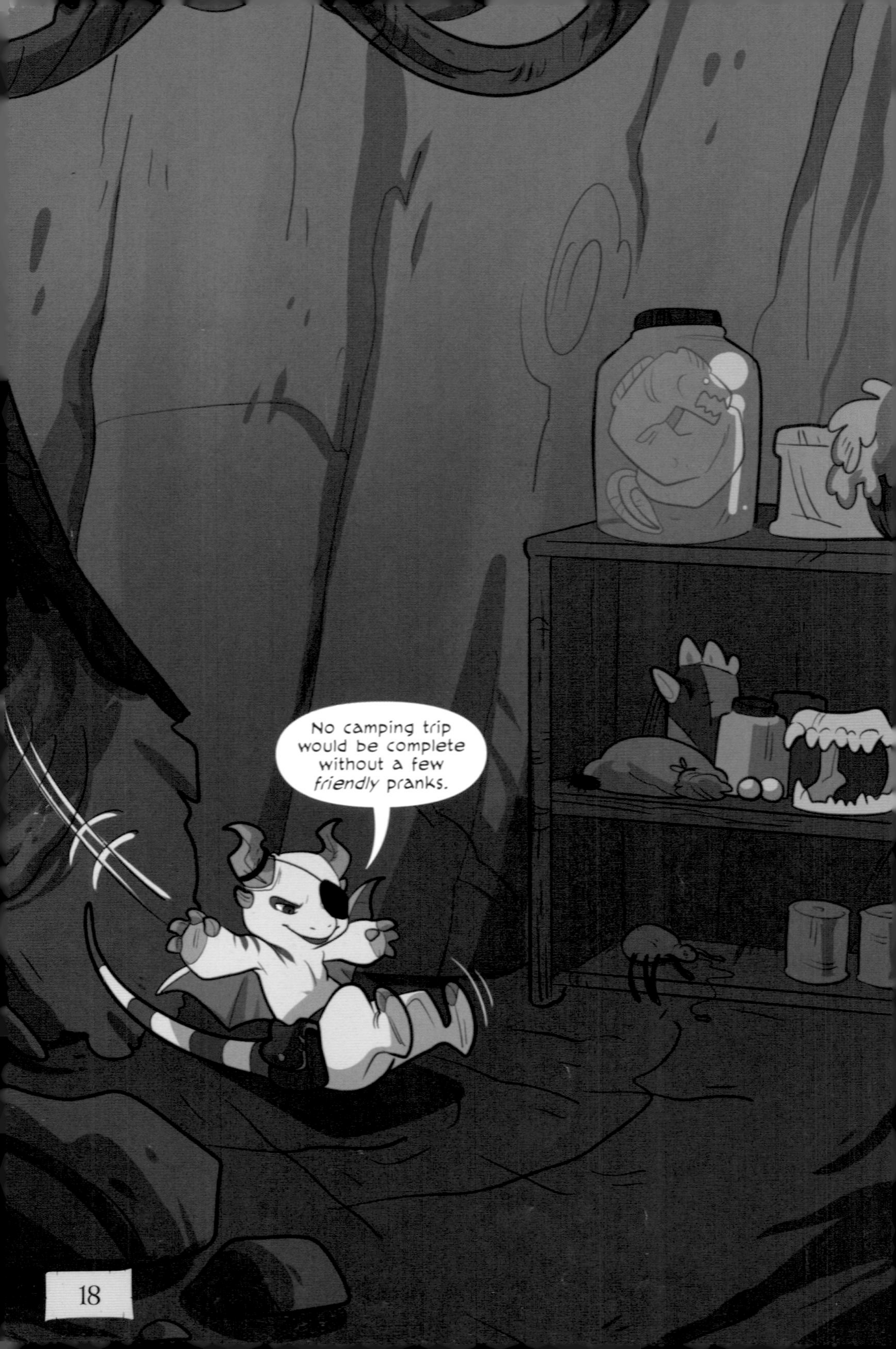
No camping trip would be complete without a few *friendly* pranks.

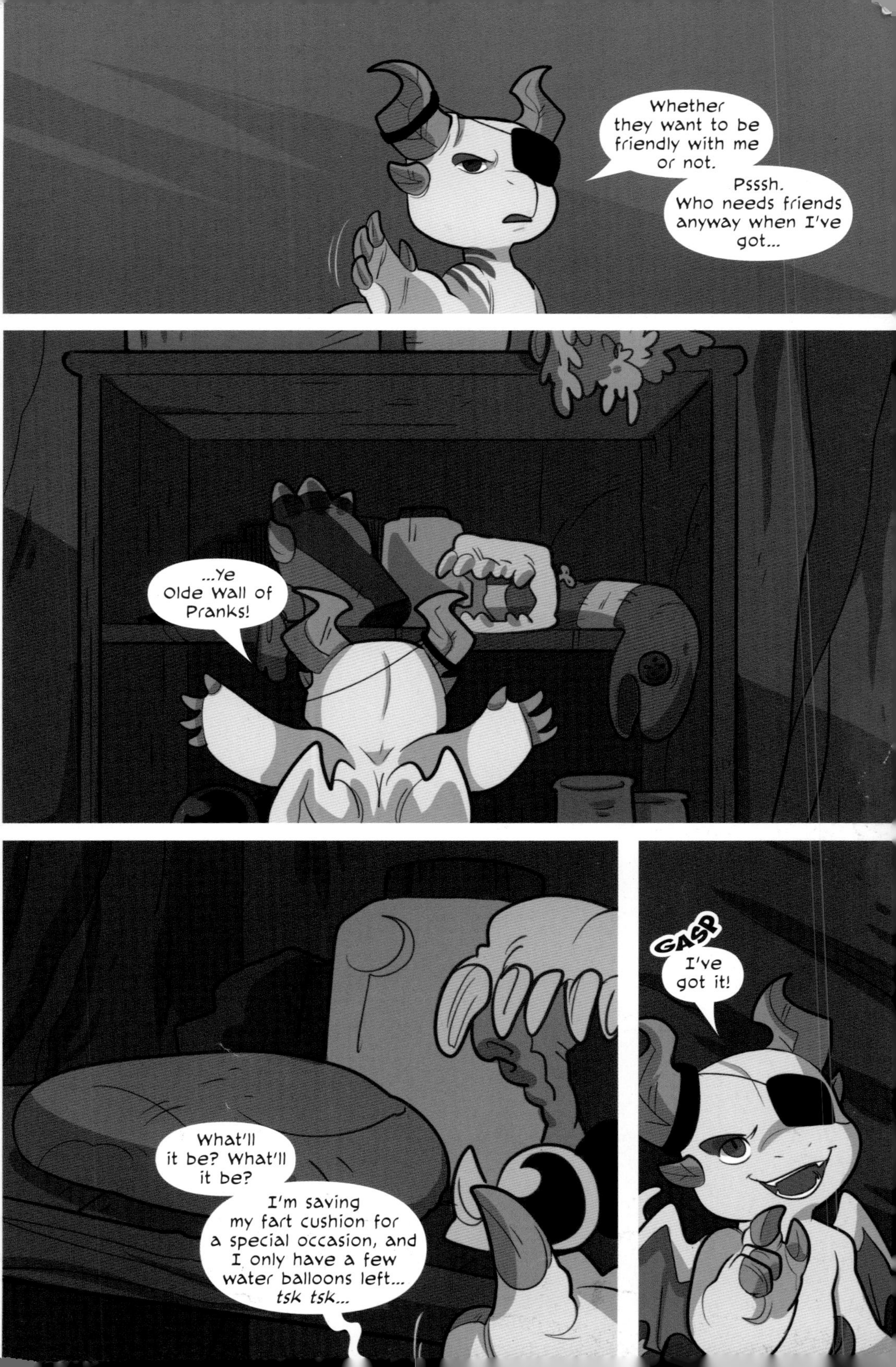
Whether they want to be friendly with me or not.
Psssh. Who needs friends anyway when I've got...
...Ye Olde Wall of Pranks!
What'll it be? What'll it be?
I'm saving my fart cushion for a special occasion, and I only have a few water balloons left... *tsk tsk*...
GASP
I've got it!

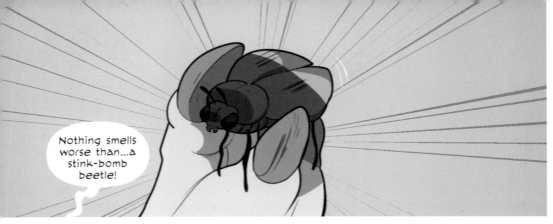

Nothing smells worse than...a stink-bomb beetle!

SNIFF
SNIFF
SNIFF

Still has that "just died" smell.

They're EXACTLY what I need!

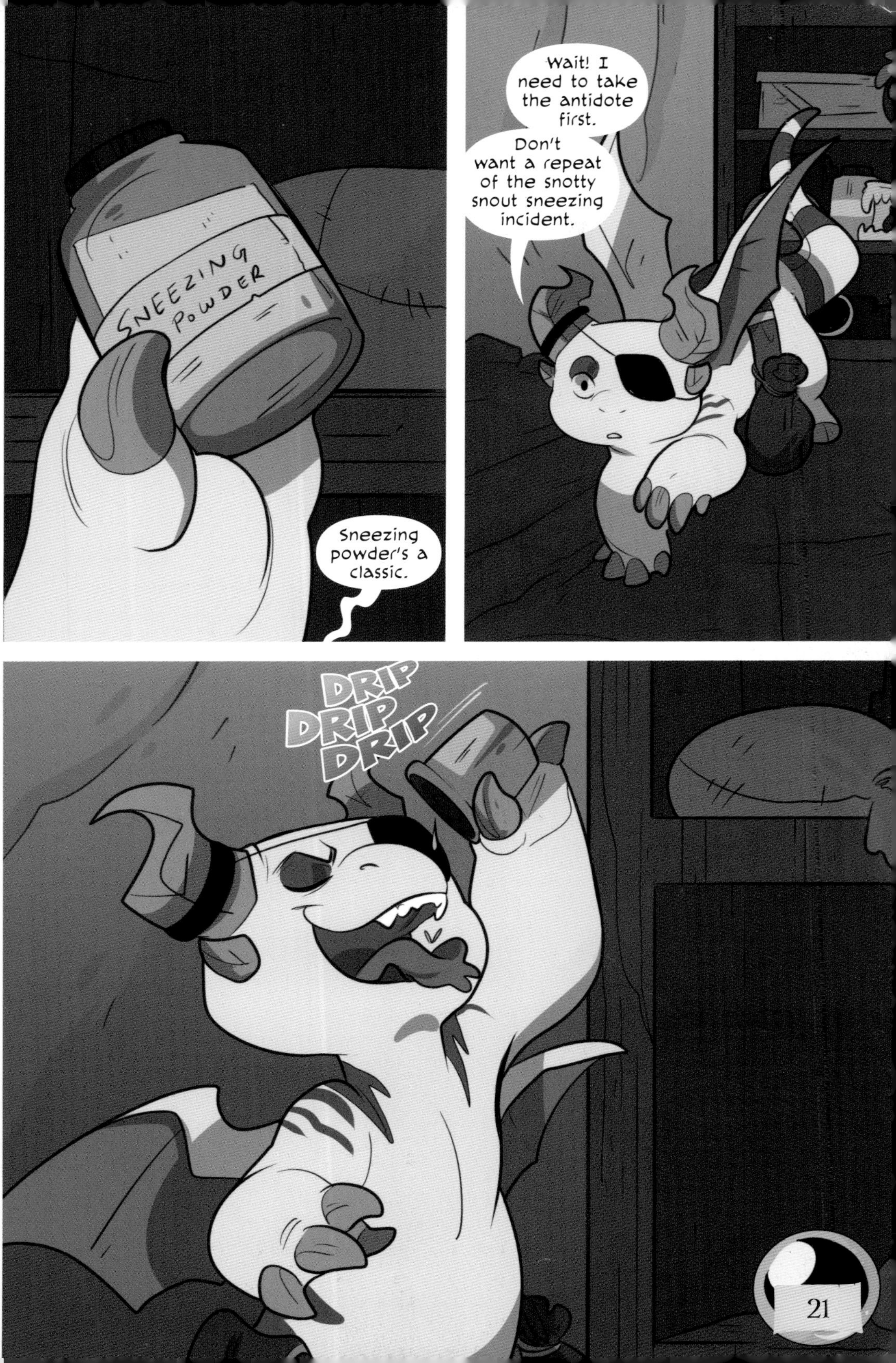
SNEEZING POWDER
Sneezing powder's a classic.
Wait! I need to take the antidote first.
Don't want a repeat of the snotty snout sneezing incident.
DRIP DRIP DRIP

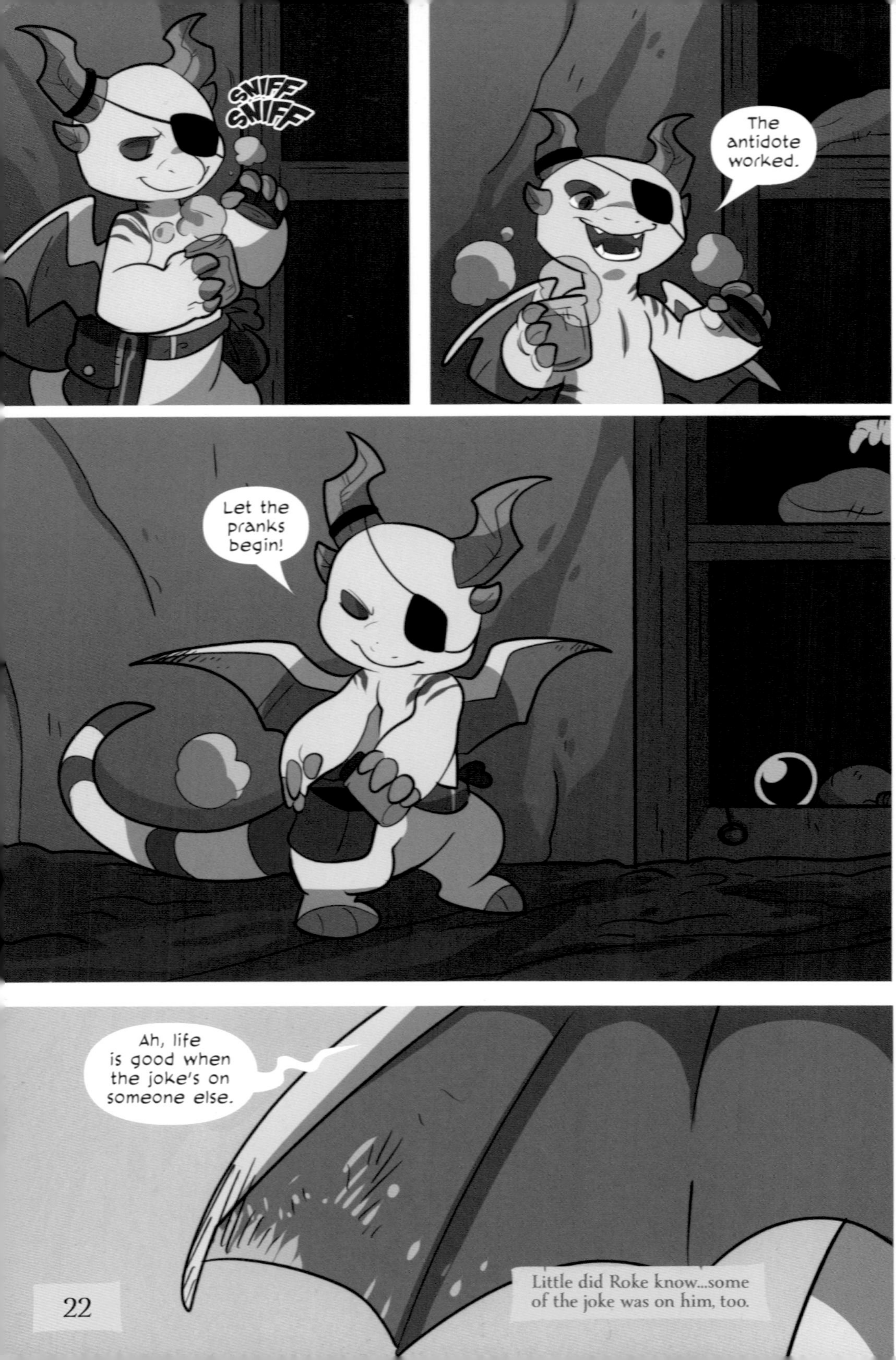
SNIFF SNIFF
The antidote worked.
Let the pranks begin!
Ah, life is good when the joke's on someone else.
Little did Roke know...some of the joke was on him, too.

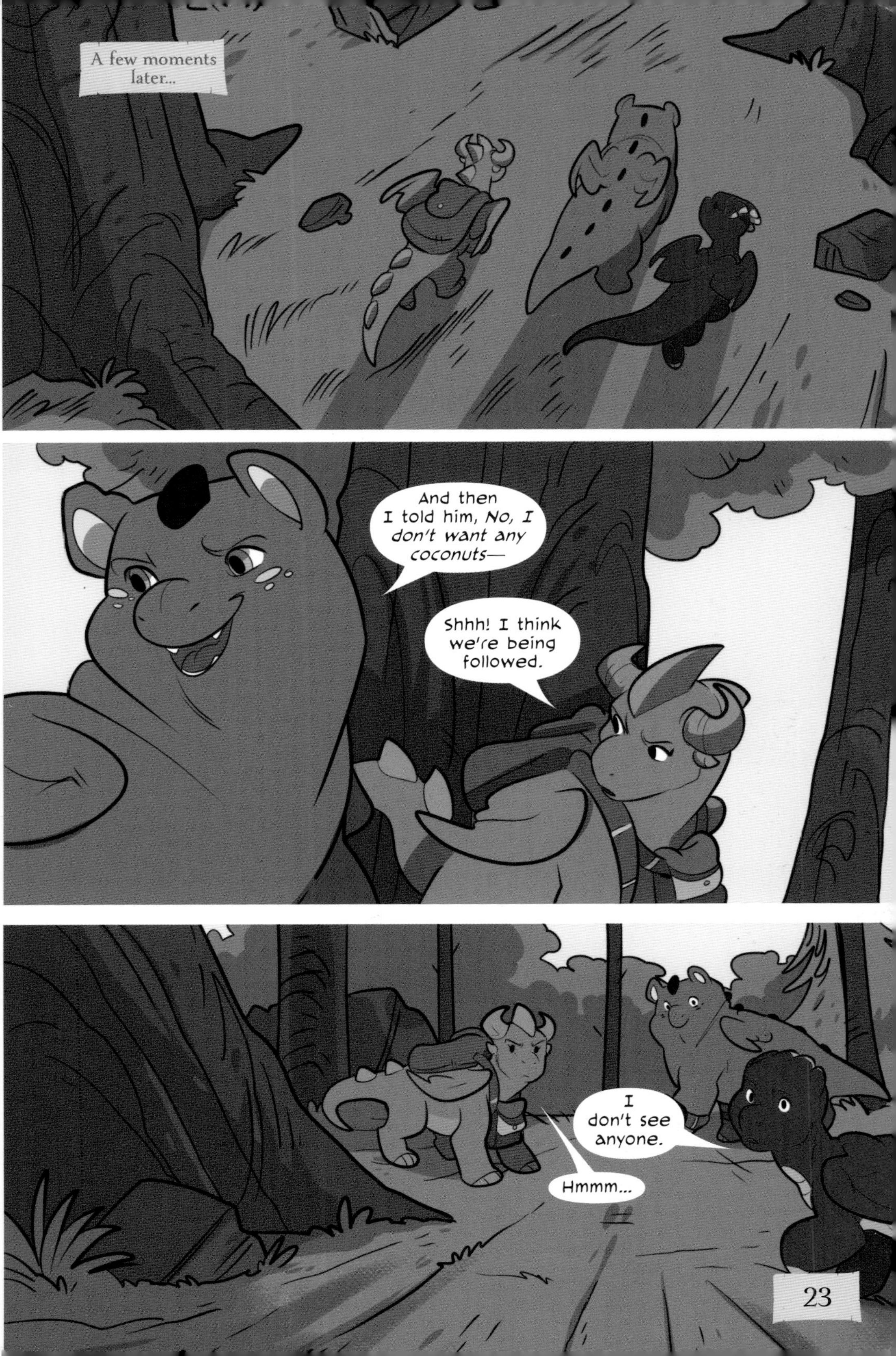

A few moments later...
And then I told him, *No, I don't want any coconuts*—
Shhh! I think we're being followed.
I don't see anyone.
Hmmm...

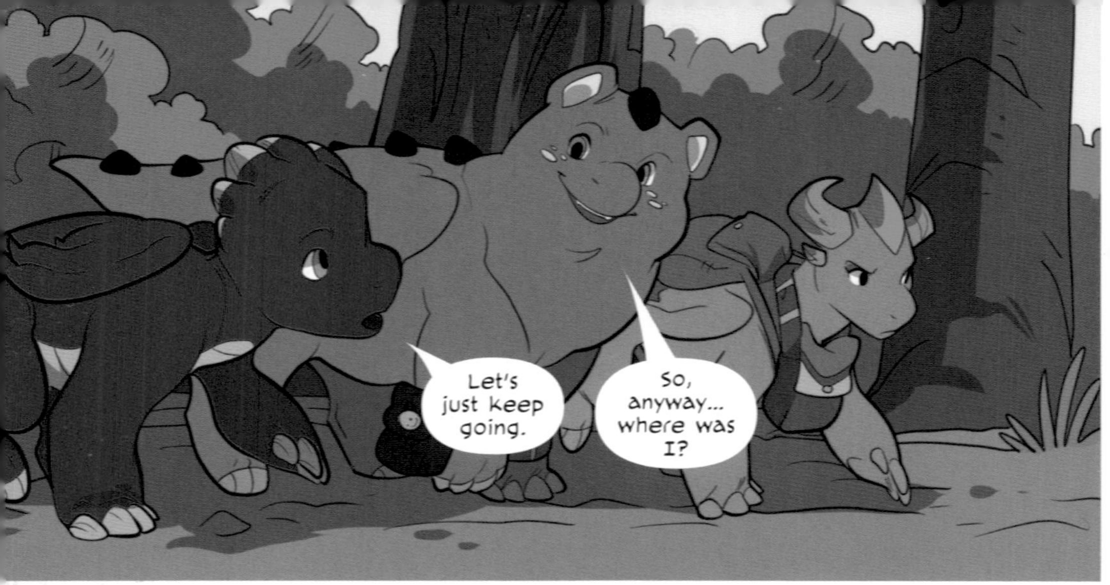
Let's just keep going.
So, anyway... where was I?

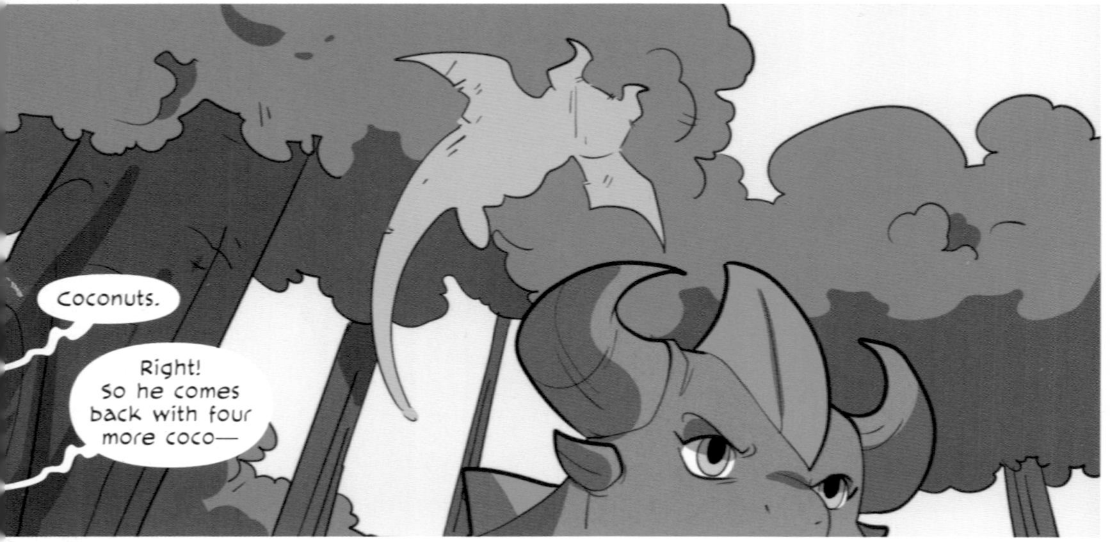
Coconuts.
Right! So he comes back with four more coco—

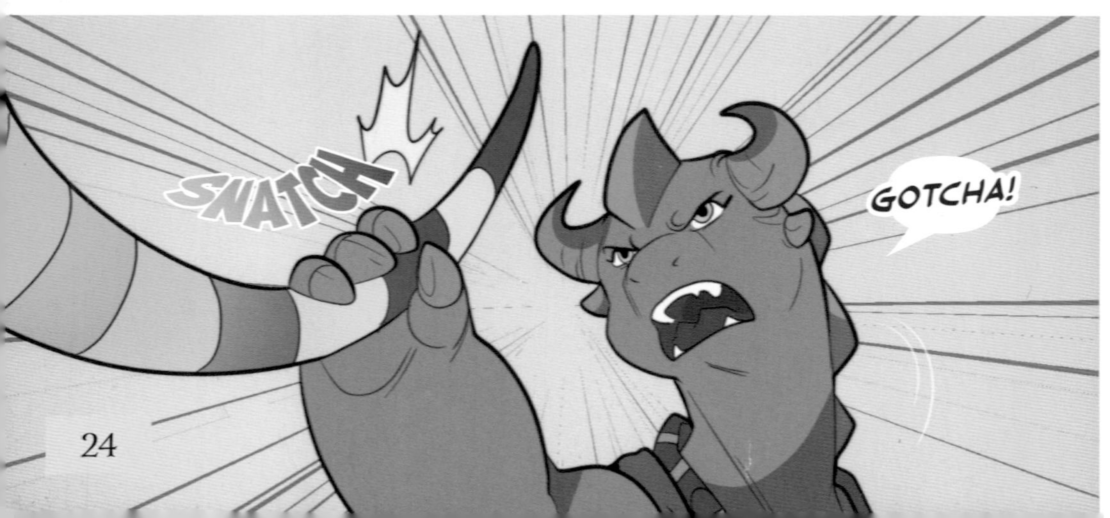
SNATCH
GOTCHA!

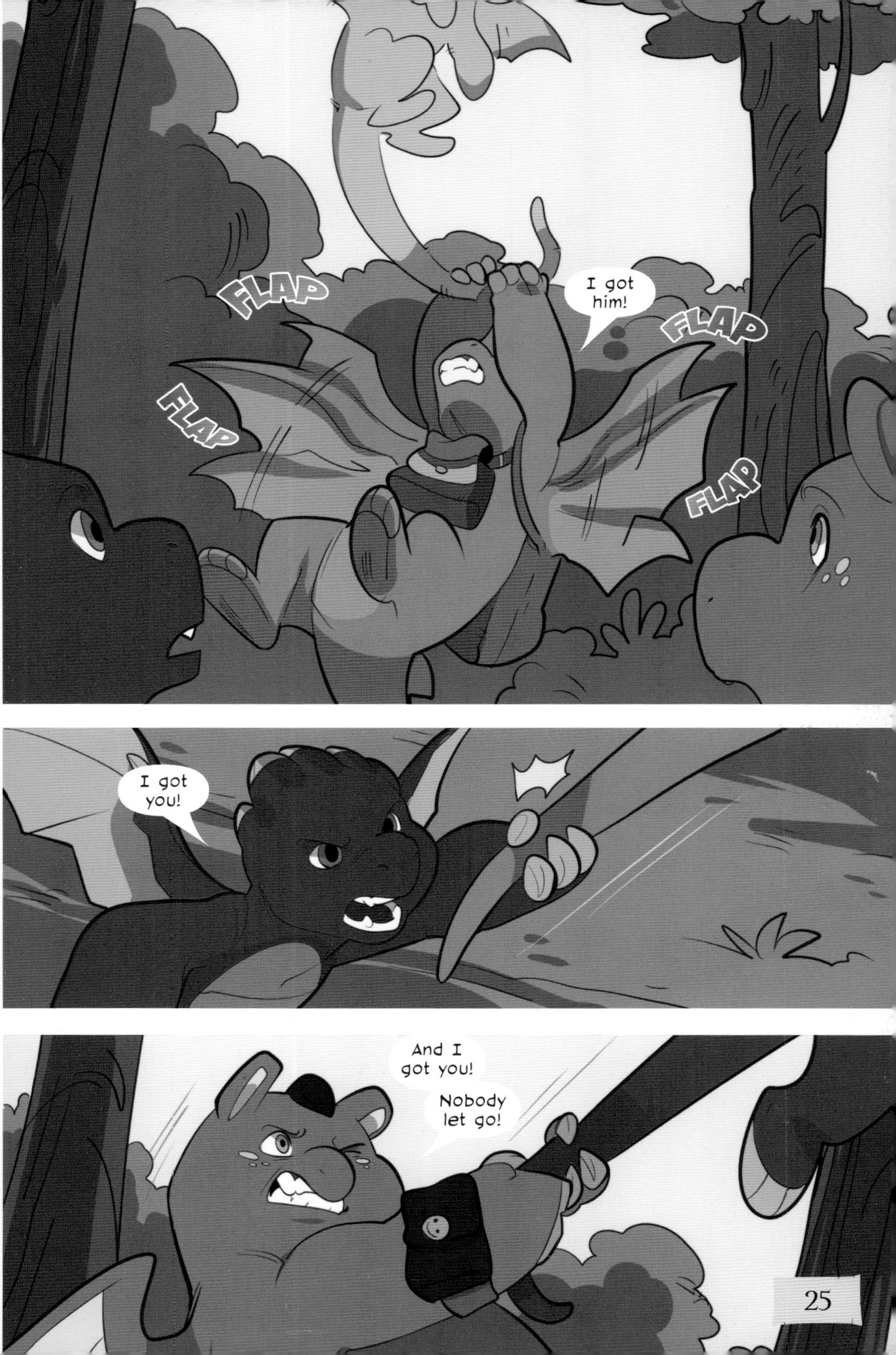
FLAP
FLAP
I got him!
FLAP
FLAP
I got you!
And I got you!
Nobody let go!

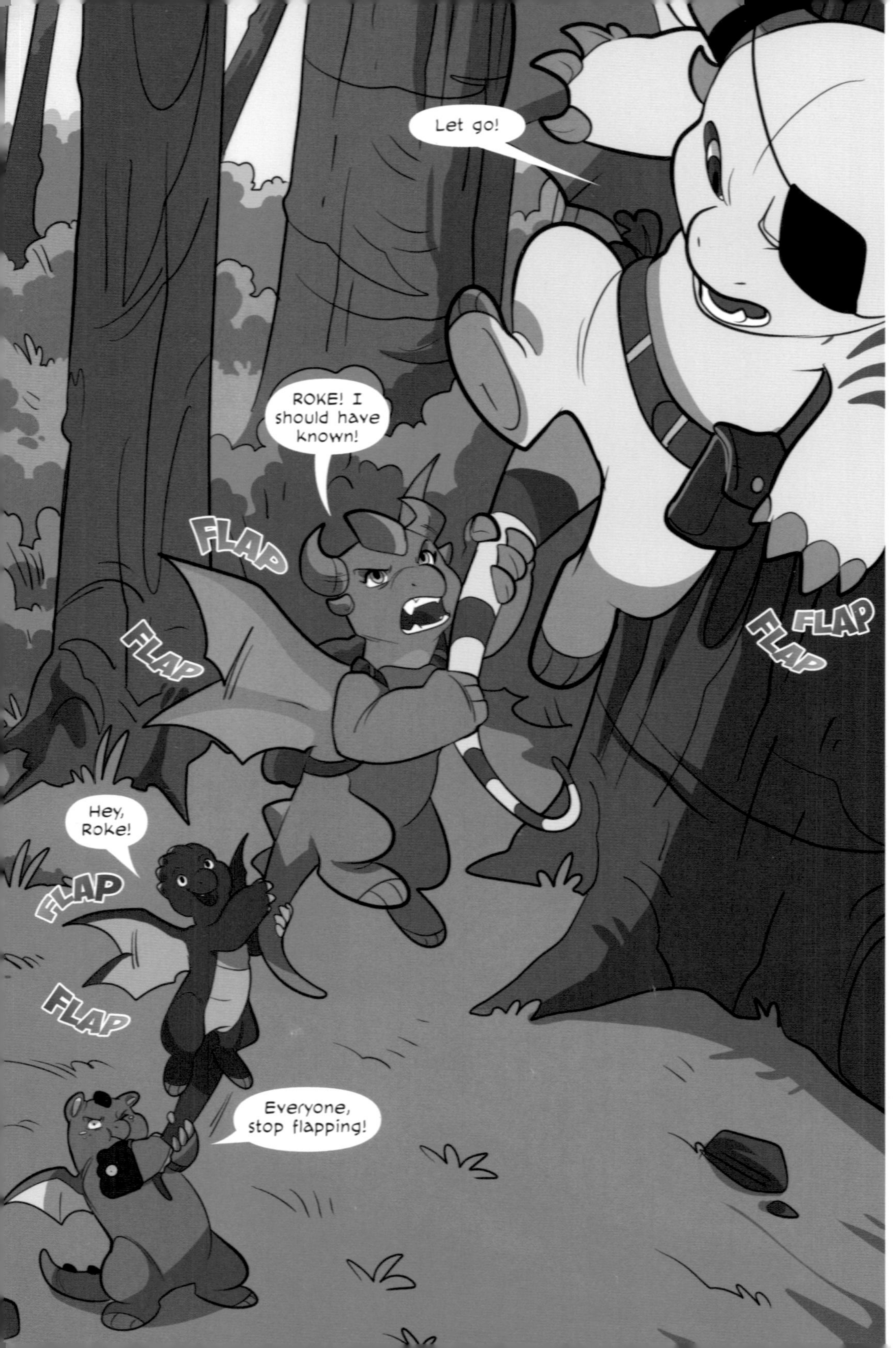
Let go!
ROKE! I should have known!
FLAP
FLAP
FLAP
FLAP
Hey, Roke!
FLAP
FLAP
Everyone, stop flapping!

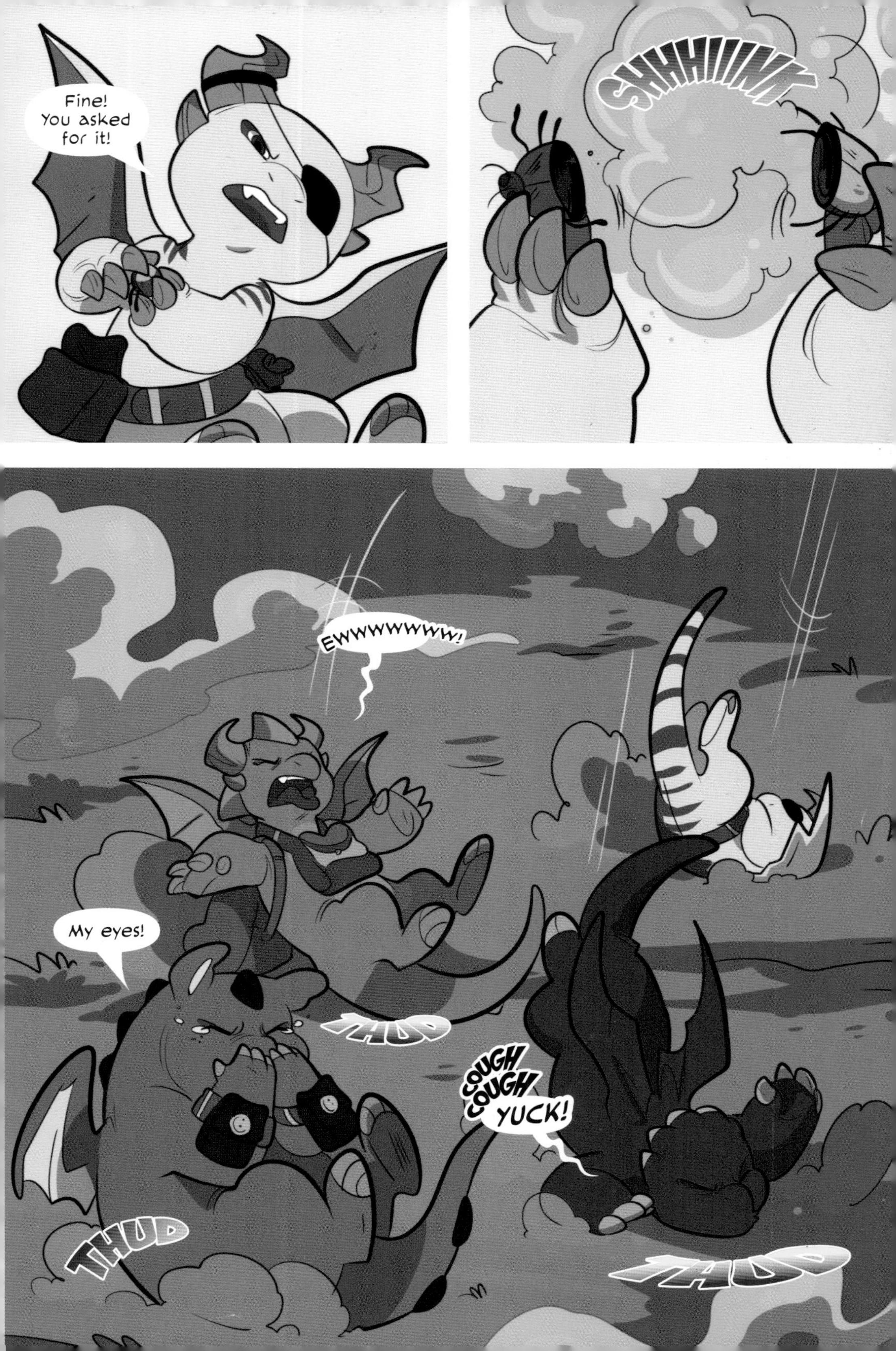

Fine! You asked for it!
SHHHIIINK
EWWWWWWW!
My eyes!
THUD
COUGH COUGH YUCK!
THUD
THUD

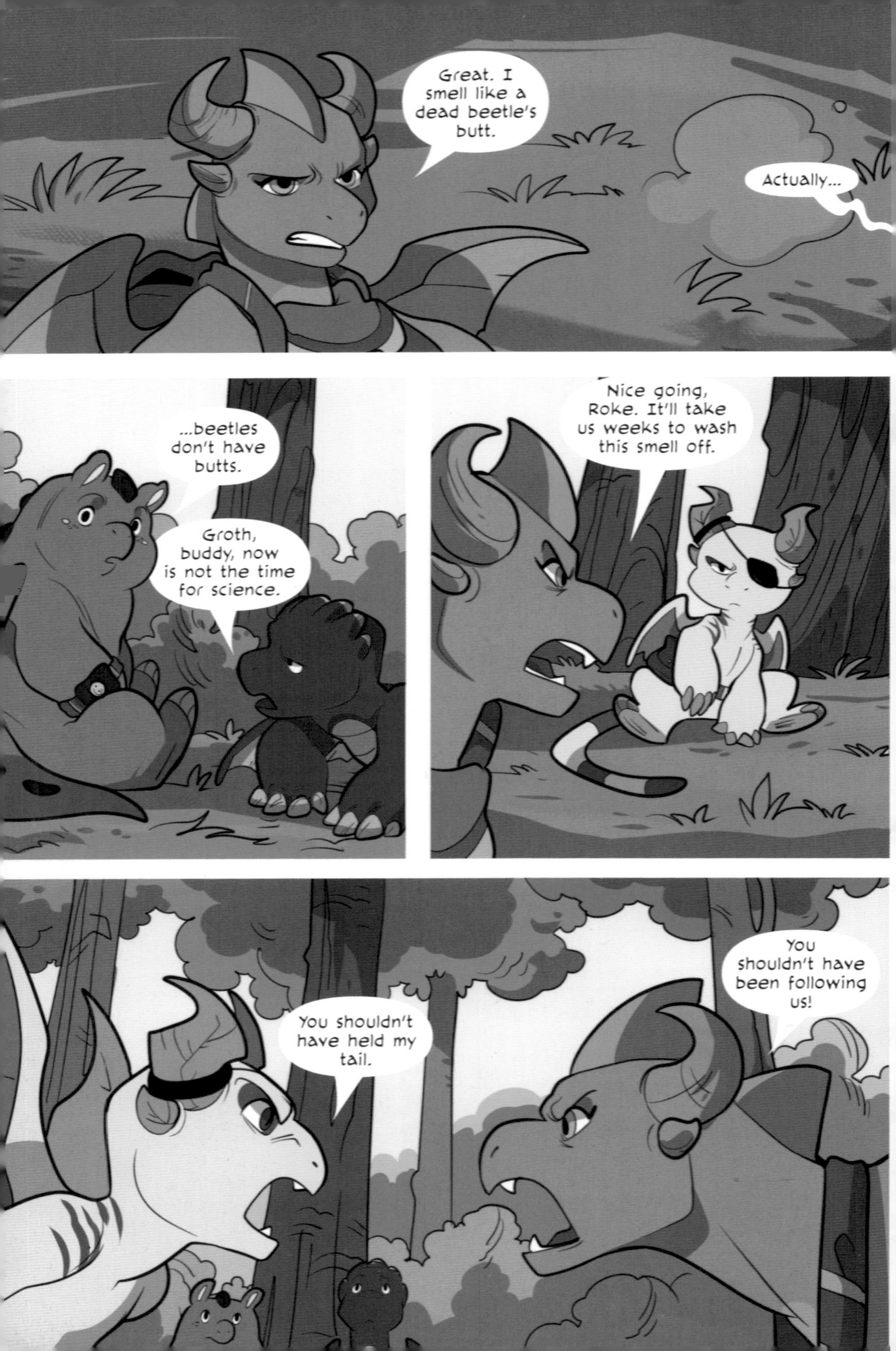
Great. I smell like a dead beetle's butt.
Actually...
...beetles don't have butts.
Groth, buddy, now is not the time for science.
Nice going, Roke. It'll take us weeks to wash this smell off.
You shouldn't have held my tail.
You shouldn't have been following us!

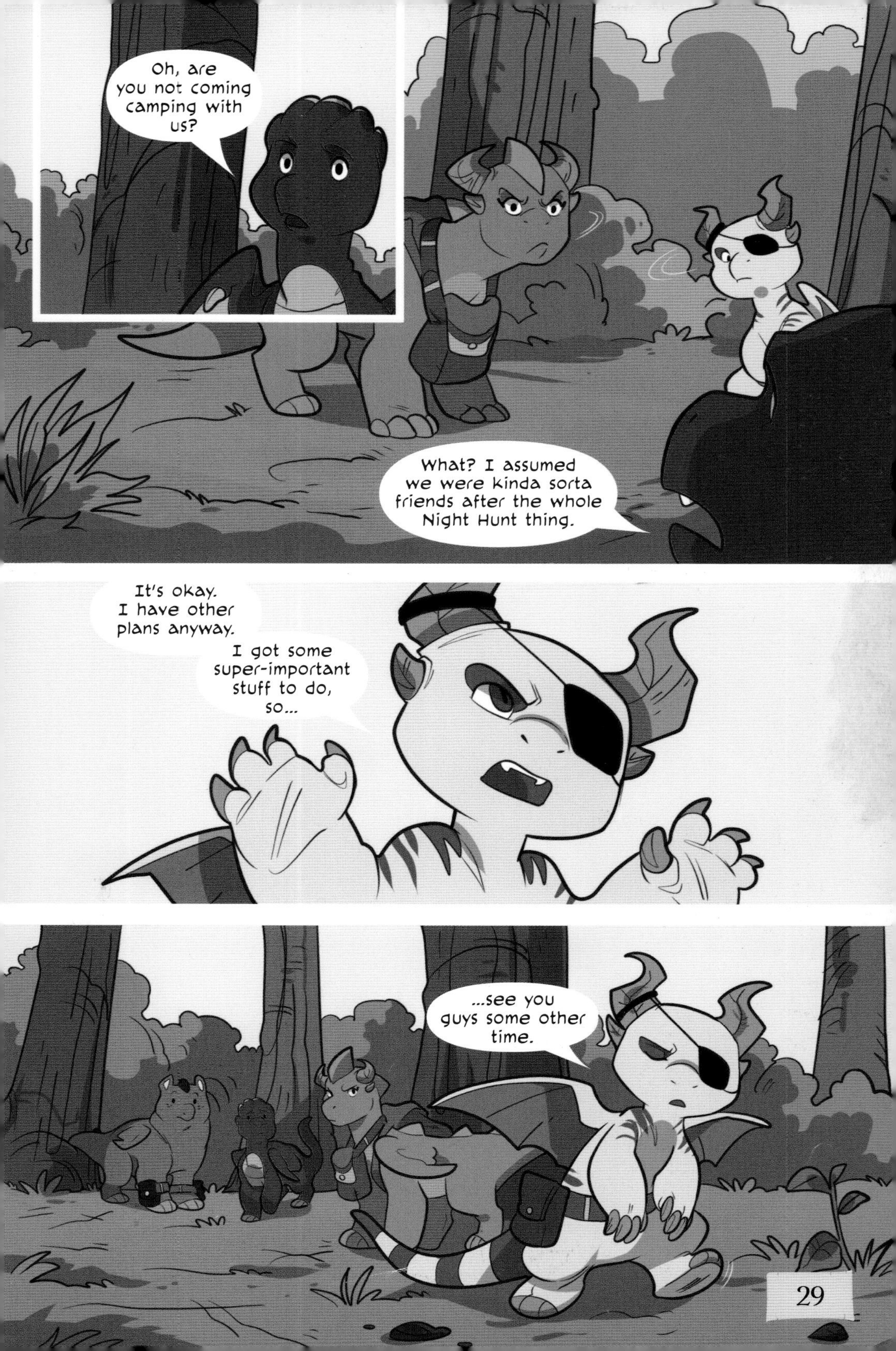
Oh, are you not coming camping with us?
What? I assumed we were kinda sorta friends after the whole Night Hunt thing.
It's okay. I have other plans anyway.
I got some super-important stuff to do, so...
...see you guys some other time.

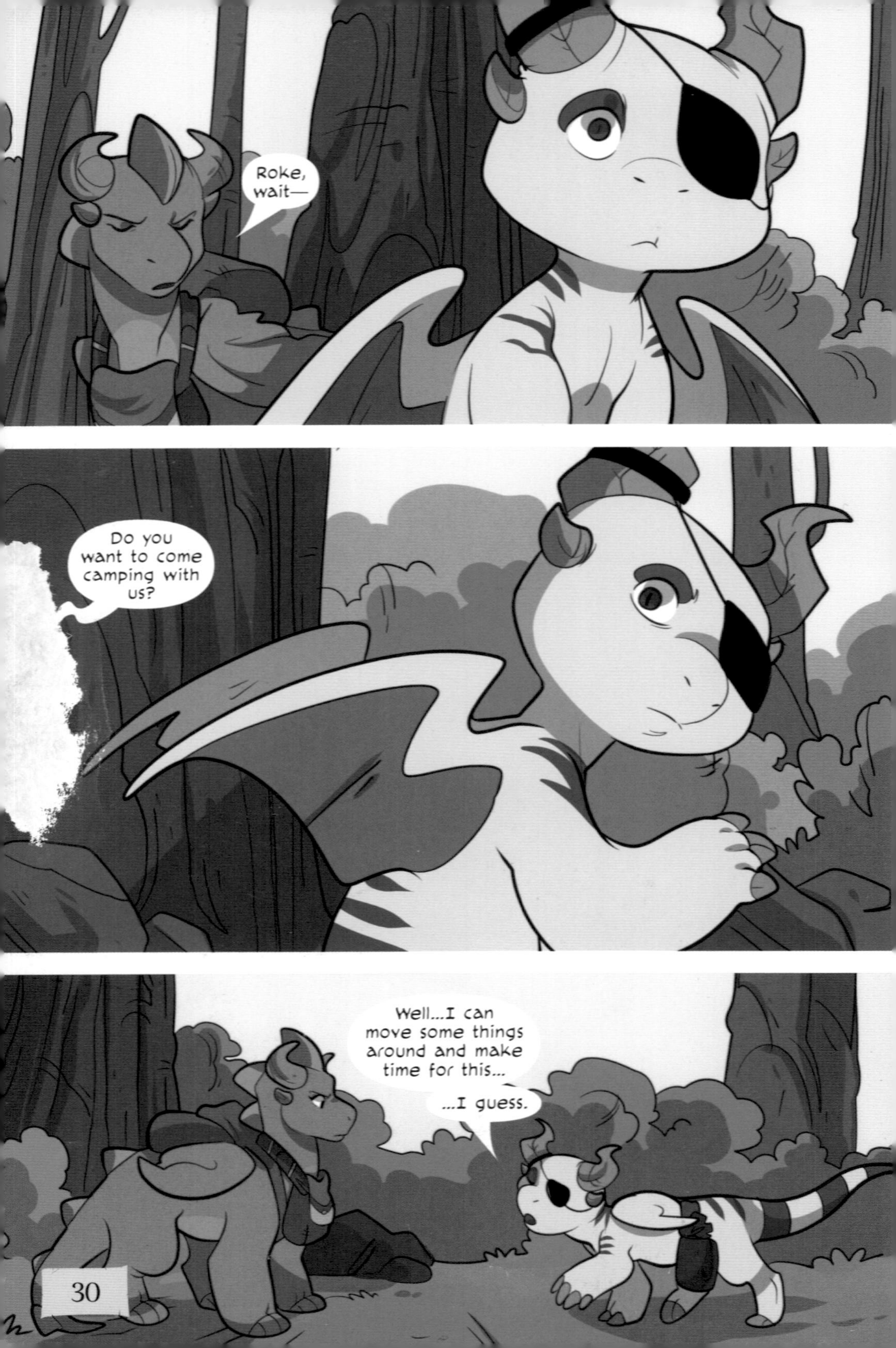
Roke, wait—
Do you want to come camping with us?
Well...I can move some things around and make time for this...
...I guess.

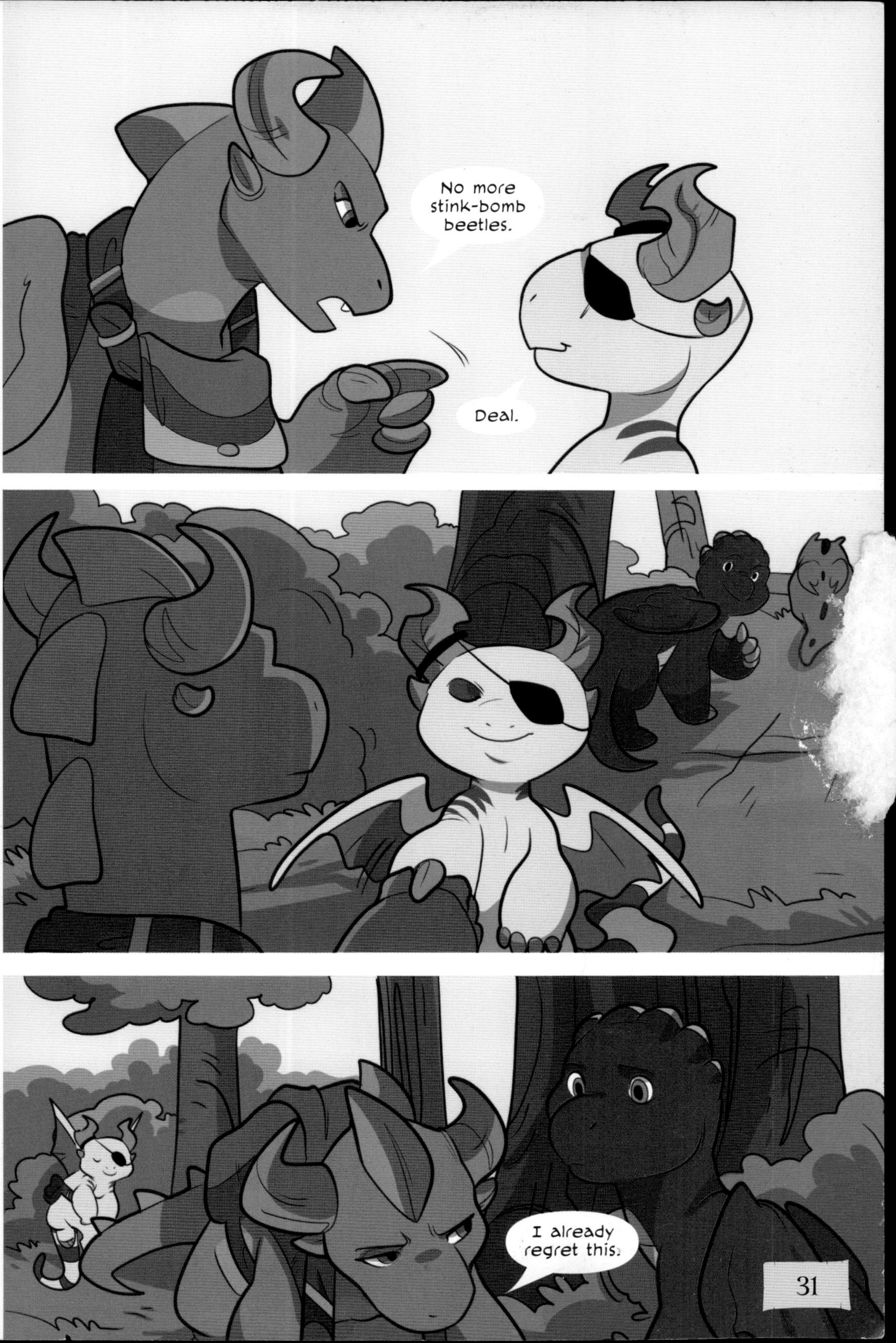
No more stink-bomb beetles.
Deal.
I already regret this.

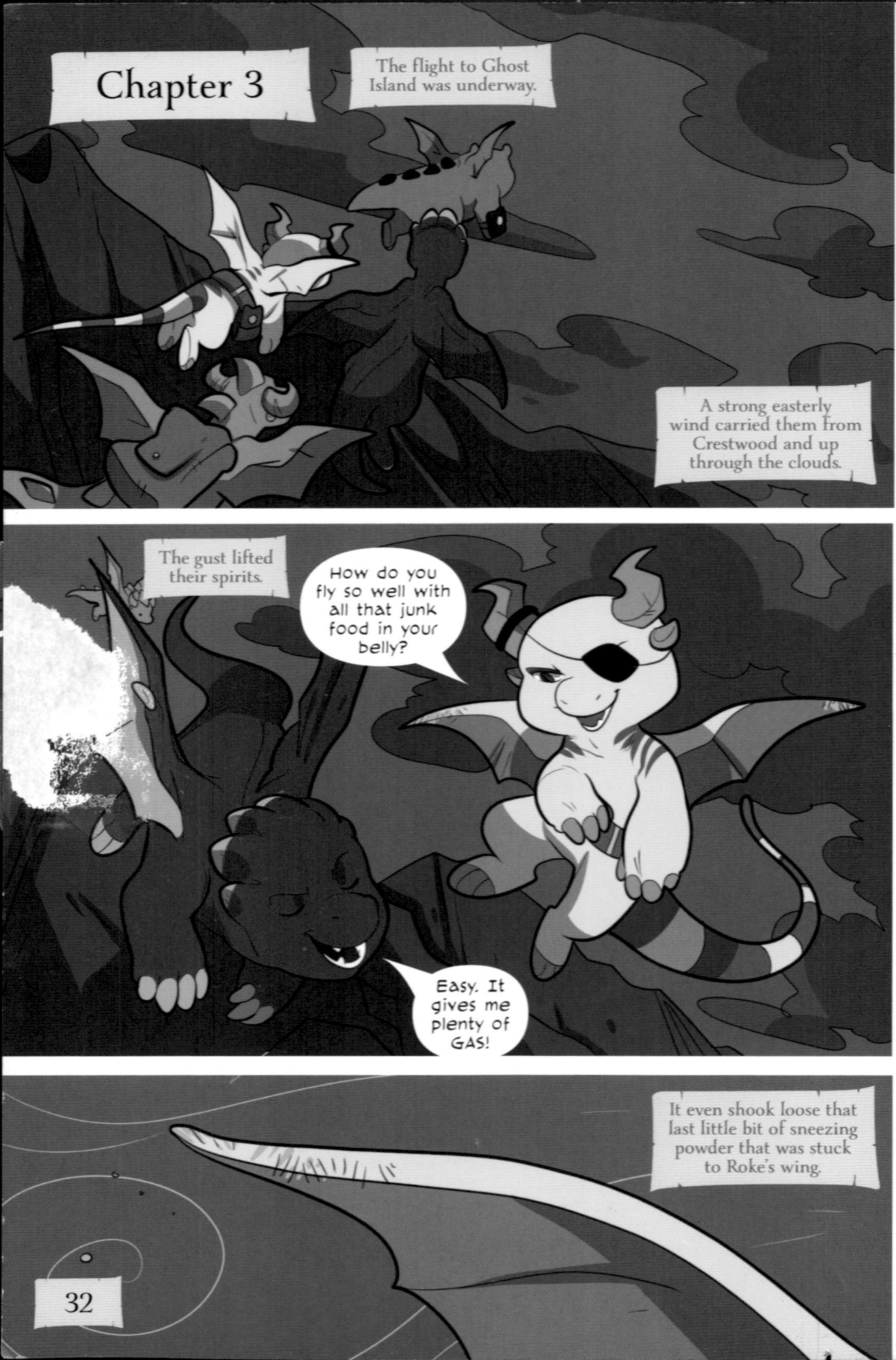
Chapter 3
The flight to Ghost Island was underway.
A strong easterly wind carried them from Crestwood and up through the clouds.
The gust lifted their spirits.
How do you fly so well with all that junk food in your belly?
Easy. It gives me plenty of GAS!
It even shook loose that last little bit of sneezing powder that was stuck to Roke's wing.

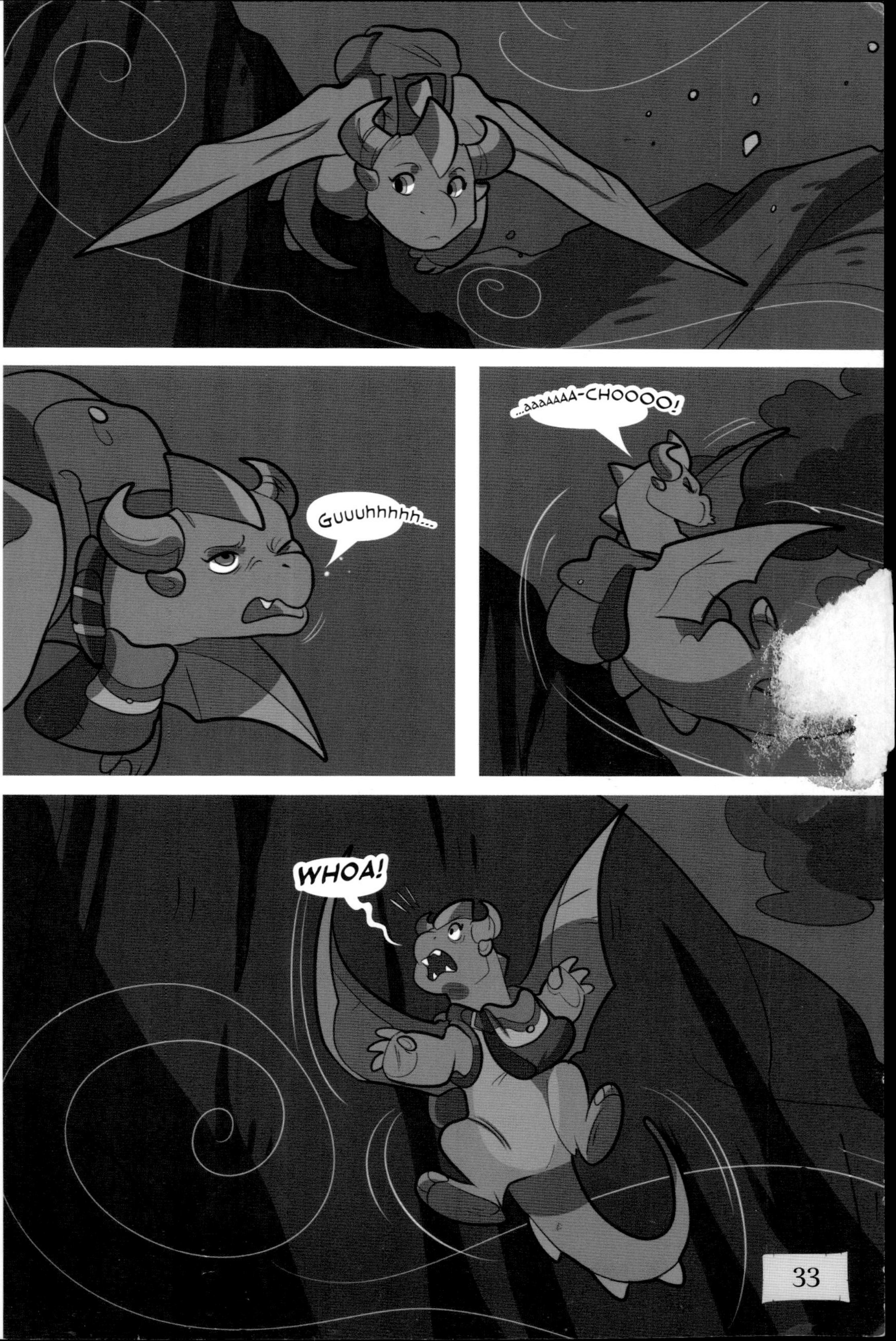

Guuuhhhhh...
...aaaaaaA-CHOOOO!
WHOA!

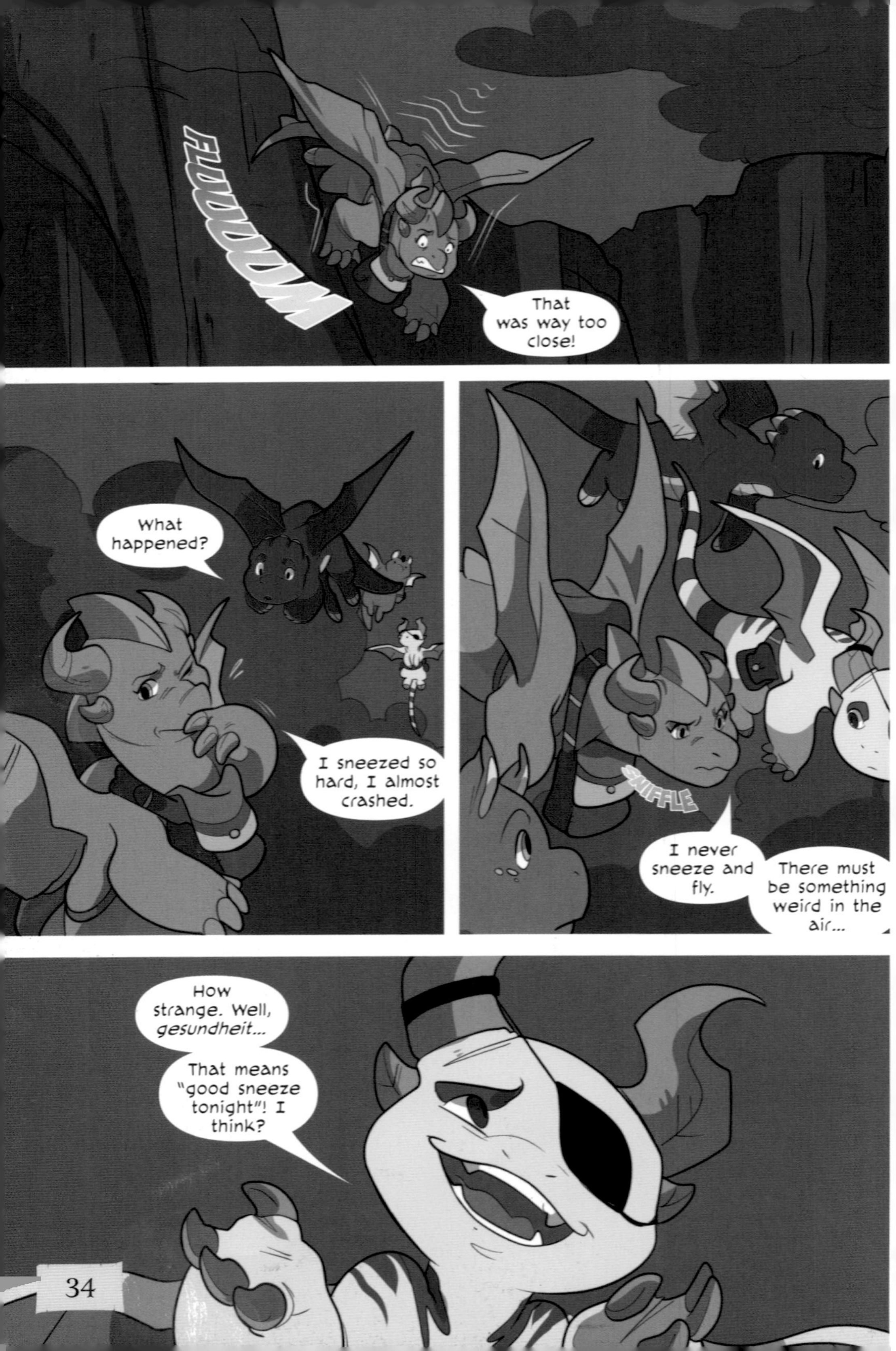
FLUUUUM
That was way too close!
What happened?
I sneezed so hard, I almost crashed.
SNIFFLE
I never sneeze and fly.
There must be something weird in the air...
How strange. Well, *gesundheit*...
That means "good sneeze tonight"! I think?

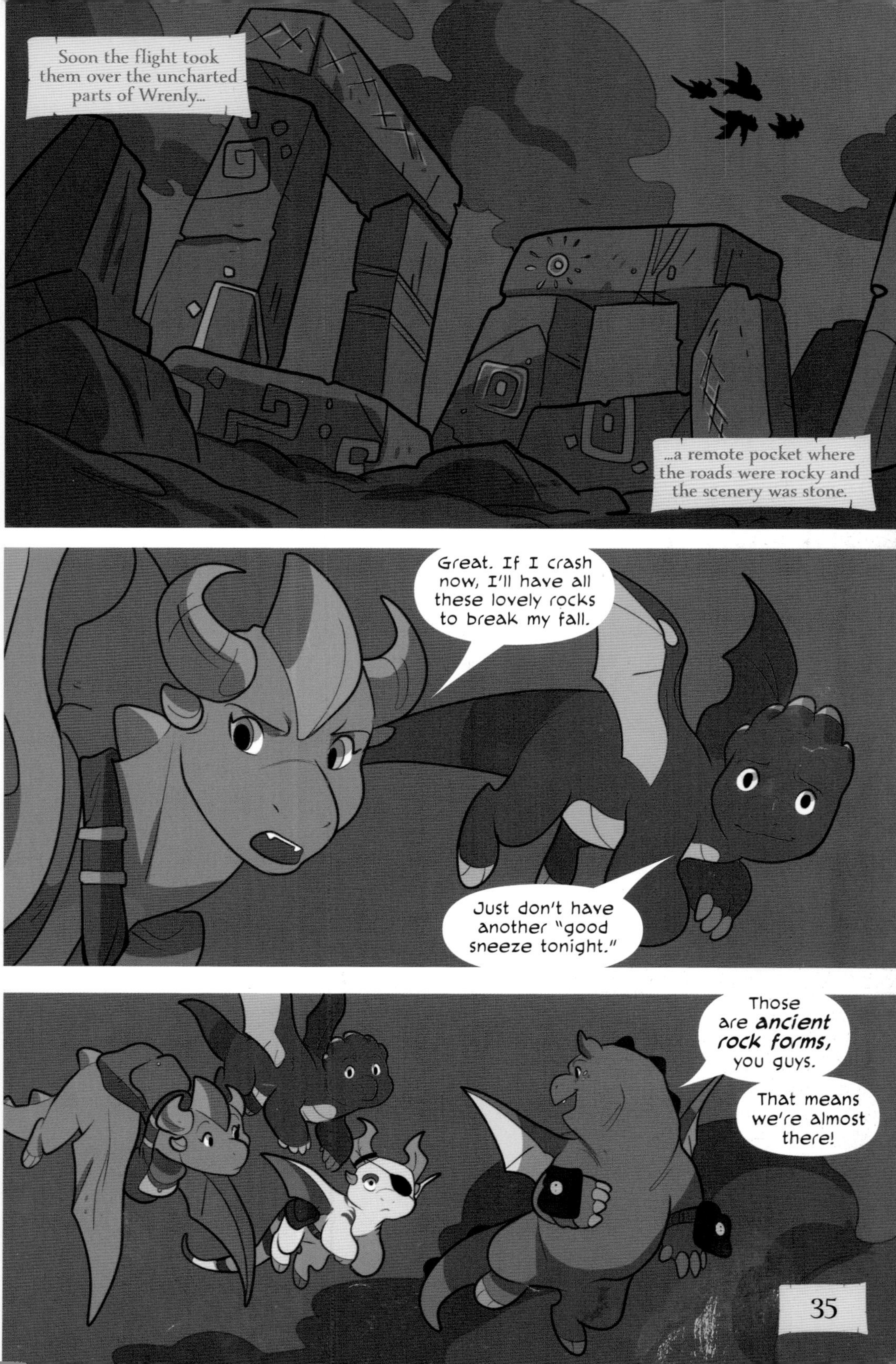
Soon the flight took them over the uncharted parts of Wrenly...
...a remote pocket where the roads were rocky and the scenery was stone.
Great. If I crash now, I'll have all these lovely rocks to break my fall.
Just don't have another "good sneeze tonight."
Those are *ancient rock forms,* you guys.
That means we're almost there!

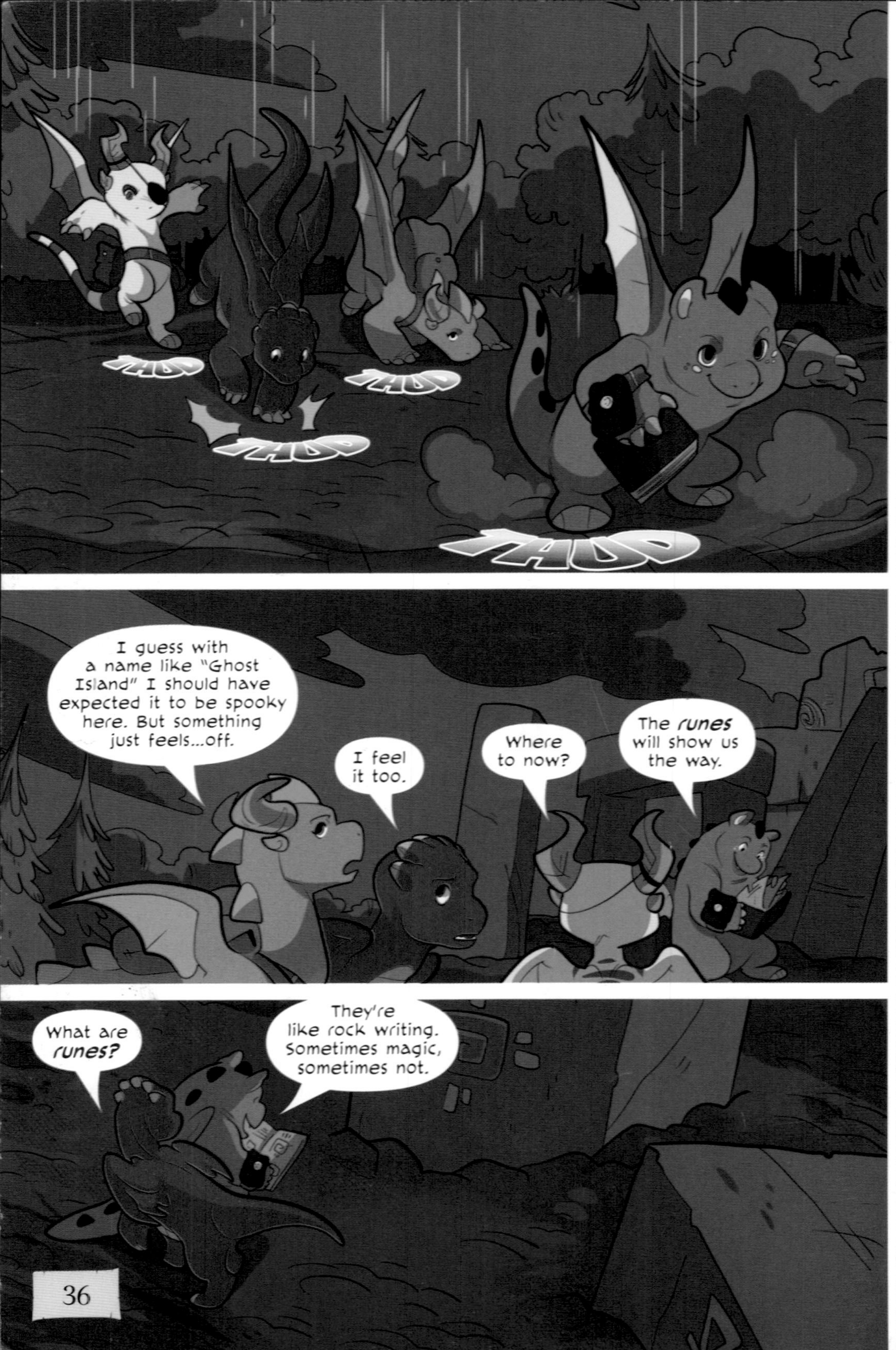
THUD
THUD
THUD
THUD
I guess with a name like "Ghost Island" I should have expected it to be spooky here. But something just feels...off.
I feel it too.
Where to now?
The *runes* will show us the way.
What are *runes?*
They're like rock writing. Sometimes magic, sometimes not.

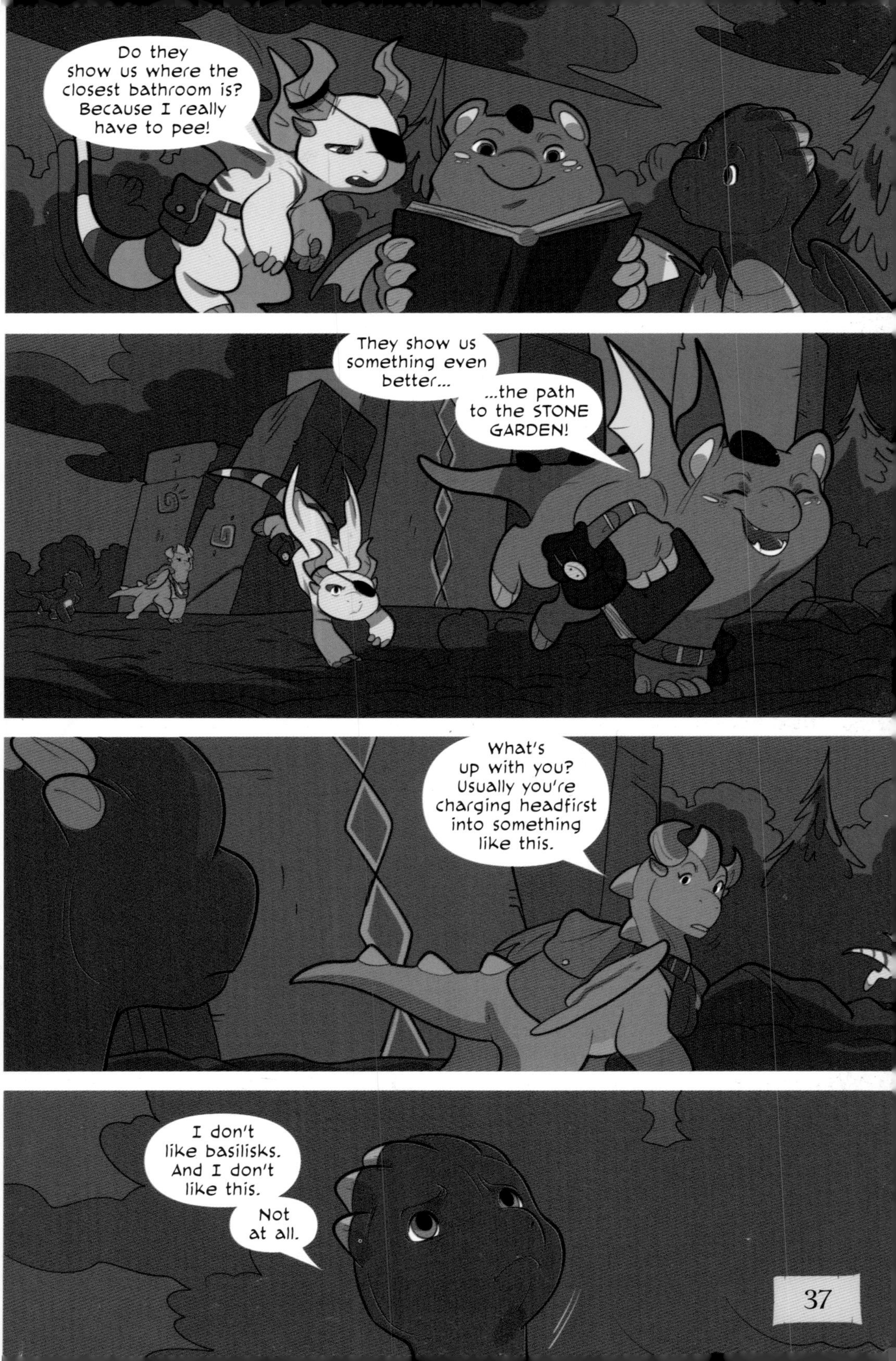
Do they show us where the closest bathroom is? Because I really have to pee!
They show us something even better...
...the path to the STONE GARDEN!
What's up with you? Usually you're charging headfirst into something like this.
I don't like basilisks. And I don't like this.
Not at all.

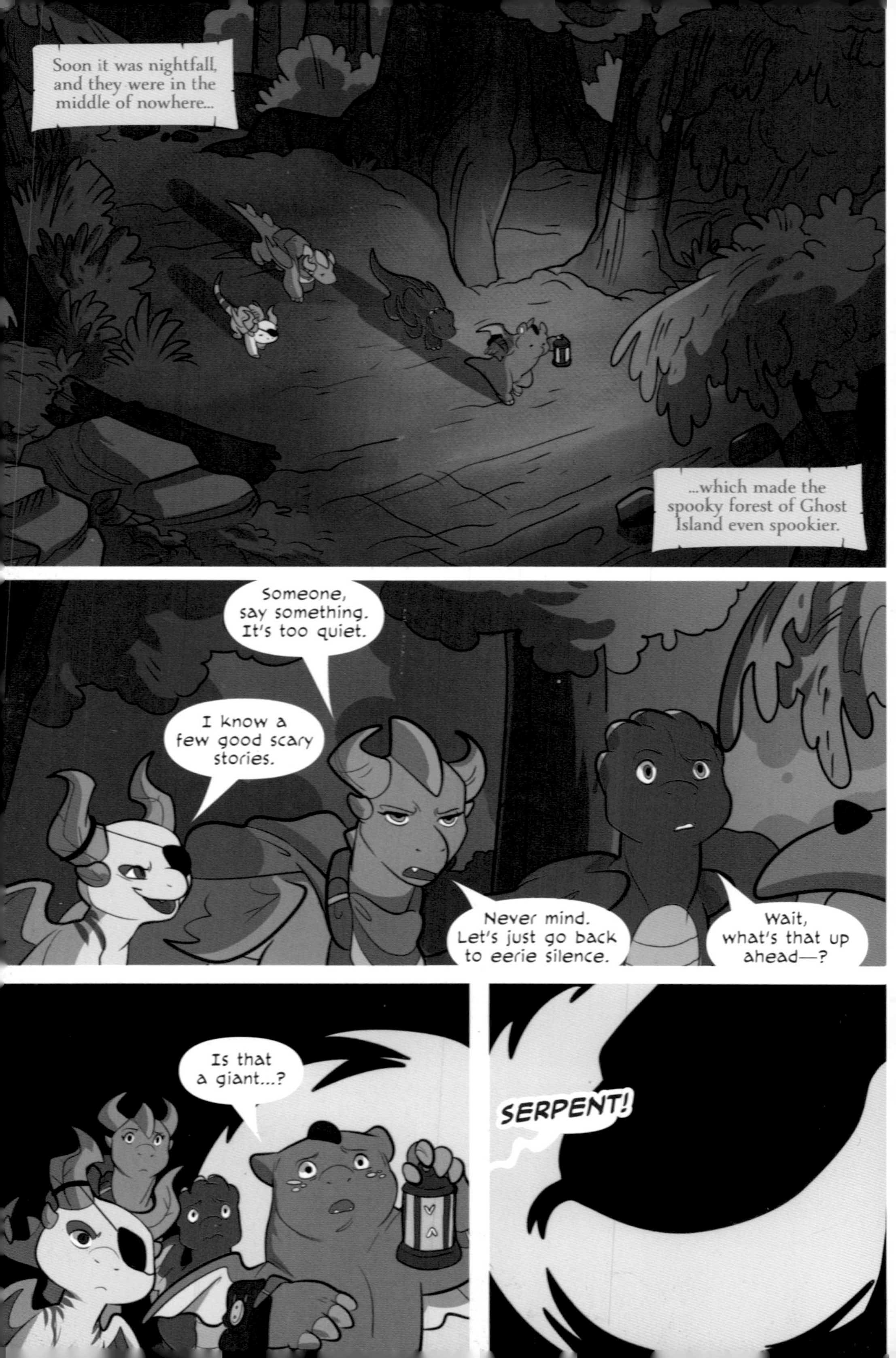

Soon it was nightfall, and they were in the middle of nowhere...
...which made the spooky forest of Ghost Island even spookier.
Someone, say something. It's too quiet.
I know a few good scary stories.
Never mind. Let's just go back to eerie silence.
Wait, what's that up ahead—?
Is that a giant...?
SERPENT!

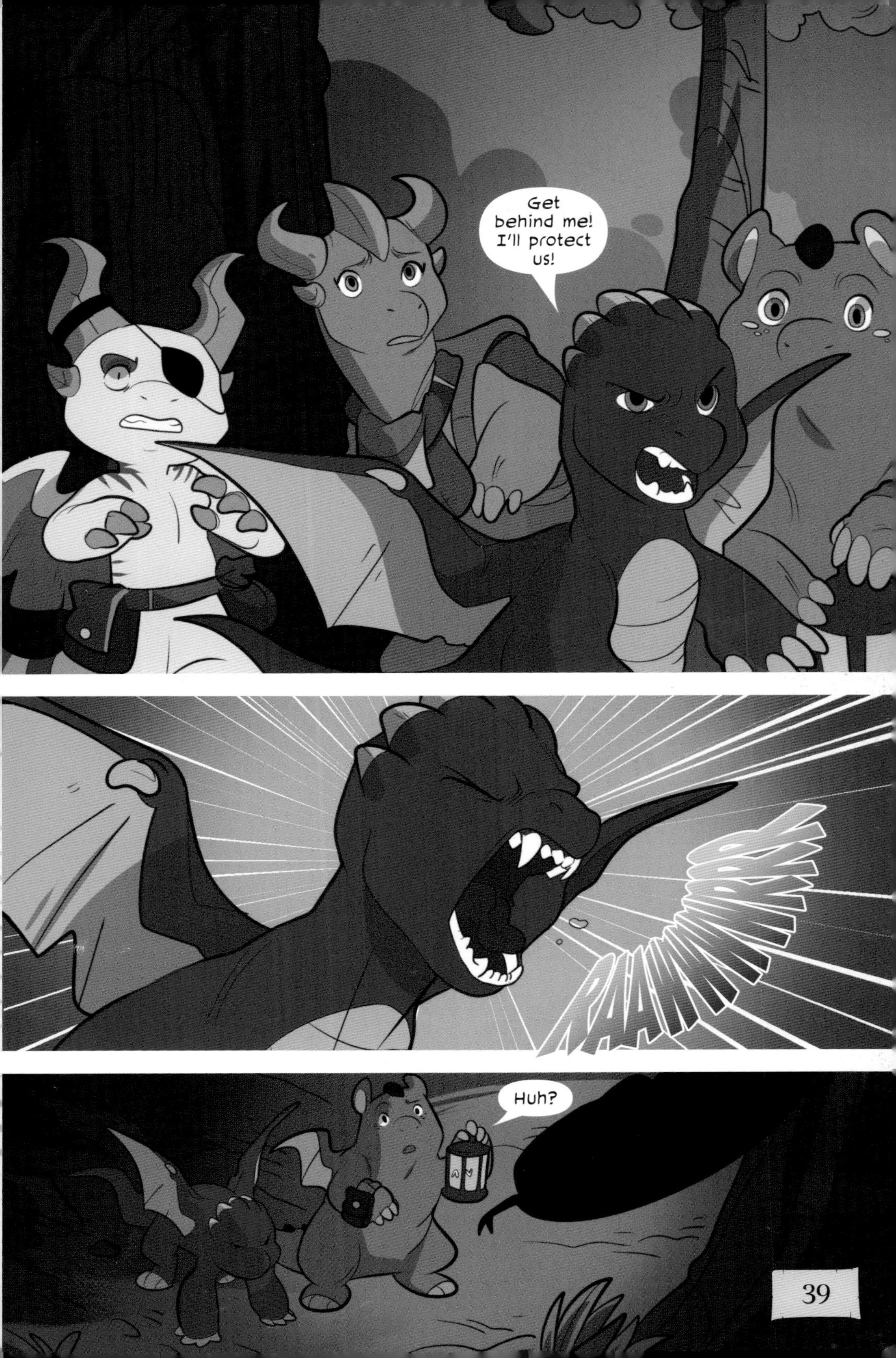
Get behind me! I'll protect us!
Huh?

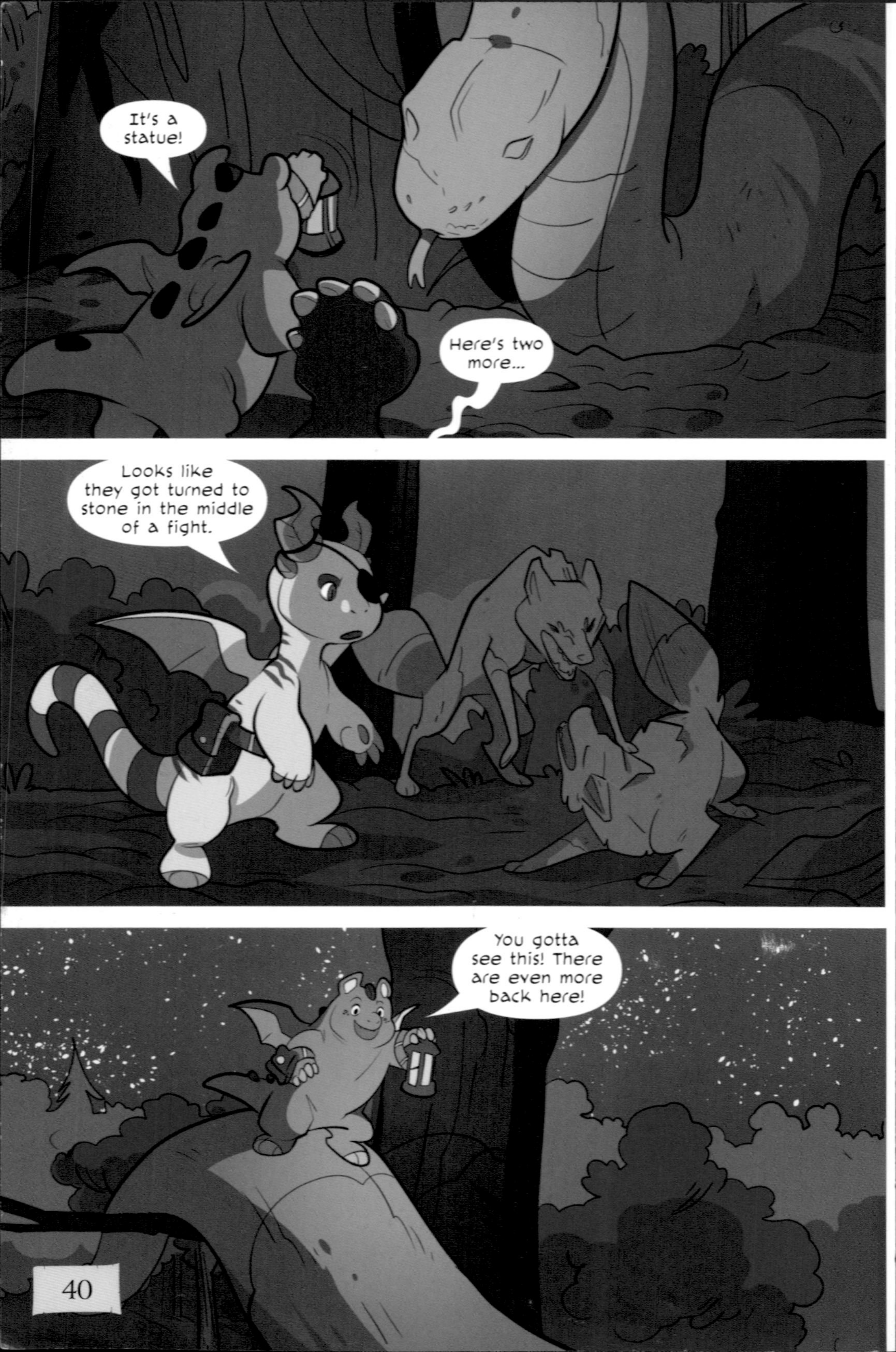
It's a statue!
Here's two more...
Looks like they got turned to stone in the middle of a fight.
You gotta see this! There are even more back here!

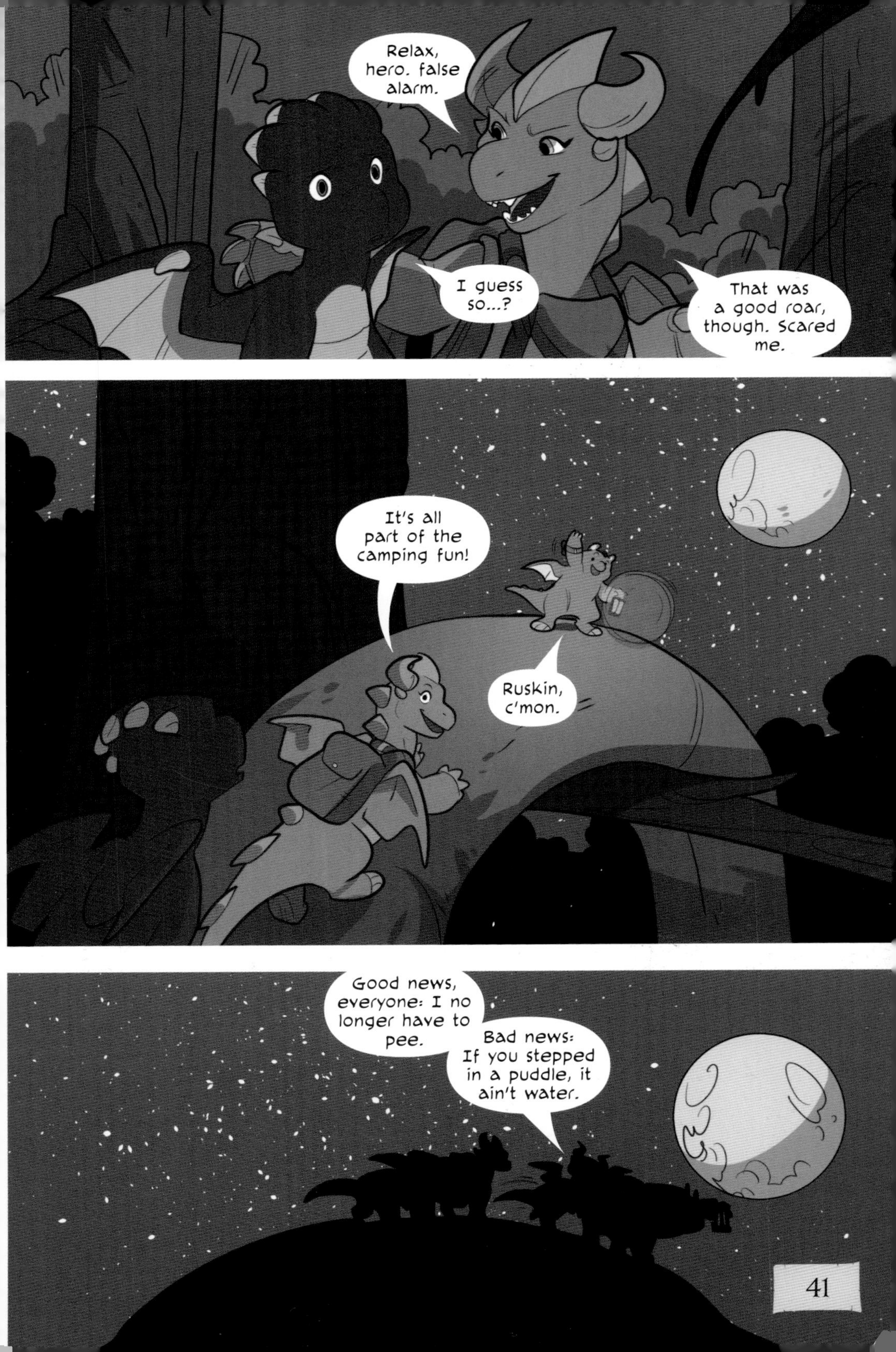
Relax, hero. false alarm.
I guess so...?
That was a good roar, though. Scared me.
It's all part of the camping fun!
Ruskin, c'mon.
Good news, everyone: I no longer have to pee.
Bad news: If you stepped in a puddle, it ain't water.

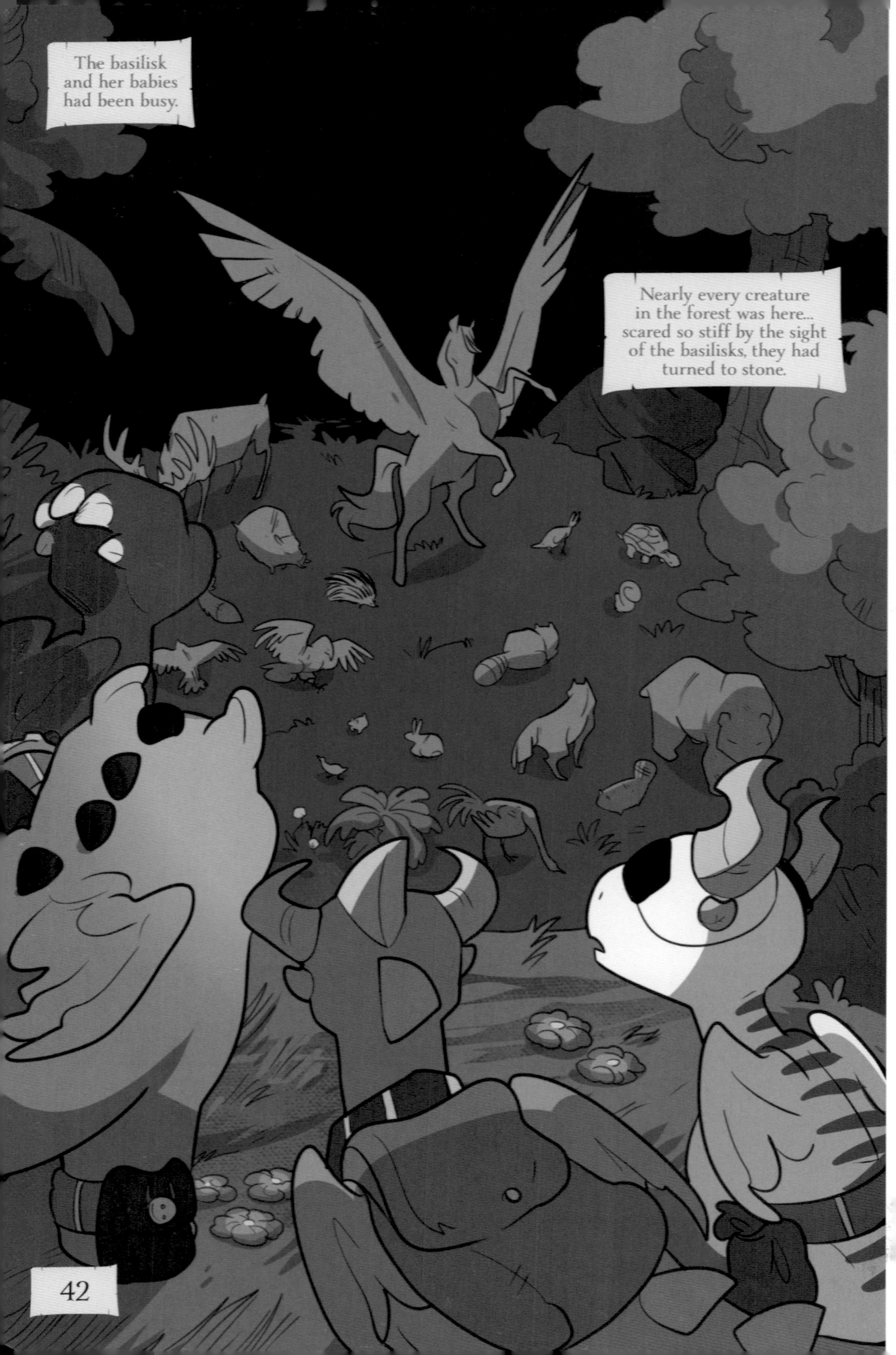
The basilisk and her babies had been busy.
Nearly every creature in the forest was here... scared so stiff by the sight of the basilisks, they had turned to stone.

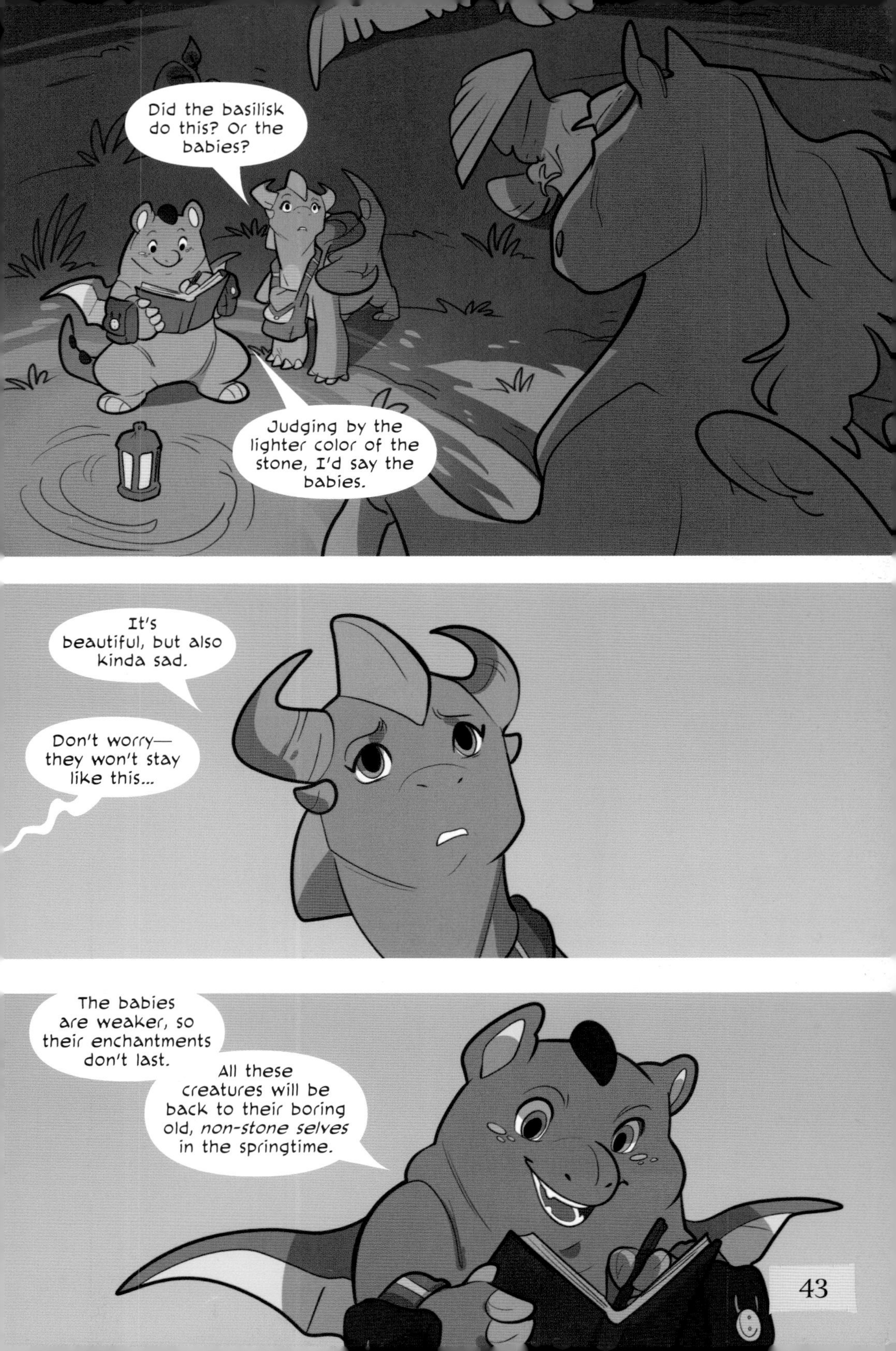
Did the basilisk do this? Or the babies?
Judging by the lighter color of the stone, I'd say the babies.
It's beautiful, but also kinda sad.
Don't worry— they won't stay like this...
The babies are weaker, so their enchantments don't last.
All these creatures will be back to their boring old, *non-stone selves* in the springtime.

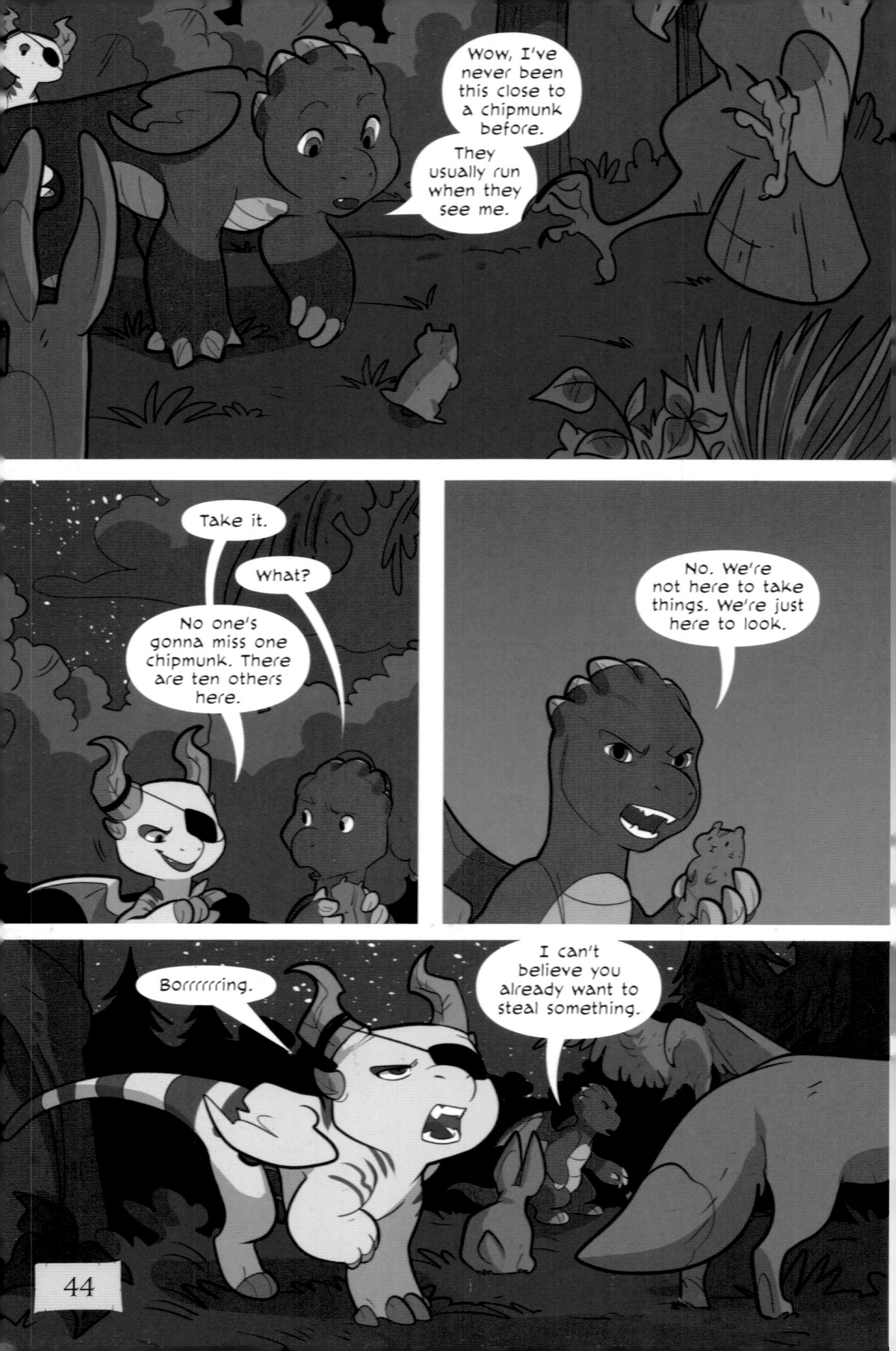
Wow, I've never been this close to a chipmunk before.
They usually run when they see me.
Take it.
What?
No one's gonna miss one chipmunk. There are ten others here.
No. We're not here to take things. We're just here to look.
Borrrrrrring.
I can't believe you already want to steal something.

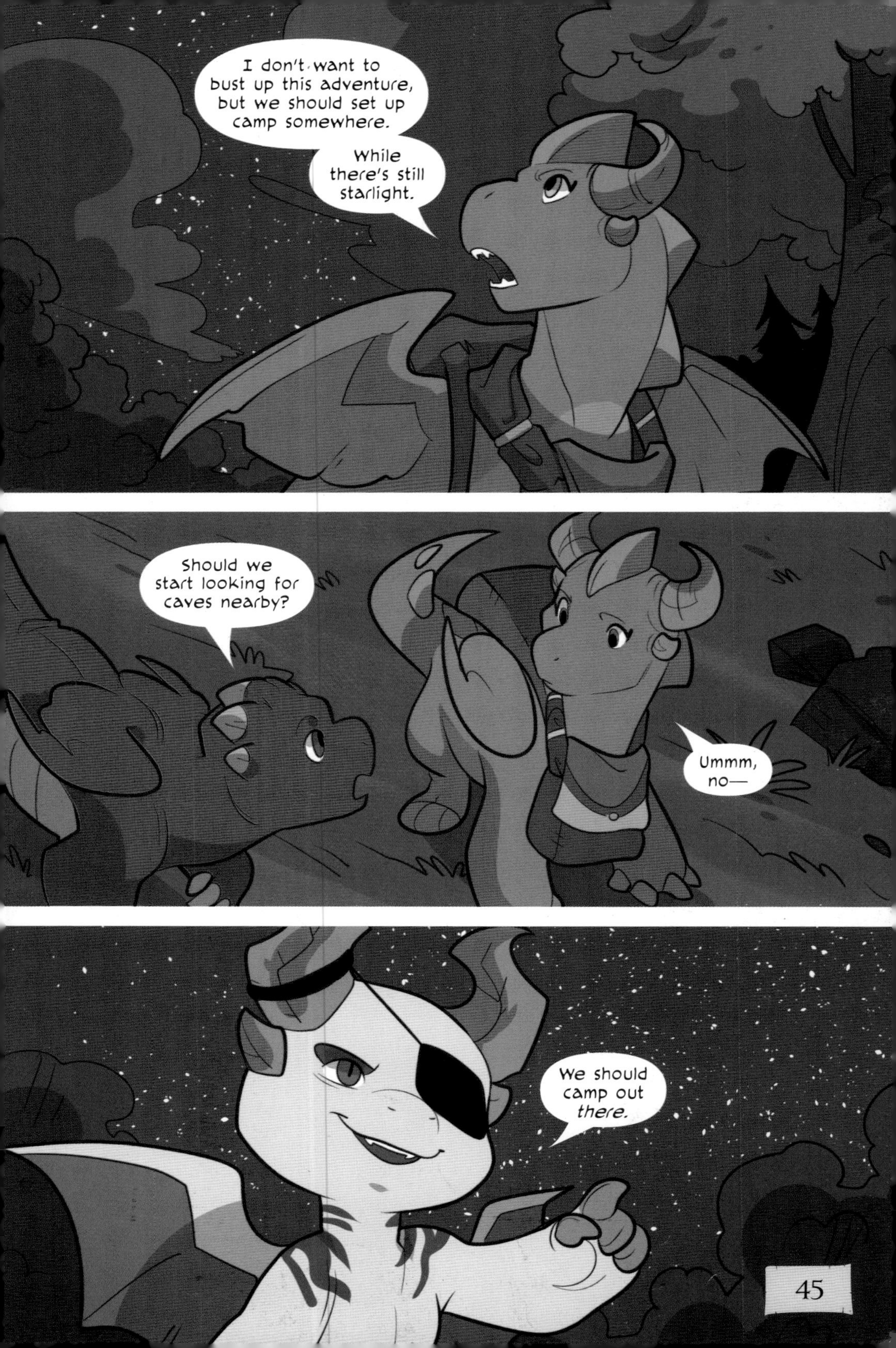
I don't want to bust up this adventure, but we should set up camp somewhere.
While there's still starlight.
Should we start looking for caves nearby?
Ummm, no—
We should camp out *there.*

Chapter 4

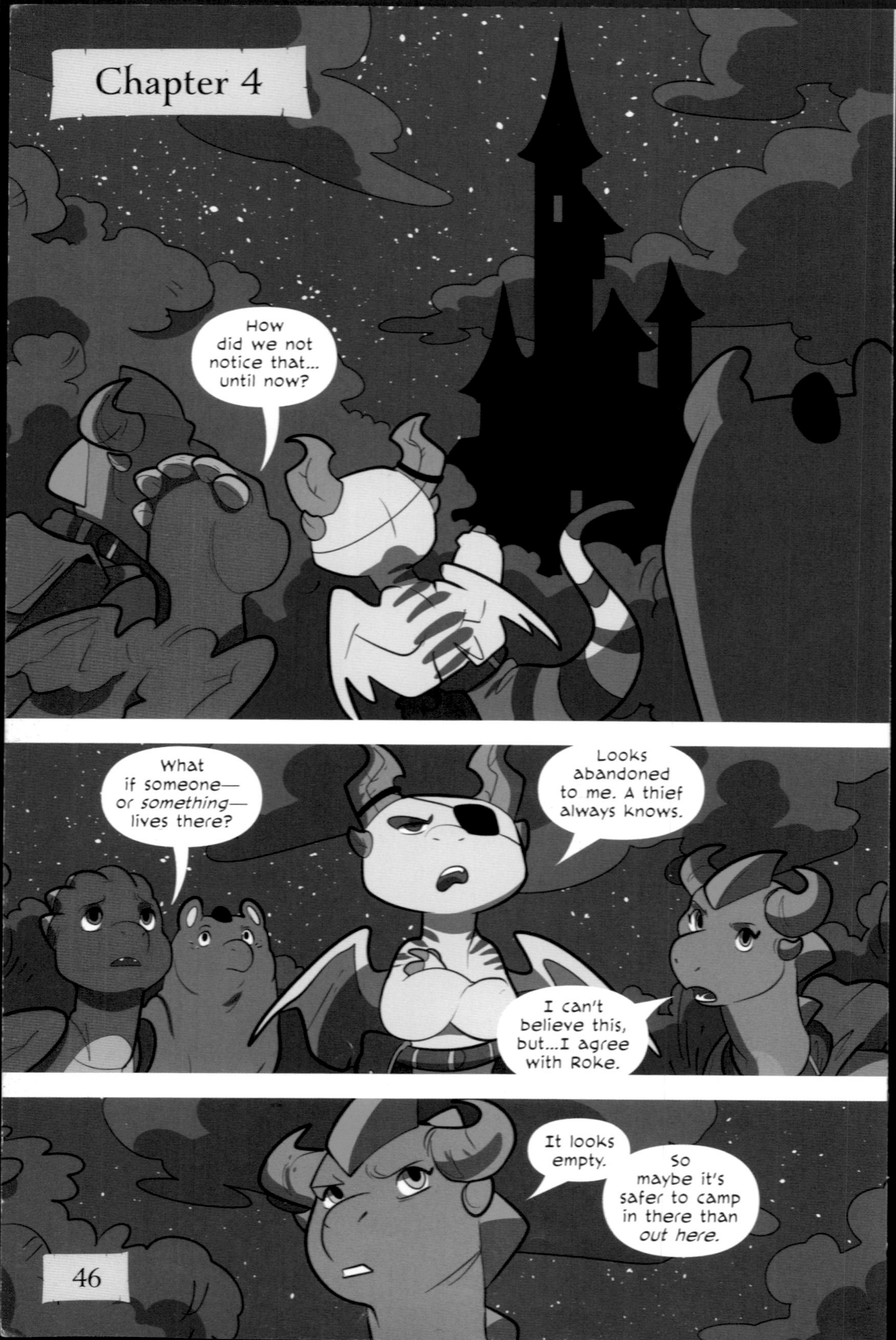
How did we not notice that... until now?
What if someone—or *something*—lives there?
Looks abandoned to me. A thief always knows.
I can't believe this, but...I agree with Roke.
It looks empty.
So maybe it's safer to camp in there than *out here.*

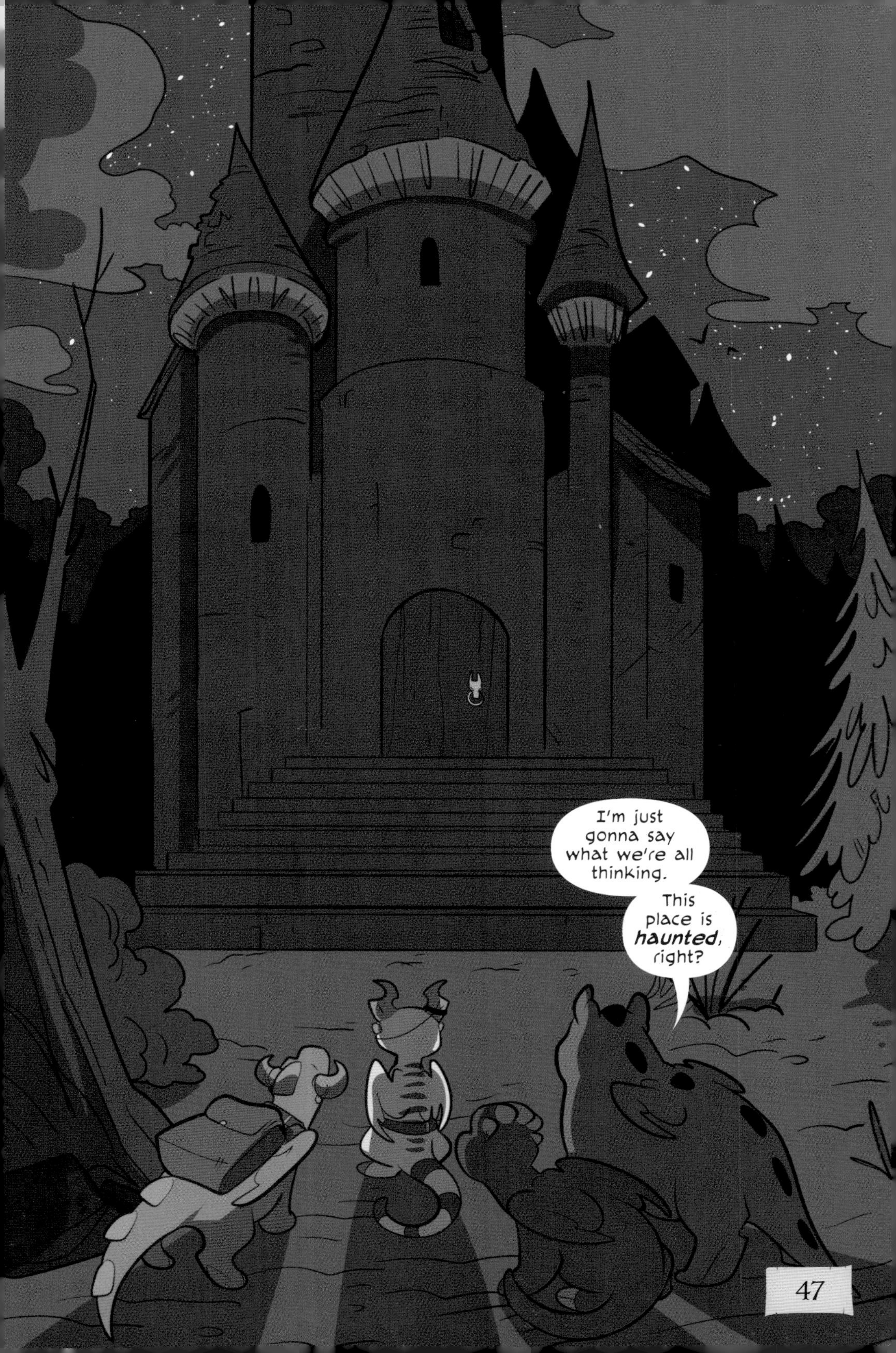
I'm just gonna say what we're all thinking.
This place is ***haunted***, right?

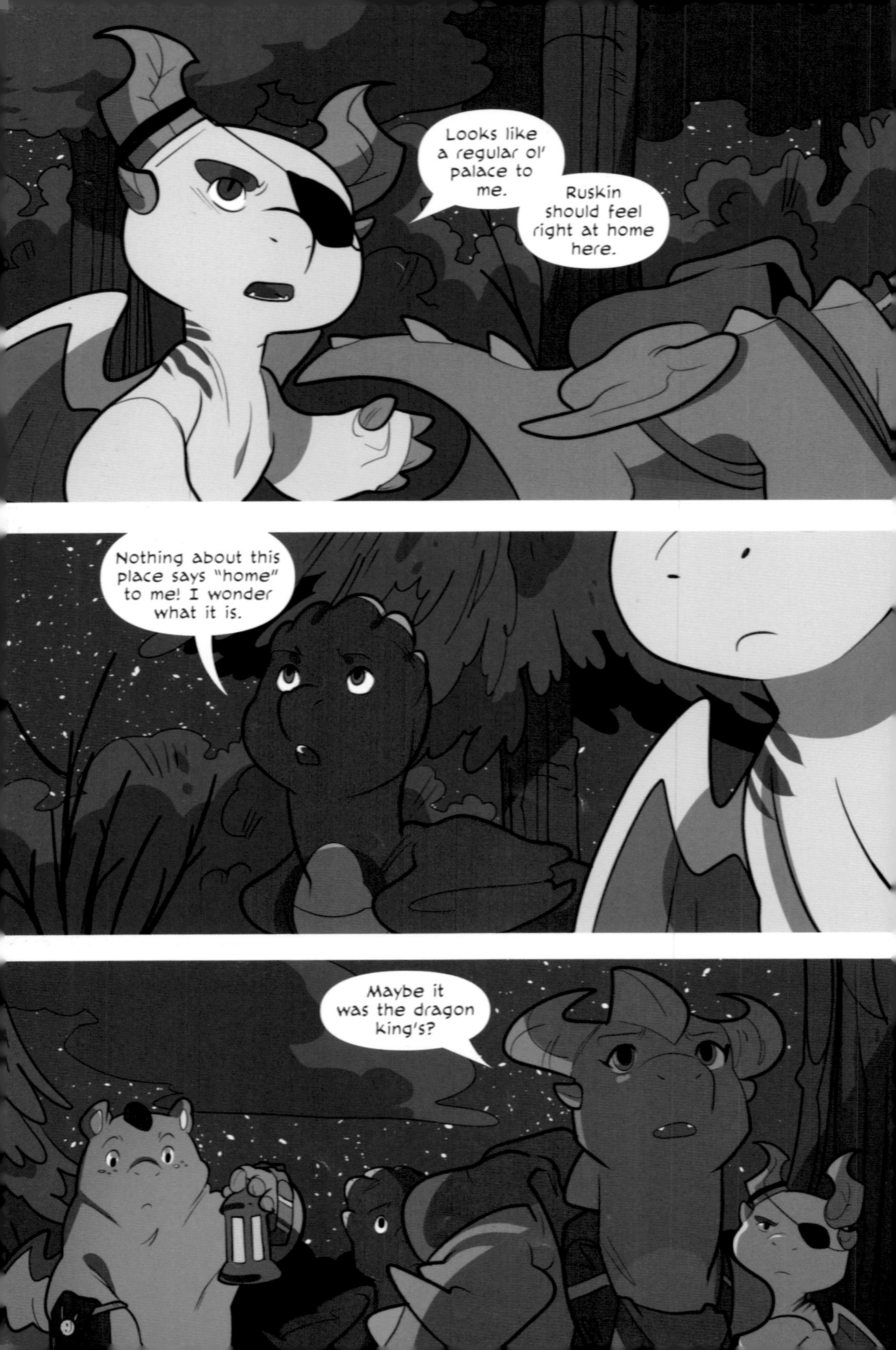
Looks like a regular ol' palace to me.
Ruskin should feel right at home here.
Nothing about this place says "home" to me! I wonder what it is.
Maybe it was the dragon king's?

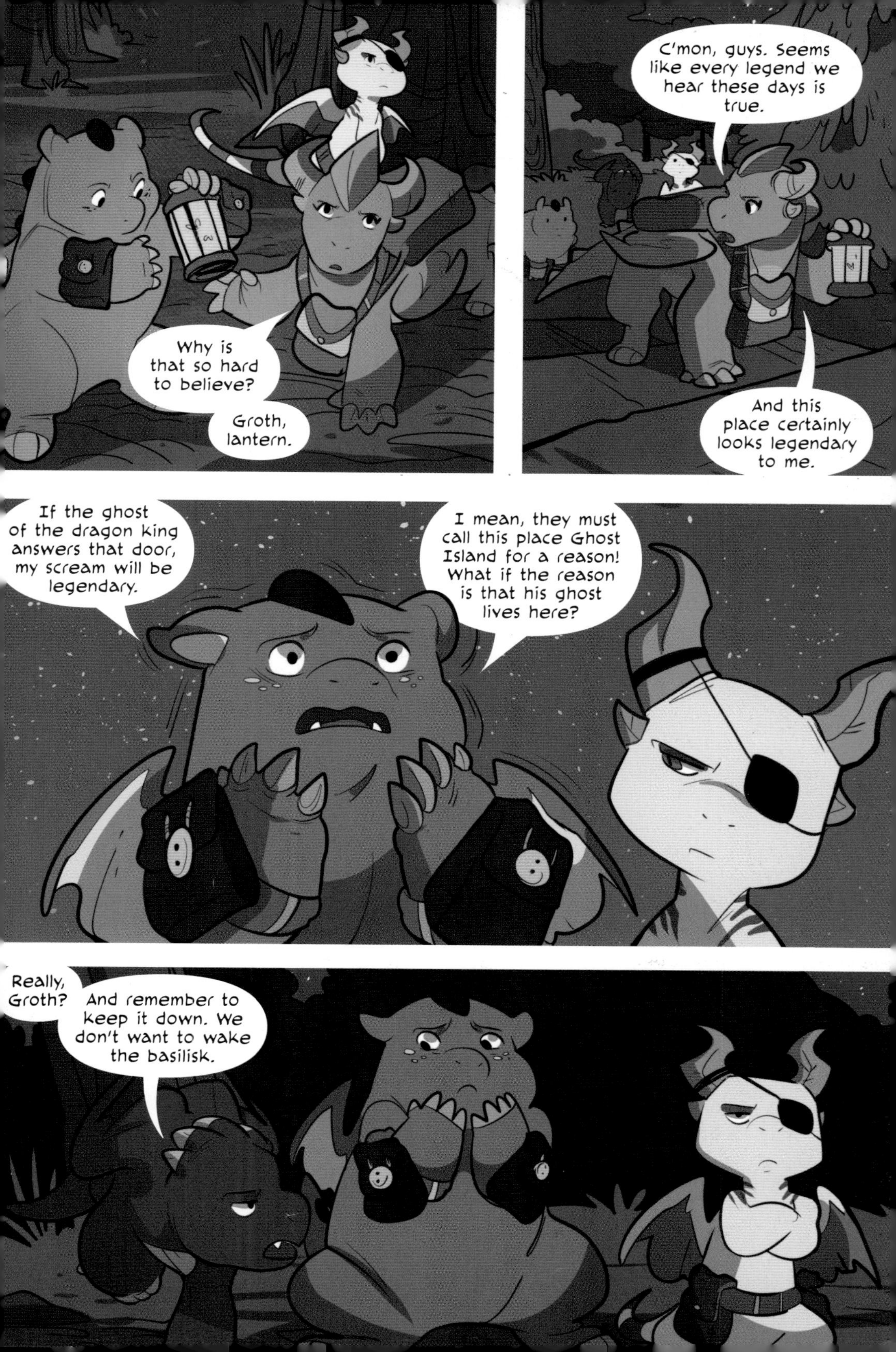
Why is that so hard to believe?
Groth, lantern.
C'mon, guys. Seems like every legend we hear these days is true.
And this place certainly looks legendary to me.
If the ghost of the dragon king answers that door, my scream will be legendary.
I mean, they must call this place Ghost Island for a reason! What if the reason is that his ghost lives here?
Really, Groth?
And remember to keep it down. We don't want to wake the basilisk.

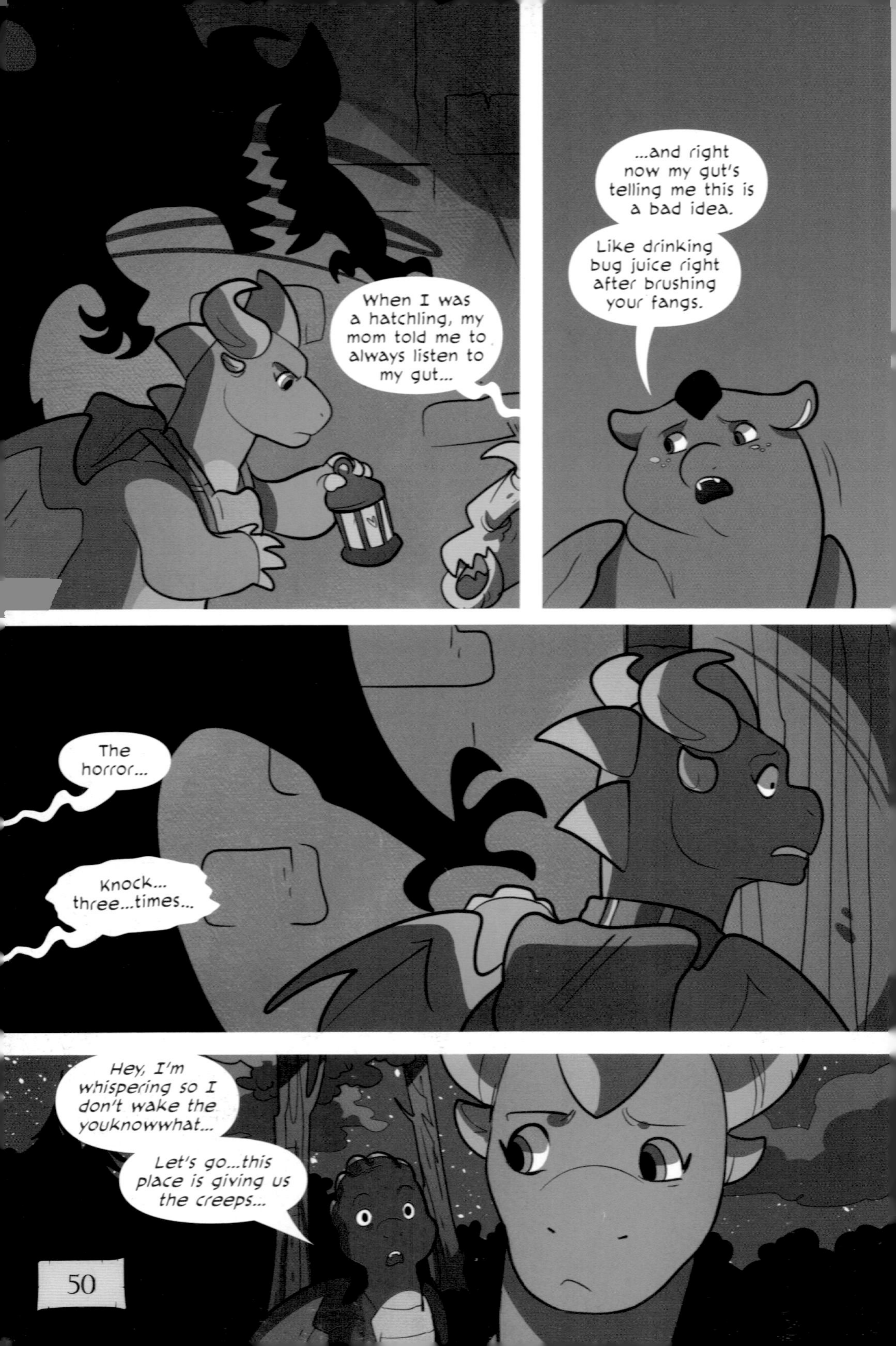
When I was a hatchling, my mom told me to always listen to my gut...
...and right now my gut's telling me this is a bad idea.
Like drinking bug juice right after brushing your fangs.
The horror...
Knock... three...times...
Hey, I'm whispering so I don't wake the youknowwhat...
Let's go...this place is giving us the creeps...

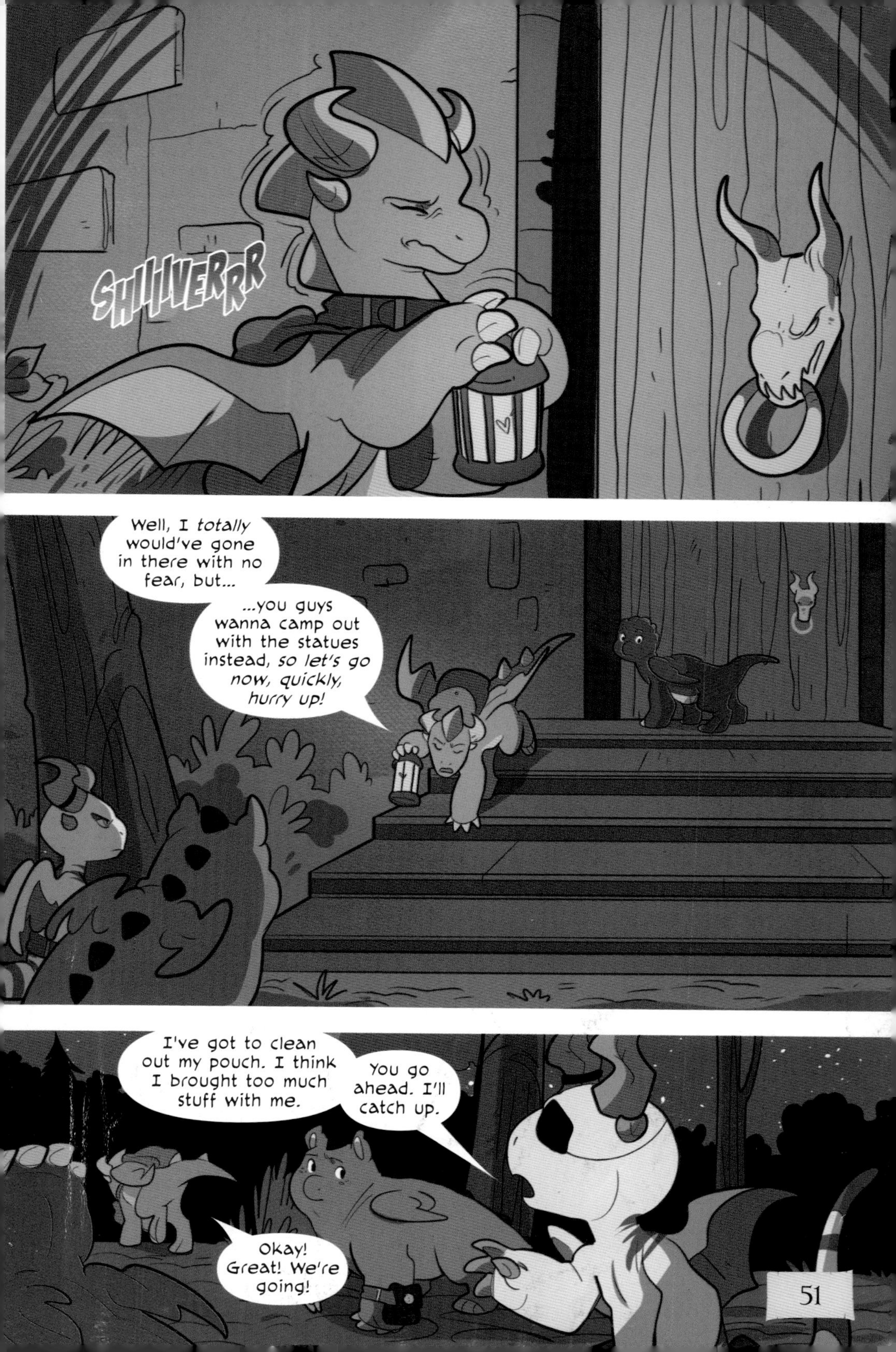
SHIIIIVERRR
Well, I *totally* would've gone in there with no fear, but...
...you guys wanna camp out with the statues instead, *so let's go now, quickly, hurry up!*
I've got to clean out my pouch. I think I brought too much stuff with me.
You go ahead. I'll catch up.
Okay! Great! We're going!

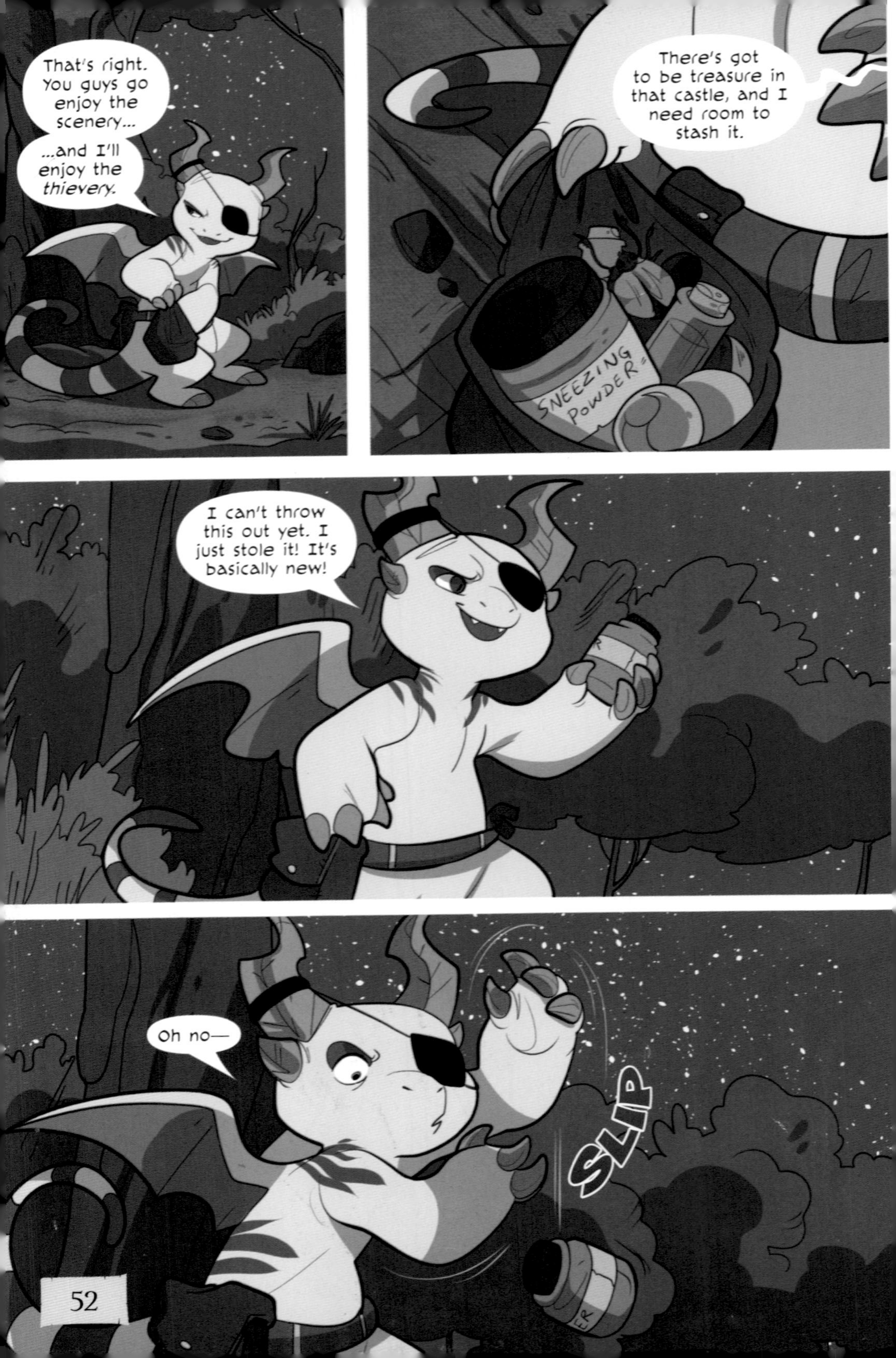

That's right. You guys go enjoy the scenery...
...and I'll enjoy the *thievery.*
There's got to be treasure in that castle, and I need room to stash it.
SNEEZING POWDER
I can't throw this out yet. I just stole it! It's basically new!
Oh no—
SLIP

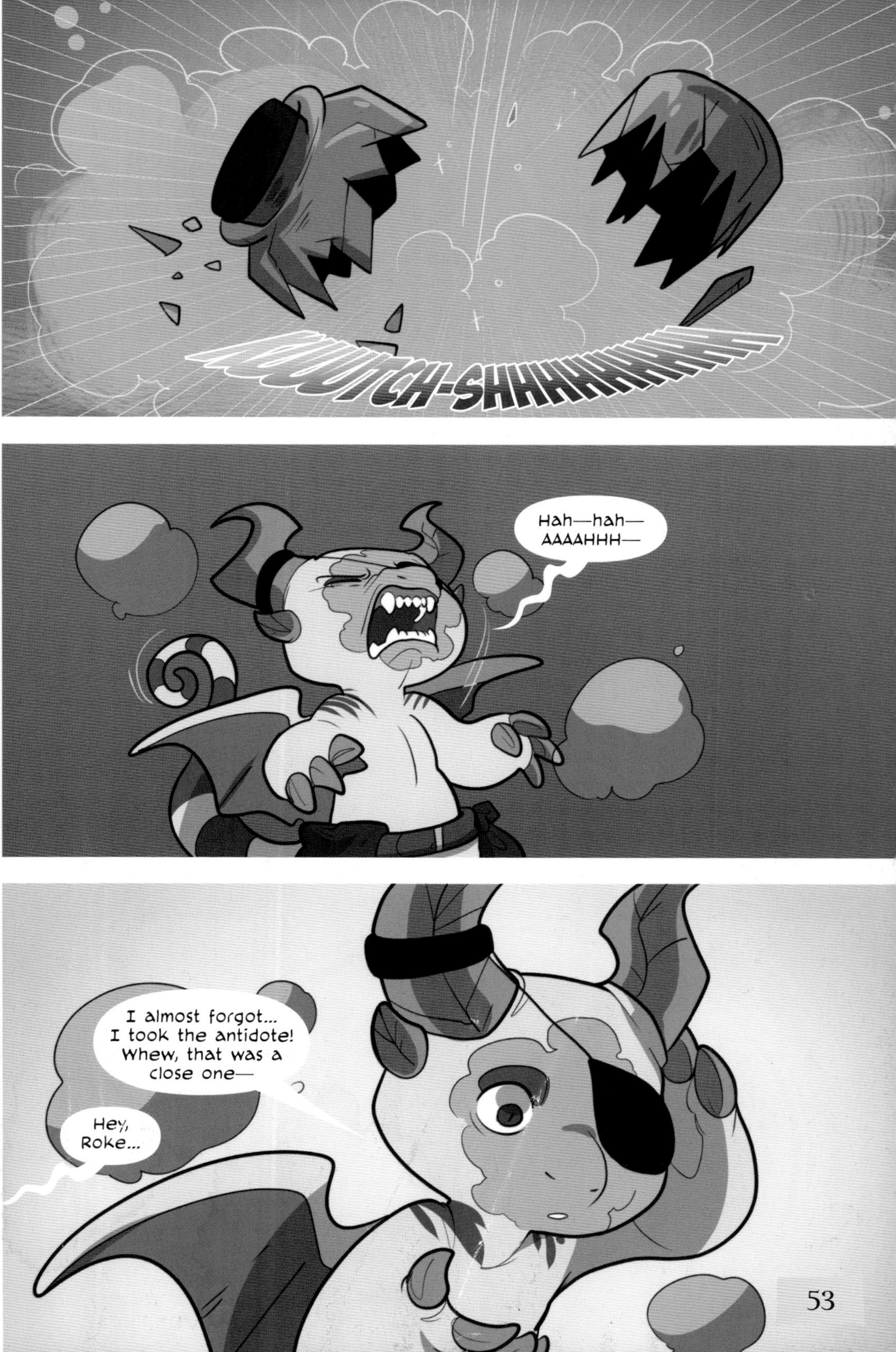
Hah—hah—
AAAAHHH—
I almost forgot... I took the antidote! Whew, that was a close one—
Hey, Roke...

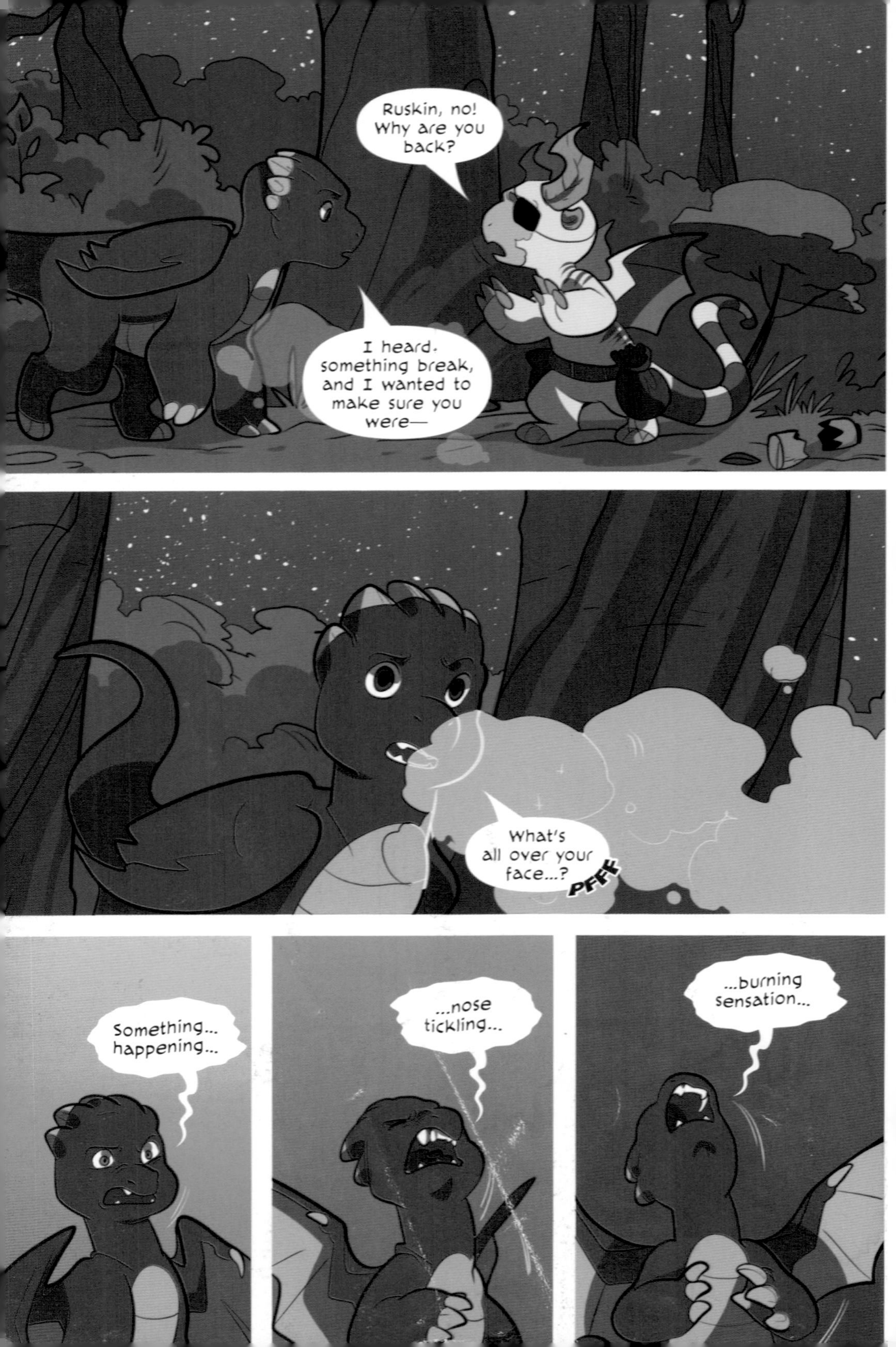
Ruskin, no! Why are you back?
I heard something break, and I wanted to make sure you were—
What's all over your face...?
PFFF
Something... happening...
...nose tickling...
...burning sensation...

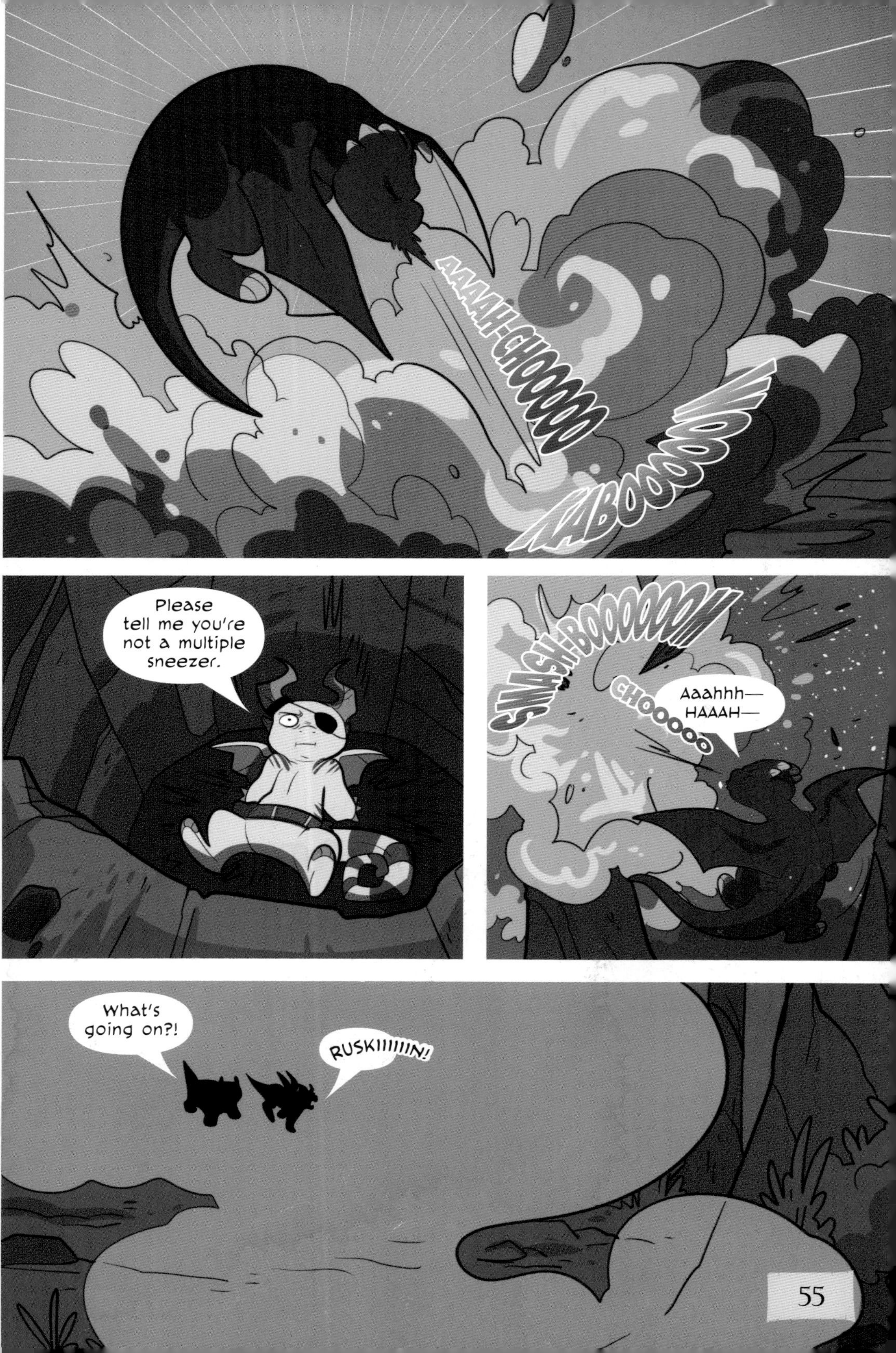
AAAAH-CHOOOOO
KABOOOOOOM
Please tell me you're not a multiple sneezer.
SMASH-BOOOOOOM
CHOOOOOO
Aaahhh—
HAAAH—
What's going on?!
RUSKIIIIIIIN!

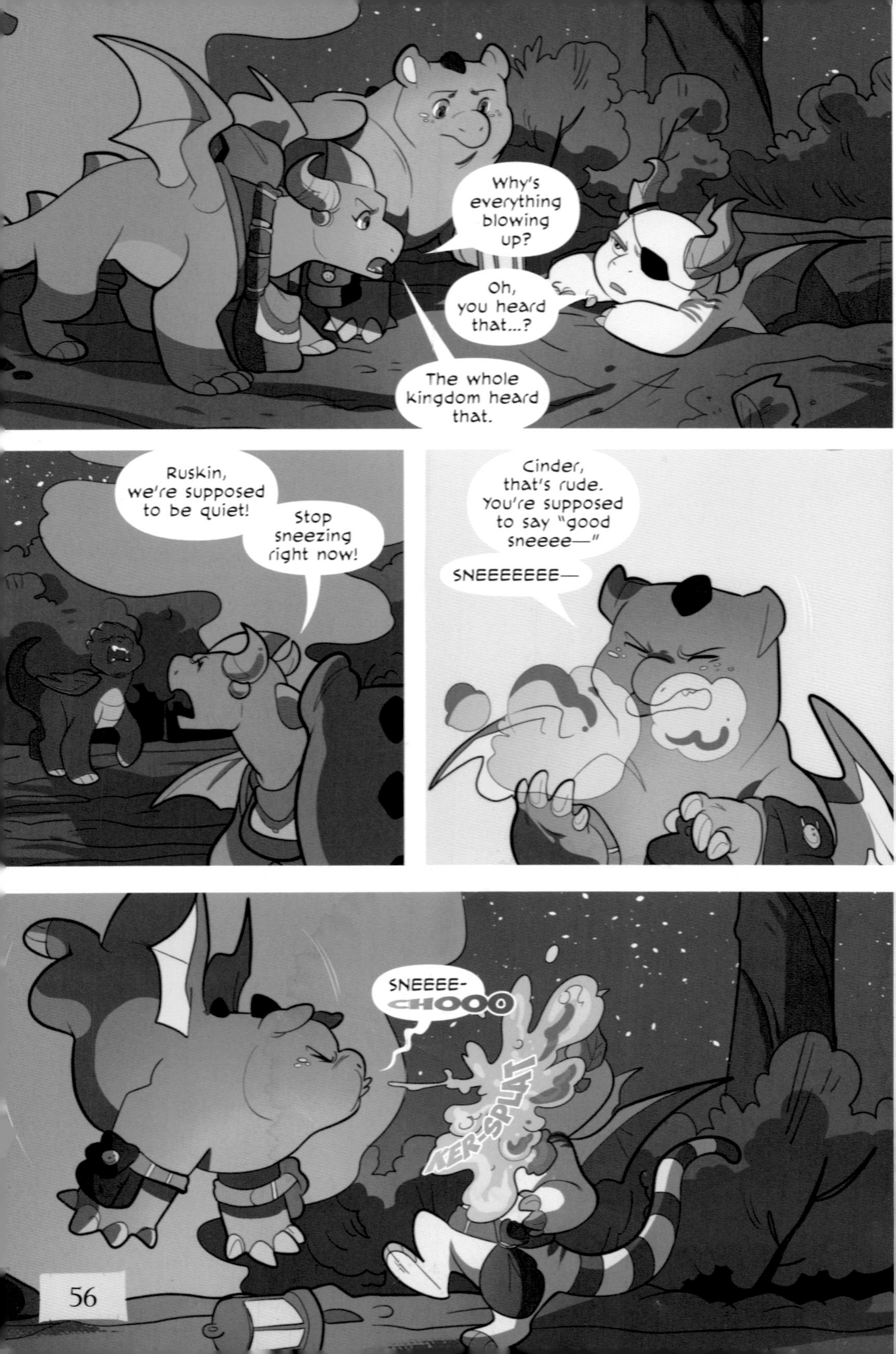
Why's everything blowing up?
Oh, you heard that...?
The whole kingdom heard that.
Ruskin, we're supposed to be quiet!
Stop sneezing right now!
Cinder, that's rude. You're supposed to say "good sneeee—"
SNEEEEEEE—
SNEEEE-CHOOO
KER-SPLAT

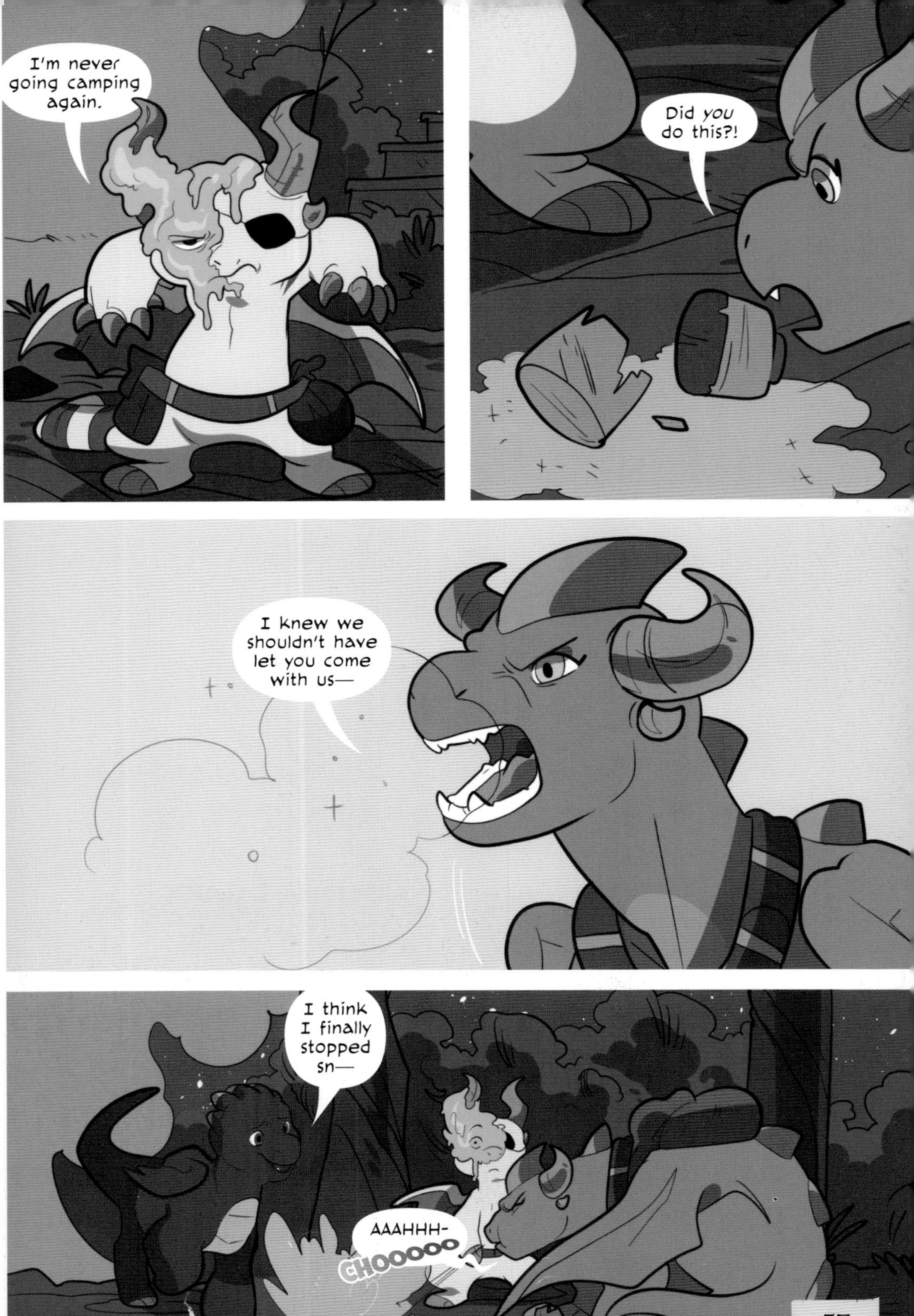
I'm never going camping again.
Did *you* do this?!
I knew we shouldn't have let you come with us—
I think I finally stopped sn—
AAAHHH-
CHOOOOO

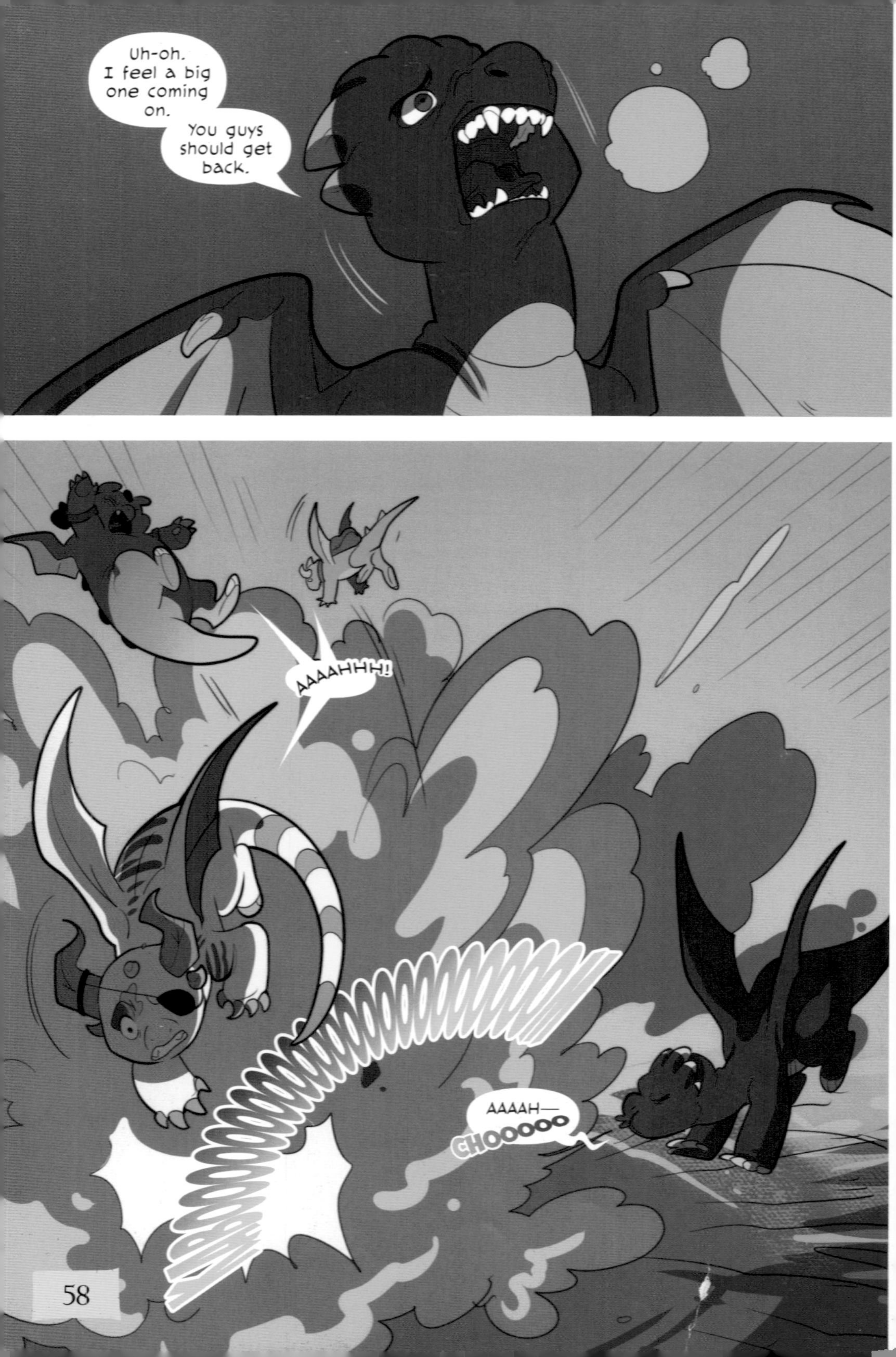
Uh-oh. I feel a big one coming on.
You guys should get back.
AAAAHHH!
AAAAH—
CHOOOOO

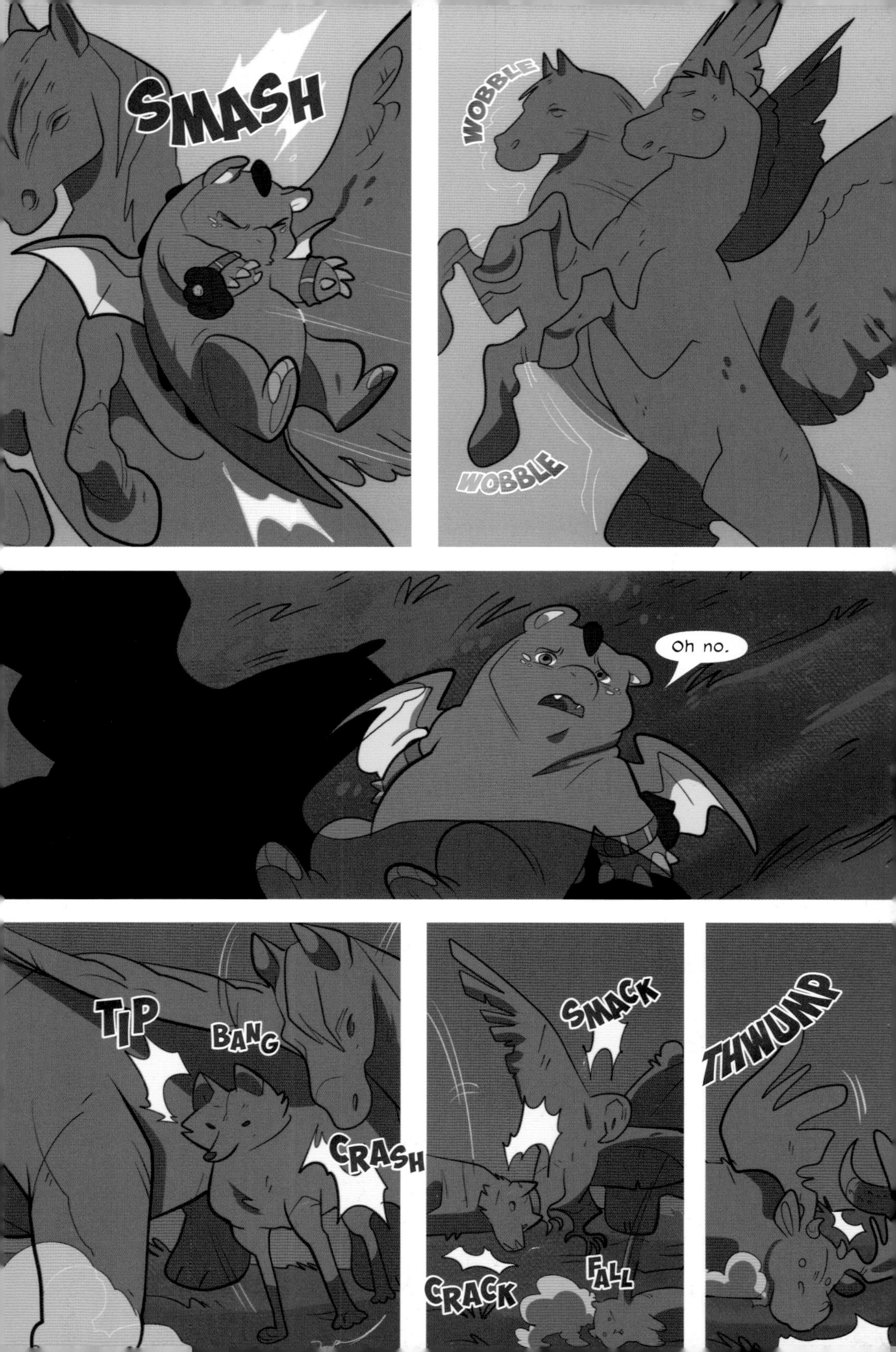
SMASH
WOBBLE
WOBBLE
Oh no.
TIP
BANG
CRASH
SMACK
CRACK
FALL
THWUMP

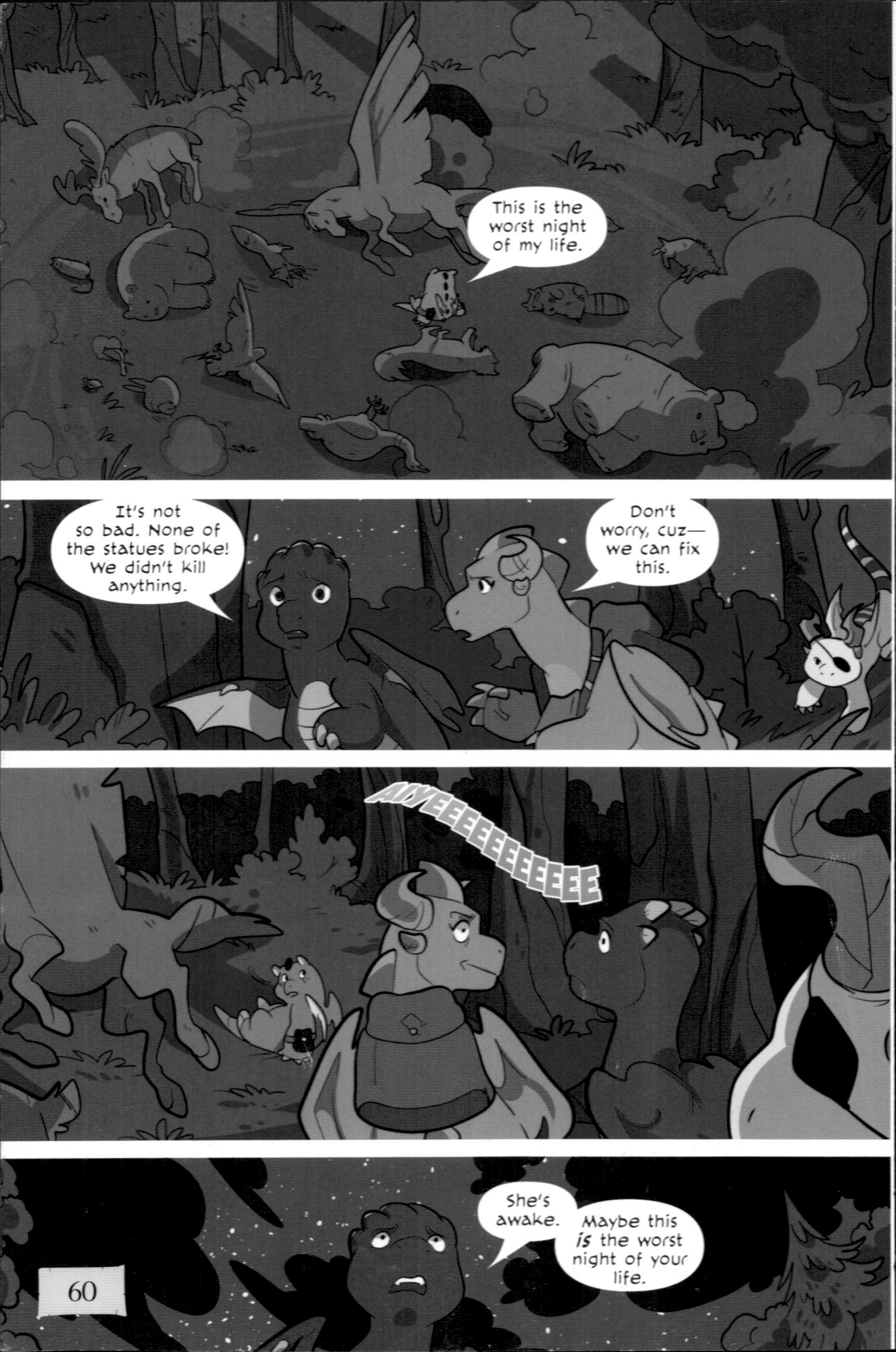
This is the worst night of my life.
It's not so bad. None of the statues broke! We didn't kill anything.
Don't worry, cuz— we can fix this.
AIYEEEEEEEEEEEE
She's awake.
Maybe this *is* the worst night of your life.

Chapter 5

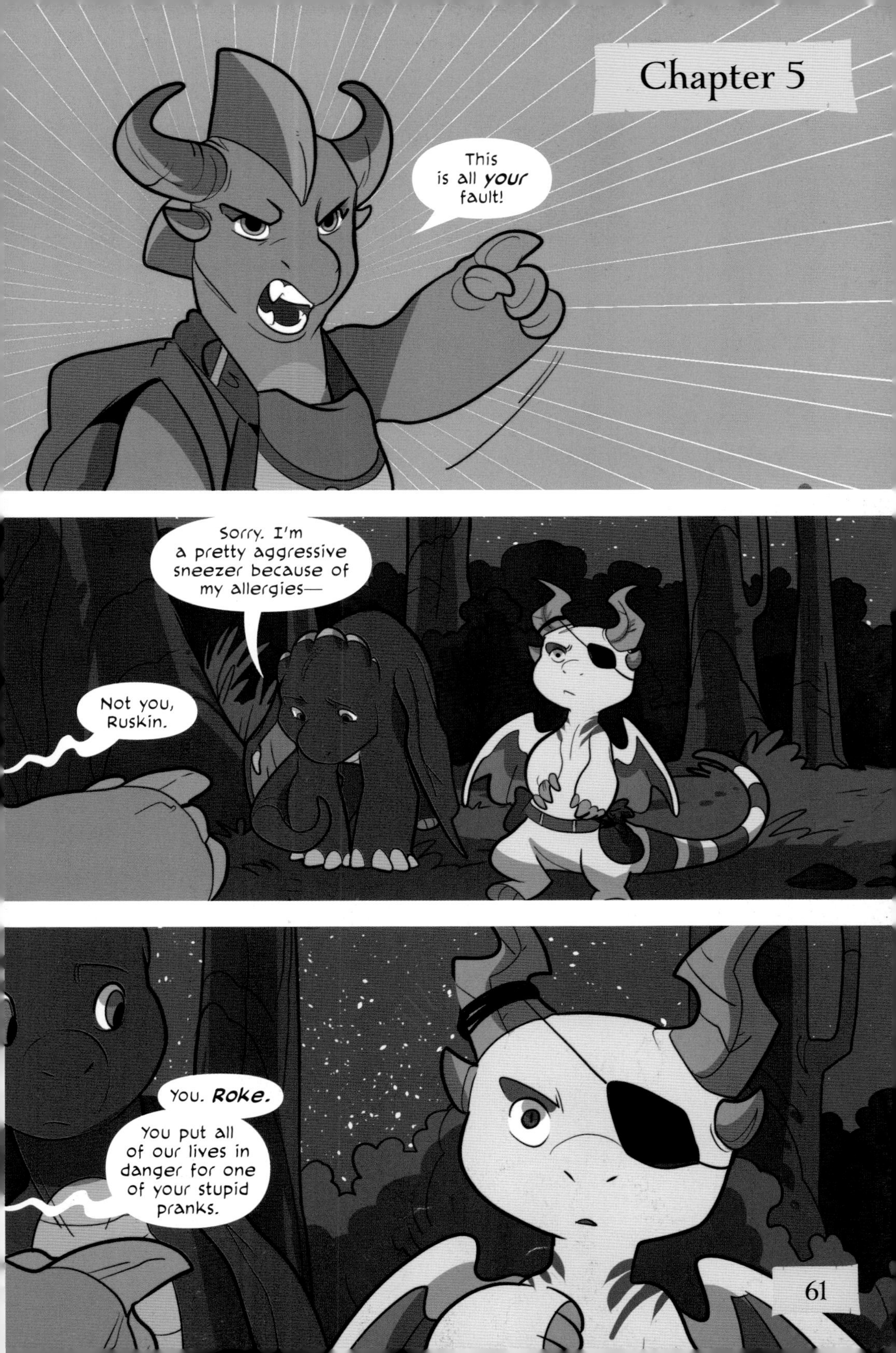

This is all *your* fault!
Sorry. I'm a pretty aggressive sneezer because of my allergies—
Not you, Ruskin.
You. **Roke.**
You put all of our lives in danger for one of your stupid pranks.

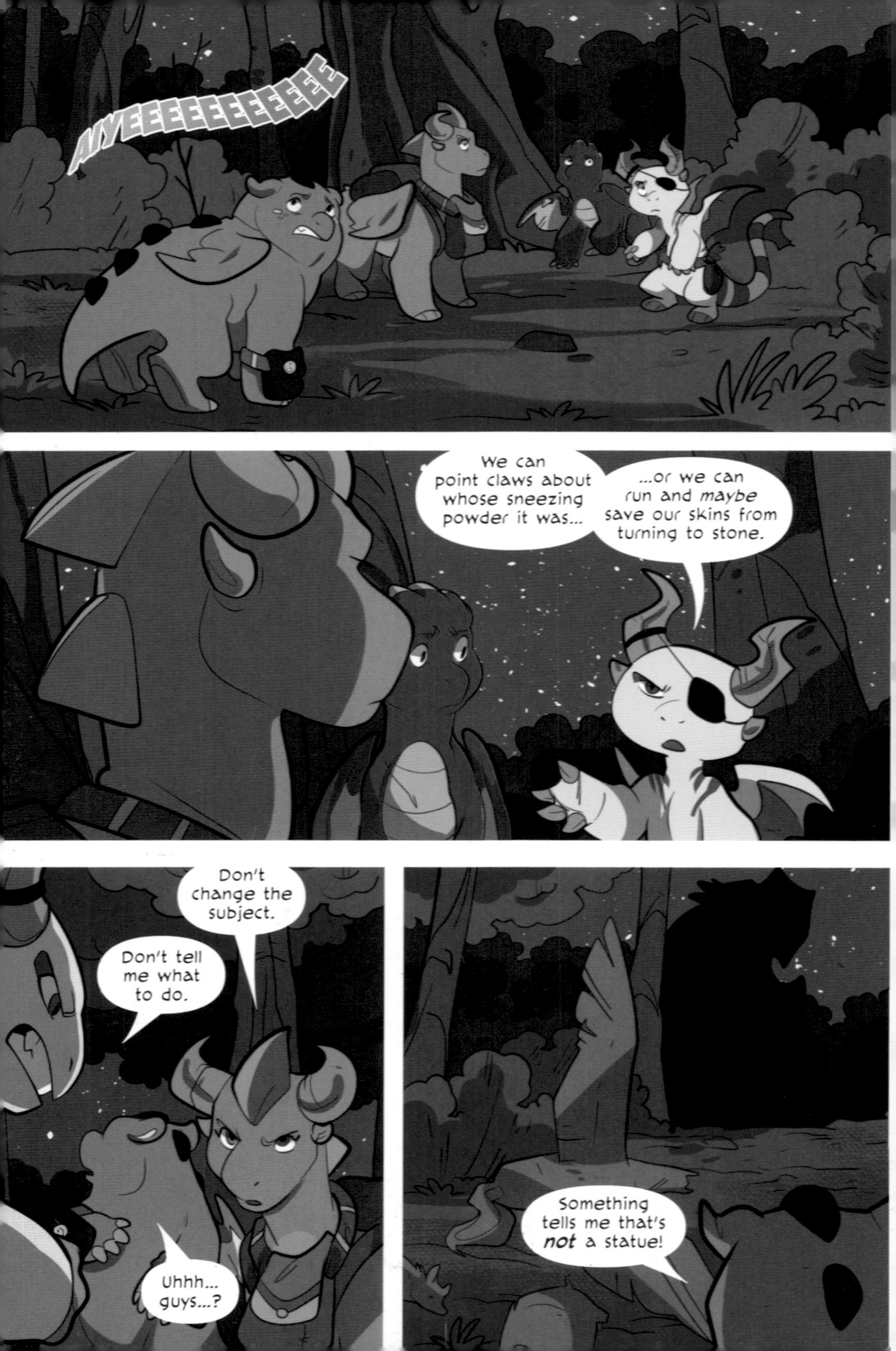
AIYEEEEEEEEEEEE
We can point claws about whose sneezing powder it was...
...or we can run and *maybe* save our skins from turning to stone.
Don't change the subject.
Don't tell me what to do.
Uhhh... guys...?
Something tells me that's *not* a statue!

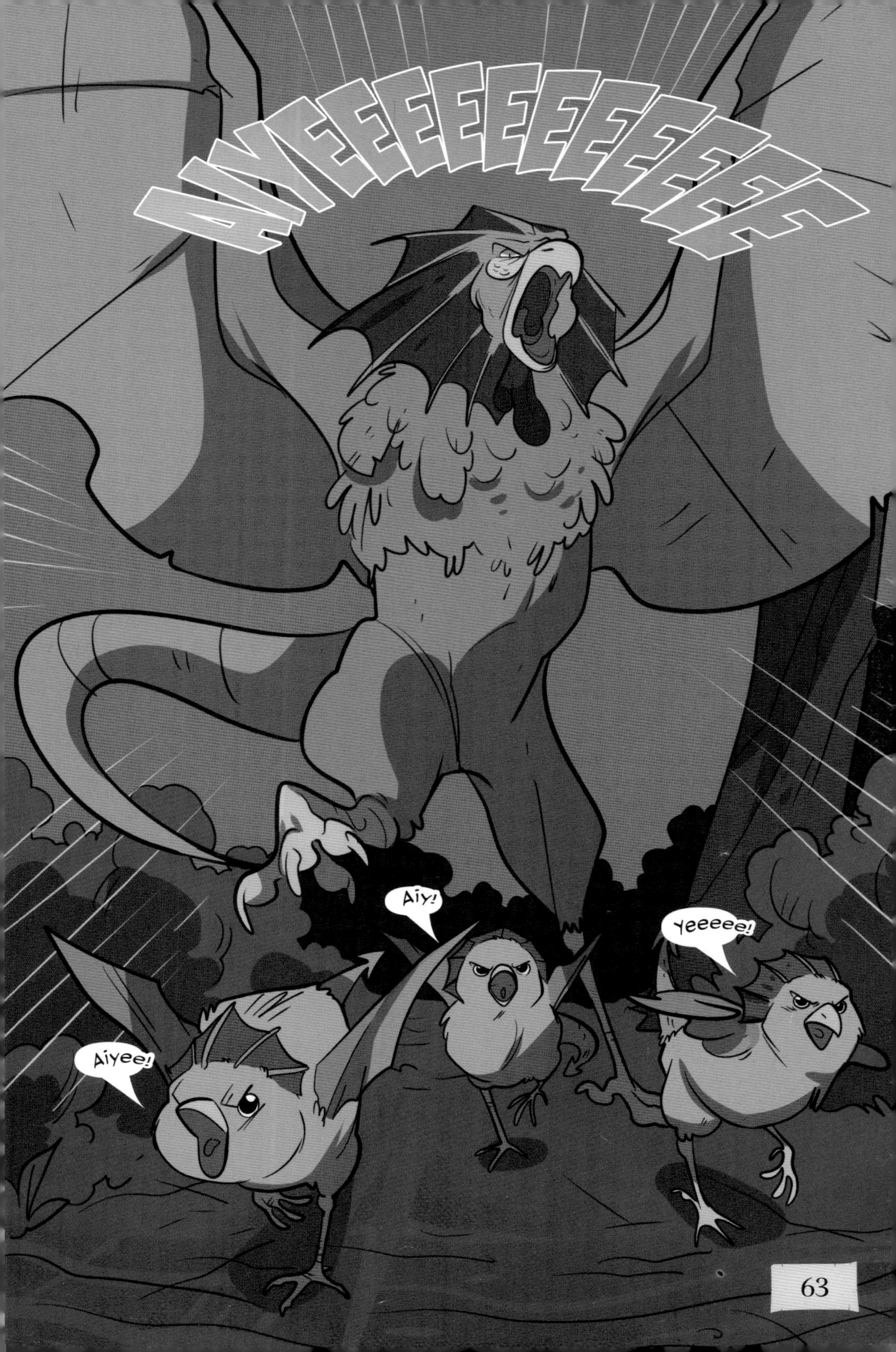
AIYEEEEEEEEEE
Aiy!
Yeeeee!
Aiyee!

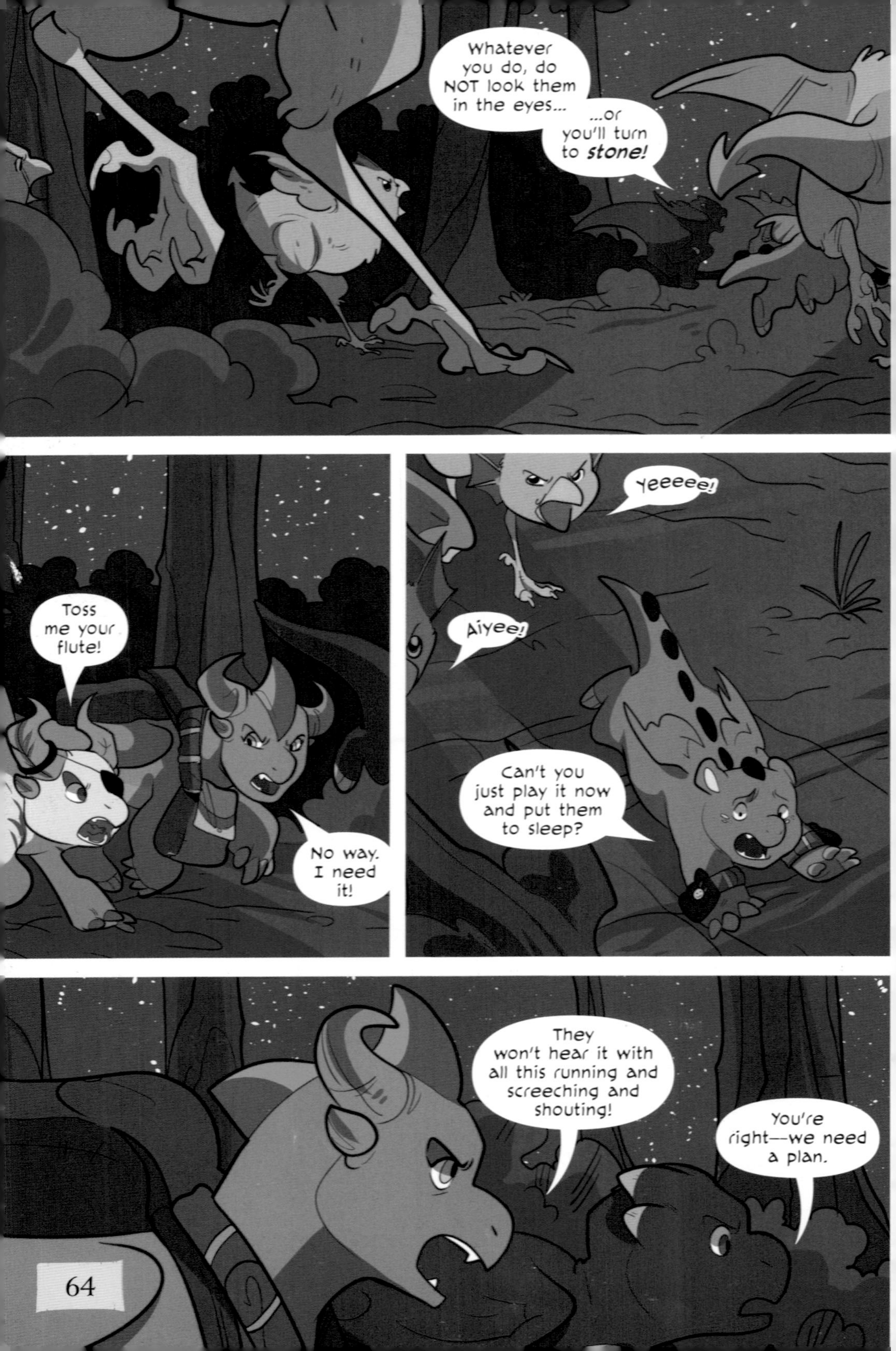
Whatever you do, do NOT look them in the eyes...
...or you'll turn to *stone!*
Toss me your flute!
No way. I need it!
Yeeeee!
Aiyee!
Can't you just play it now and put them to sleep?
They won't hear it with all this running and screeching and shouting!
You're right—we need a plan.

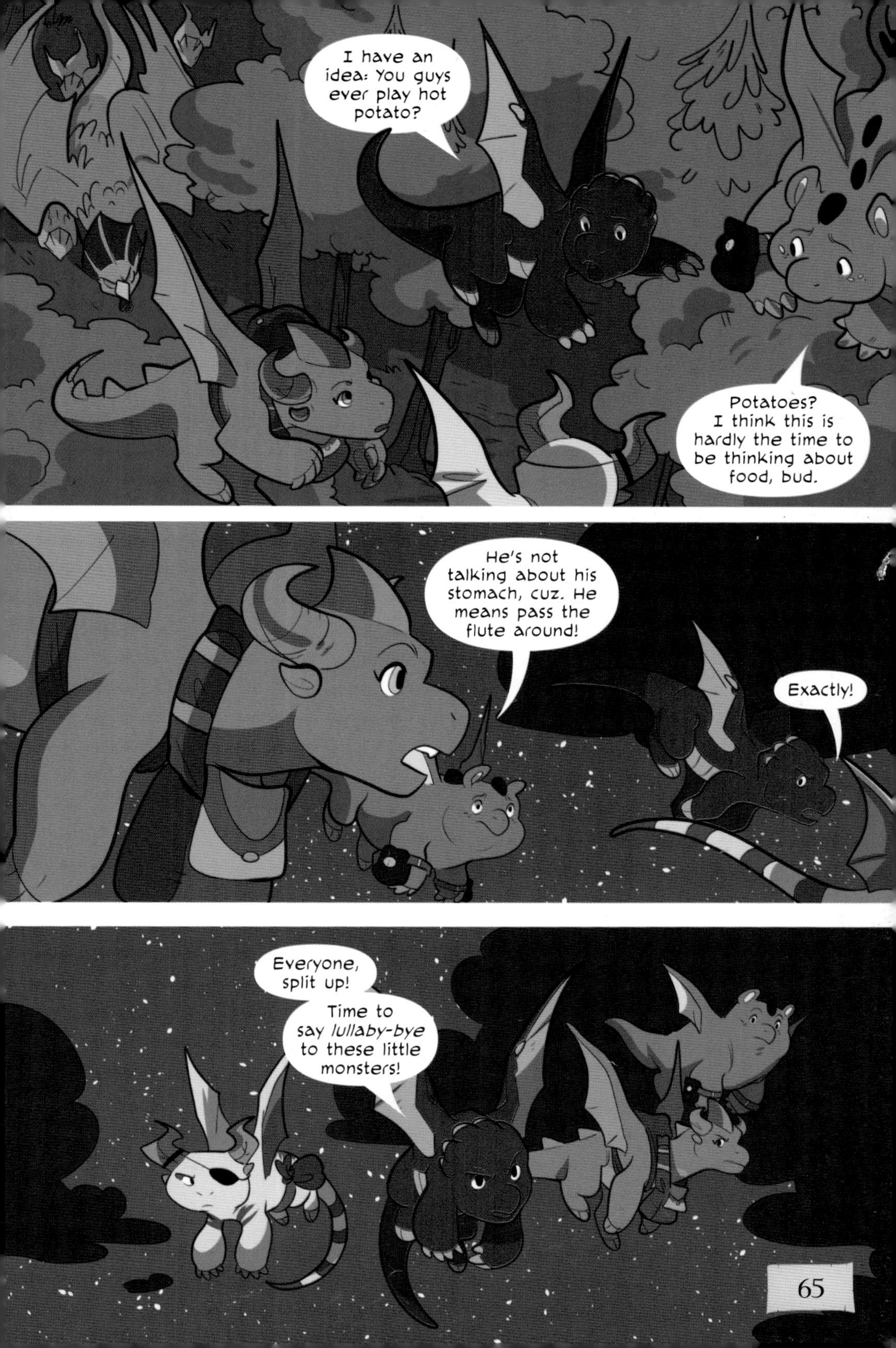
I have an idea: You guys ever play hot potato?
Potatoes? I think this is hardly the time to be thinking about food, bud.
He's not talking about his stomach, cuz. He means pass the flute around!
Exactly!
Everyone, split up!
Time to say *lullaby-bye* to these little monsters!

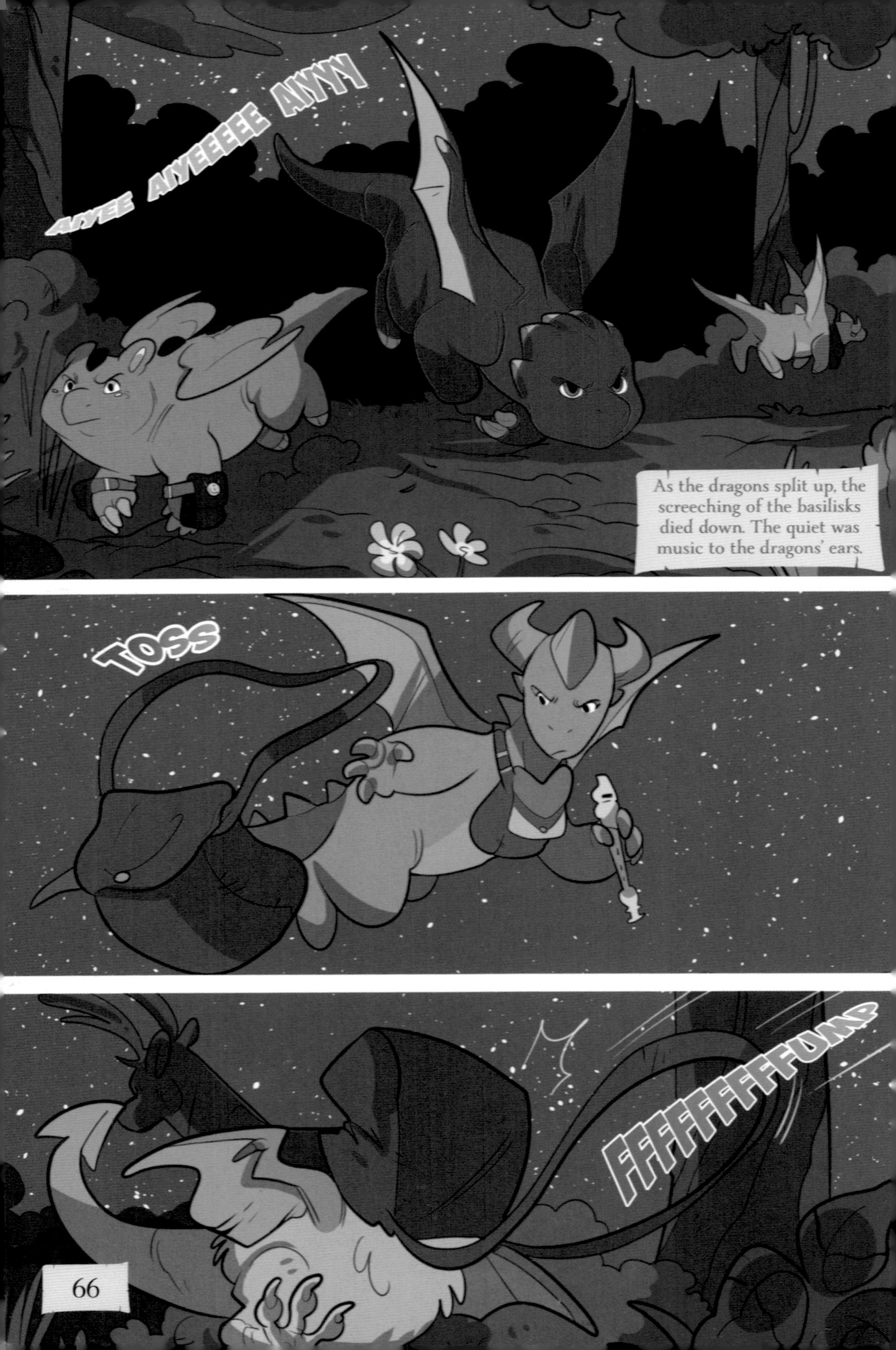
AIYEE AIYEEEEEE AIYYY
As the dragons split up, the screeching of the basilisks died down. The quiet was music to the dragons' ears.
TOSS
FFFFFFFFFUMP

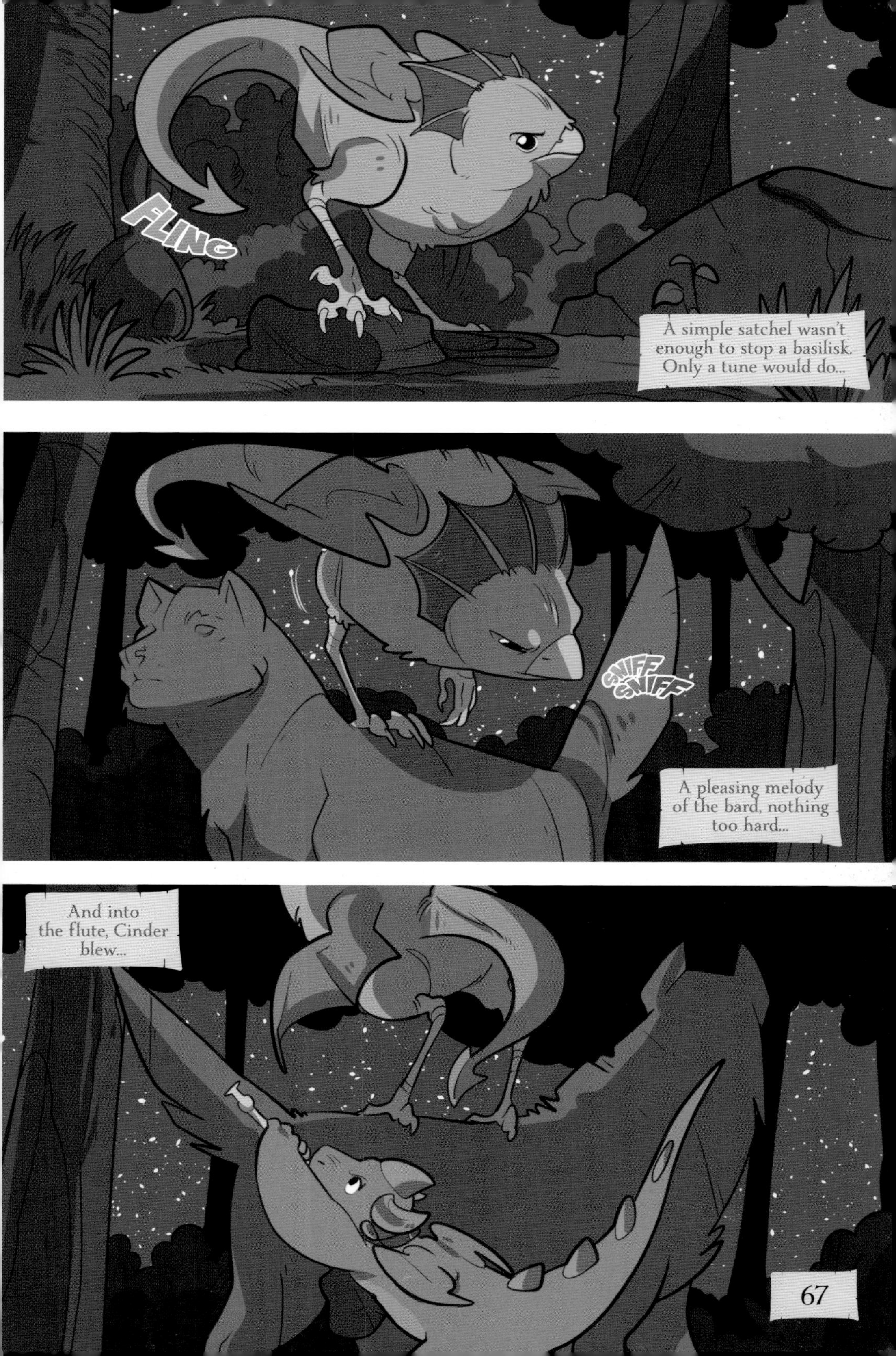
FLING
A simple satchel wasn't enough to stop a basilisk. Only a tune would do...
SNIFF SNIFF
A pleasing melody of the bard, nothing too hard...
And into the flute, Cinder blew...

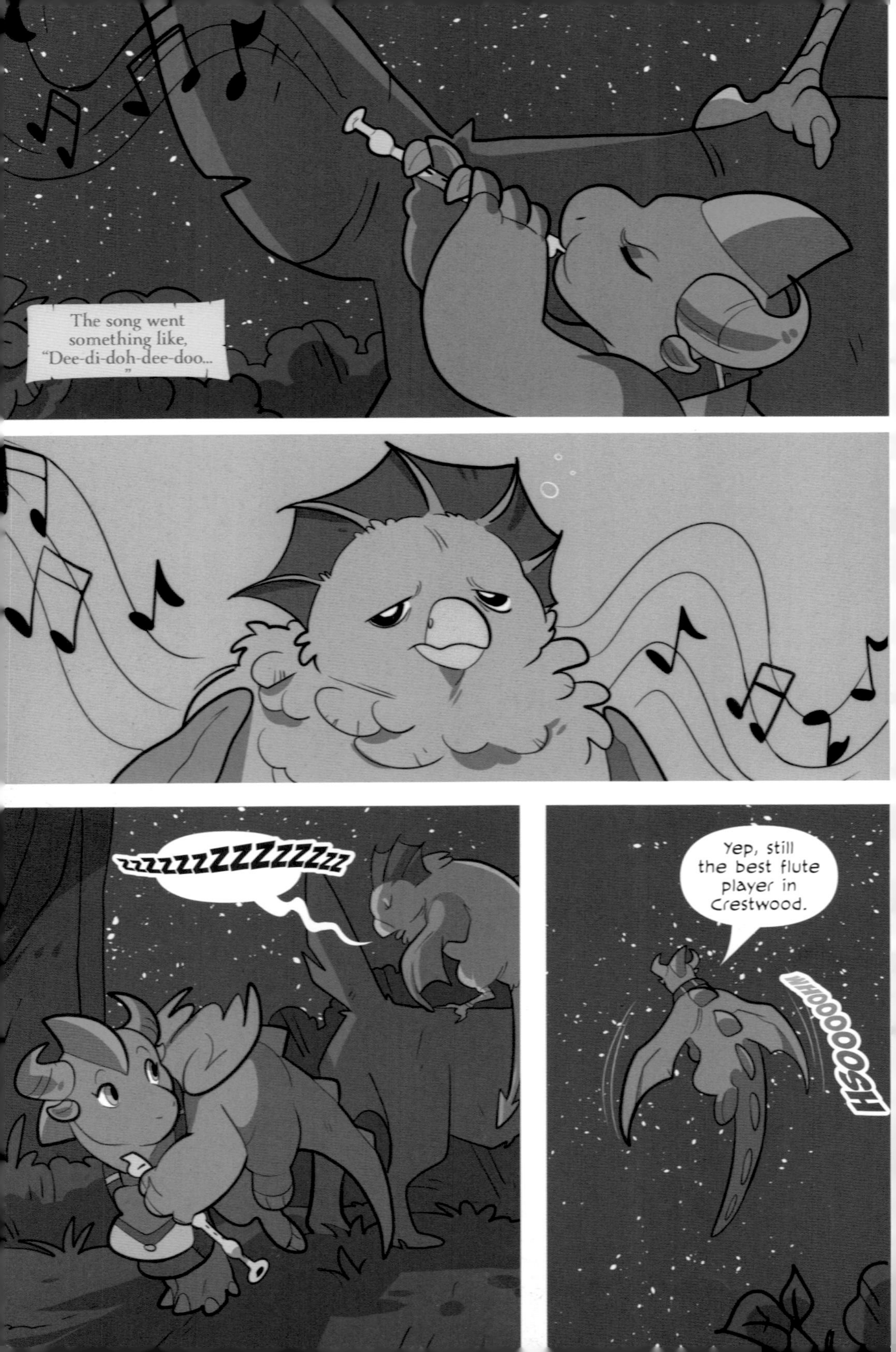
The song went something like, "Dee-di-doh-dee-doo... "
zzzzzzZZZZZZZzz
Yep, still the best flute player in Crestwood.
WHOOOOOOSH

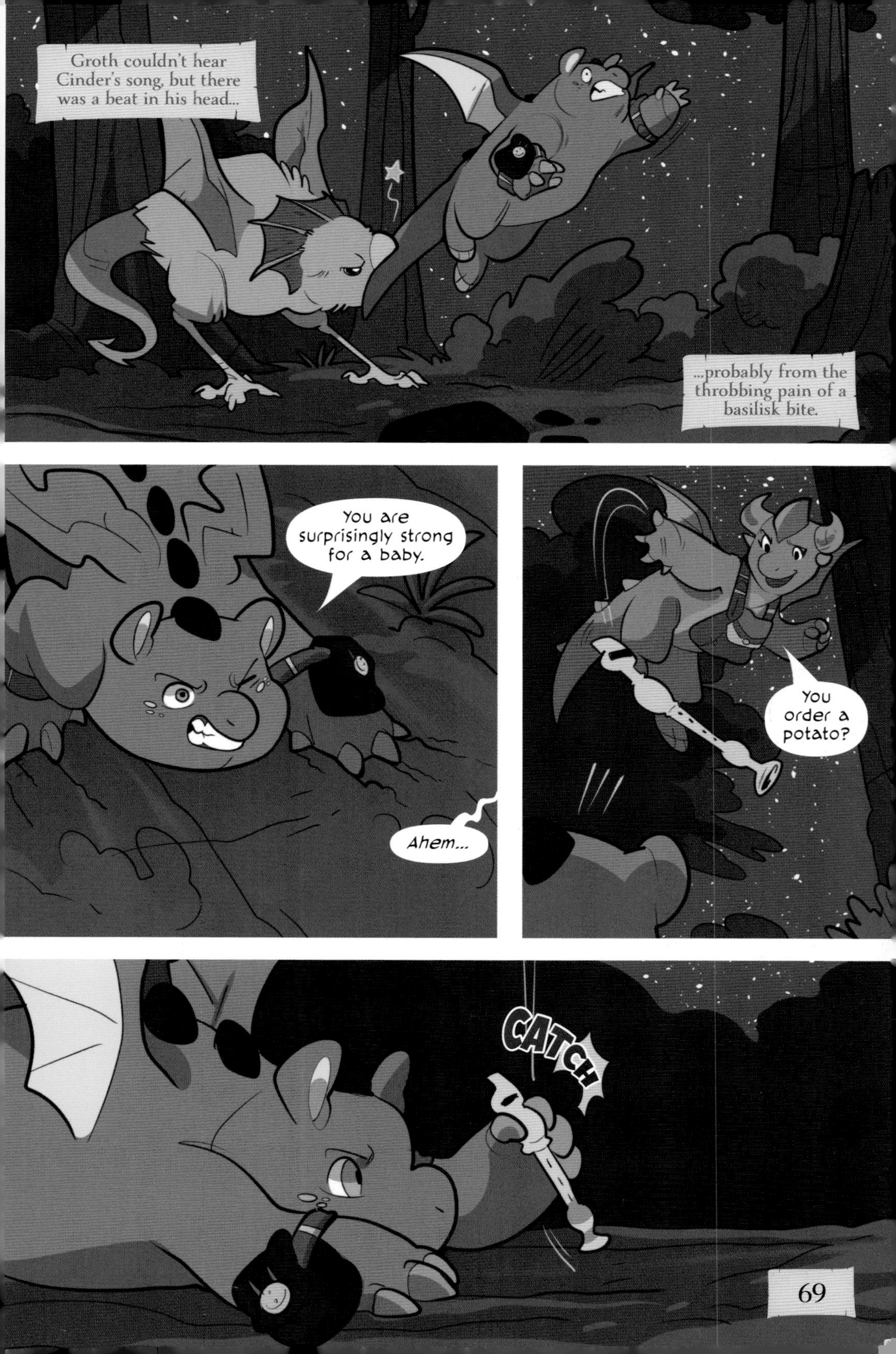

Groth couldn't hear Cinder's song, but there was a beat in his head...
...probably from the throbbing pain of a basilisk bite.
You are surprisingly strong for a baby.
Ahem...
You order a potato?
CATCH

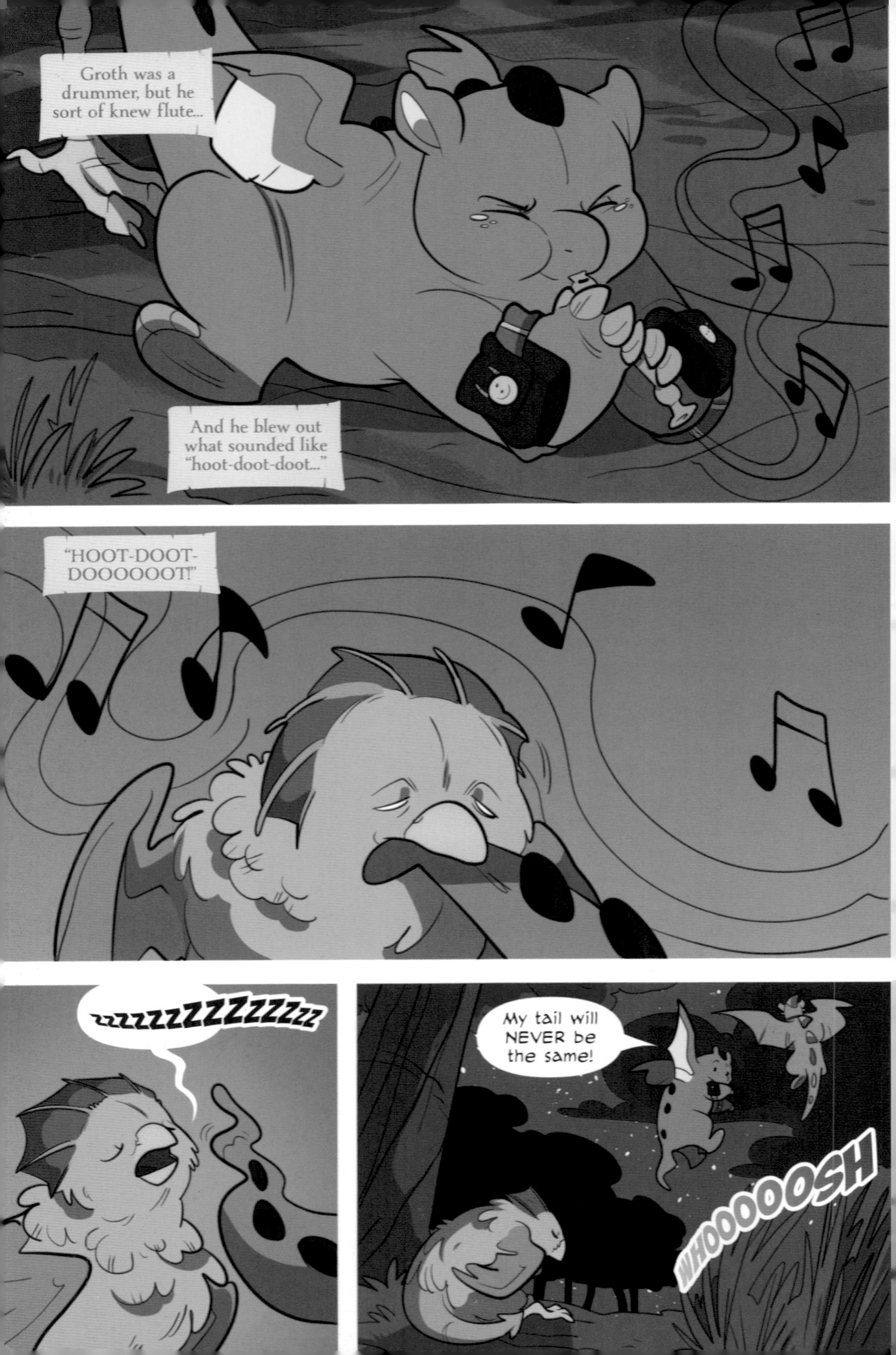
Groth was a drummer, but he sort of knew flute...
And he blew out what sounded like "hoot-doot-doot..."
"HOOT-DOOT-DOOOOOOT!"
zzzzzzZZZZZZZzz
My tail will NEVER be the same!
WHOOOOOOSH

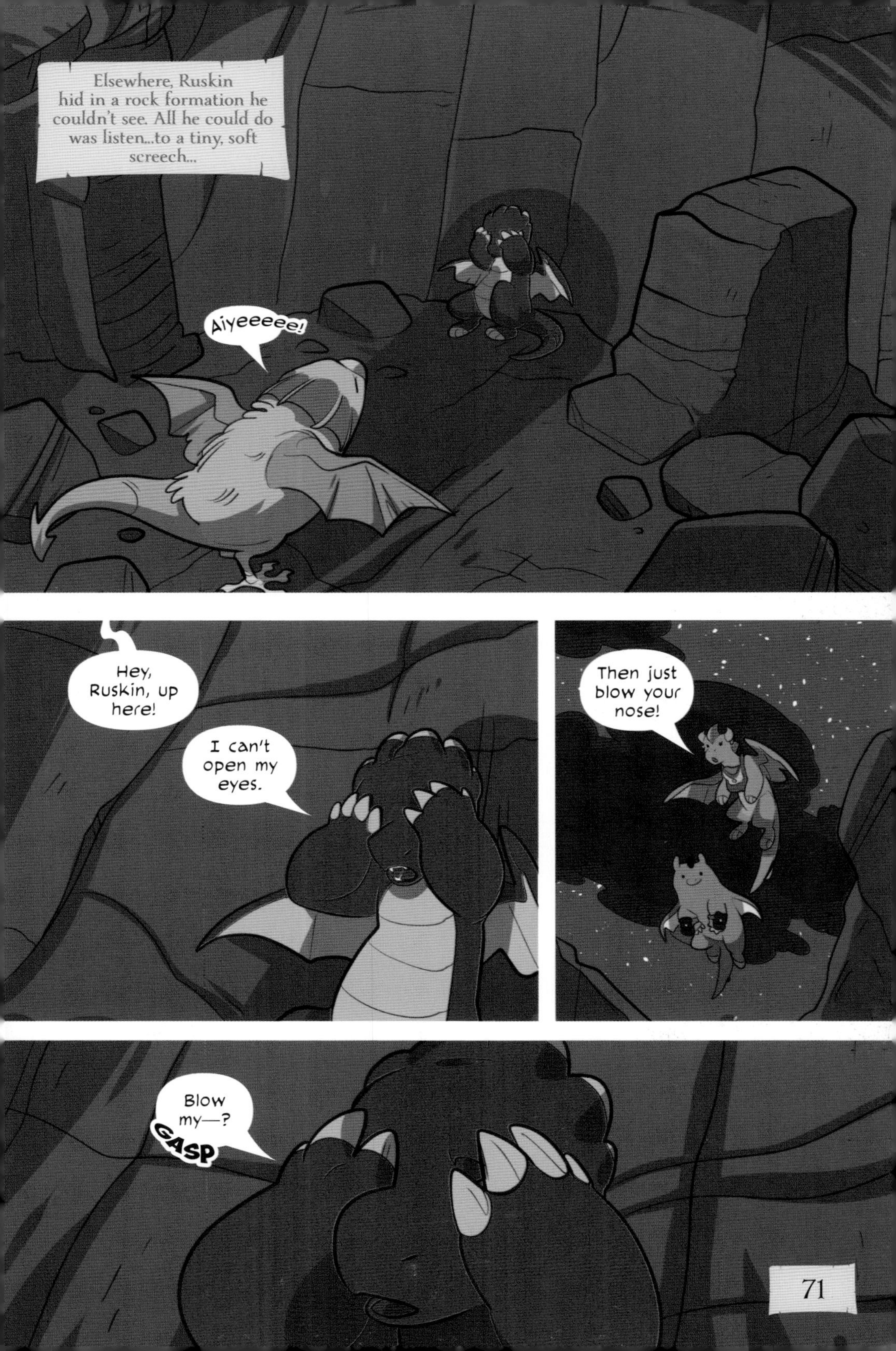
Elsewhere, Ruskin hid in a rock formation he couldn't see. All he could do was listen...to a tiny, soft screech...
Aiyeeeee!
Hey, Ruskin, up here!
I can't open my eyes.
Then just blow your nose!
Blow my—?
GASP

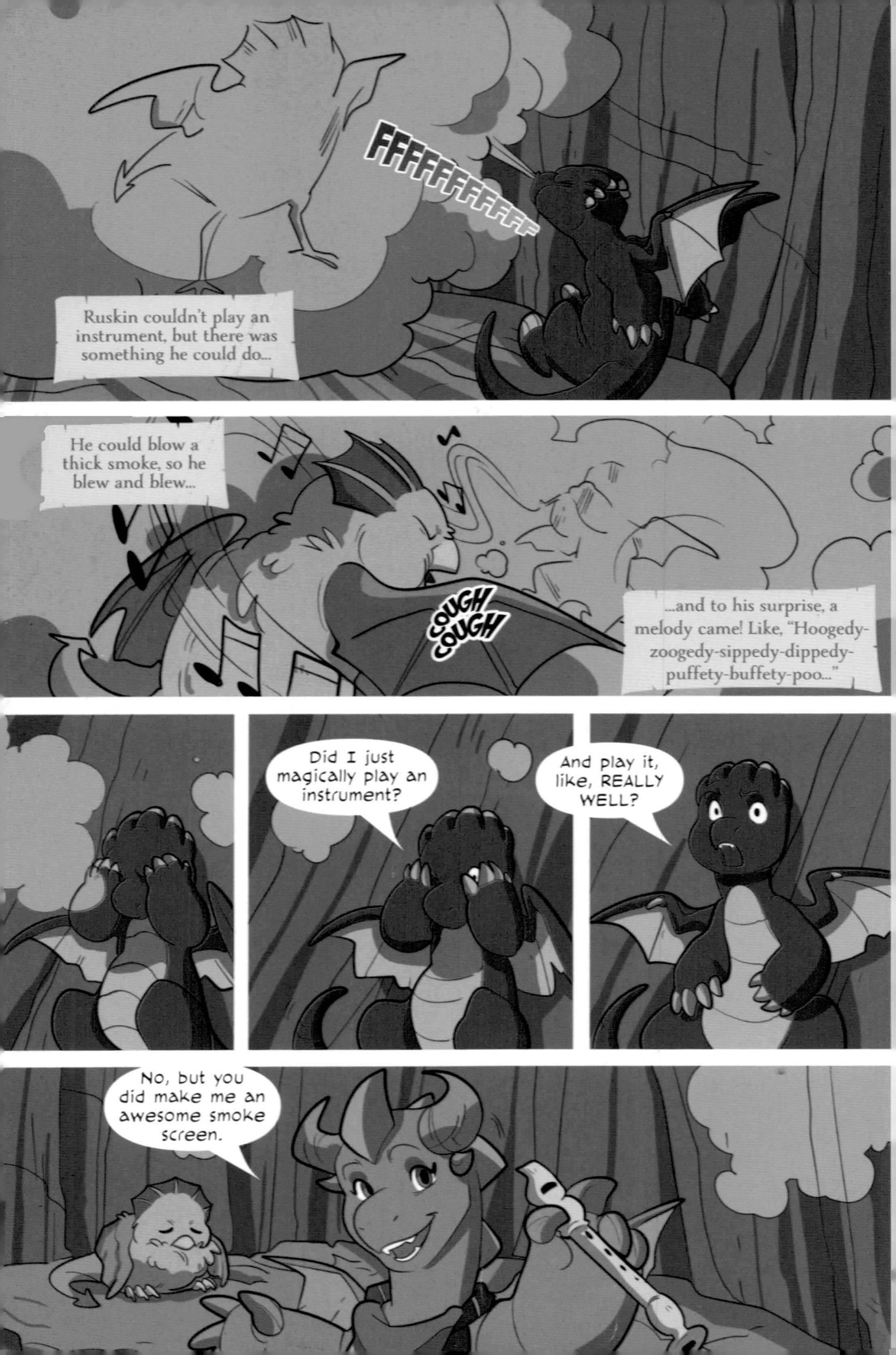
FFFFFFFFFFFFF
Ruskin couldn't play an instrument, but there was something he could do...
He could blow a thick smoke, so he blew and blew...
COUGH COUGH
...and to his surprise, a melody came! Like, "Hoogedy-zoogedy-sippedy-dippedy-puffety-buffety-poo..."
Did I just magically play an instrument?
And play it, like, REALLY WELL?
No, but you did make me an awesome smoke screen.

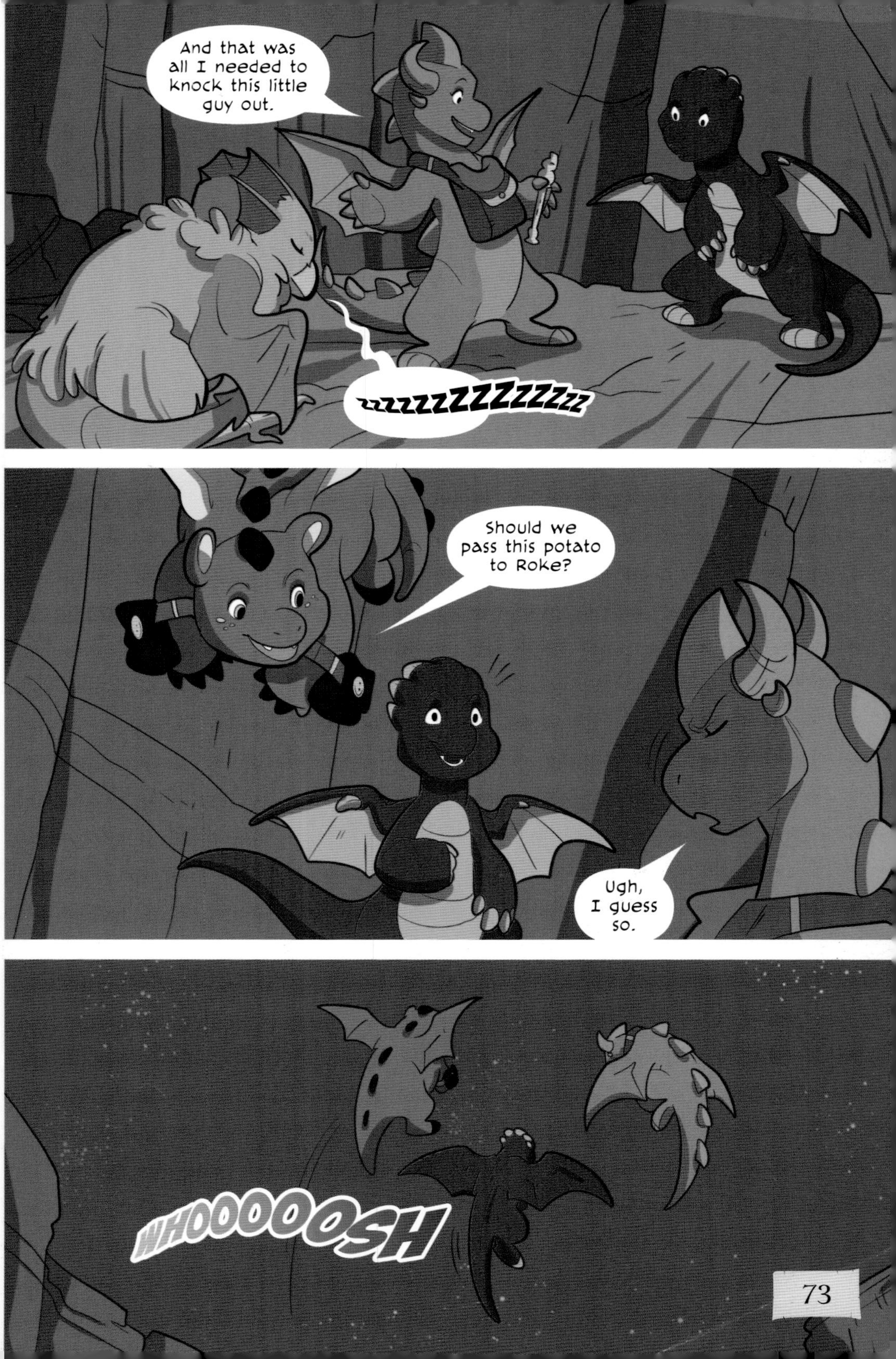
And that was all I needed to knock this little guy out.
zzzzzzZZZZZZzz
Should we pass this potato to Roke?
Ugh, I guess so.
WHOOOOOOSH

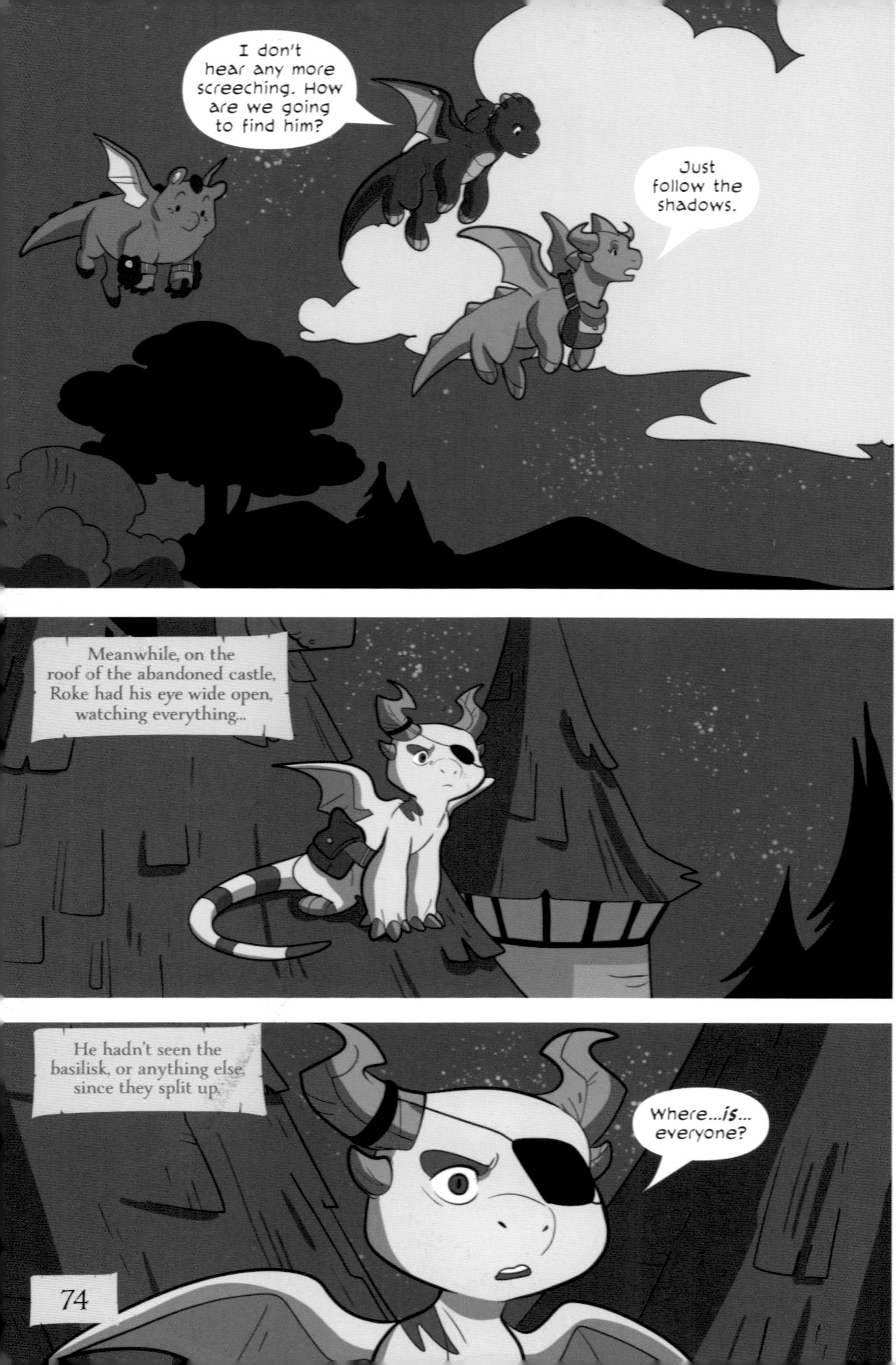
I don't hear any more screeching. How are we going to find him?
Just follow the shadows.
Meanwhile, on the roof of the abandoned castle, Roke had his eye wide open, watching everything...
He hadn't seen the basilisk, or anything else, since they split up.
Where...*is*... everyone?

And where is that disgusting-looking basilisk?

Probably somewhere licking its feathers.

This place isn't that spooky.

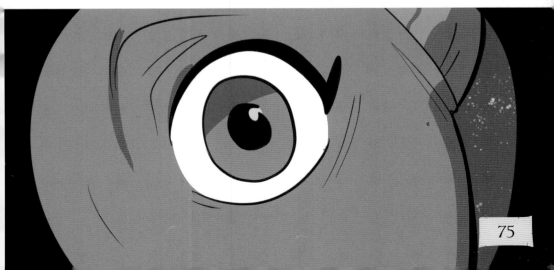

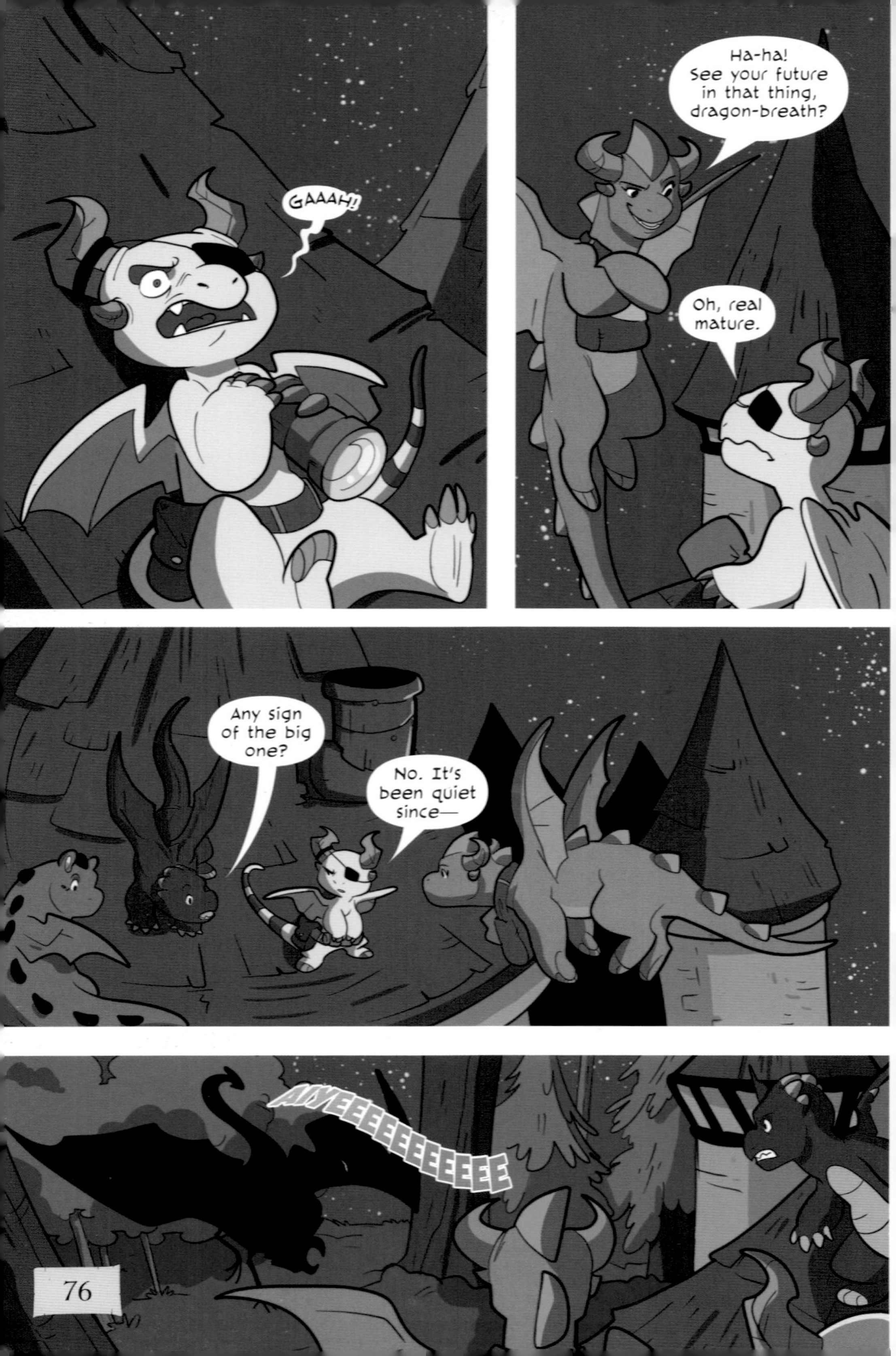
GAAAH!
Ha-ha! See your future in that thing, dragon-breath?
Oh, real mature.
Any sign of the big one?
No. It's been quiet since—
AIYEEEEEEEEEEEE

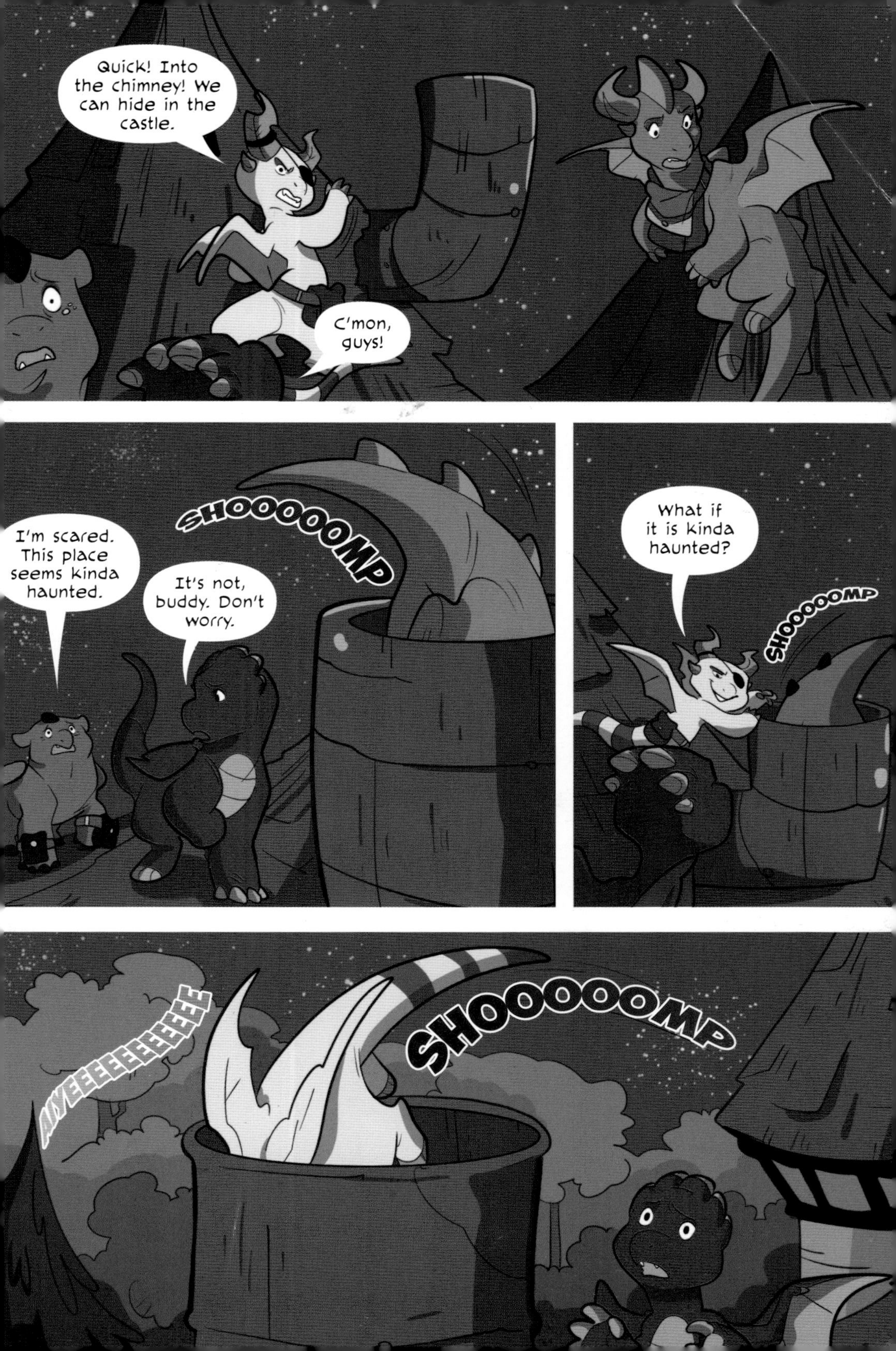

Quick! Into the chimney! We can hide in the castle.
C'mon, guys!
SHOOOOOOMP
I'm scared. This place seems kinda haunted.
It's not, buddy. Don't worry.
What if it is kinda haunted?
SHOOOOOMP
AIYEEEEEEEEEE
SHOOOOOOMP

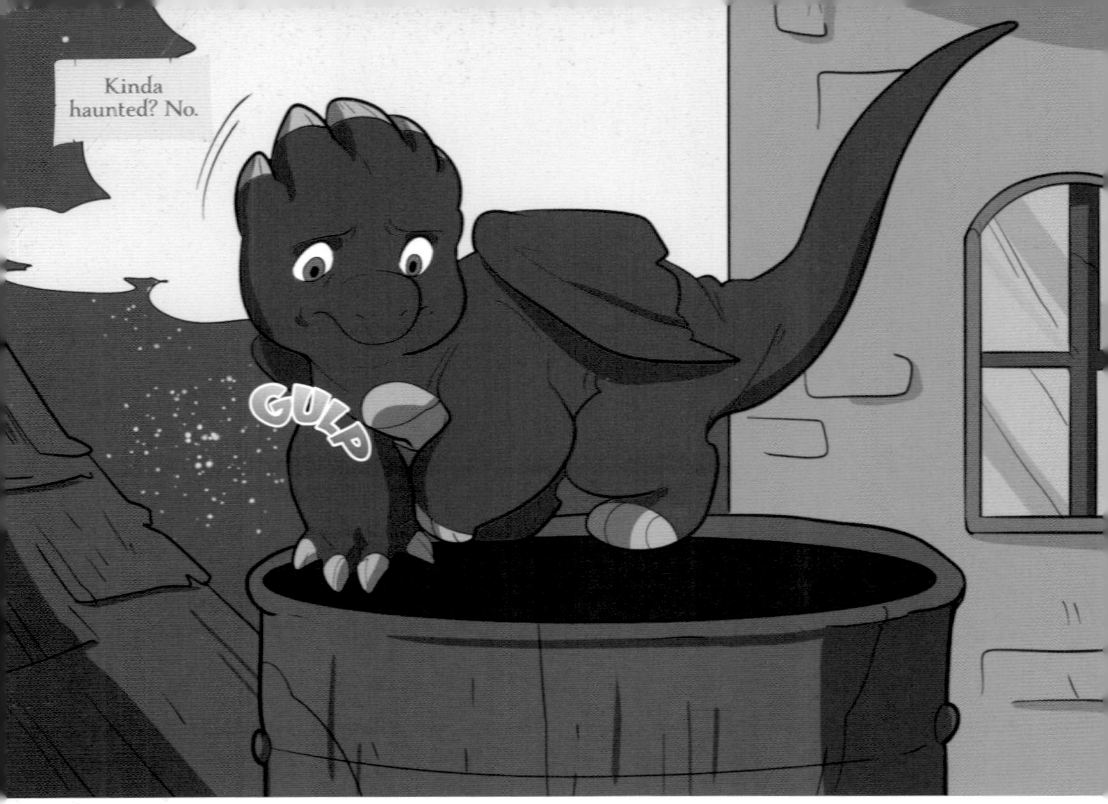
Kinda haunted? No.
GULP

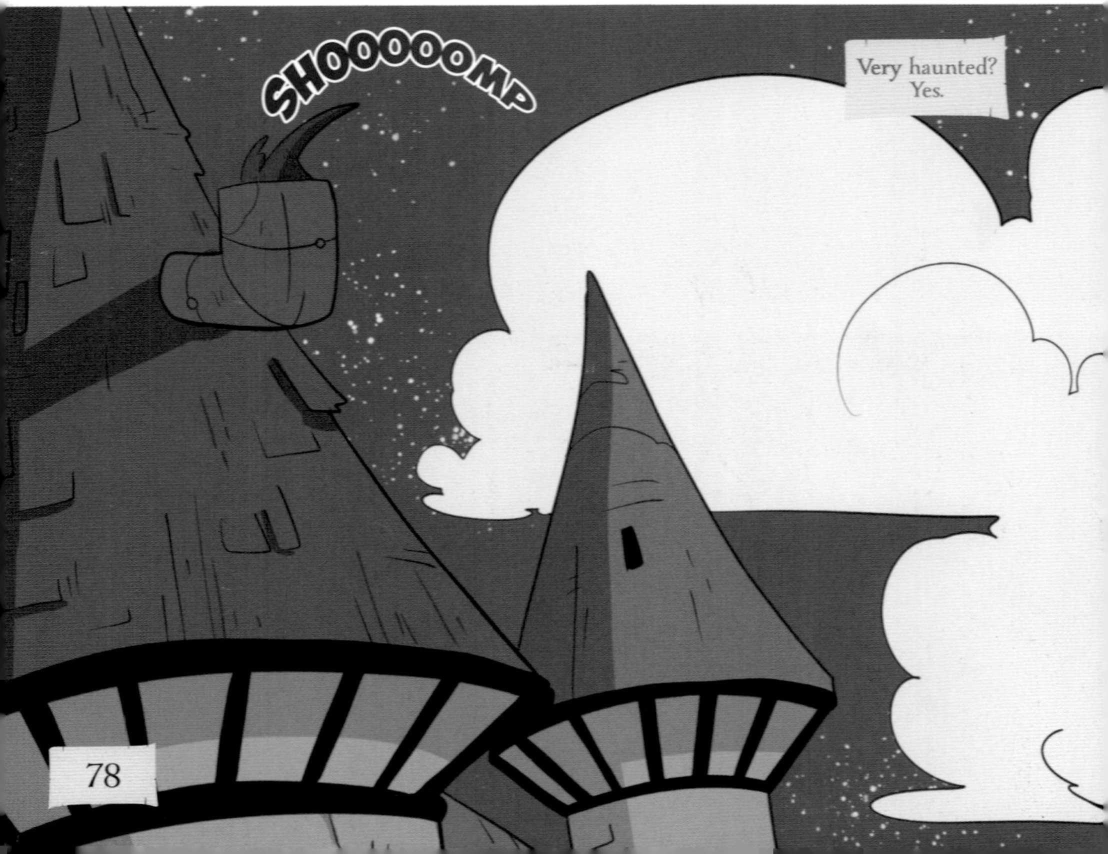
SHOOOOOOMP
Very haunted? Yes.

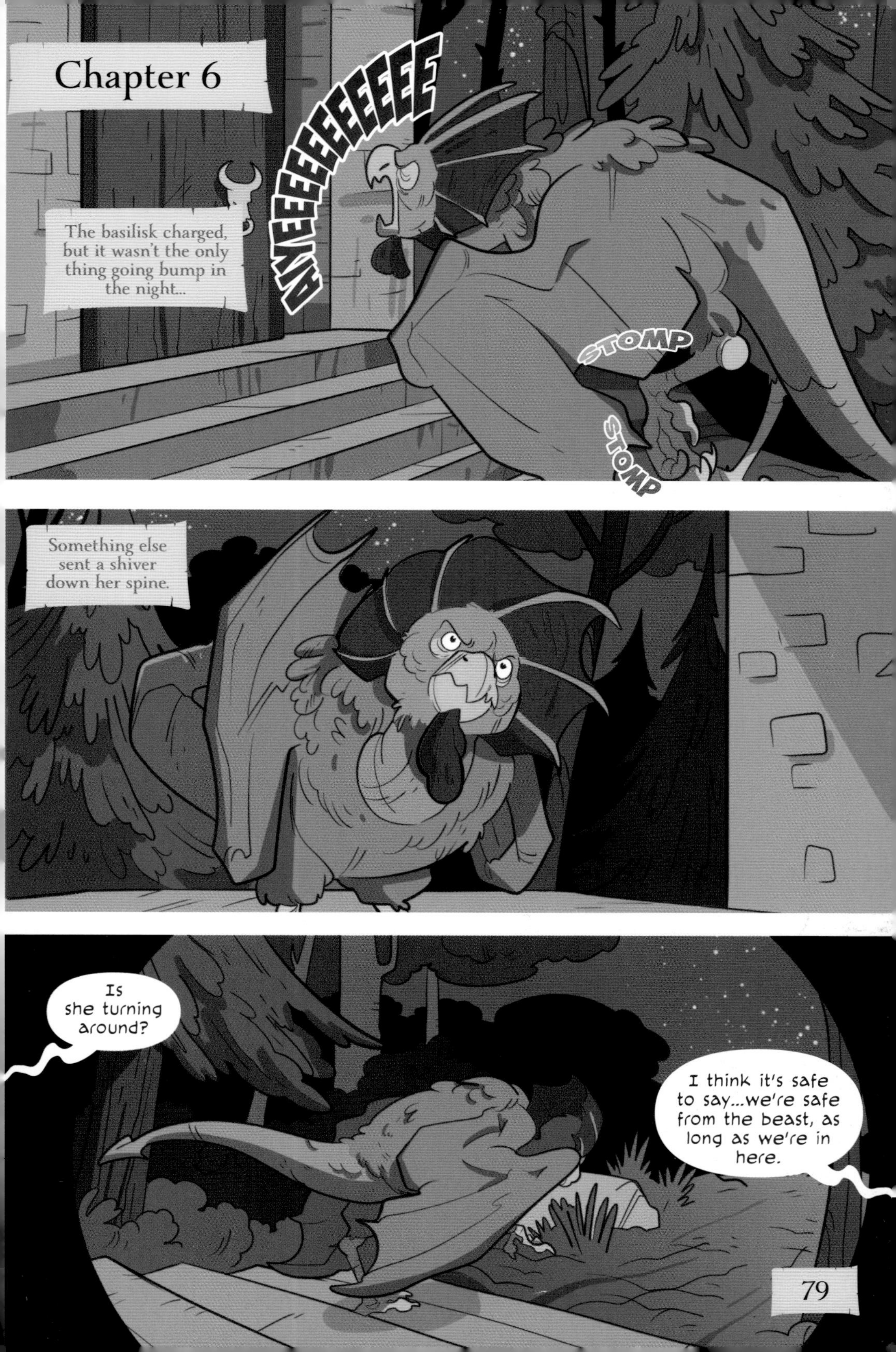
Chapter 6
The basilisk charged, but it wasn't the only thing going bump in the night...
AYEEEEEEEEEEE
STOMP
STOMP
Something else sent a shiver down her spine.
Is she turning around?
I think it's safe to say...we're safe from the beast, as long as we're in here.

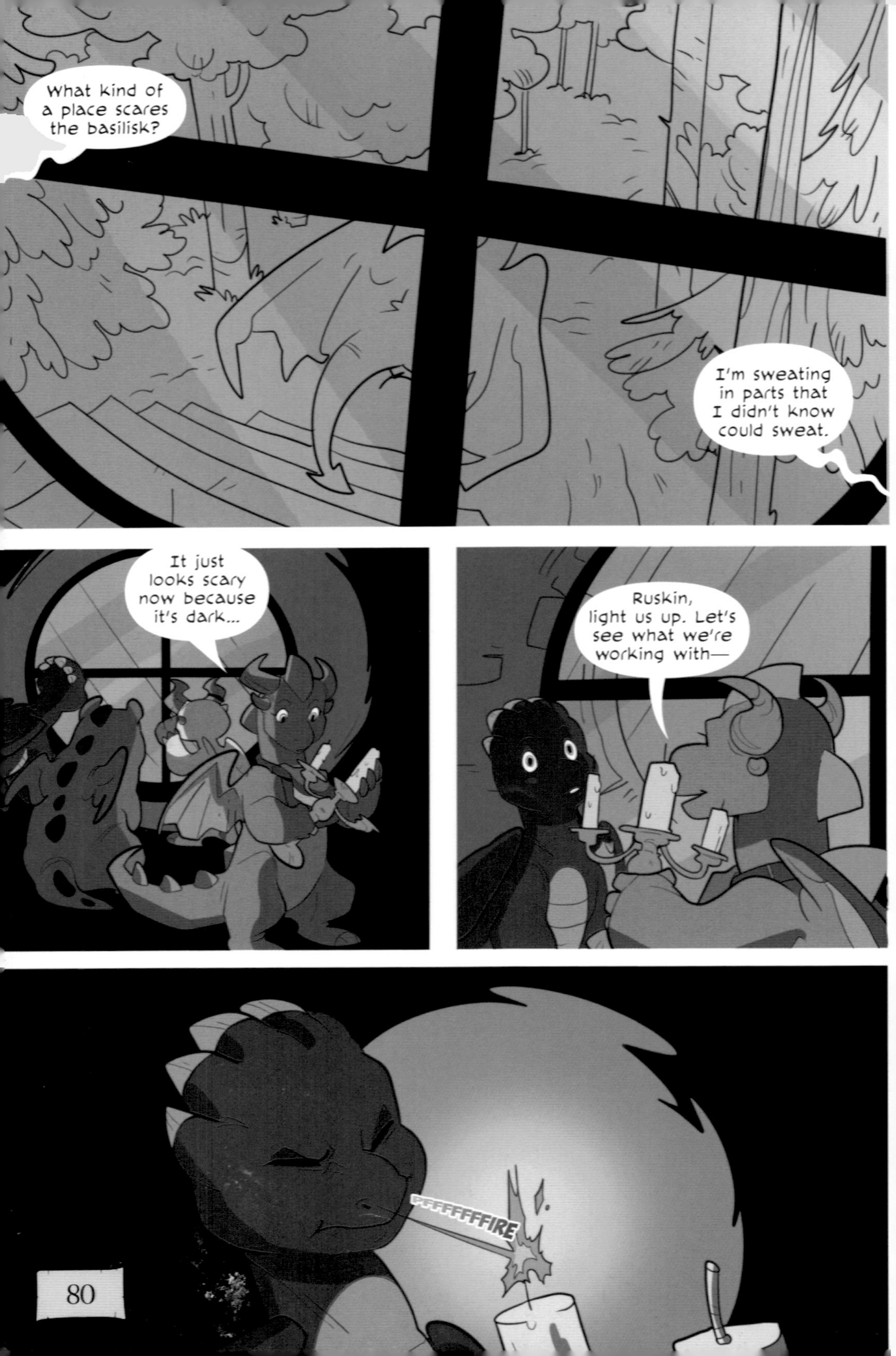
What kind of a place scares the basilisk?
I'm sweating in parts that I didn't know could sweat.
It just looks scary now because it's dark...
Ruskin, light us up. Let's see what we're working with—
PFFFFFFFIRE

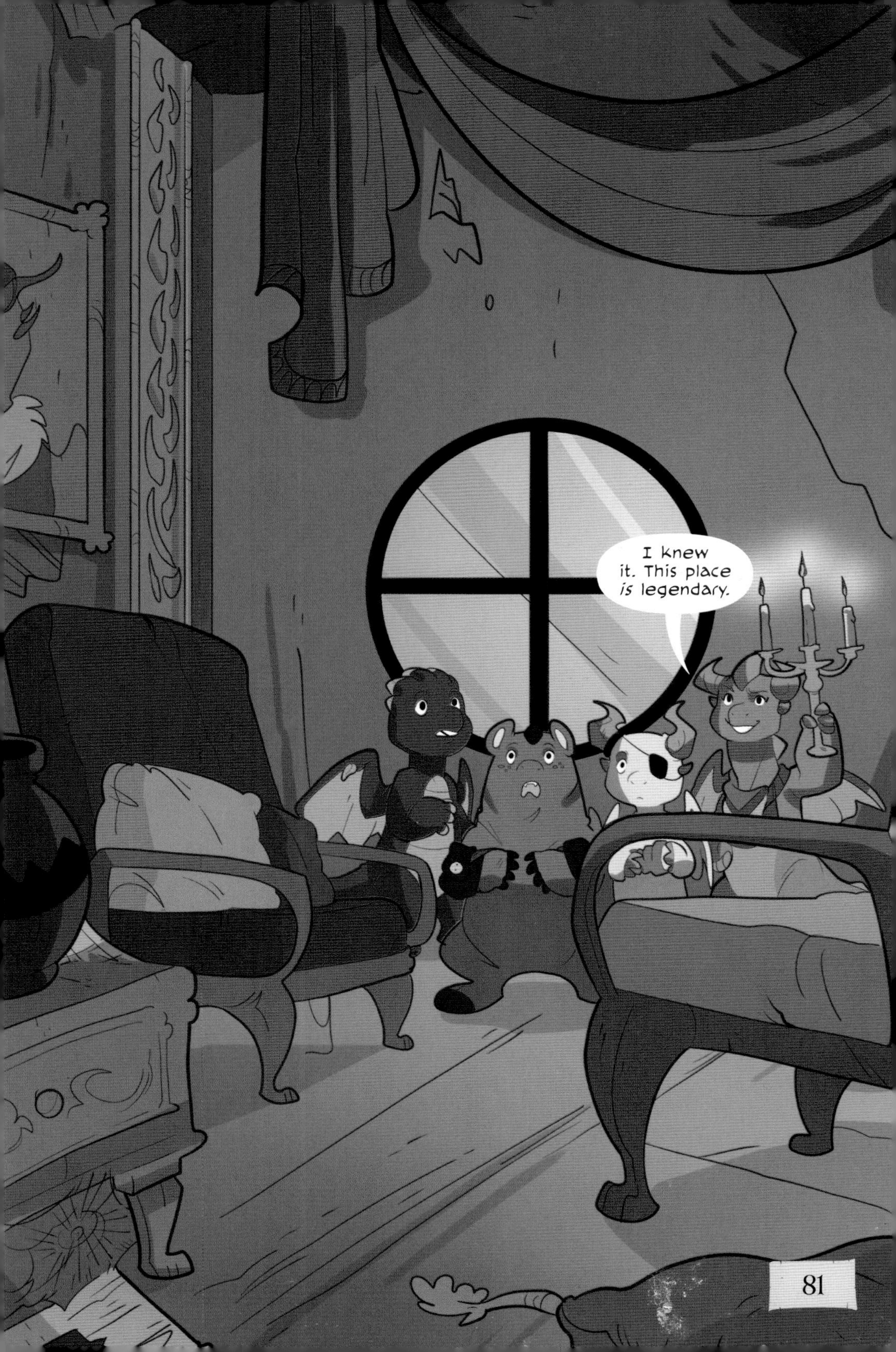
I knew it. This place is legendary.

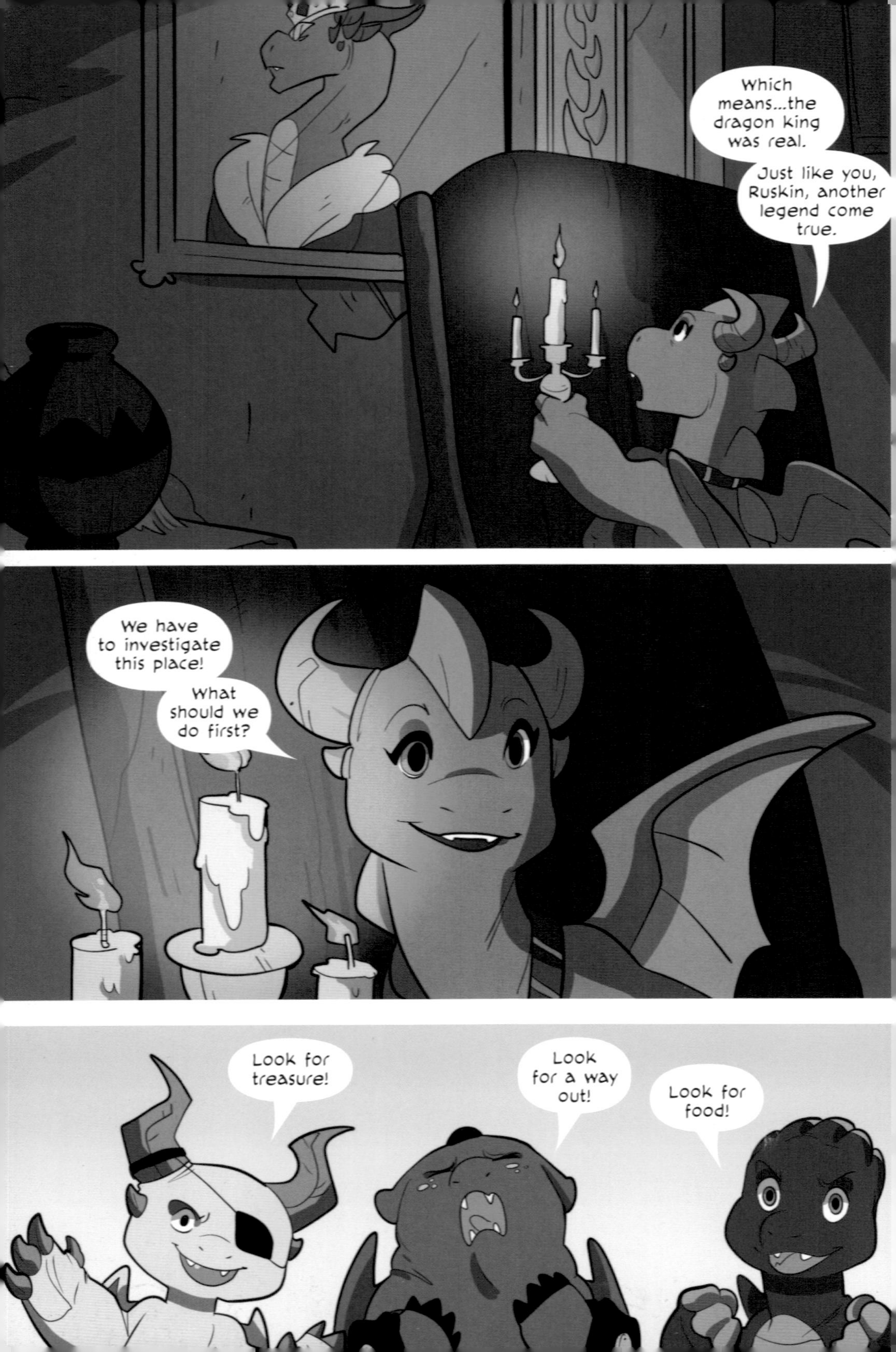
Which means...the dragon king was real.
Just like you, Ruskin, another legend come true.
We have to investigate this place!
What should we do first?
Look for treasure!
Look for a way out!
Look for food!

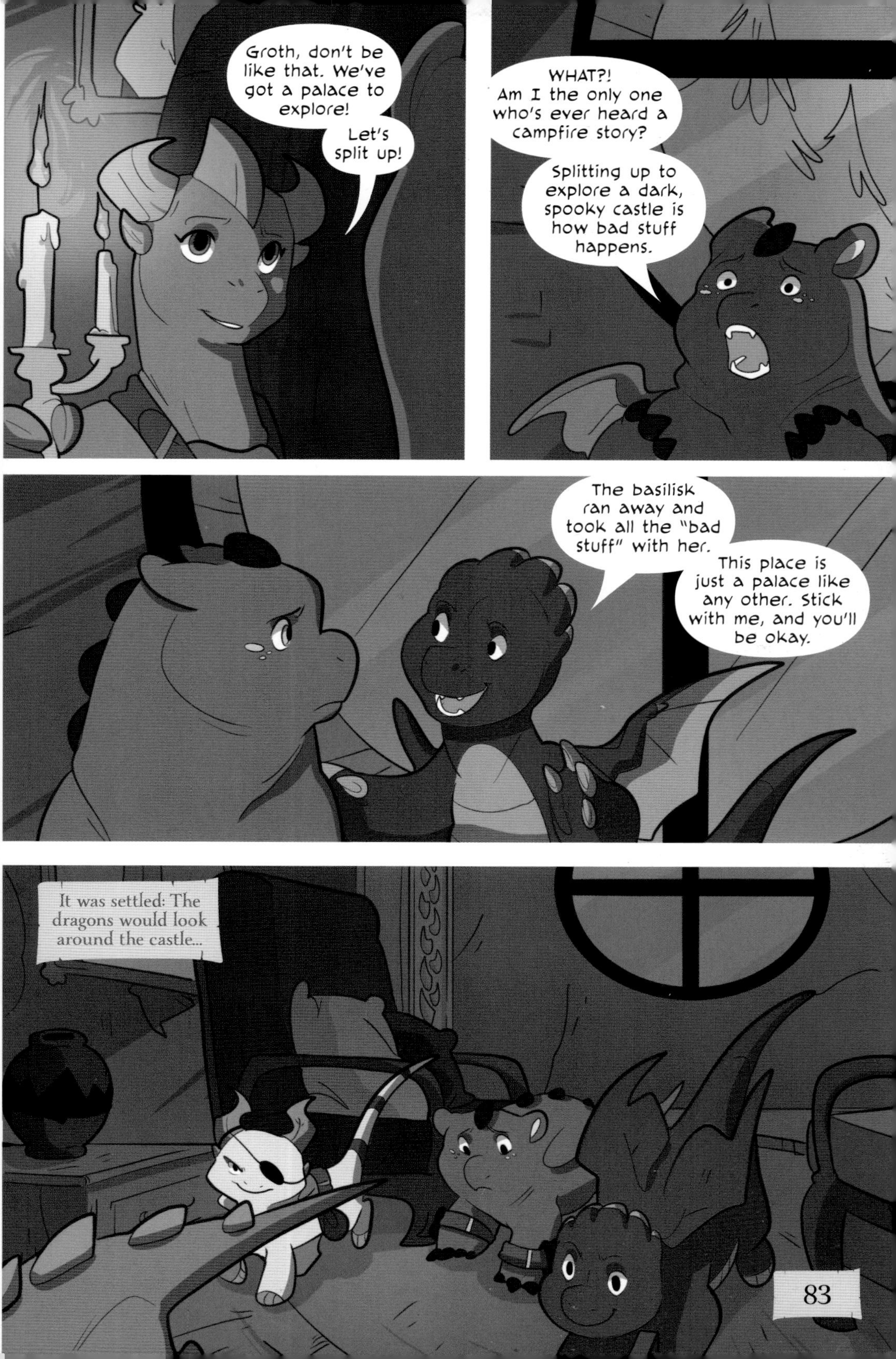
Groth, don't be like that. We've got a palace to explore!
Let's split up!
WHAT?! Am I the only one who's ever heard a campfire story?
Splitting up to explore a dark, spooky castle is how bad stuff happens.
The basilisk ran away and took all the "bad stuff" with her.
This place is just a palace like any other. Stick with me, and you'll be okay.
It was settled: The dragons would look around the castle...

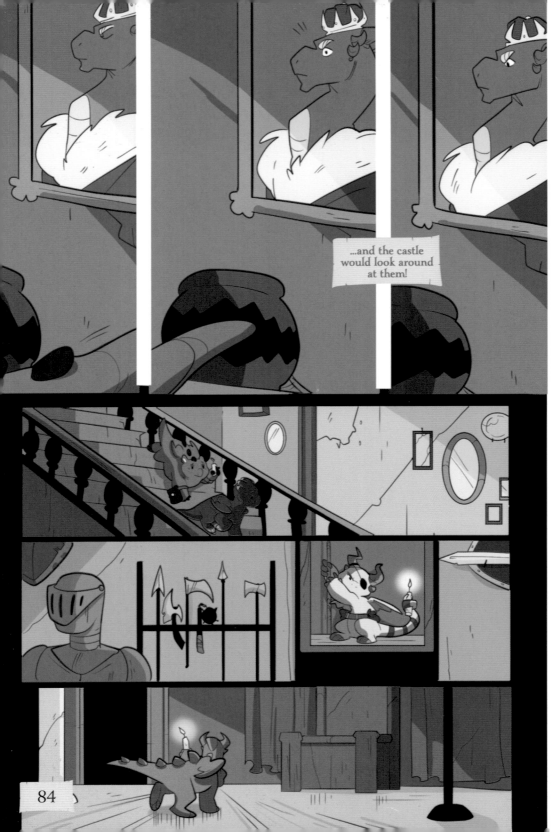

...and the castle would look around at them!

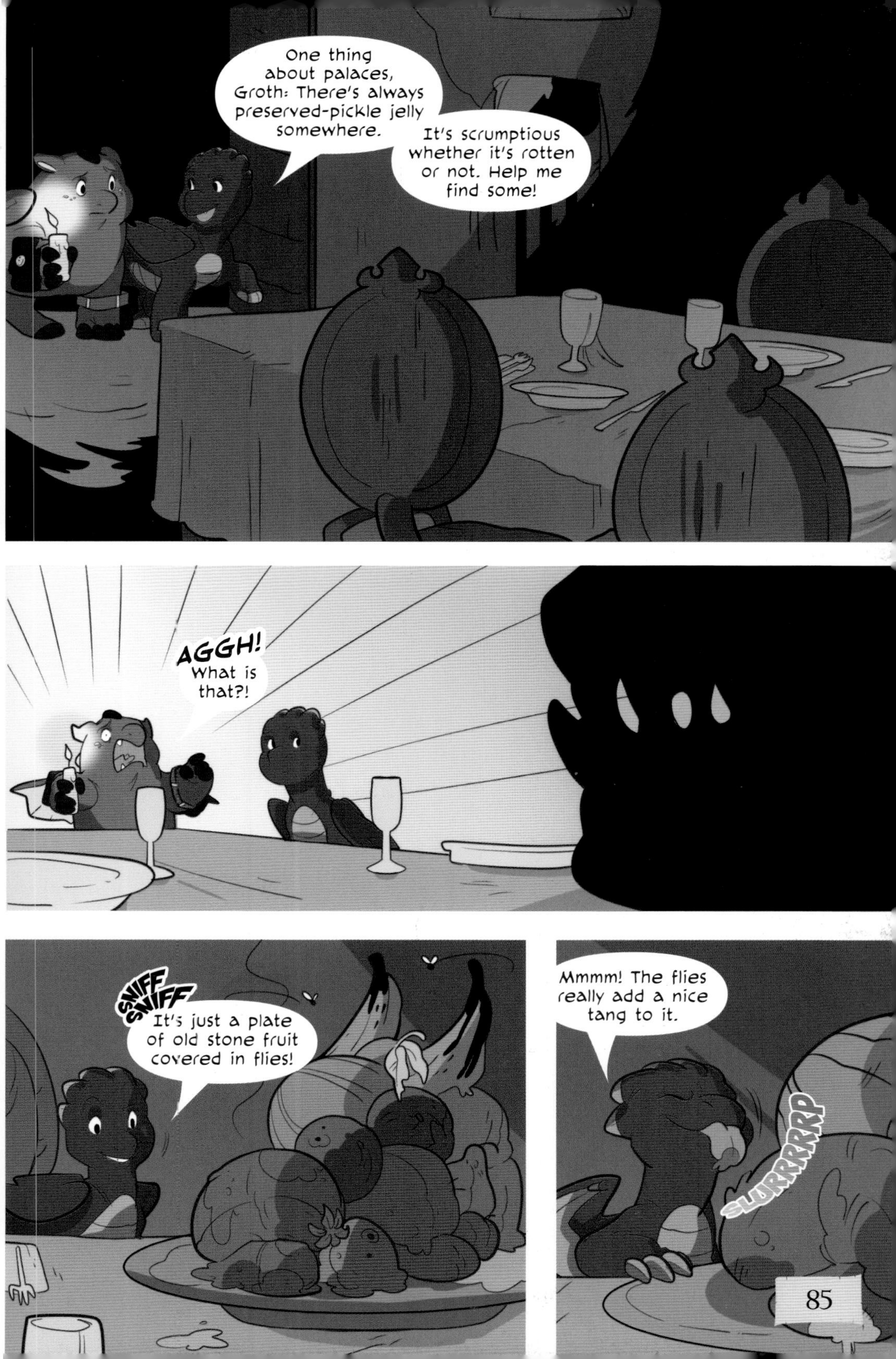
One thing about palaces, Groth: There's always preserved-pickle jelly somewhere.
It's scrumptious whether it's rotten or not. Help me find some!
AGGH! What is that?!
SNIFF SNIFF
It's just a plate of old stone fruit covered in flies!
Mmmm! The flies really add a nice tang to it.
SLURRRRRP

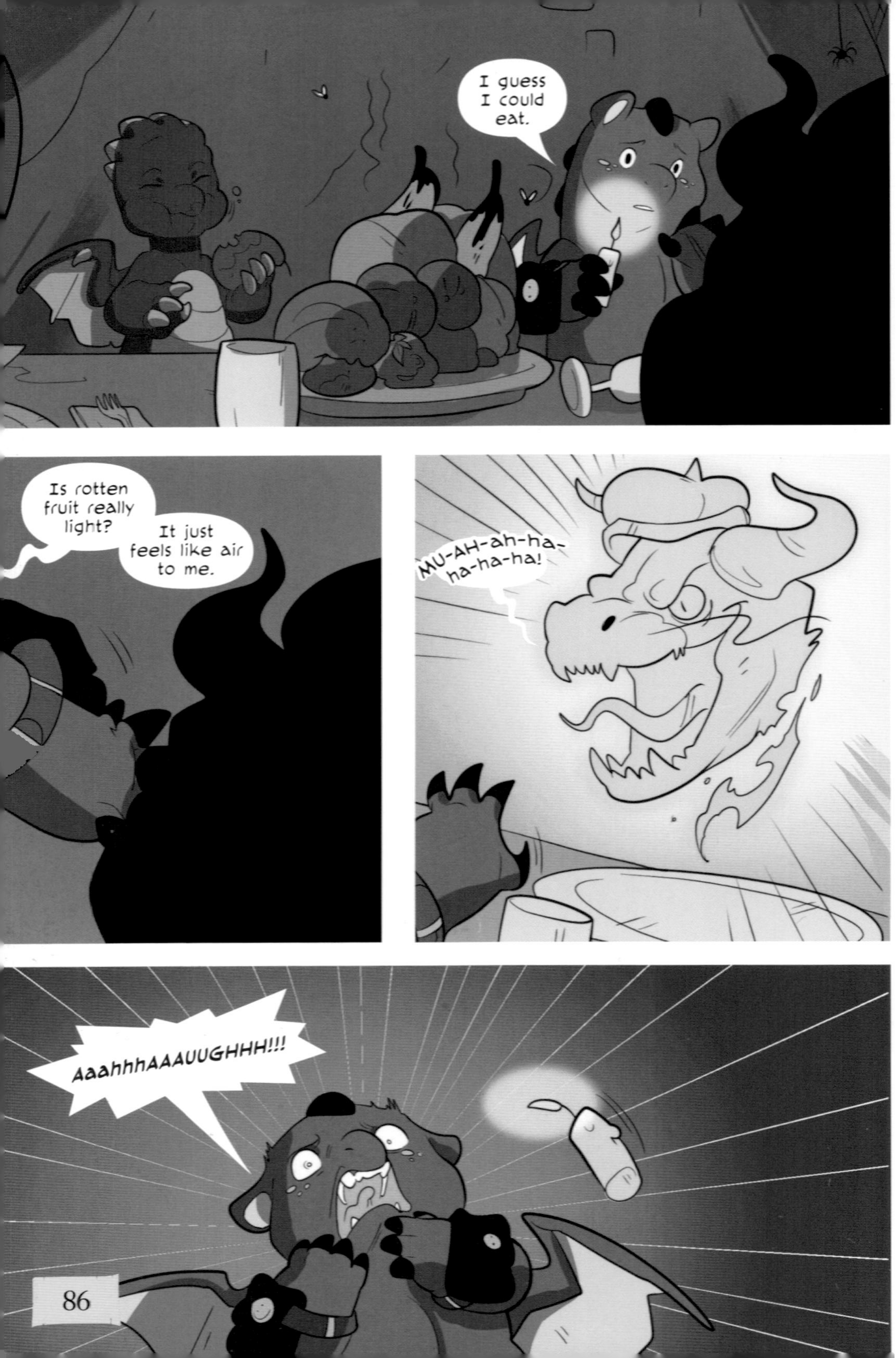

I guess I could eat.
Is rotten fruit really light?
It just feels like air to me.
MU-AH-ah-ha-ha-ha-ha!
AaahhhAAAUUGHHH!!!

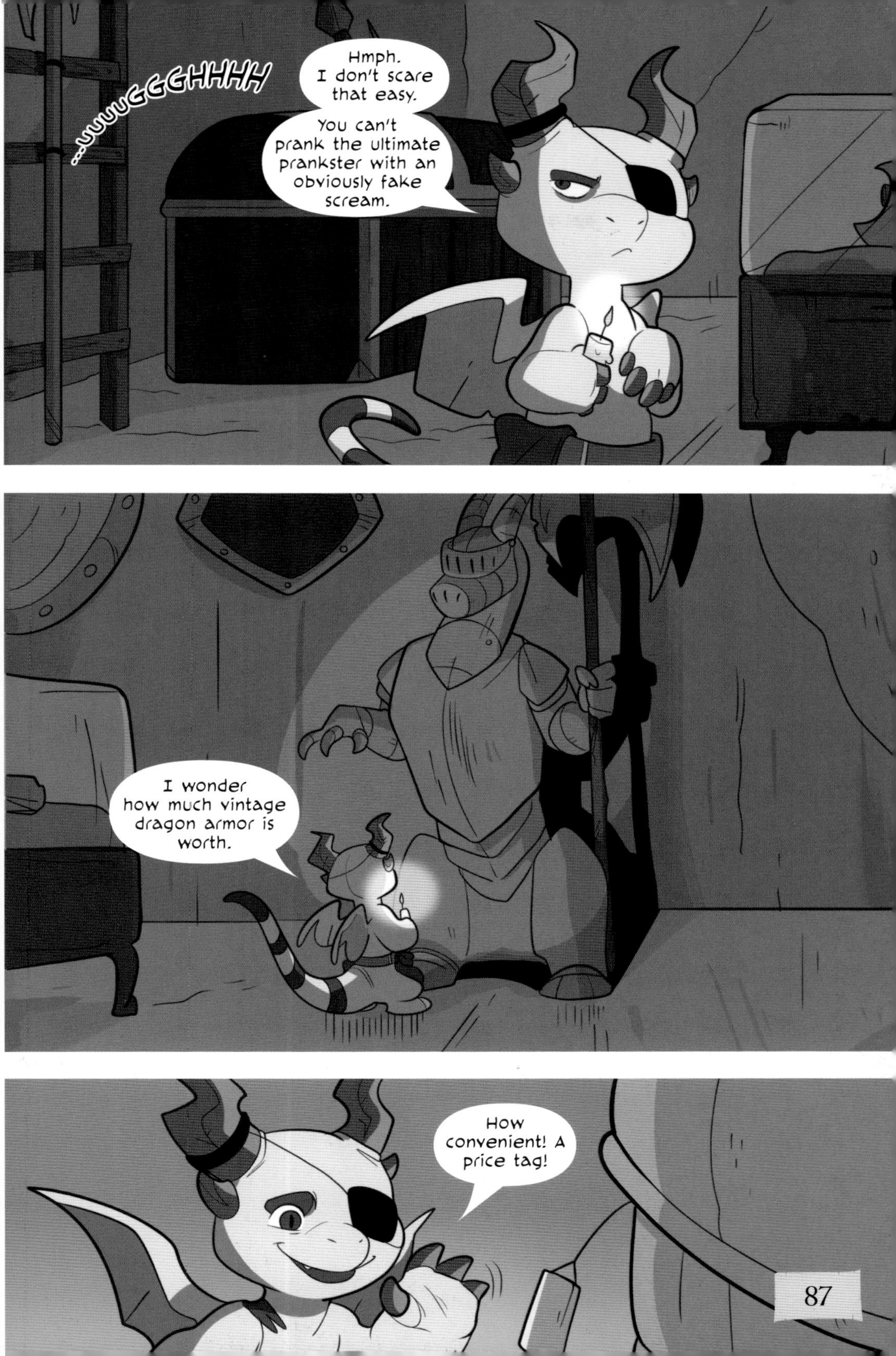
...UUUUGGGHHHH
Hmph. I don't scare that easy.
You can't prank the ultimate prankster with an obviously fake scream.
I wonder how much vintage dragon armor is worth.
How convenient! A price tag!

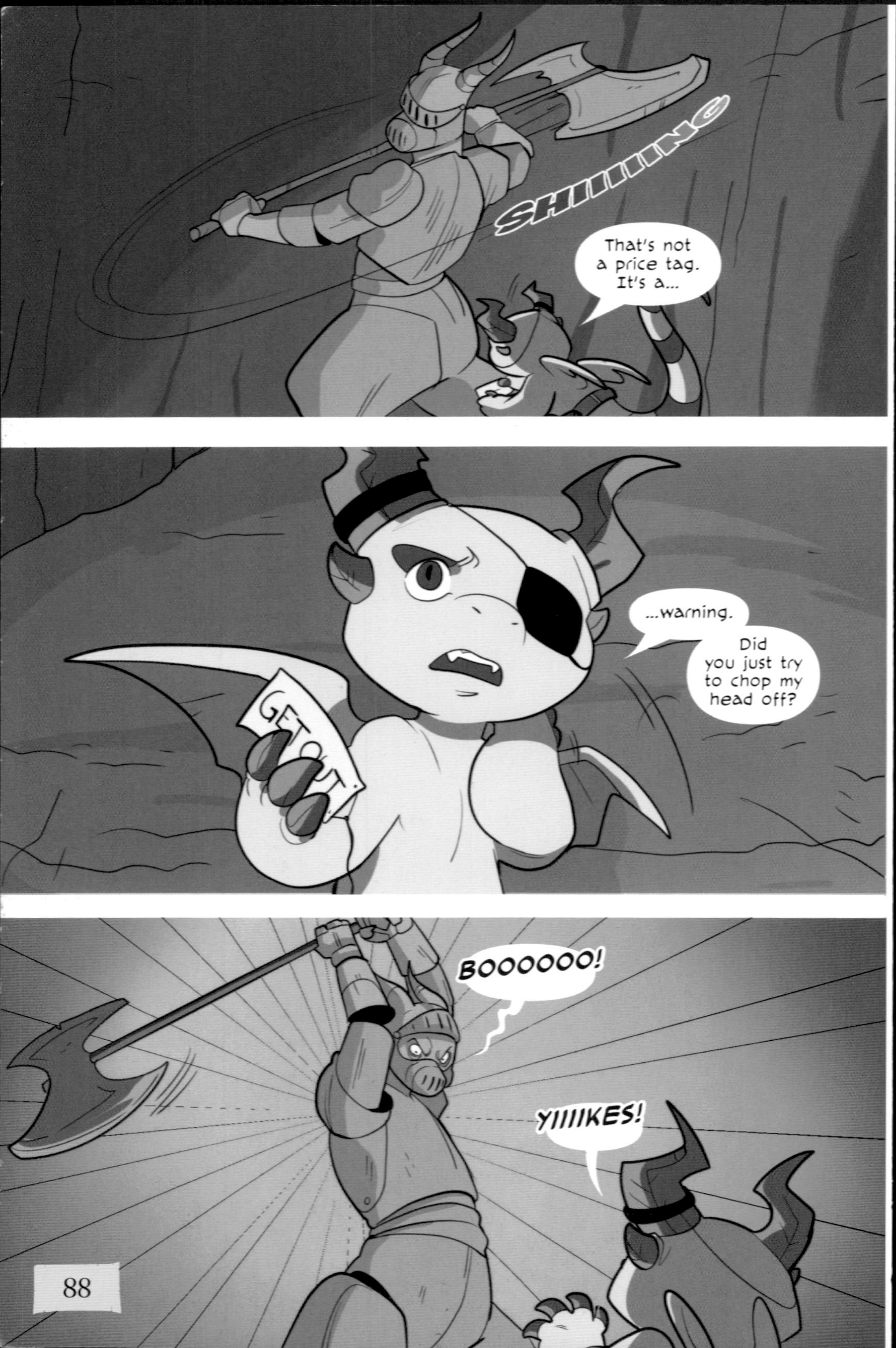
SHIIIIIING
That's not a price tag. It's a...
...warning.
Did you just try to chop my head off?
GET OUT
BOOOOOO!
YIIIIKES!

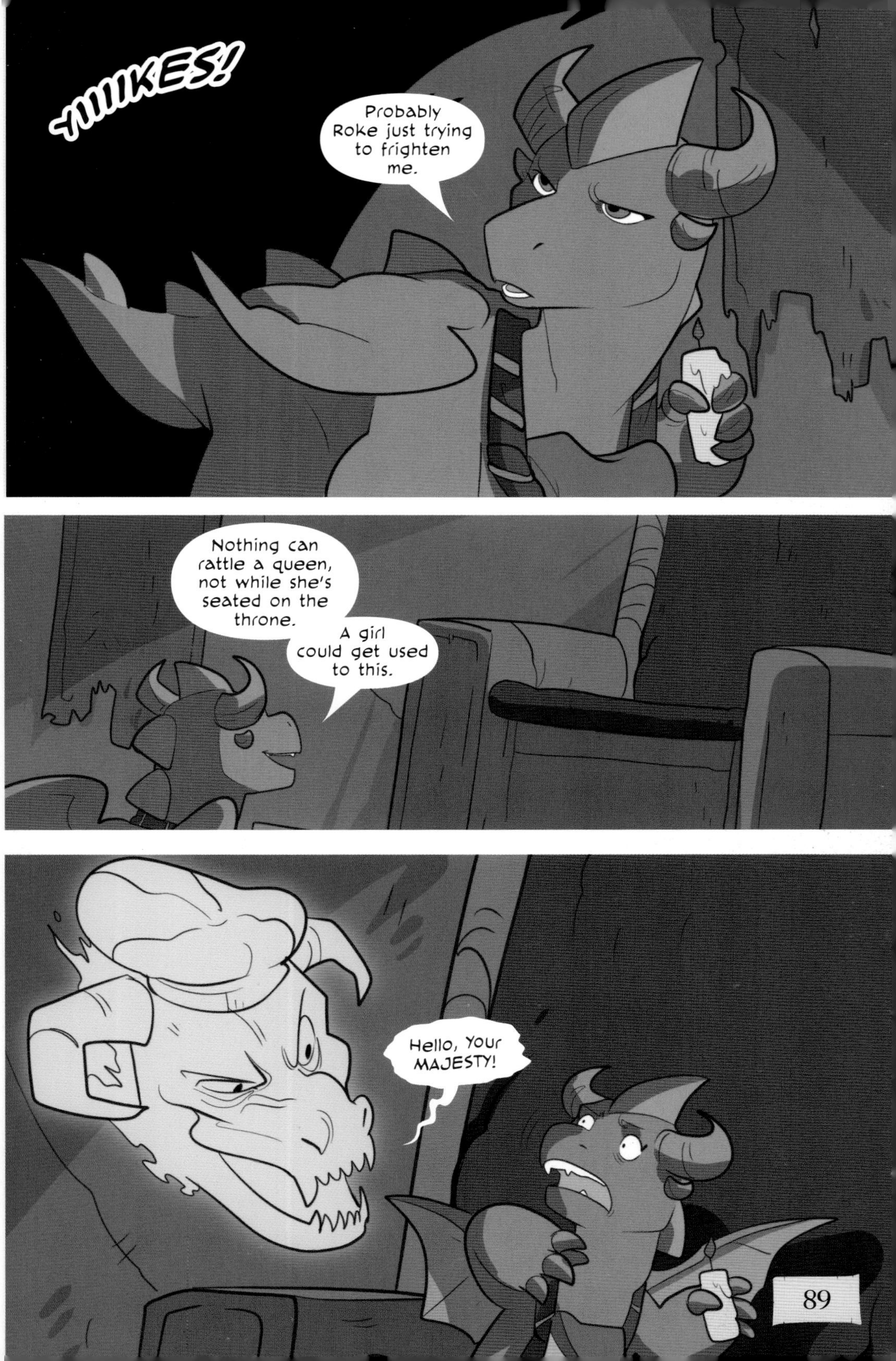
-IIIIKES!
Probably Roke just trying to frighten me.
Nothing can rattle a queen, not while she's seated on the throne.
A girl could get used to this.
Hello, Your MAJESTY!

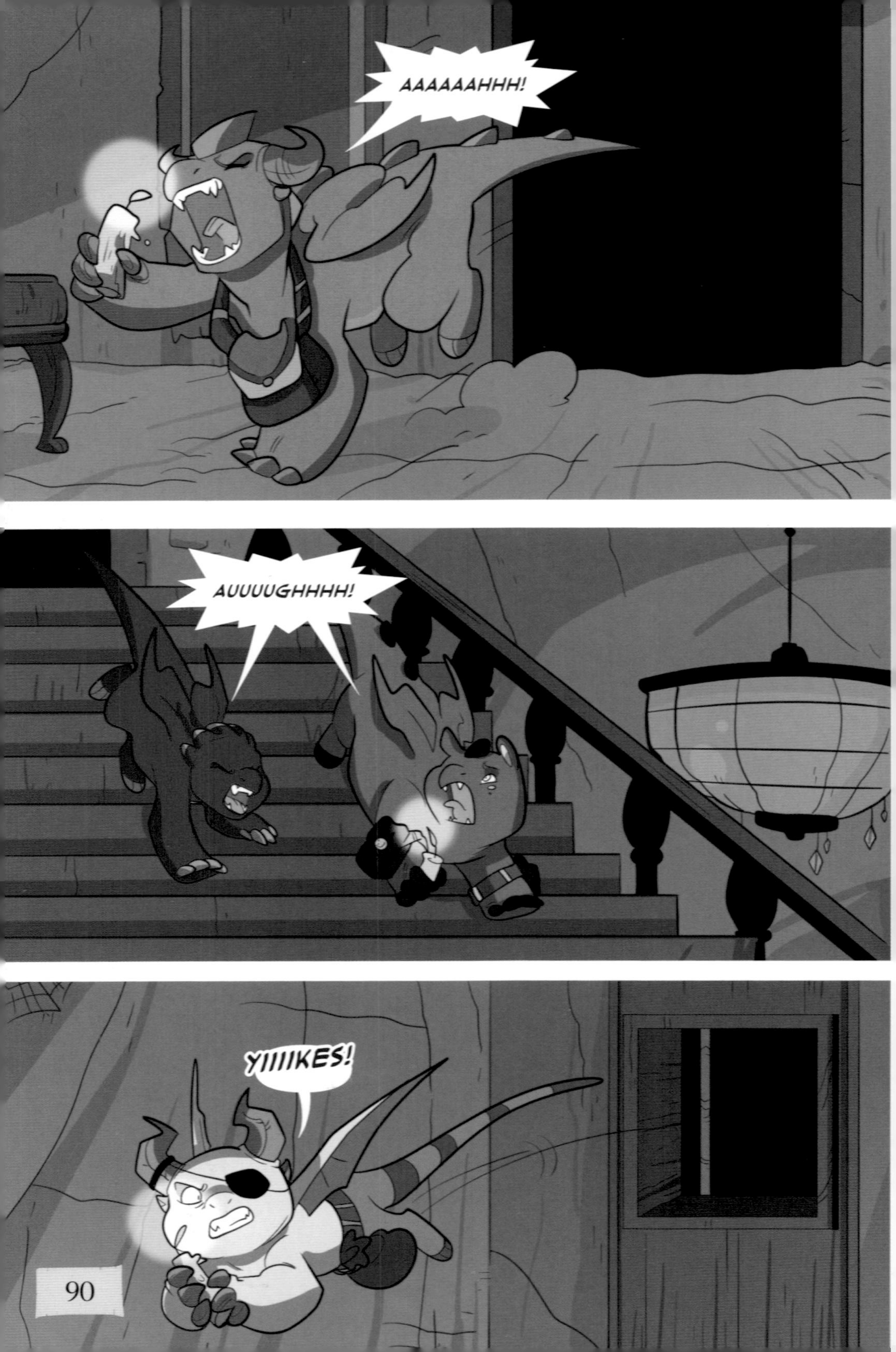

AAAAAAHHH!
AUUUUGHHHH!
YIIIIKES!

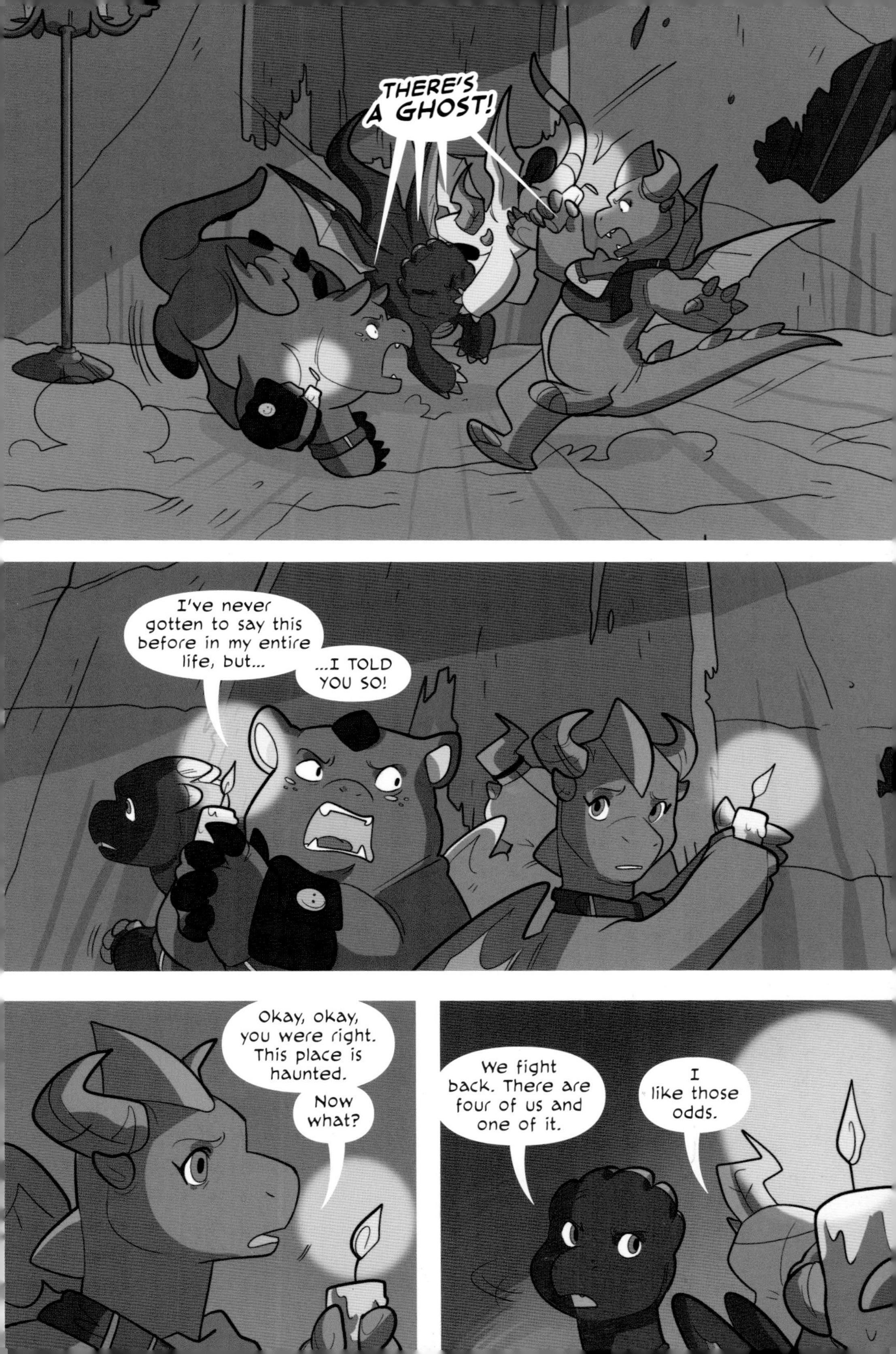
THERE'S A GHOST!
I've never gotten to say this before in my entire life, but...
...I TOLD YOU SO!
Okay, okay, you were right. This place is haunted.
Now what?
We fight back. There are four of us and one of it.
I like those odds.

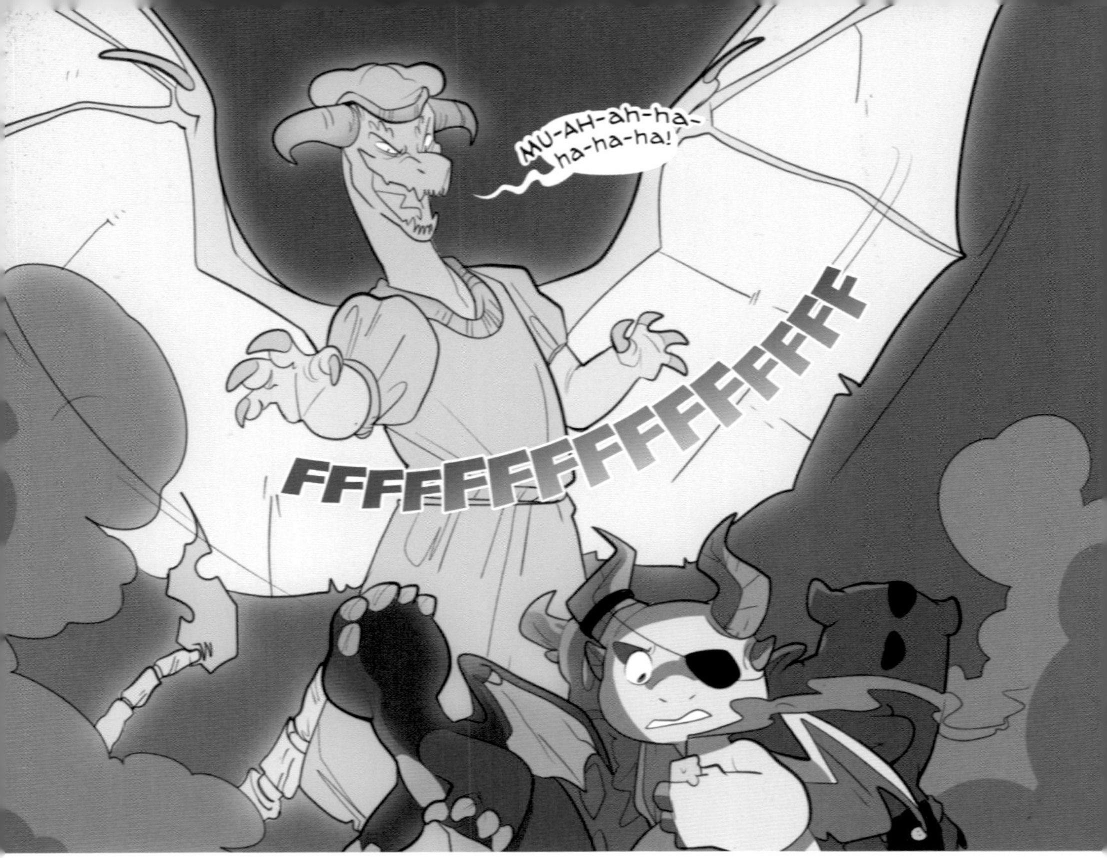
MU-AH-ah-ha-ha-ha-ha!
FFFFFFFFFFFFFFFFFFF

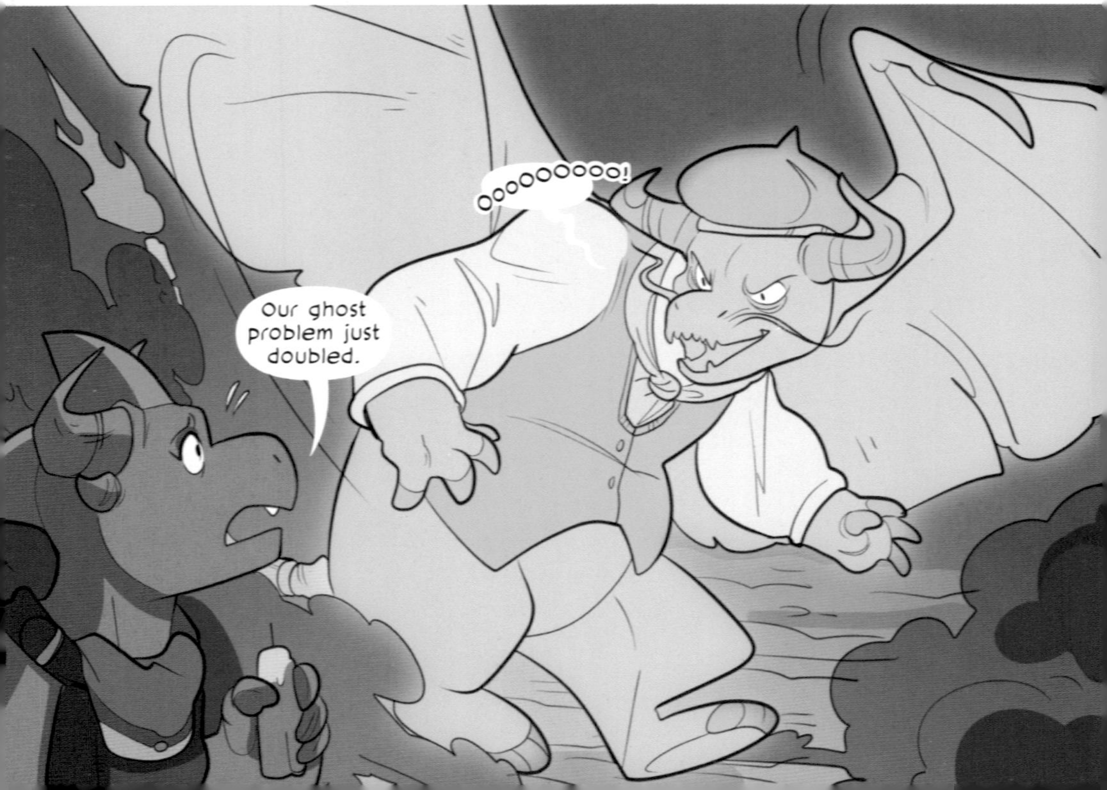
OOOOOOOOO!
Our ghost problem just doubled.

Chapter 7

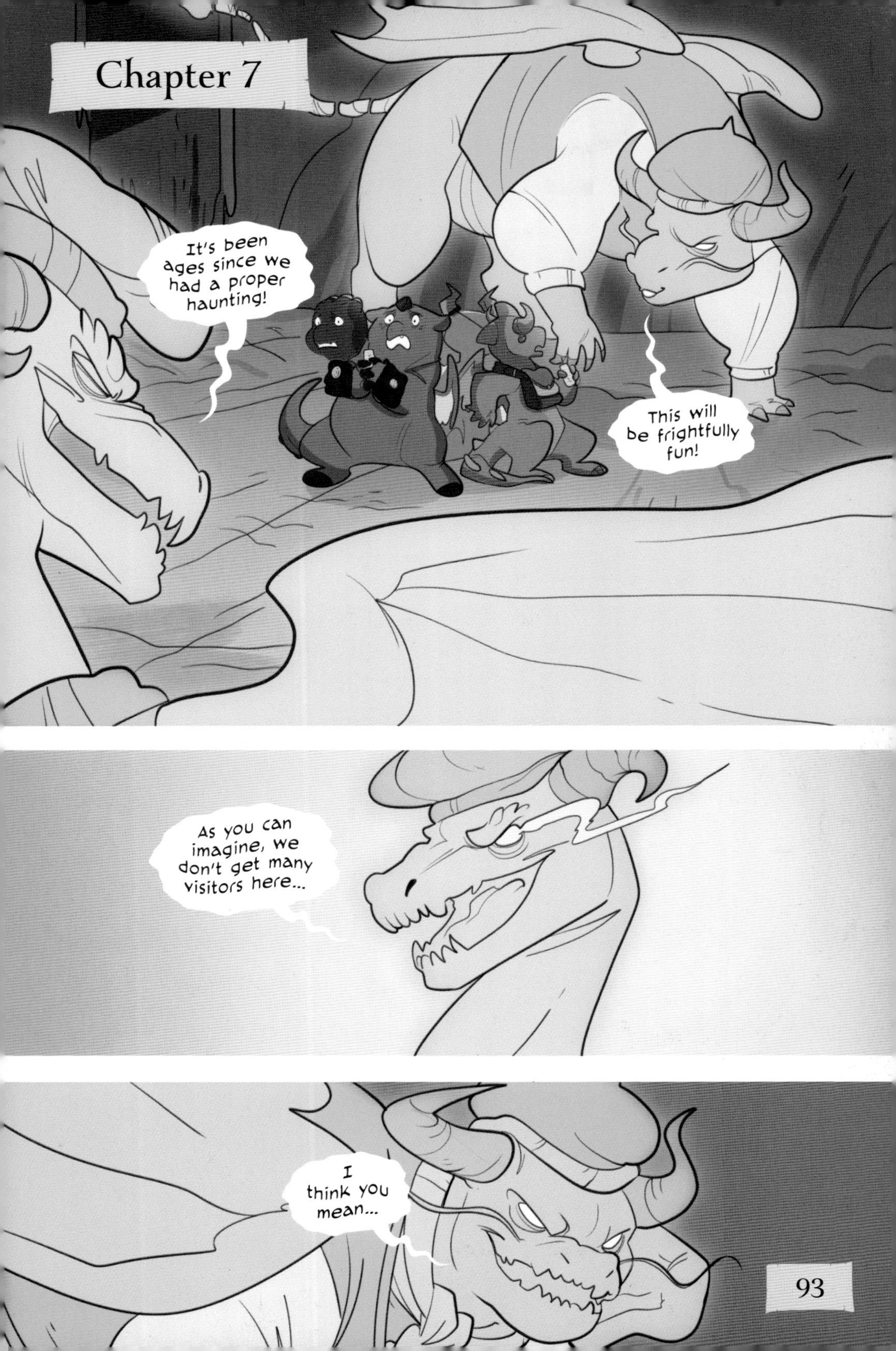

It's been ages since we had a proper haunting!
This will be frightfully fun!
As you can imagine, we don't get many visitors here...
I think you mean...

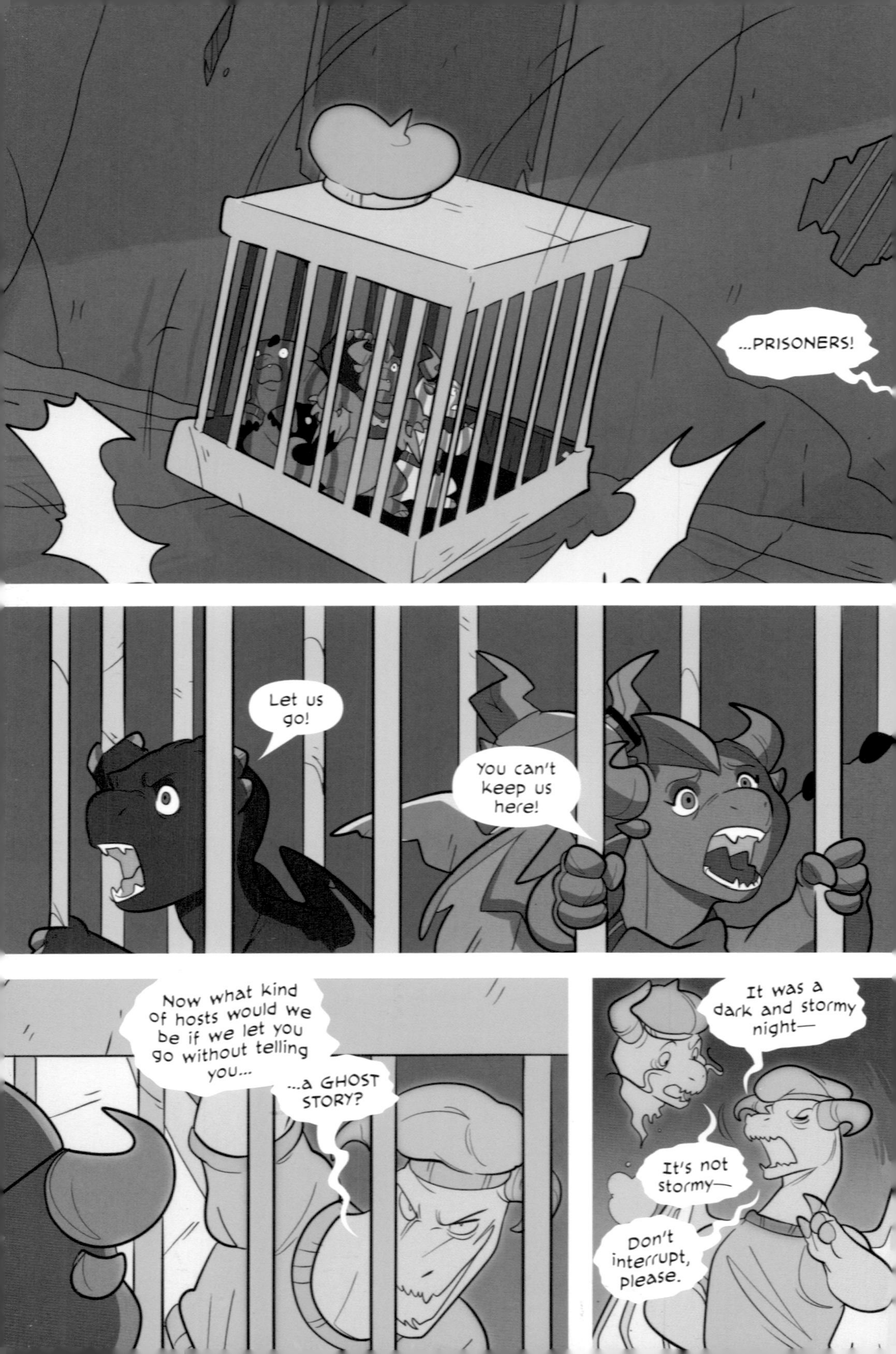
...PRISONERS!
Let us go!
You can't keep us here!
Now what kind of hosts would we be if we let you go without telling you...
...a GHOST STORY?
It was a dark and stormy night—
It's not stormy—
Don't interrupt, please.

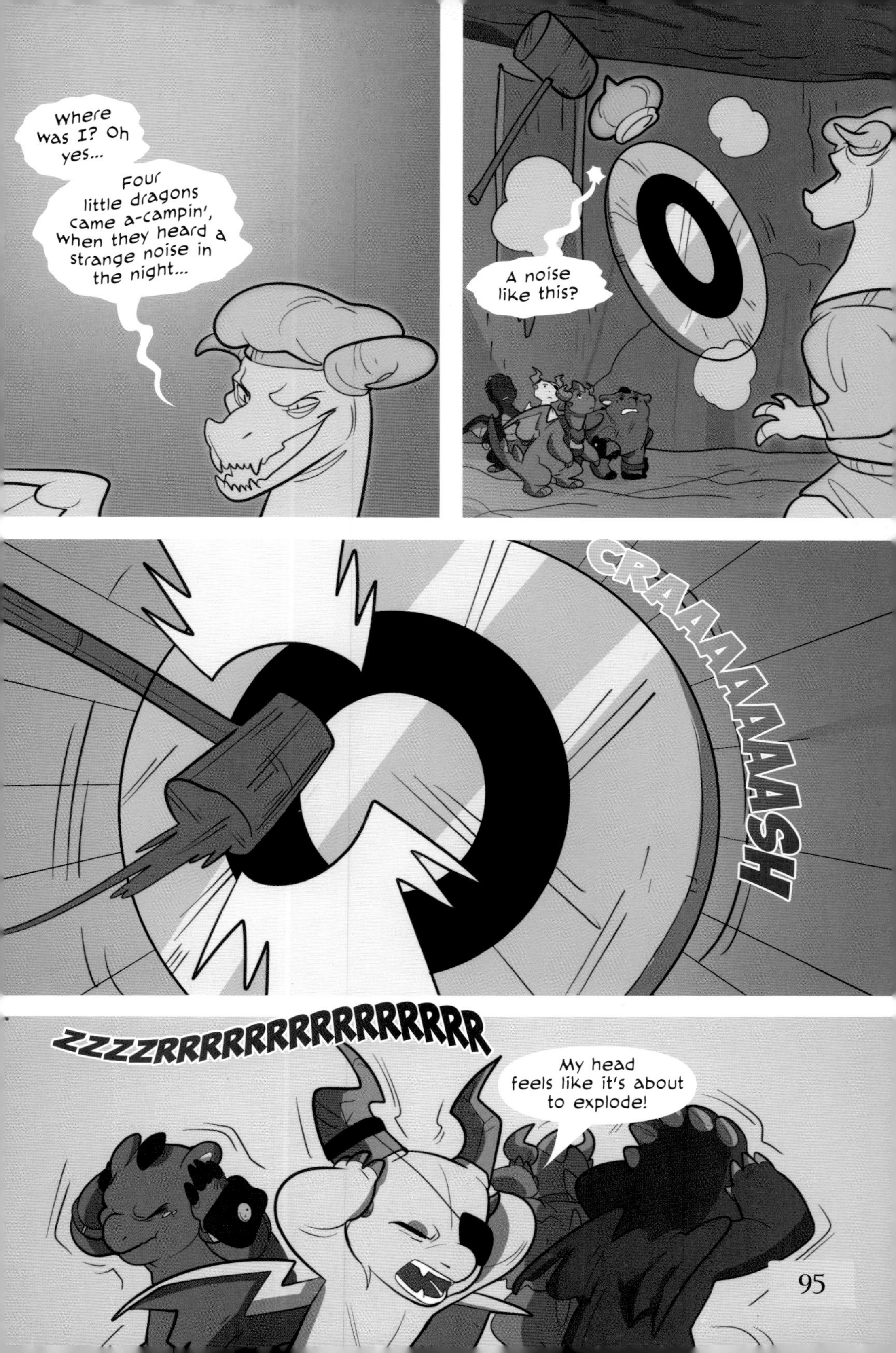
Where was I? Oh yes...
Four little dragons came a-campin', when they heard a strange noise in the night...
A noise like this?
CRAAAAAAASH!
ZZZZRRRRRRRRRRRRRRR
My head feels like it's about to explode!

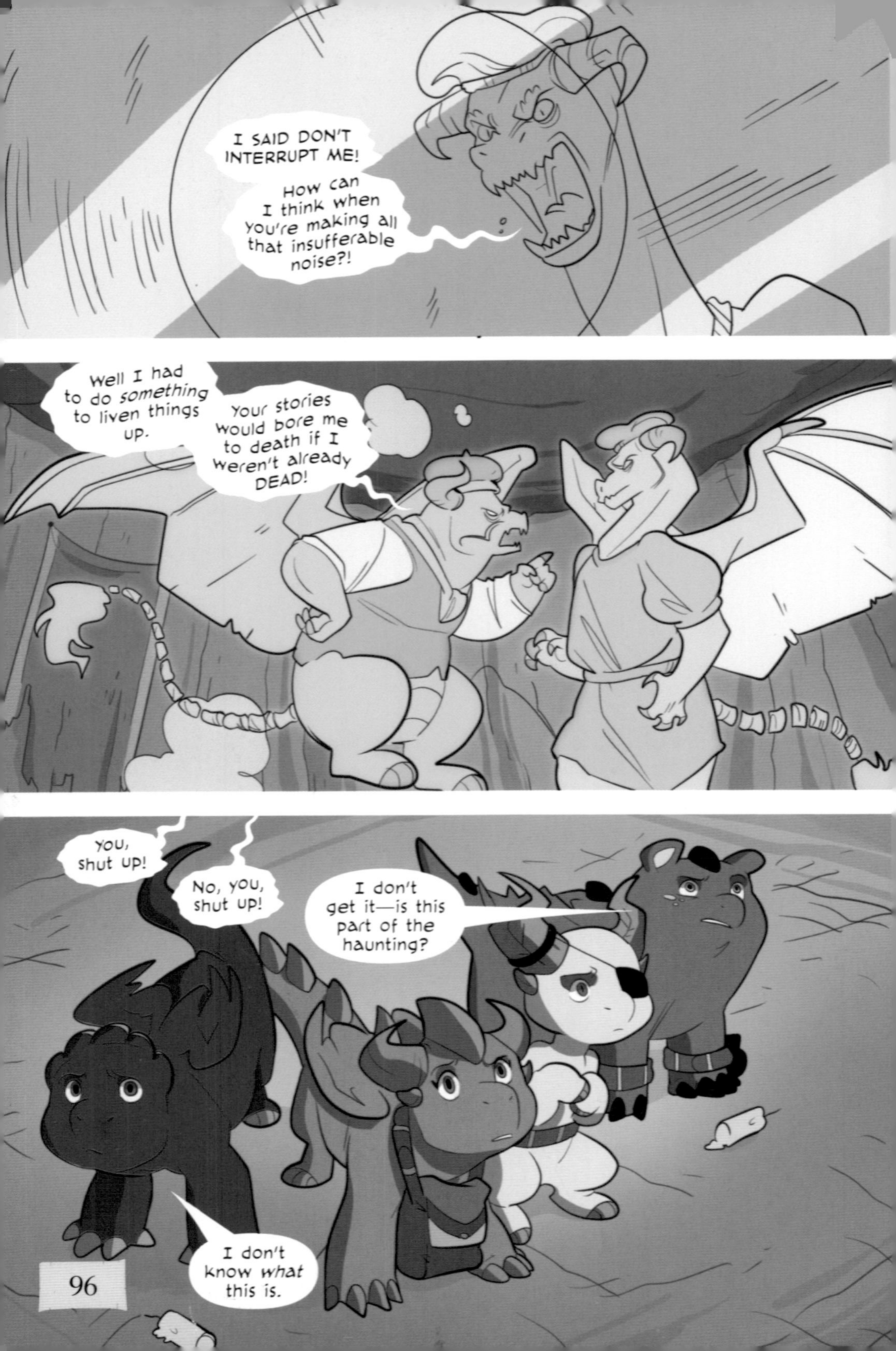
I SAID DON'T INTERRUPT ME!
How can I think when you're making all that insufferable noise?!
Well I had to do *something* to liven things up.
Your stories would bore me to death if I weren't already DEAD!
You, shut up!
No, you, shut up!
I don't get it—is this part of the haunting?
I don't know *what* this is.

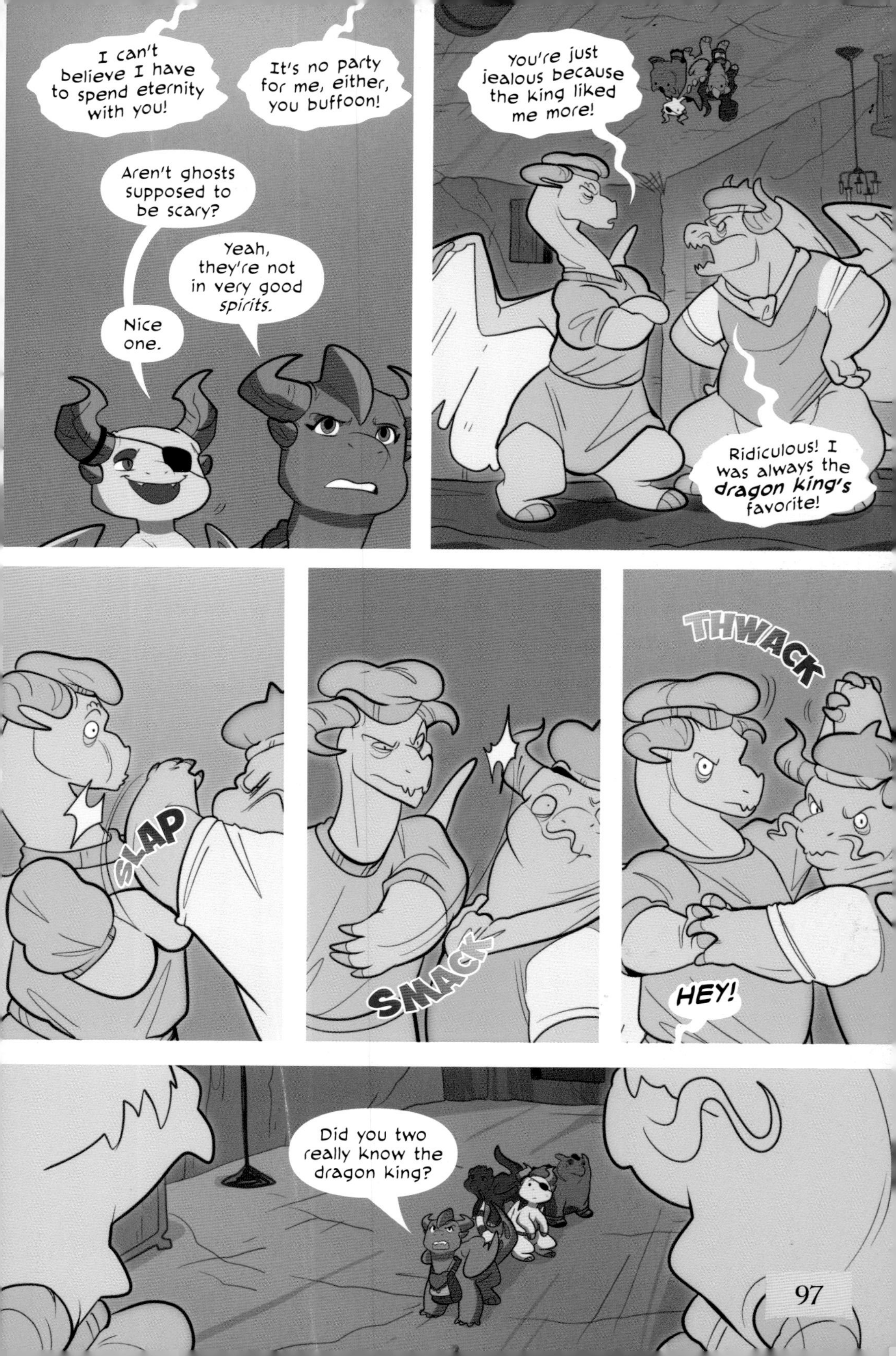
I can't believe I have to spend eternity with you!
It's no party for me, either, you buffoon!
Aren't ghosts supposed to be scary?
Yeah, they're not in very good *spirits.*
Nice one.
You're just jealous because the king liked me more!
Ridiculous! I was always the ***dragon king's*** favorite!
SLAP
SMACK
THWACK
HEY!
Did you two really know the dragon king?

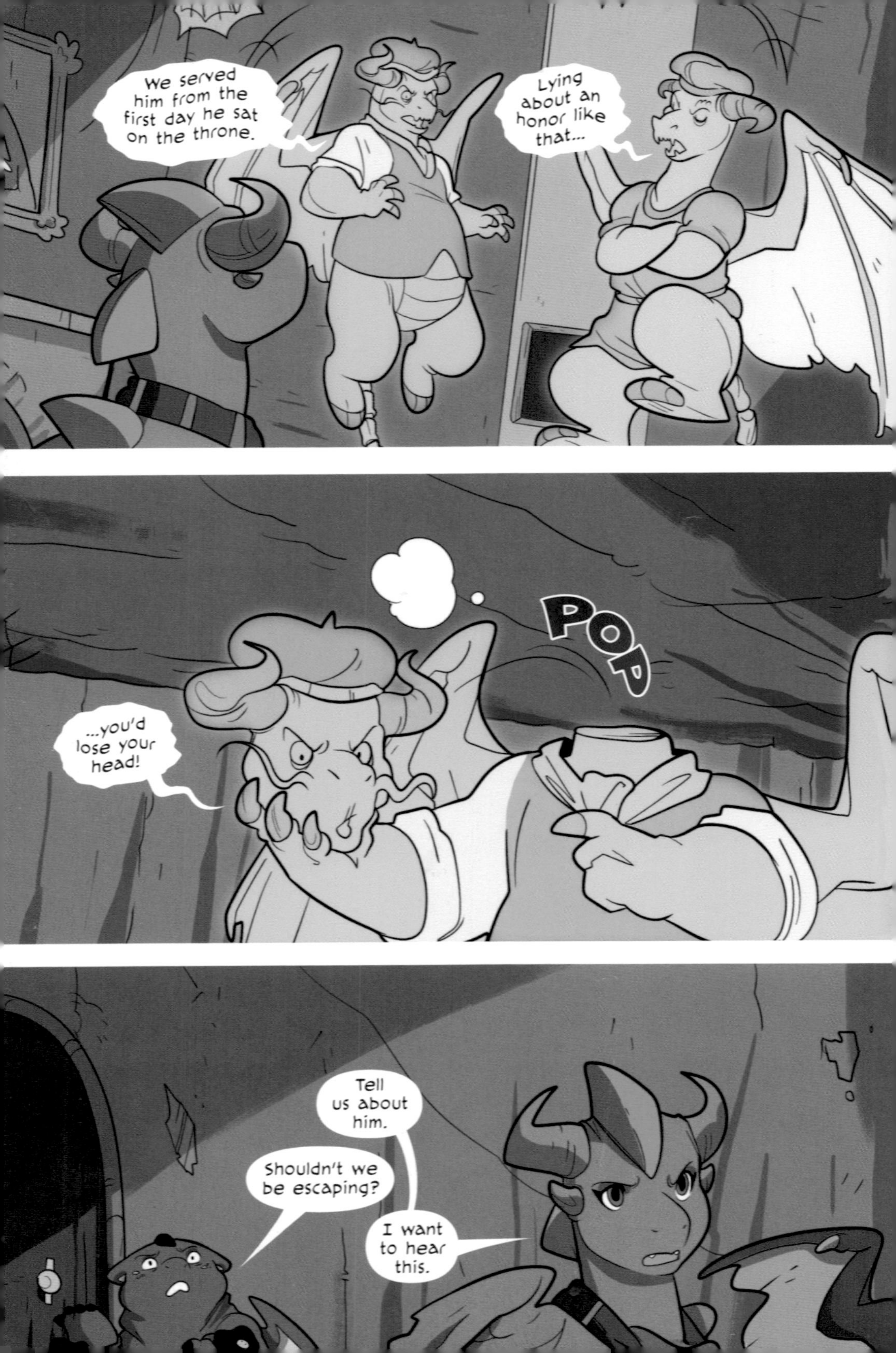
We served him from the first day he sat on the throne.
Lying about an honor like that...
POP
...you'd lose your head!
Tell us about him.
Shouldn't we be escaping?
I want to hear this.

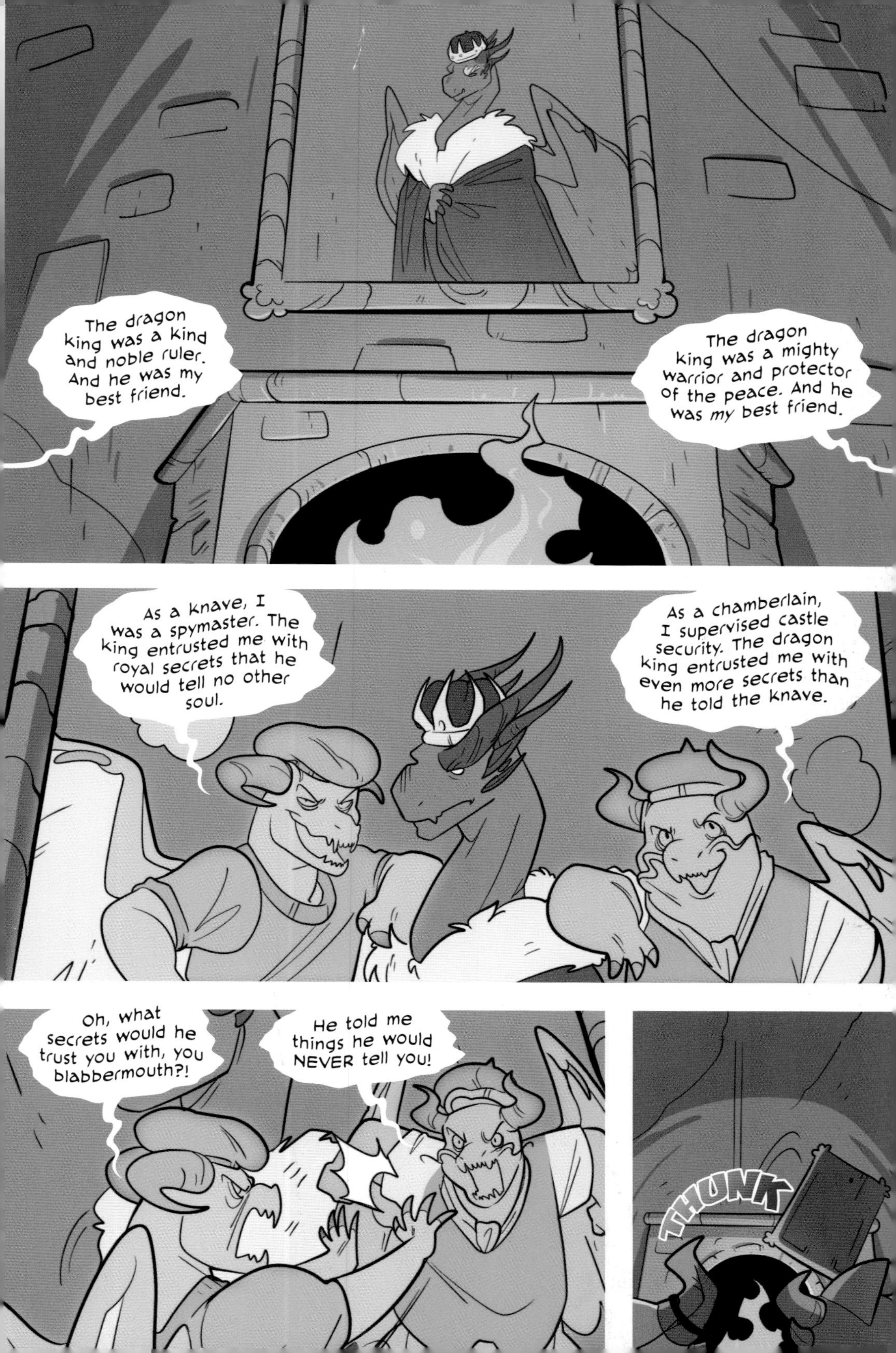
The dragon king was a kind and noble ruler. And he was my best friend.
The dragon king was a mighty warrior and protector of the peace. And he was *my* best friend.
As a knave, I was a spymaster. The king entrusted me with royal secrets that he would tell no other soul.
As a chamberlain, I supervised castle security. The dragon king entrusted me with even more secrets than he told the knave.
Oh, what secrets would he trust you with, you blabbermouth?!
He told me things he would NEVER tell you!
THUNK

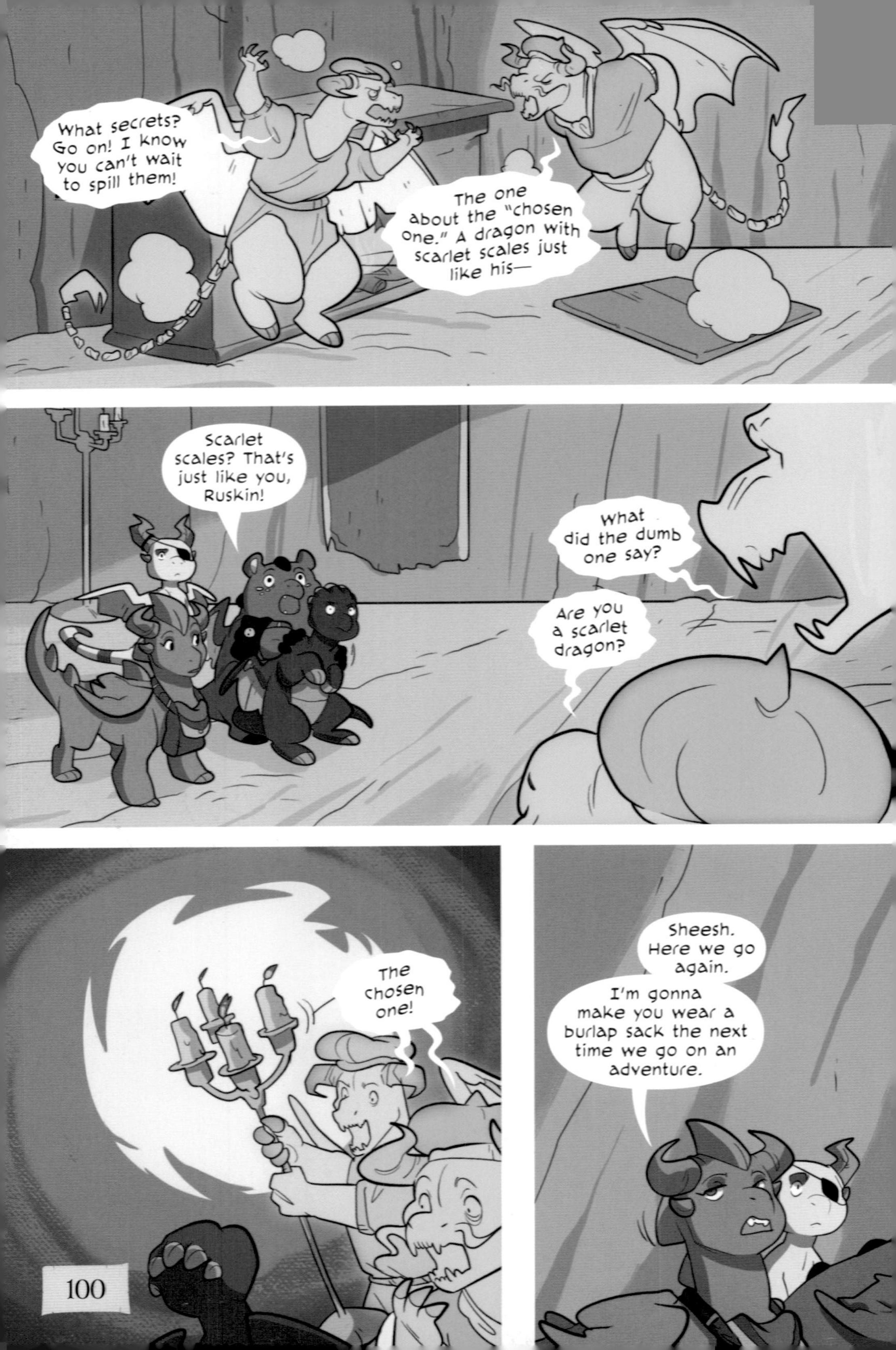
What secrets? Go on! I know you can't wait to spill them!
The one about the "chosen one." A dragon with scarlet scales just like his—
Scarlet scales? That's just like you, Ruskin!
What did the dumb one say?
Are you a scarlet dragon?
The chosen one!
Sheesh. Here we go again.
I'm gonna make you wear a burlap sack the next time we go on an adventure.

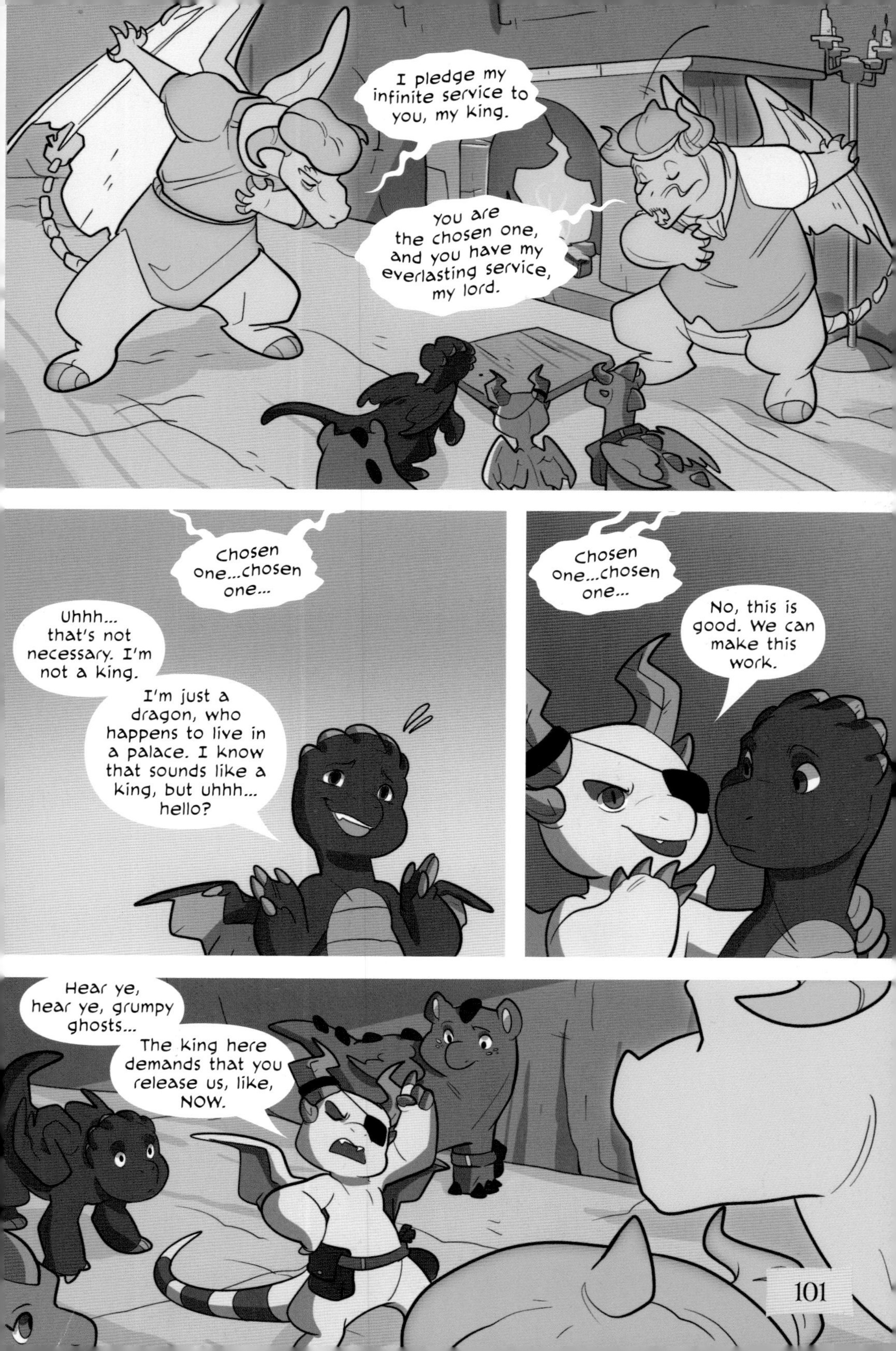
I pledge my infinite service to you, my king.
You are the chosen one, and you have my everlasting service, my lord.
Chosen one...chosen one...
Uhhh... that's not necessary. I'm not a king.
I'm just a dragon, who happens to live in a palace. I know that sounds like a king, but uhhh... hello?
Chosen one...chosen one...
No, this is good. We can make this work.
Hear ye, hear ye, grumpy ghosts...
The king here demands that you release us, like, NOW.

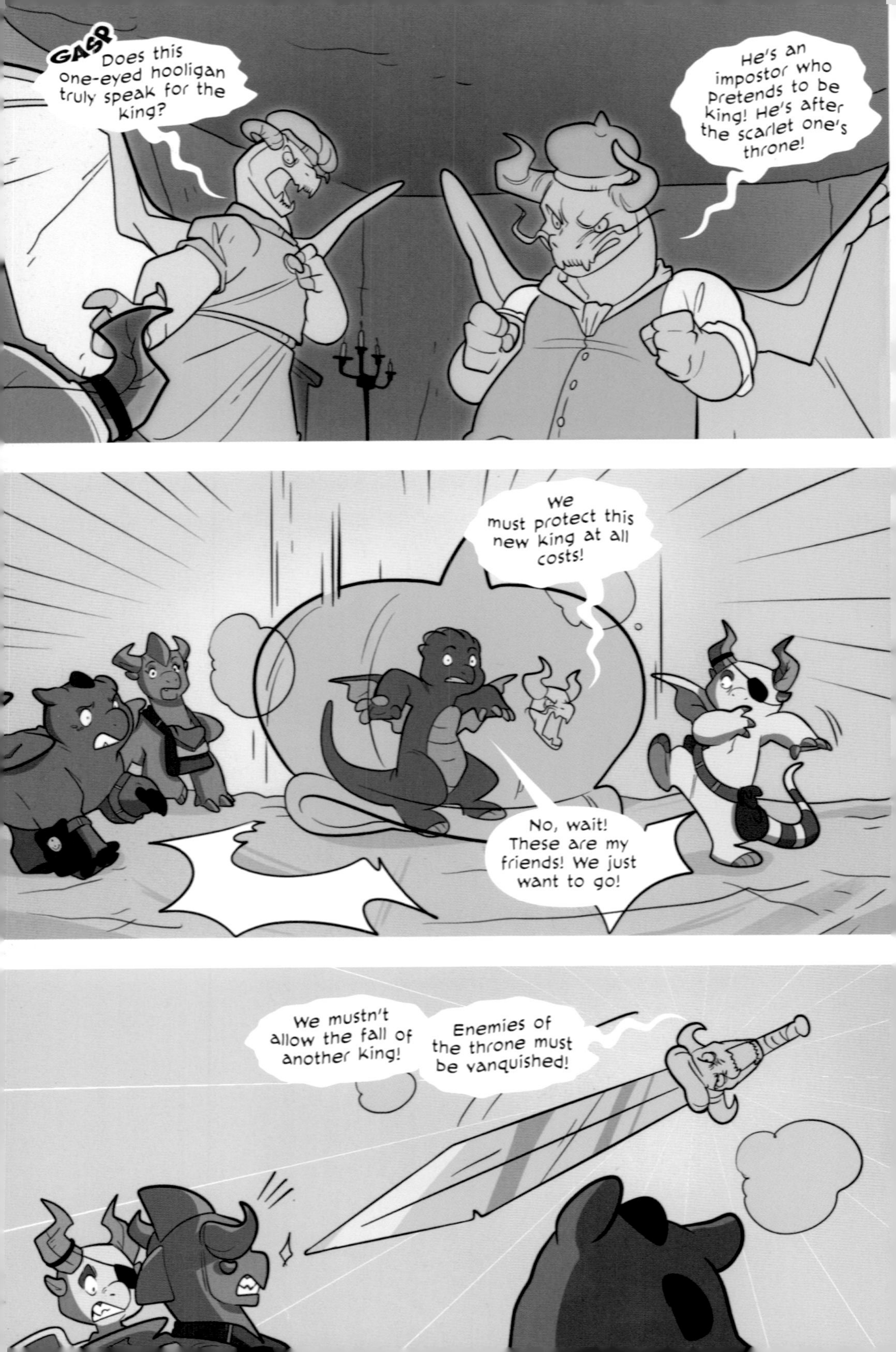
GASP
Does this one-eyed hooligan truly speak for the king?
He's an impostor who pretends to be king! He's after the scarlet one's throne!
We must protect this new king at all costs!
No, wait! These are my friends! We just want to go!
We mustn't allow the fall of another king!
Enemies of the throne must be vanquished!

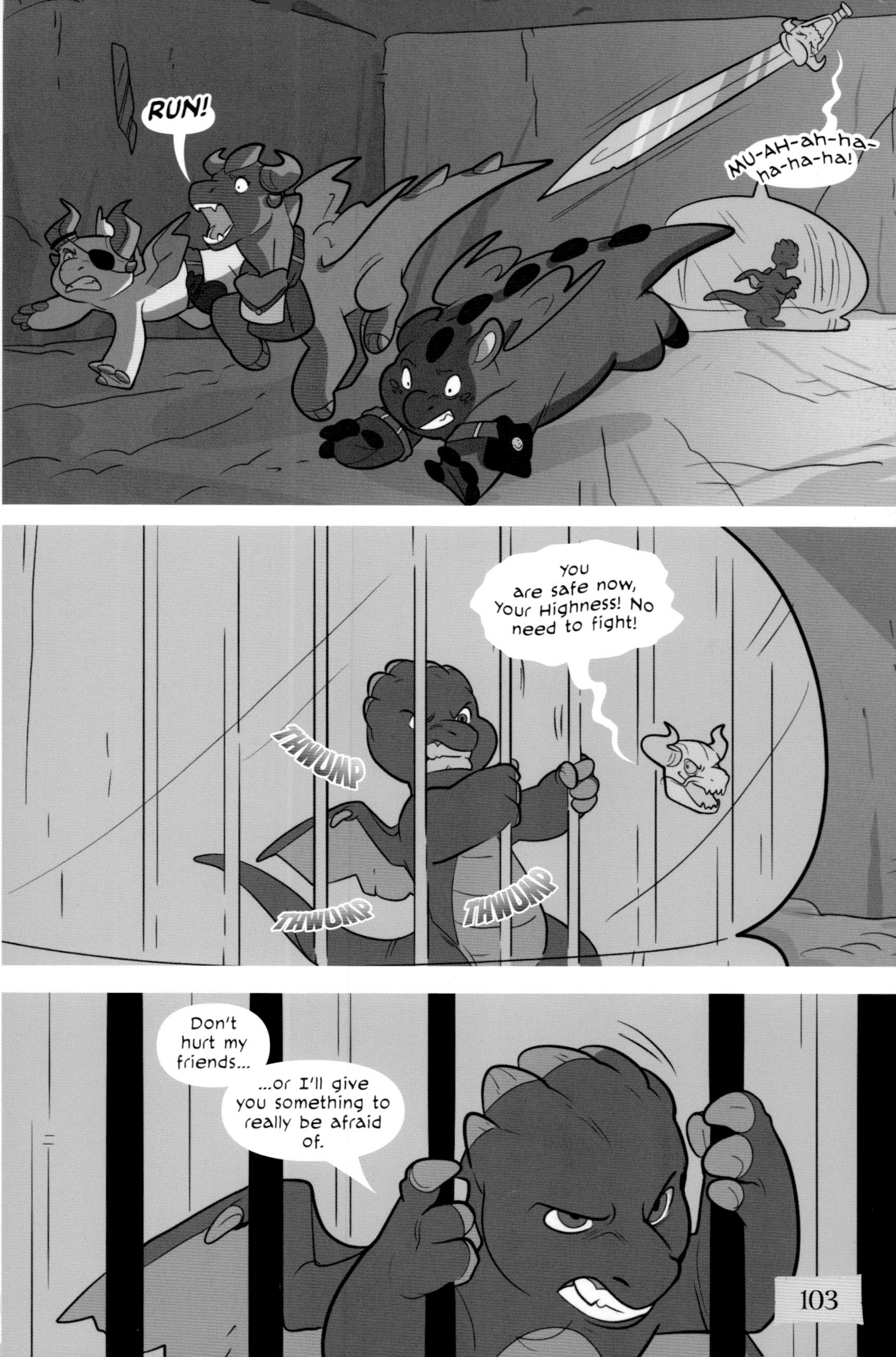
RUN!
MU-AH-ah-ha-ha-ha-ha!
You are safe now, Your Highness! No need to fight!
THWUMP
THWUMP
THWUMP
Don't hurt my friends...
...or I'll give you something to really be afraid of.

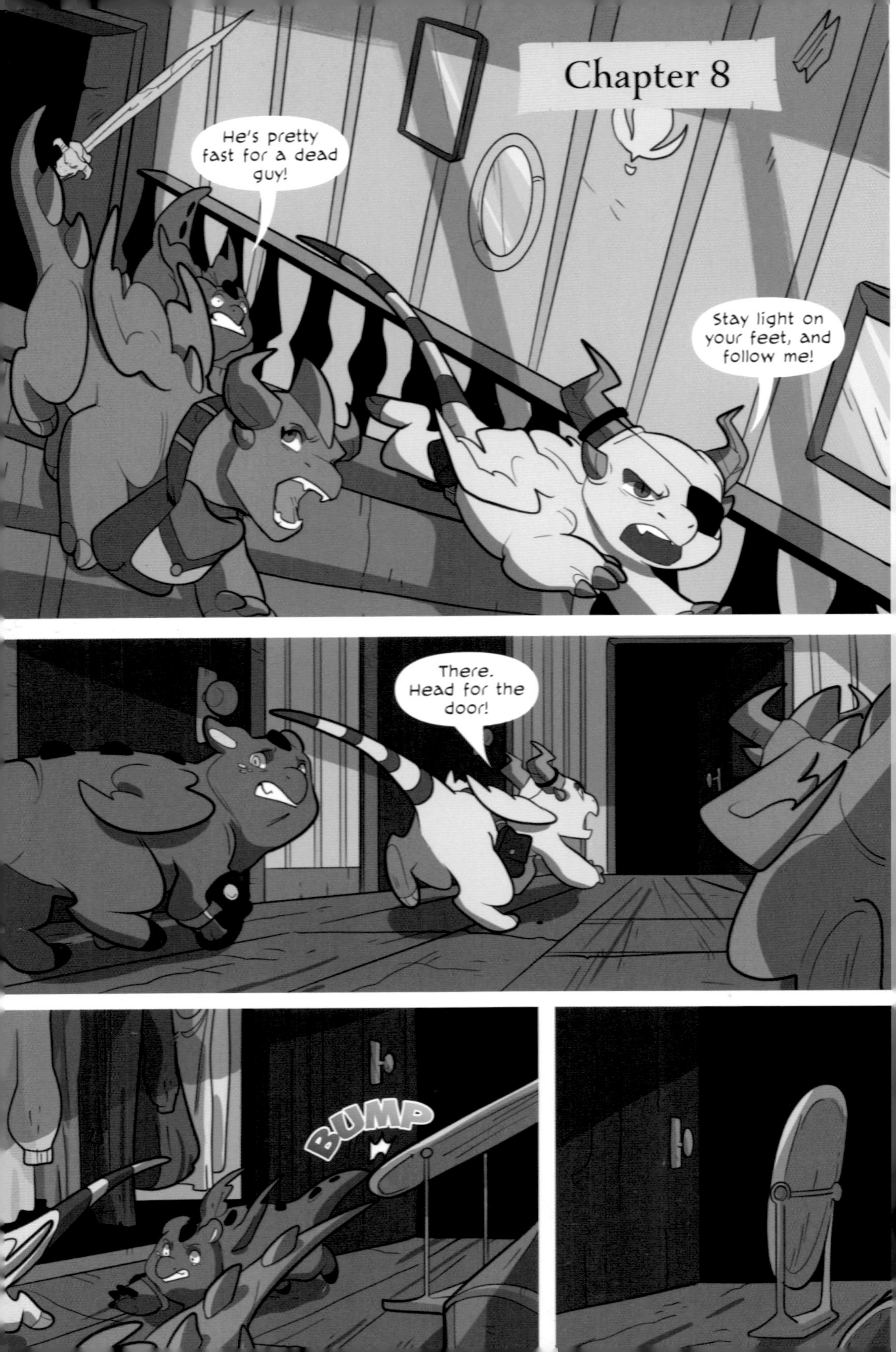
Chapter 8
He's pretty fast for a dead guy!
Stay light on your feet, and follow me!
There. Head for the door!
BUMP

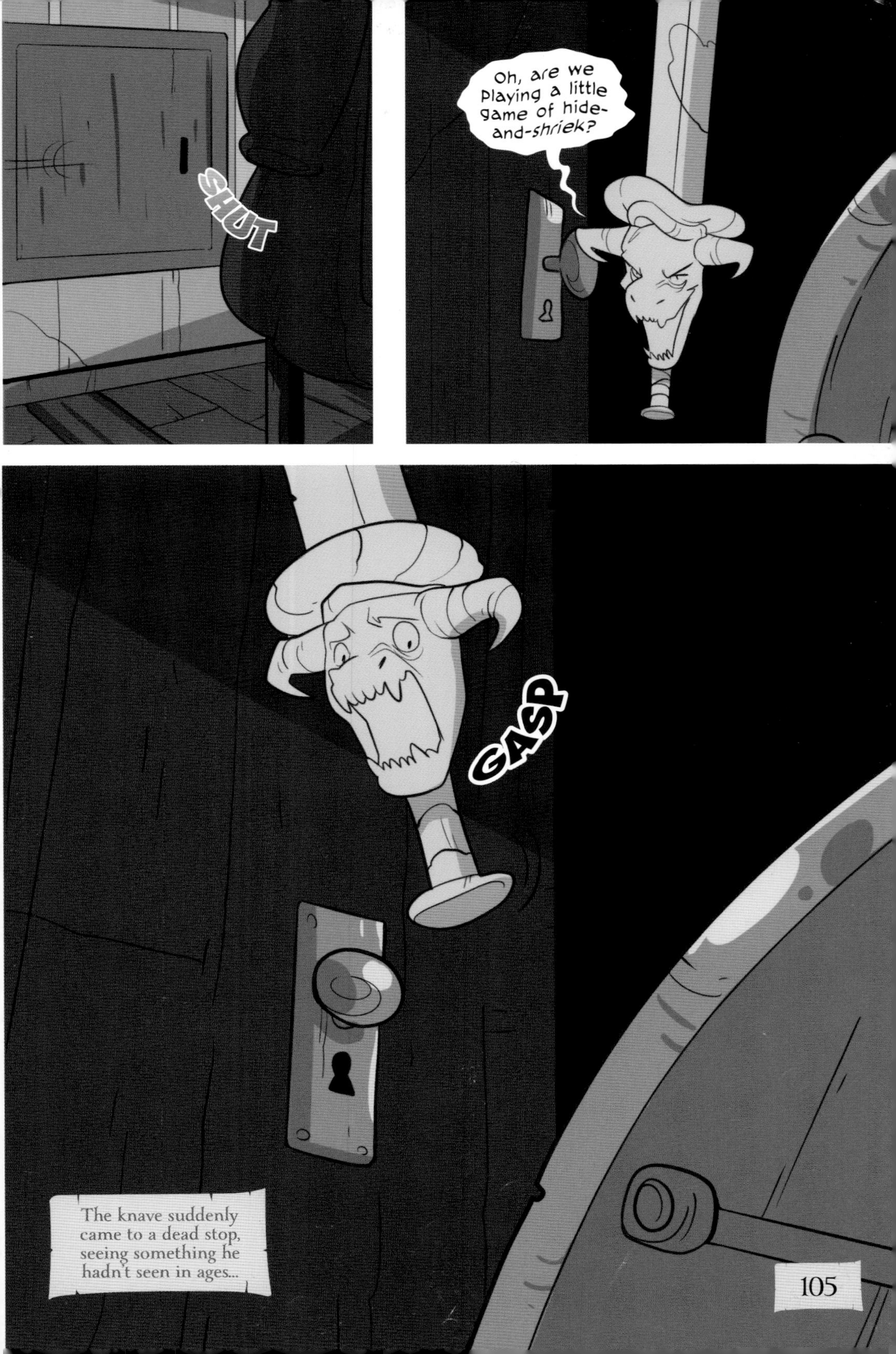
SHUT
Oh, are we playing a little game of hide-and-*shriek*?
GASP
The knave suddenly came to a dead stop, seeing something he hadn't seen in ages...

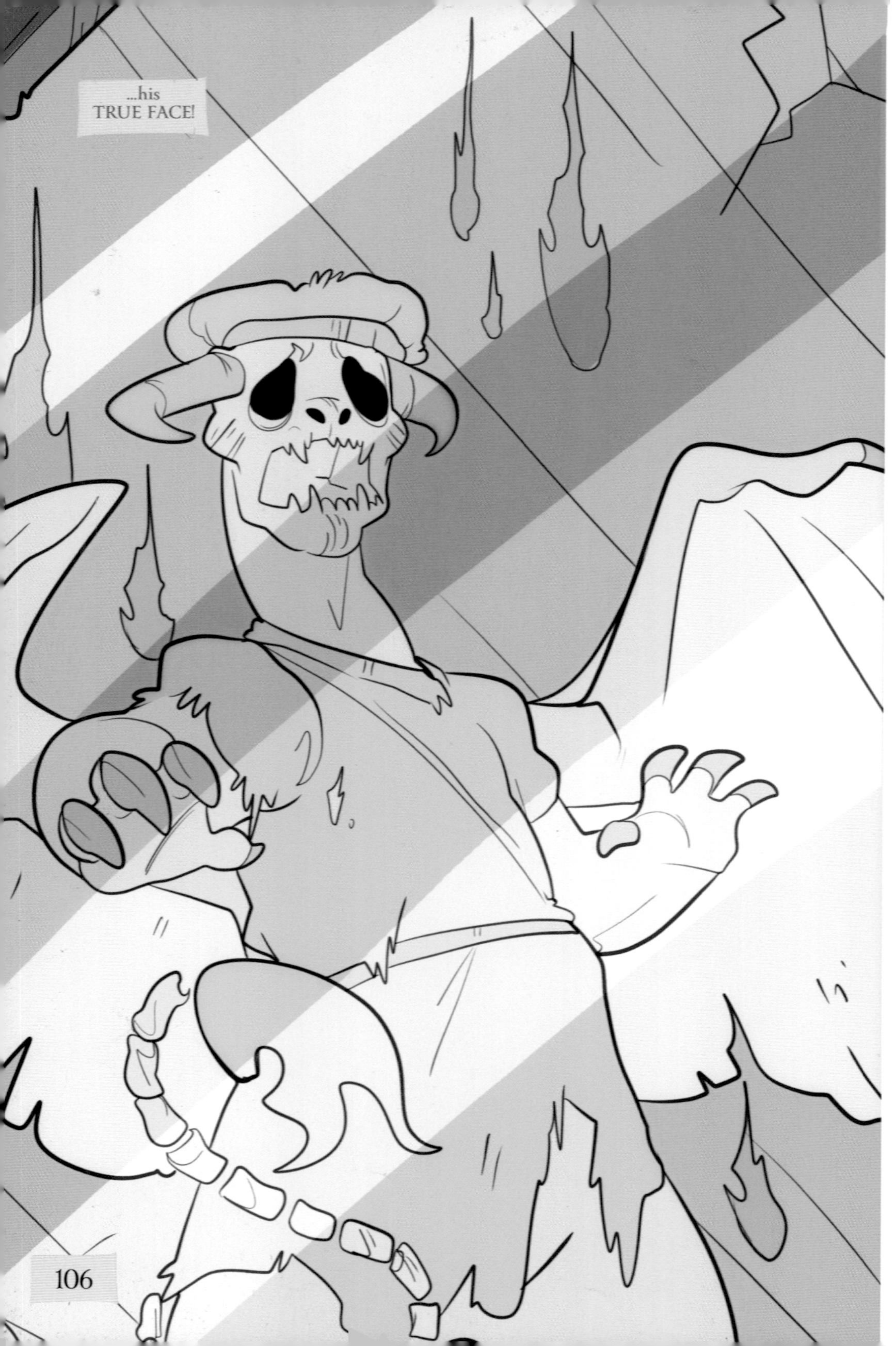
...his
TRUE FACE!

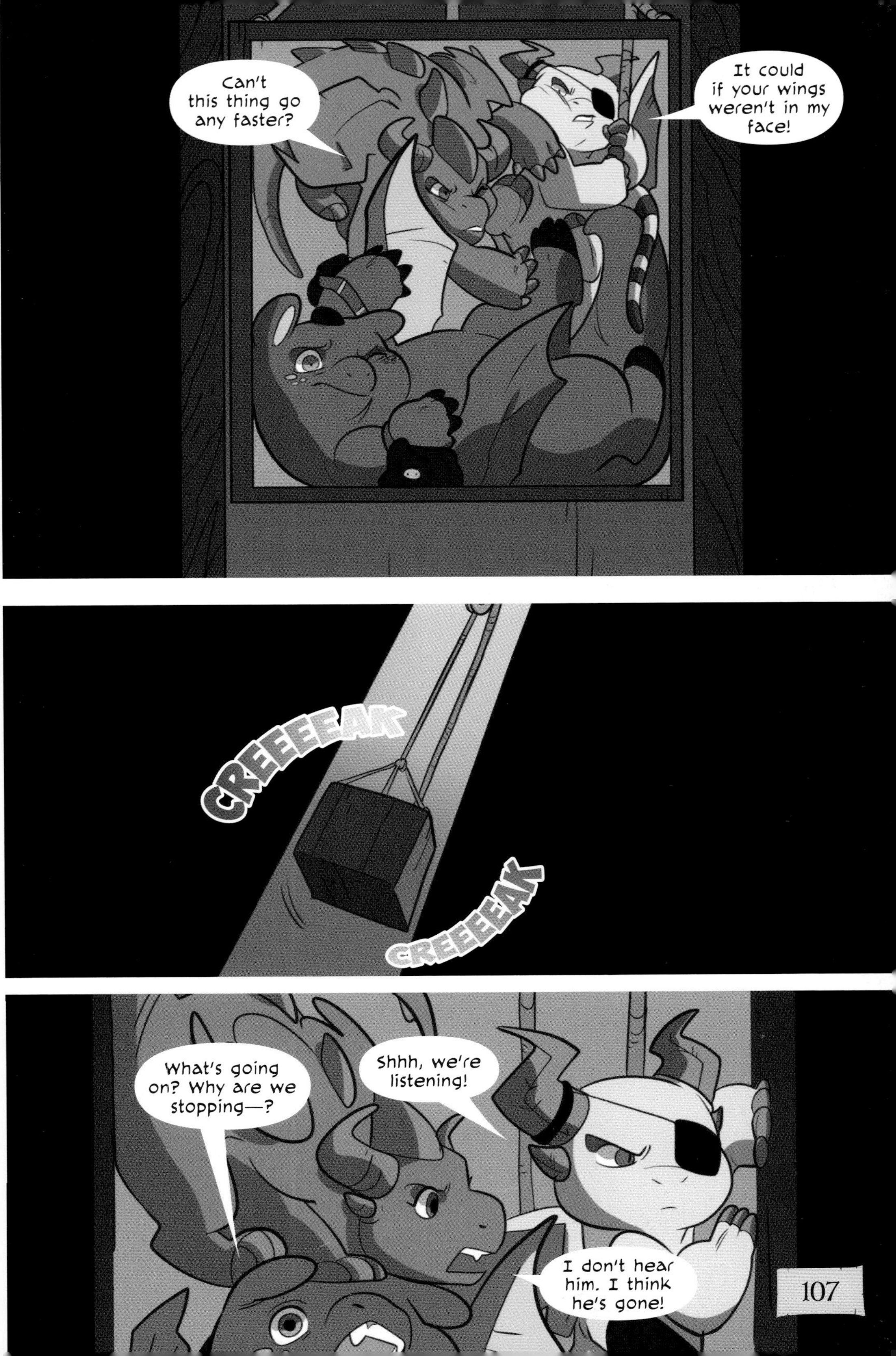
Can't this thing go any faster?
It could if your wings weren't in my face!
CREEEEAK
CREEEEAK
What's going on? Why are we stopping—?
Shhh, we're listening!
I don't hear him. I think he's gone!

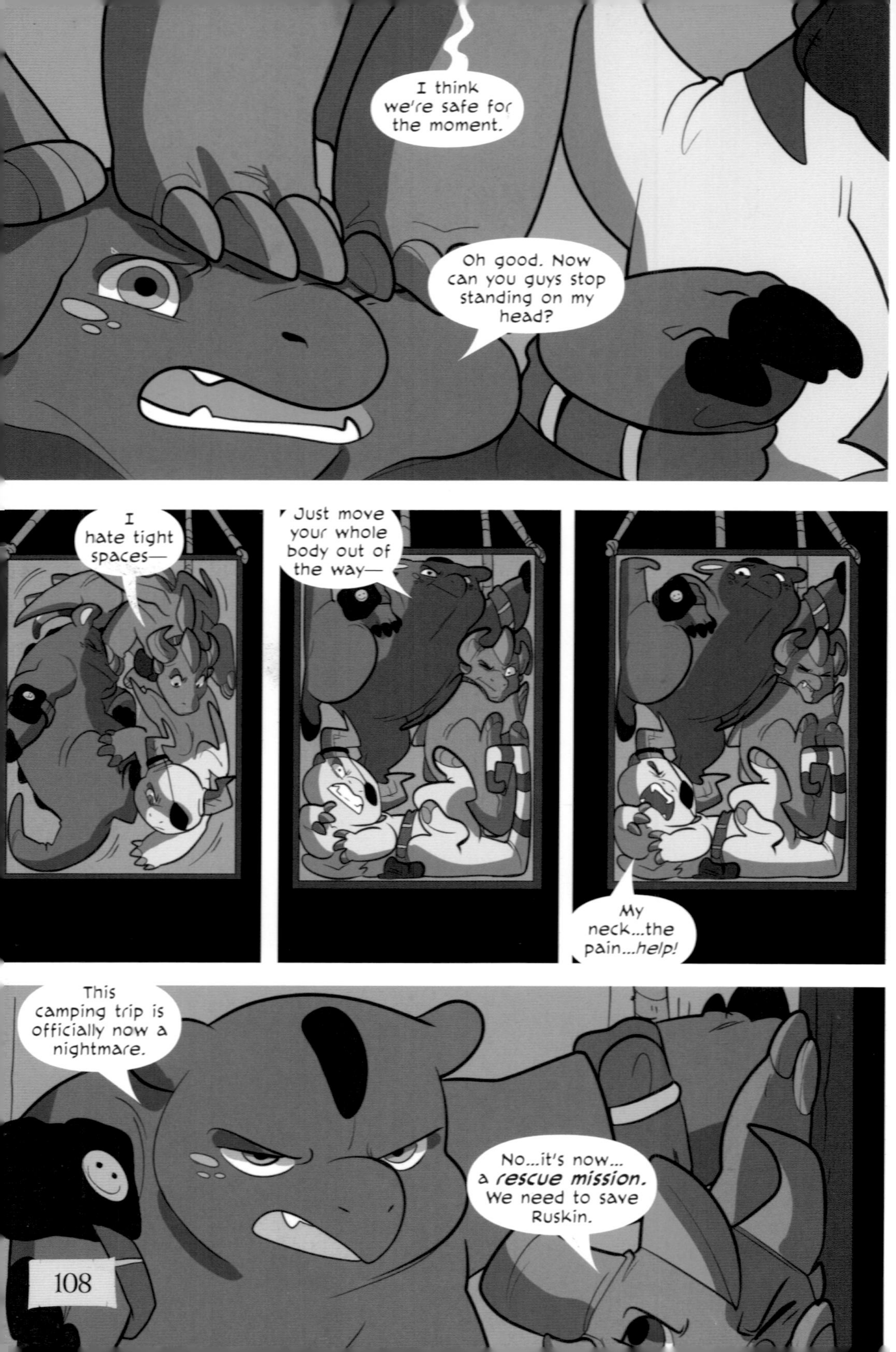
I think we're safe for the moment.
Oh good. Now can you guys stop standing on my head?
I hate tight spaces—
Just move your whole body out of the way—
My neck...the pain...*help!*
This camping trip is officially now a nightmare.
No...it's now... a ***rescue mission.*** We need to save Ruskin.

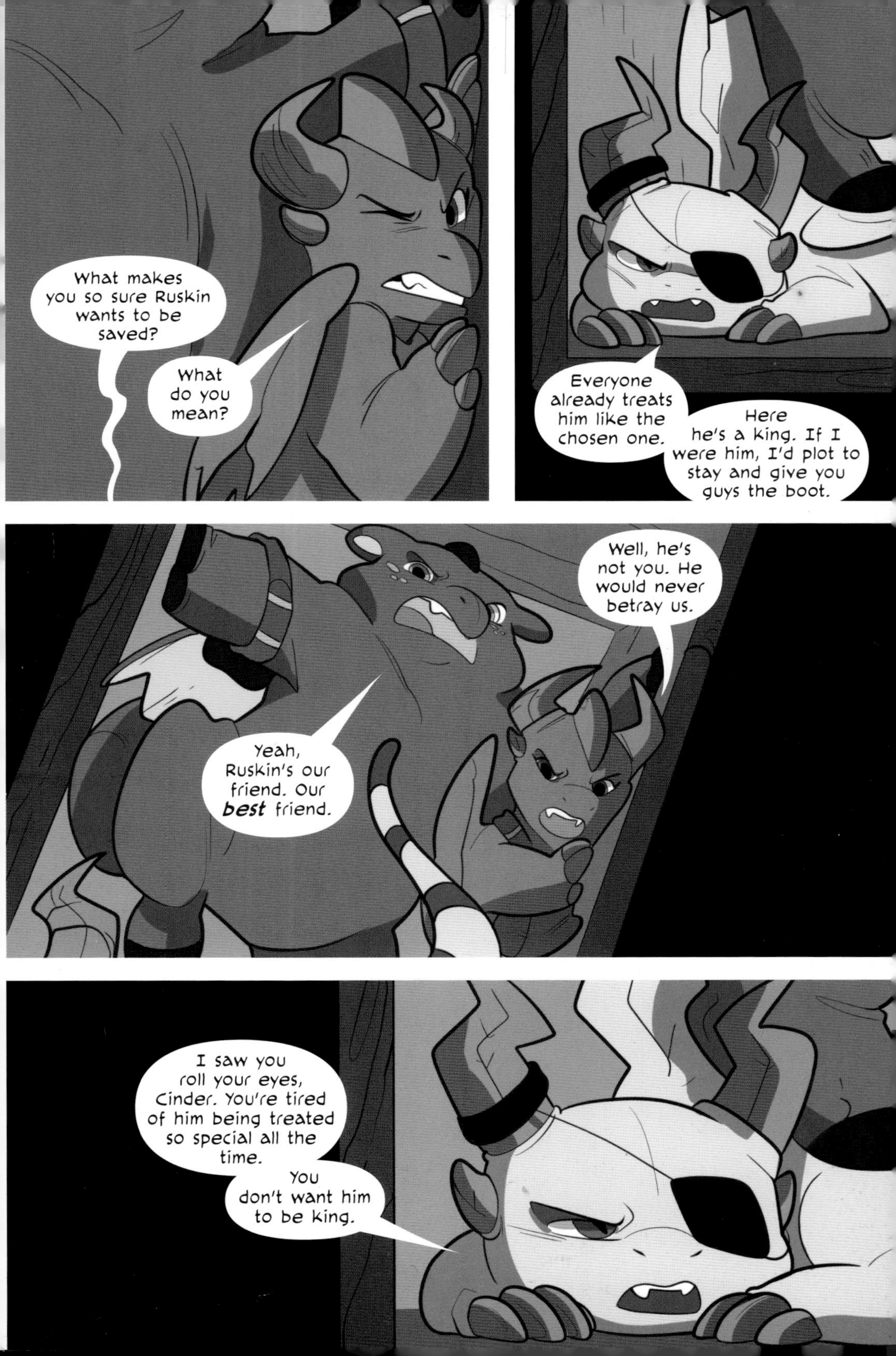
What makes you so sure Ruskin wants to be saved?
What do you mean?
Everyone already treats him like the chosen one.
Here he's a king. If I were him, I'd plot to stay and give you guys the boot.
Well, he's not you. He would never betray us.
Yeah, Ruskin's our friend. Our **best** friend.
I saw you roll your eyes, Cinder. You're tired of him being treated so special all the time.
You don't want him to be king.

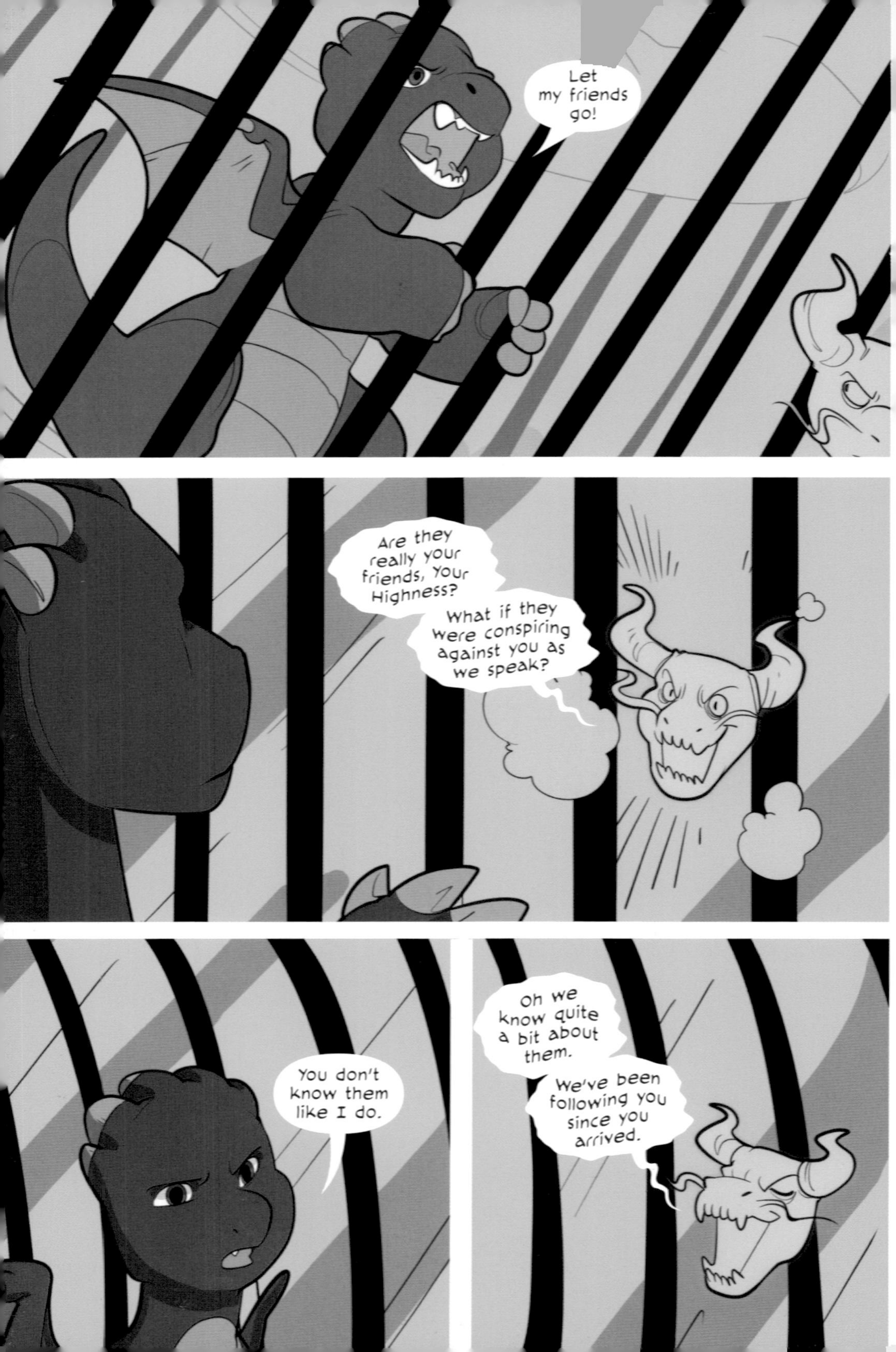
Let my friends go!
Are they really your friends, Your Highness?
What if they were conspiring against you as we speak?
You don't know them like I do.
Oh we know quite a bit about them.
We've been following you since you arrived.

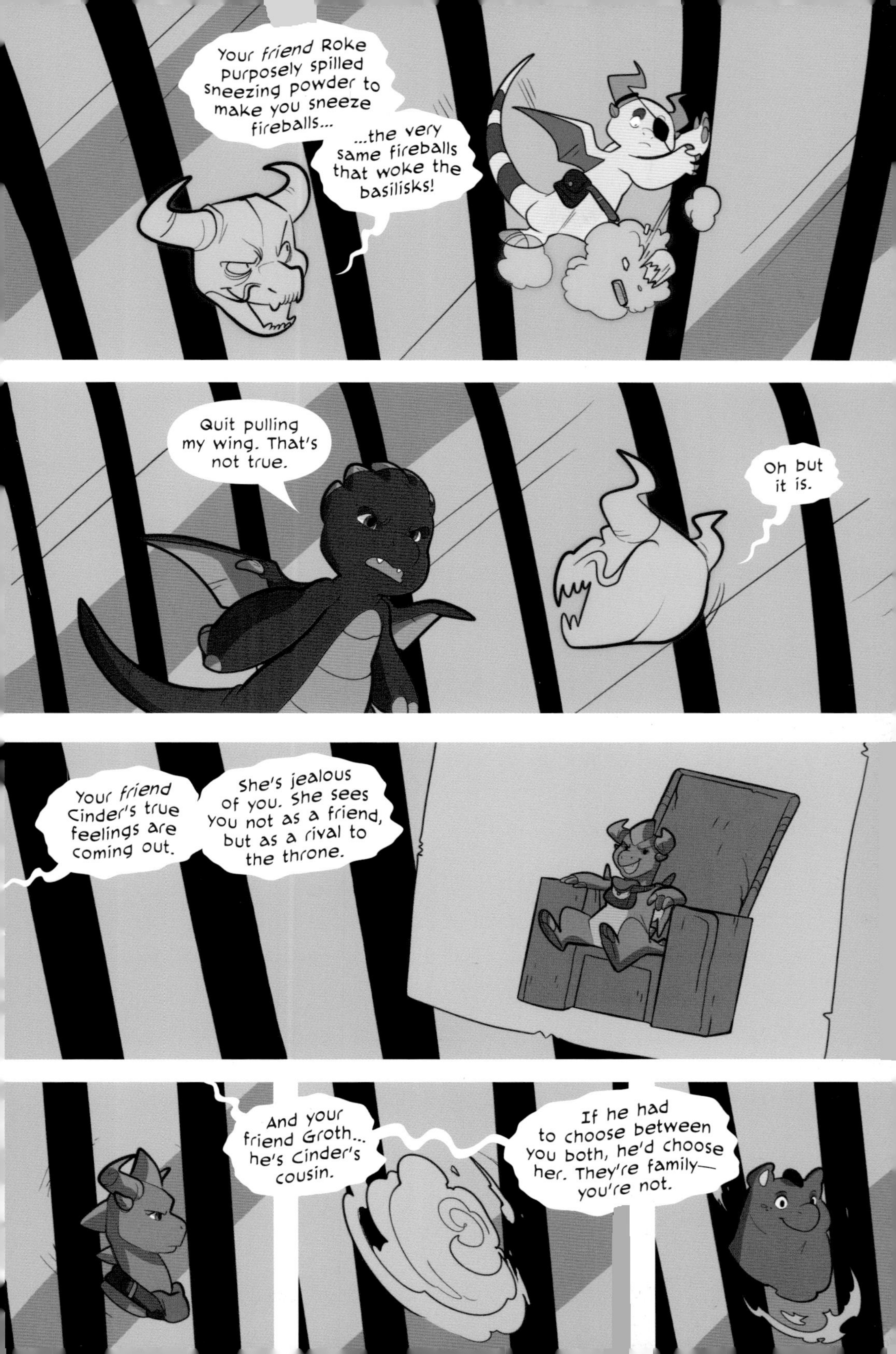
Your *friend* Roke purposely spilled sneezing powder to make you sneeze fireballs...
...the very same fireballs that woke the basilisks!
Quit pulling my wing. That's not true.
Oh but it is.
Your *friend* Cinder's true feelings are coming out.
She's jealous of you. She sees you not as a friend, but as a rival to the throne.
And your friend Groth... he's Cinder's cousin.
If he had to choose between you both, he'd choose her. They're family— you're not.

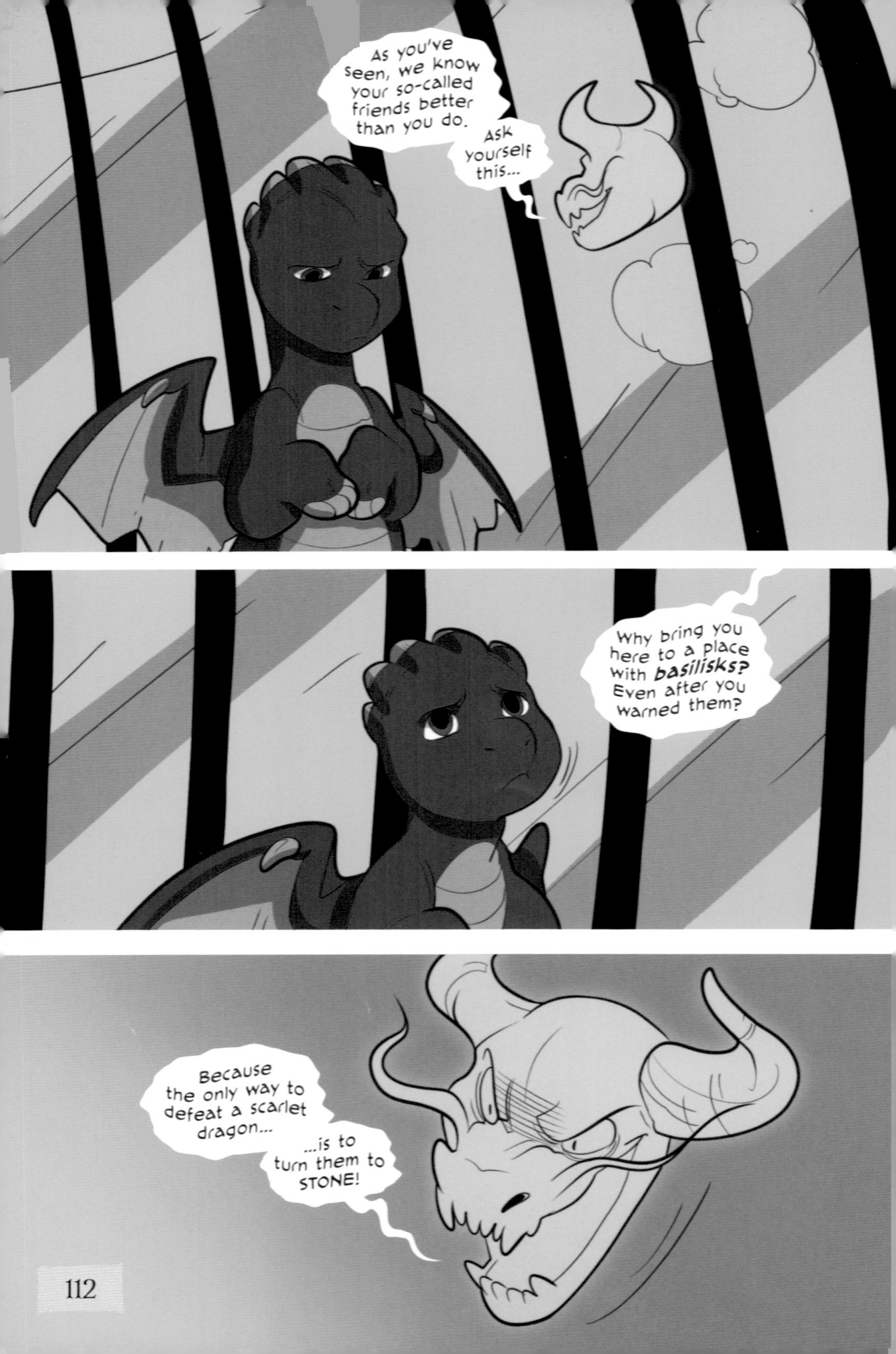
As you've seen, we know your so-called friends better than you do.
Ask yourself this...
Why bring you here to a place with *basilisks?* Even after you warned them?
Because the only way to defeat a scarlet dragon...
...is to turn them to STONE!

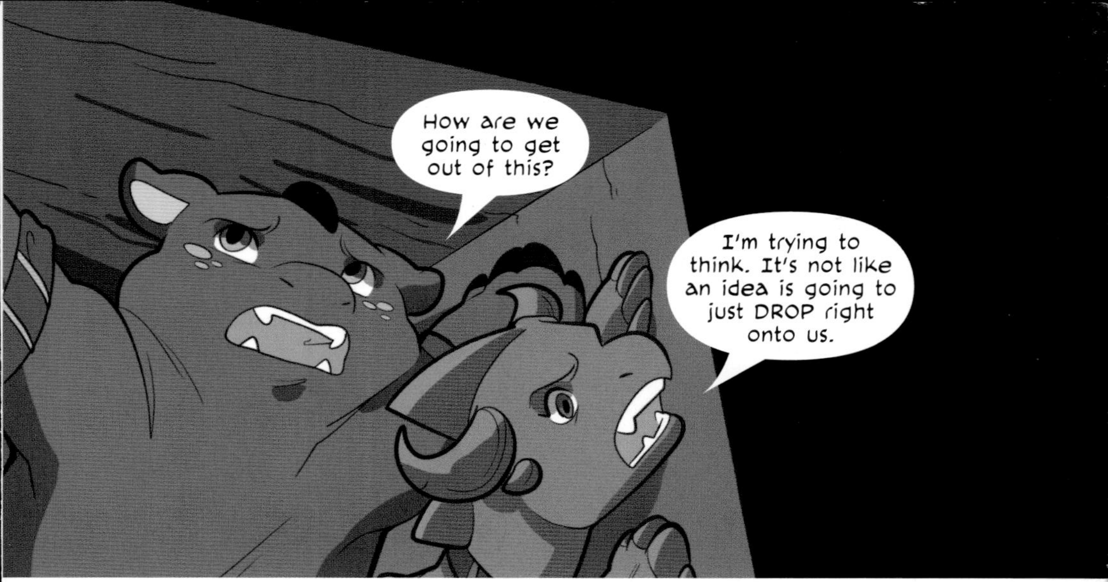
How are we going to get out of this?
I'm trying to think. It's not like an idea is going to just DROP right onto us.

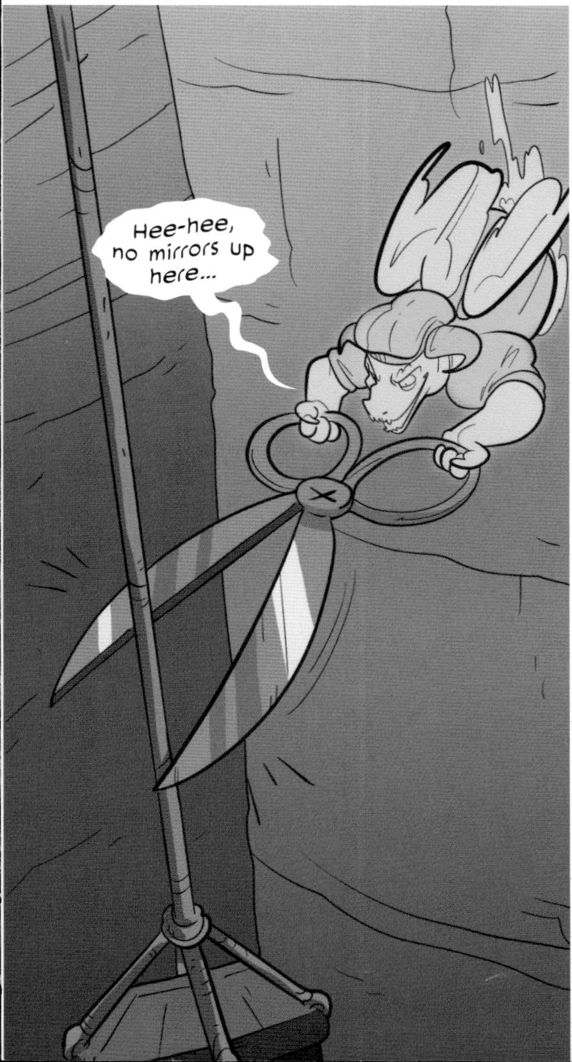
Hee-hee, no mirrors up here...

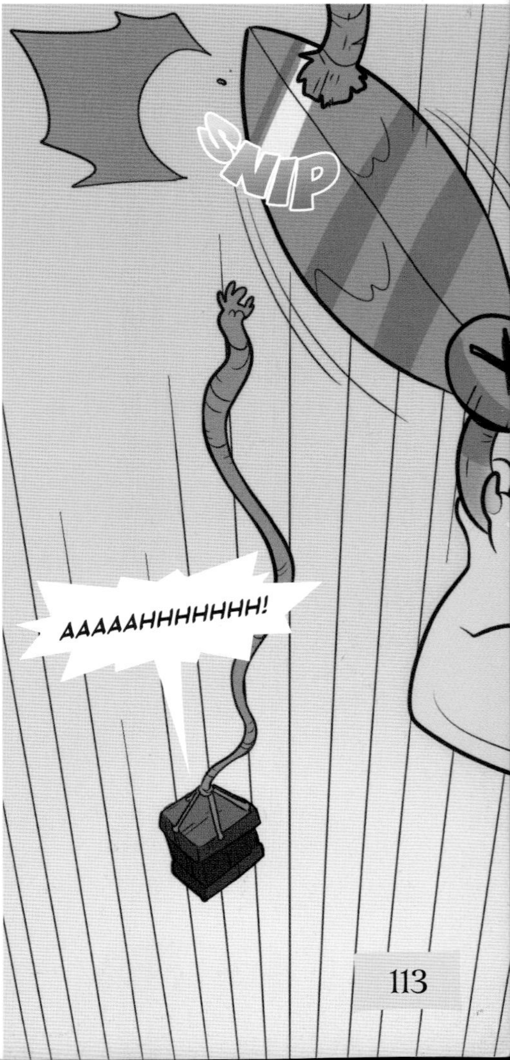
SNIP
AAAAAHHHHHHH!

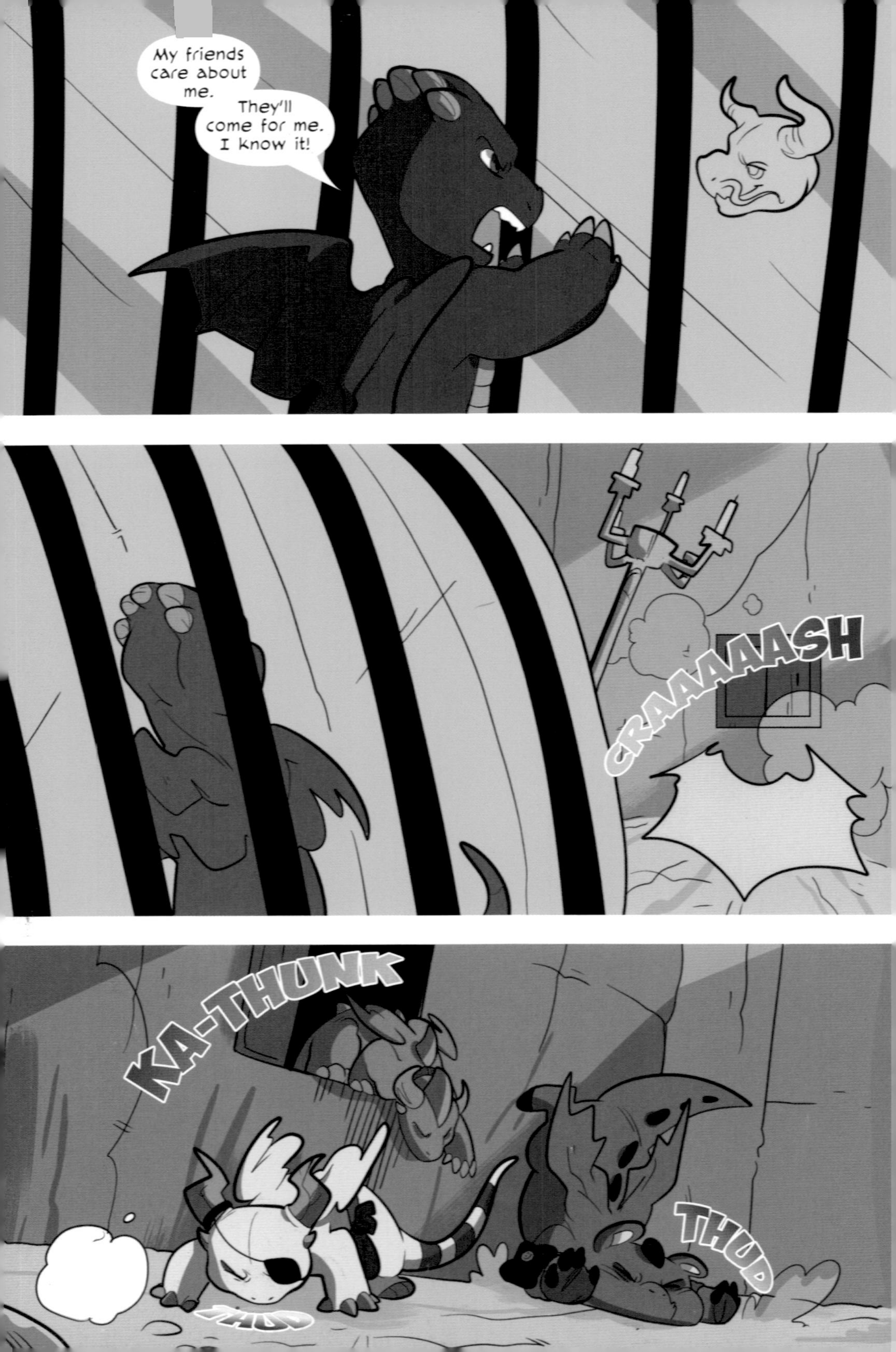

My friends care about me.
They'll come for me. I know it!
CRAAAAAASH
KA-THUNK
THUD
THUD

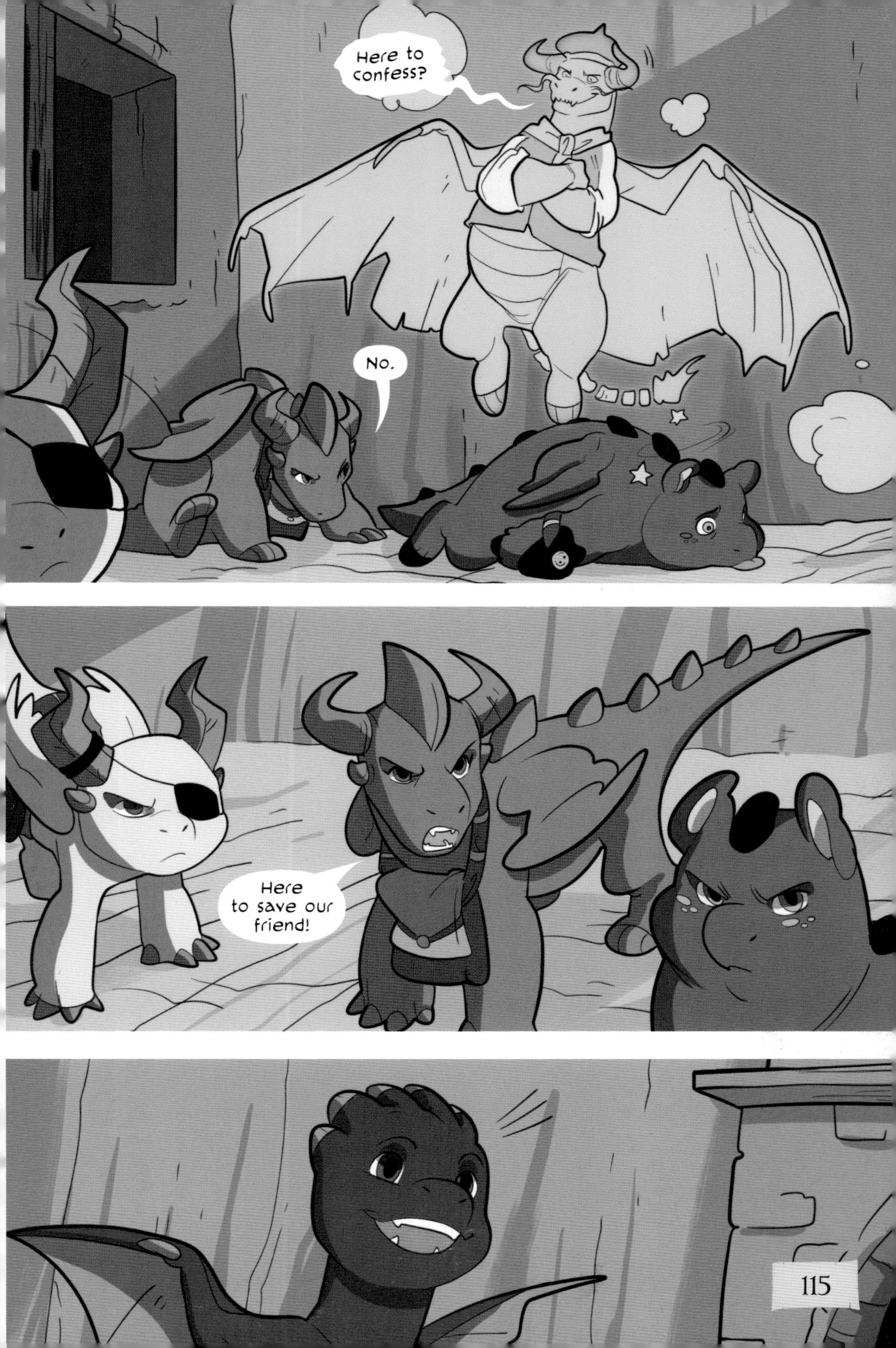
Here to confess?
No.
Here to save our friend!

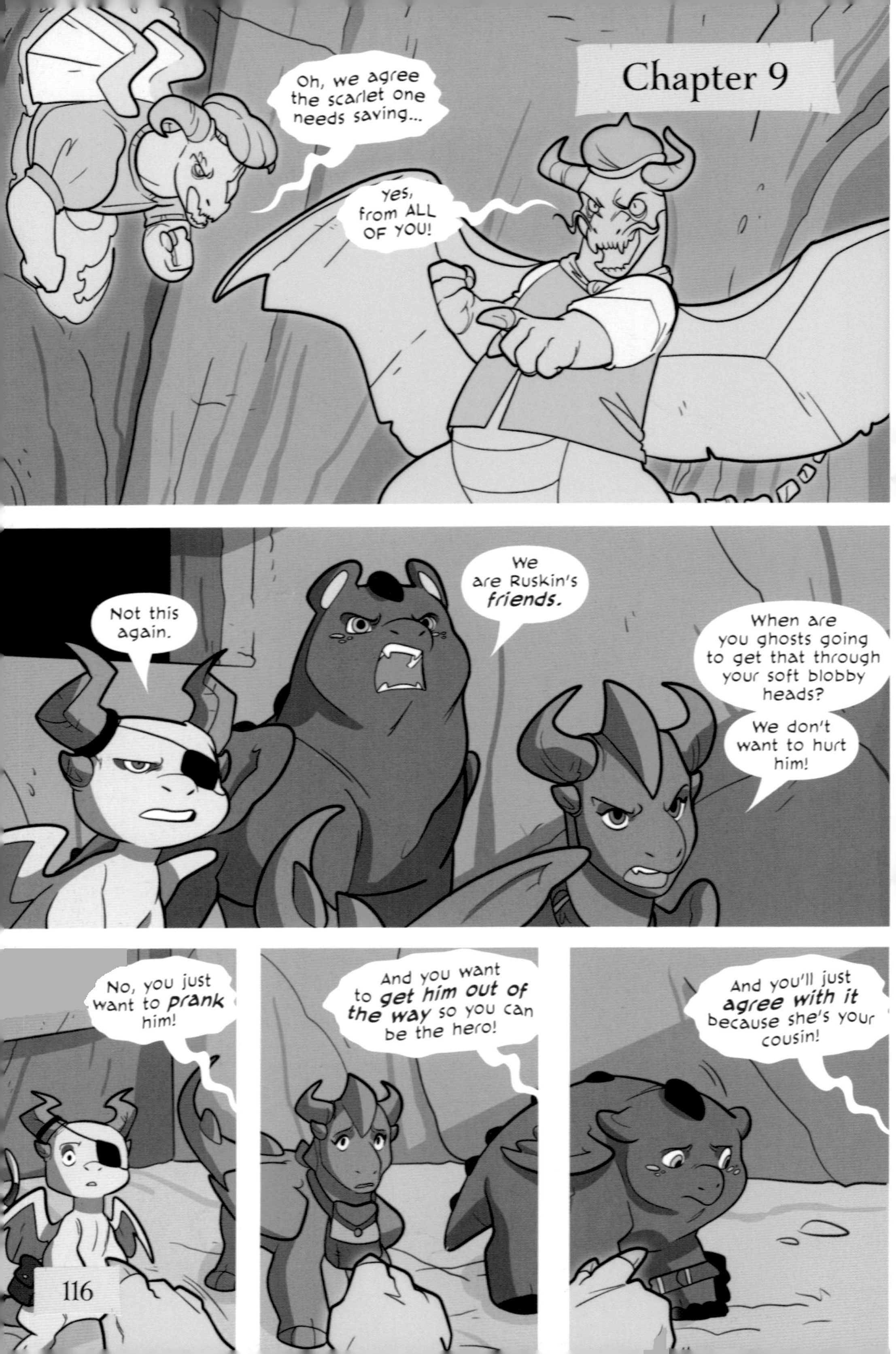
Chapter 9
Oh, we agree the scarlet one needs saving...
Yes, from ALL OF YOU!
Not this again.
We are Ruskin's *friends.*
When are you ghosts going to get that through your soft blobby heads?
We don't want to hurt him!
No, you just want to *prank* him!
And you want to ***get him out of the way*** so you can be the hero!
And you'll just ***agree with it*** because she's your cousin!

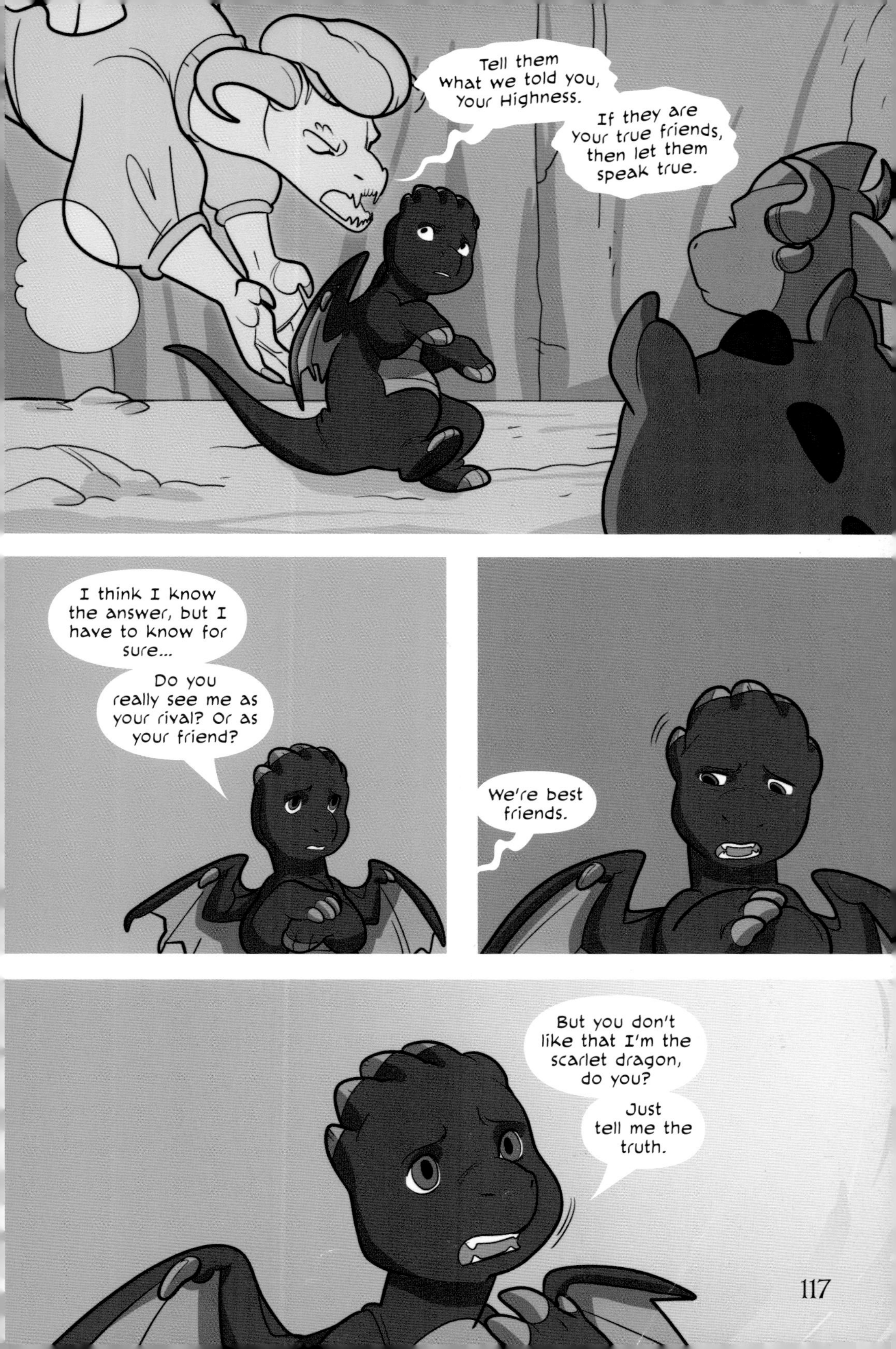
Tell them what we told you, Your Highness.
If they are your true friends, then let them speak true.
I think I know the answer, but I have to know for sure...
Do you really see me as your rival? Or as your friend?
We're best friends.
But you don't like that I'm the scarlet dragon, do you?
Just tell me the truth.

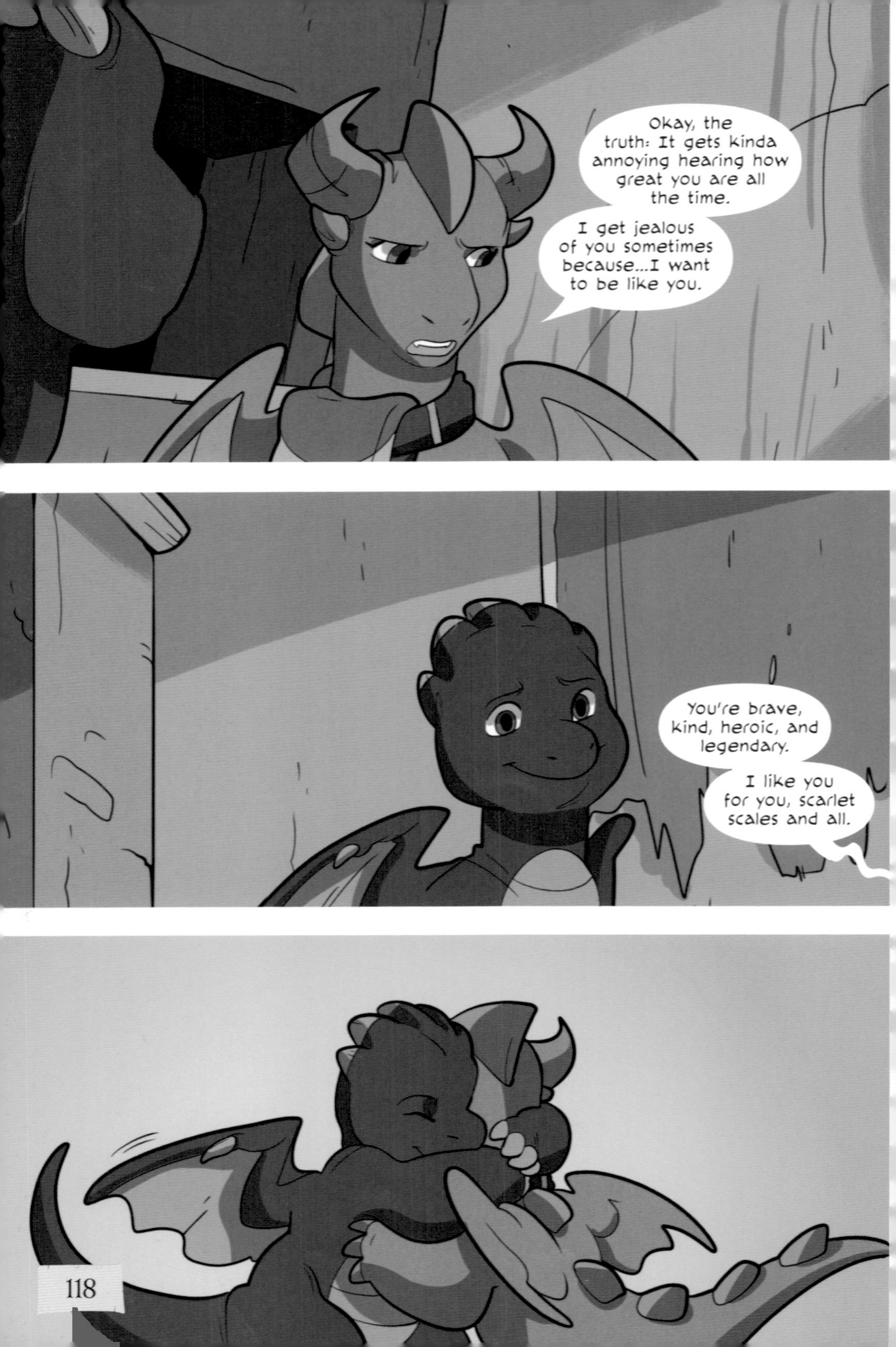
Okay, the truth: It gets kinda annoying hearing how great you are all the time.
I get jealous of you sometimes because...I want to be like you.
You're brave, kind, heroic, and legendary.
I like you for you, scarlet scales and all.

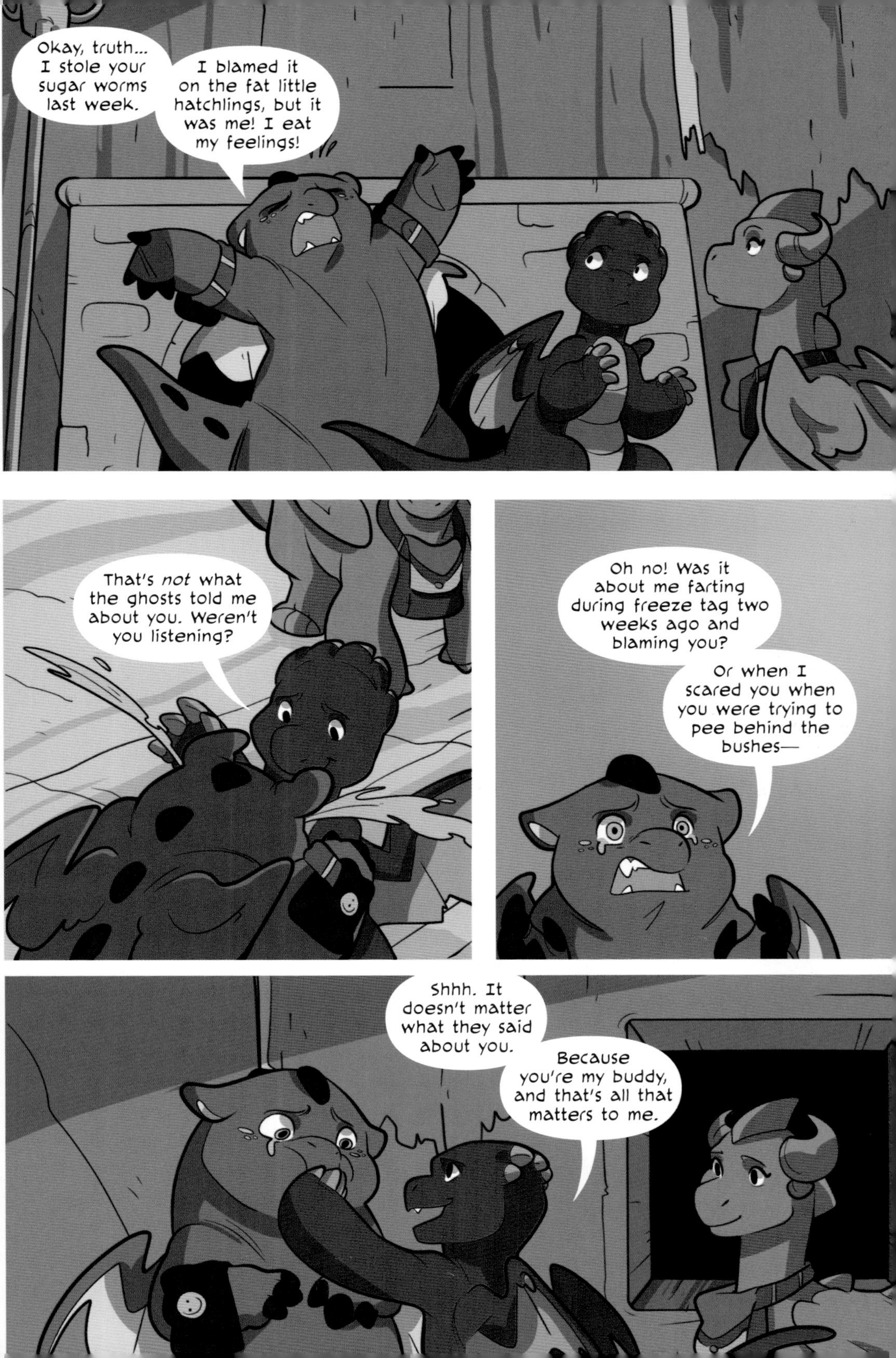
Okay, truth... I stole your sugar worms last week.
I blamed it on the fat little hatchlings, but it was me! I eat my feelings!
That's *not* what the ghosts told me about you. Weren't you listening?
Oh no! Was it about me farting during freeze tag two weeks ago and blaming you?
Or when I scared you when you were trying to pee behind the bushes—
Shhh. It doesn't matter what they said about you.
Because you're my buddy, and that's all that matters to me.

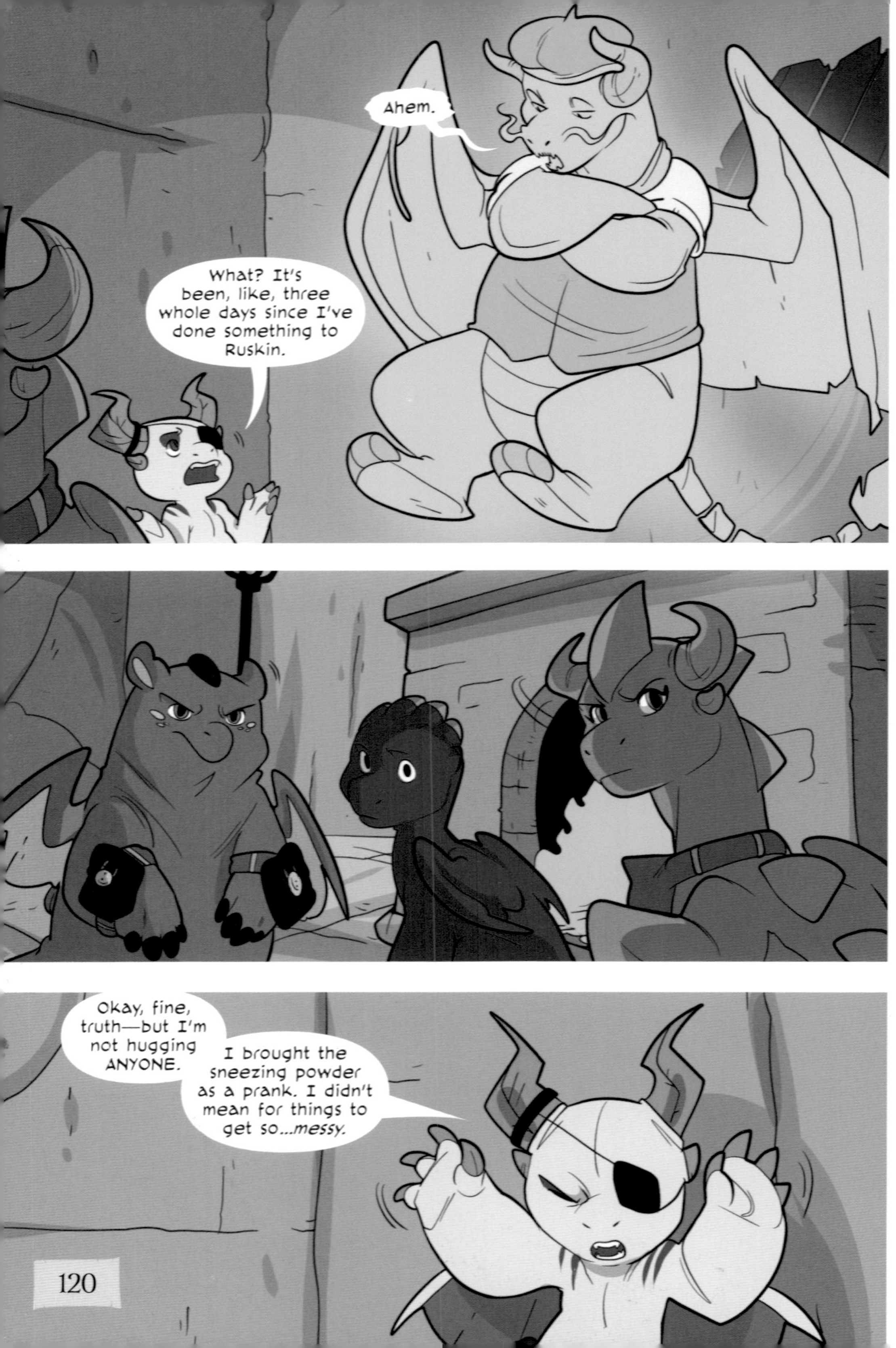
Ahem.
What? It's been, like, three whole days since I've done something to Ruskin.
Okay, fine, truth—but I'm not hugging ANYONE.
I brought the sneezing powder as a prank. I didn't mean for things to get so...*messy.*

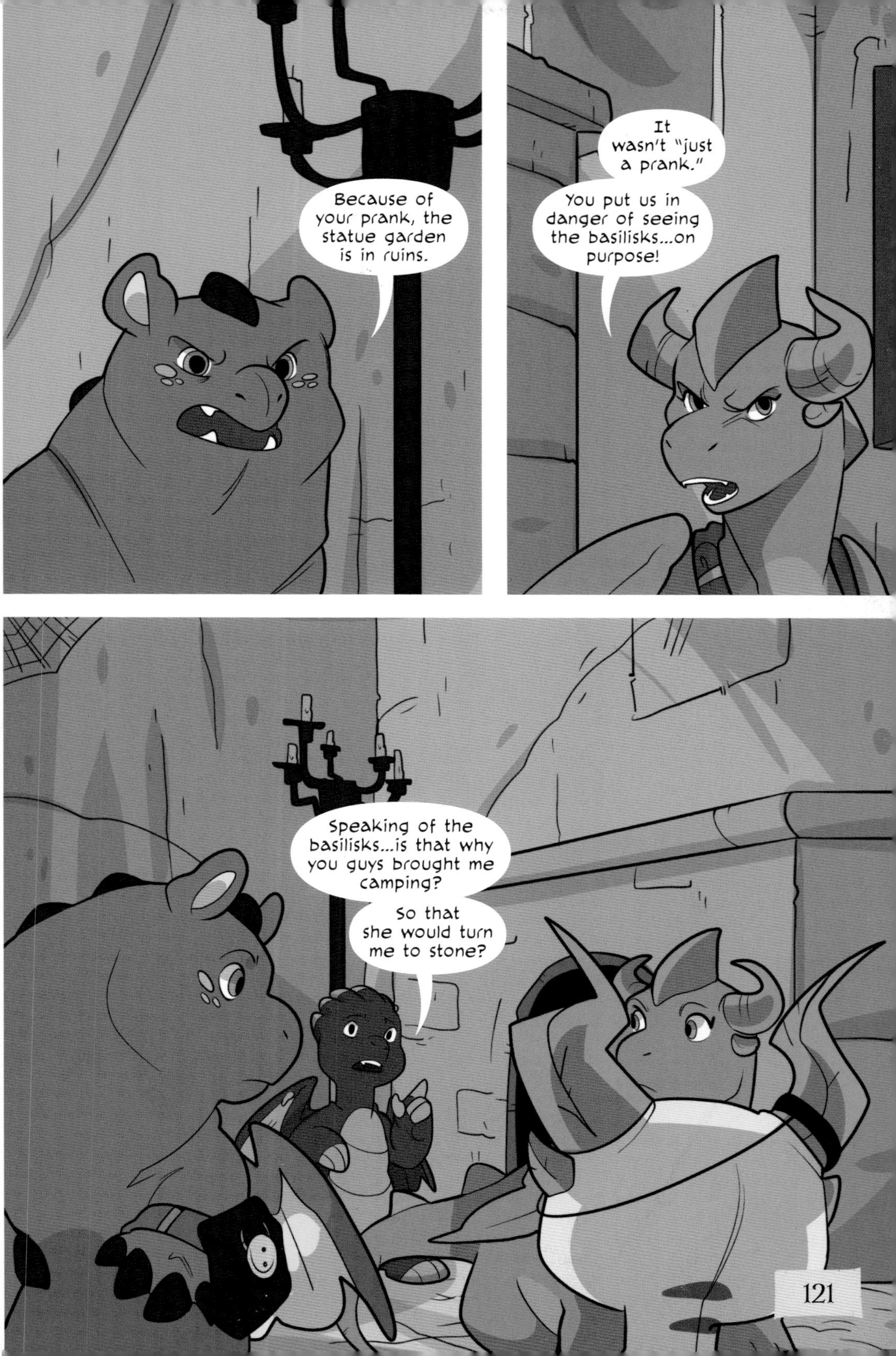
Because of your prank, the statue garden is in ruins.
It wasn't "just a prank."
You put us in danger of seeing the basilisks...on purpose!
Speaking of the basilisks...is that why you guys brought me camping?
So that she would turn me to stone?

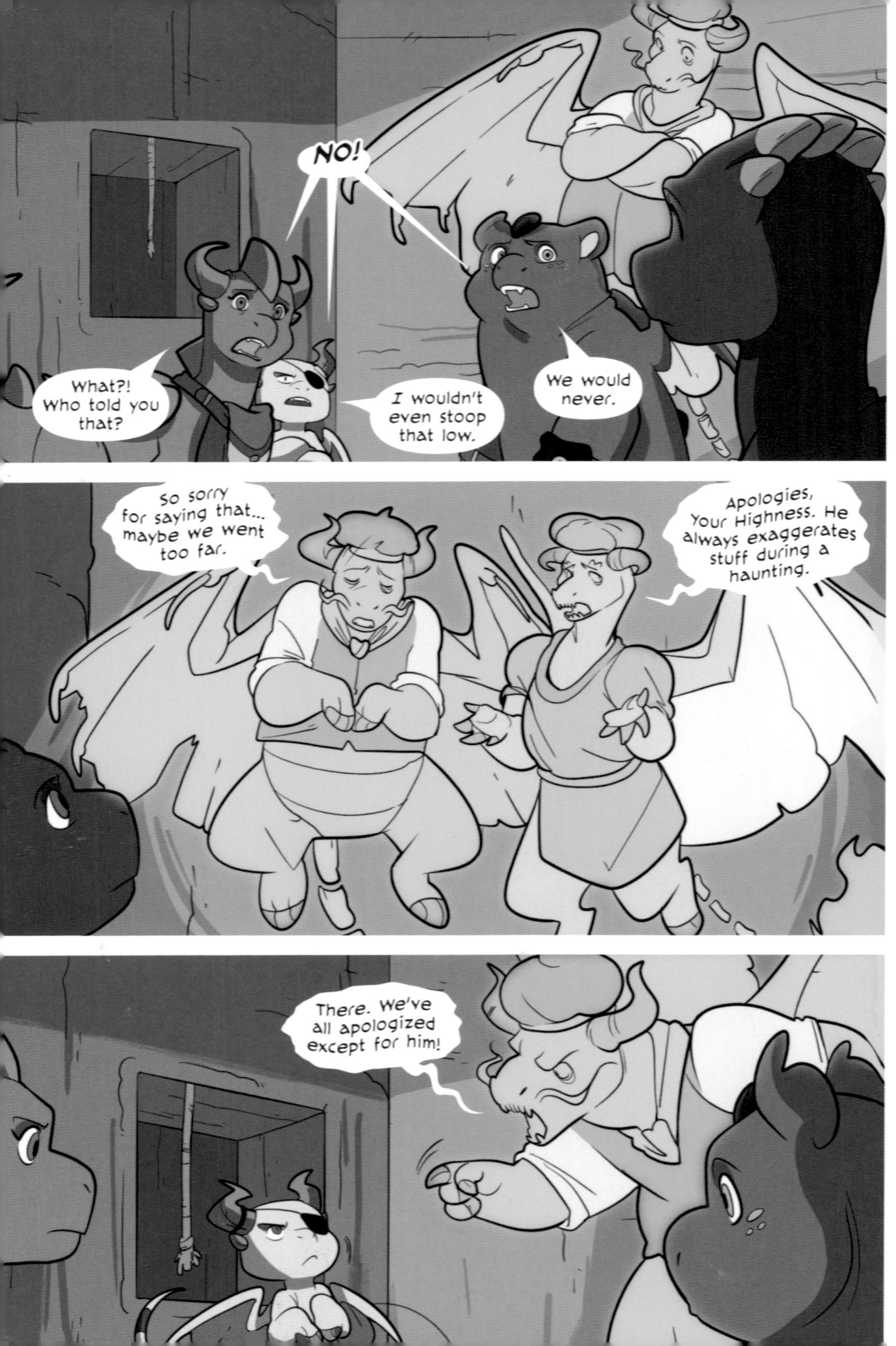
NO!
What?! Who told you that?
I wouldn't even stoop that low.
We would never.
So sorry for saying that... maybe we went too far.
Apologies, Your Highness. He always exaggerates stuff during a haunting.
There. We've all apologized except for him!

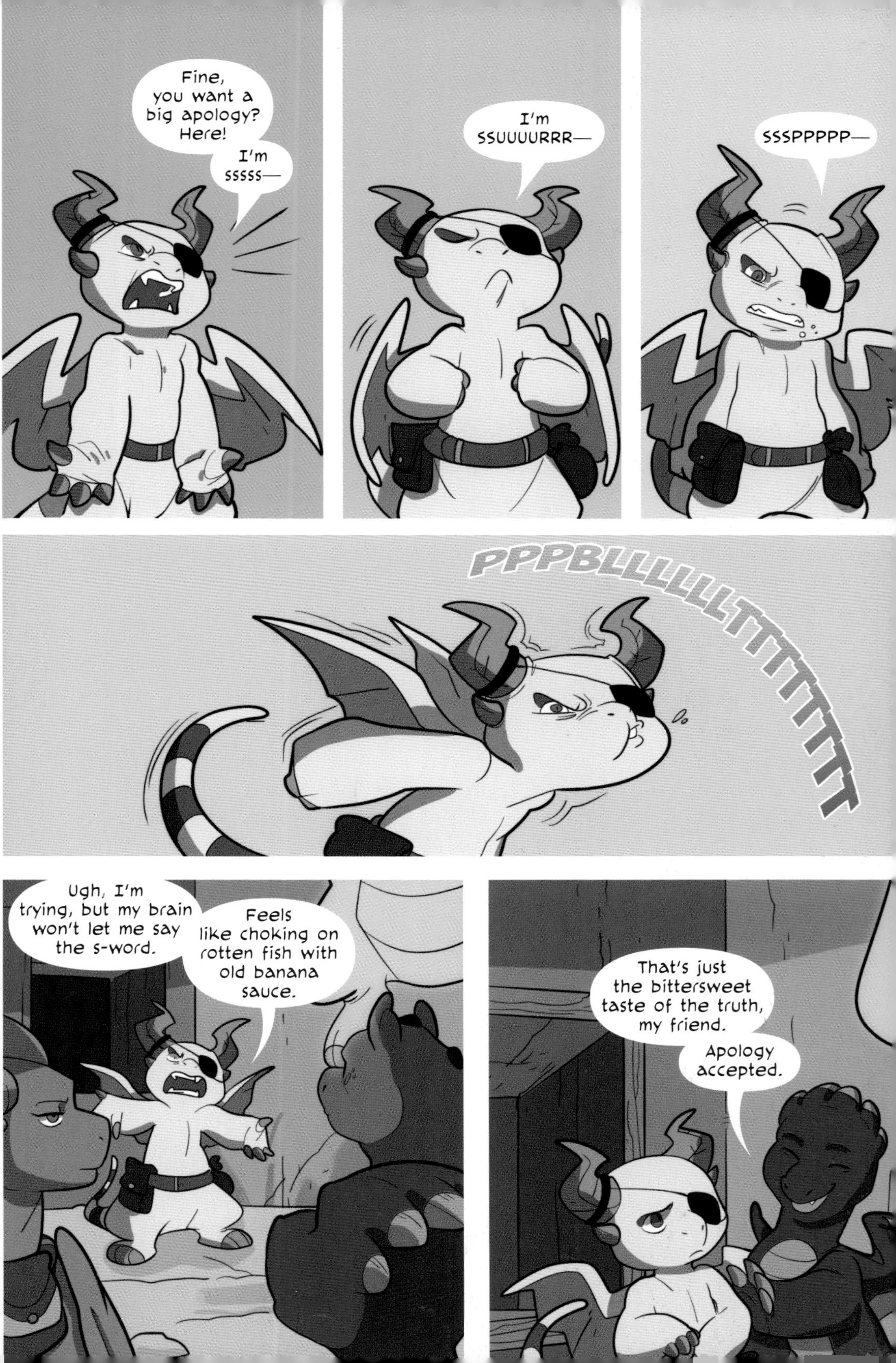
Fine, you want a big apology? Here!
I'm sssss—
I'm SSUUUURRR—
SSSPPPPP—
PPPBLLLLLLTTTTTTTT
Ugh, I'm trying, but my brain won't let me say the s-word.
Feels like choking on rotten fish with old banana sauce.
That's just the bittersweet taste of the truth, my friend.
Apology accepted.

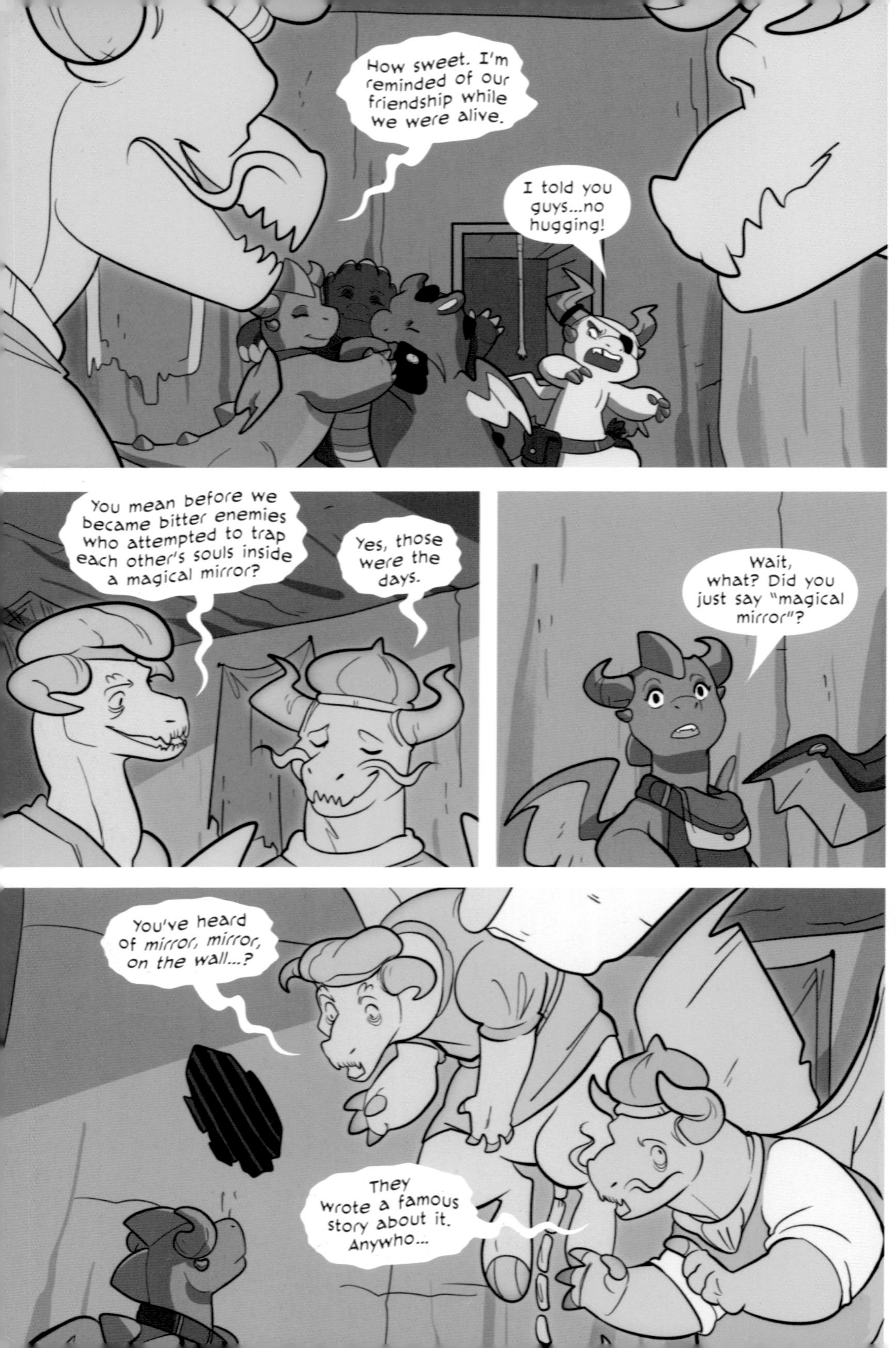
How sweet. I'm reminded of our friendship while we were alive.
I told you guys...no hugging!
You mean before we became bitter enemies who attempted to trap each other's souls inside a magical mirror?
Yes, those were the days.
Wait, what? Did you just say "magical mirror"?
You've heard of *mirror, mirror, on the wall*...?
They wrote a famous story about it. Anywho...

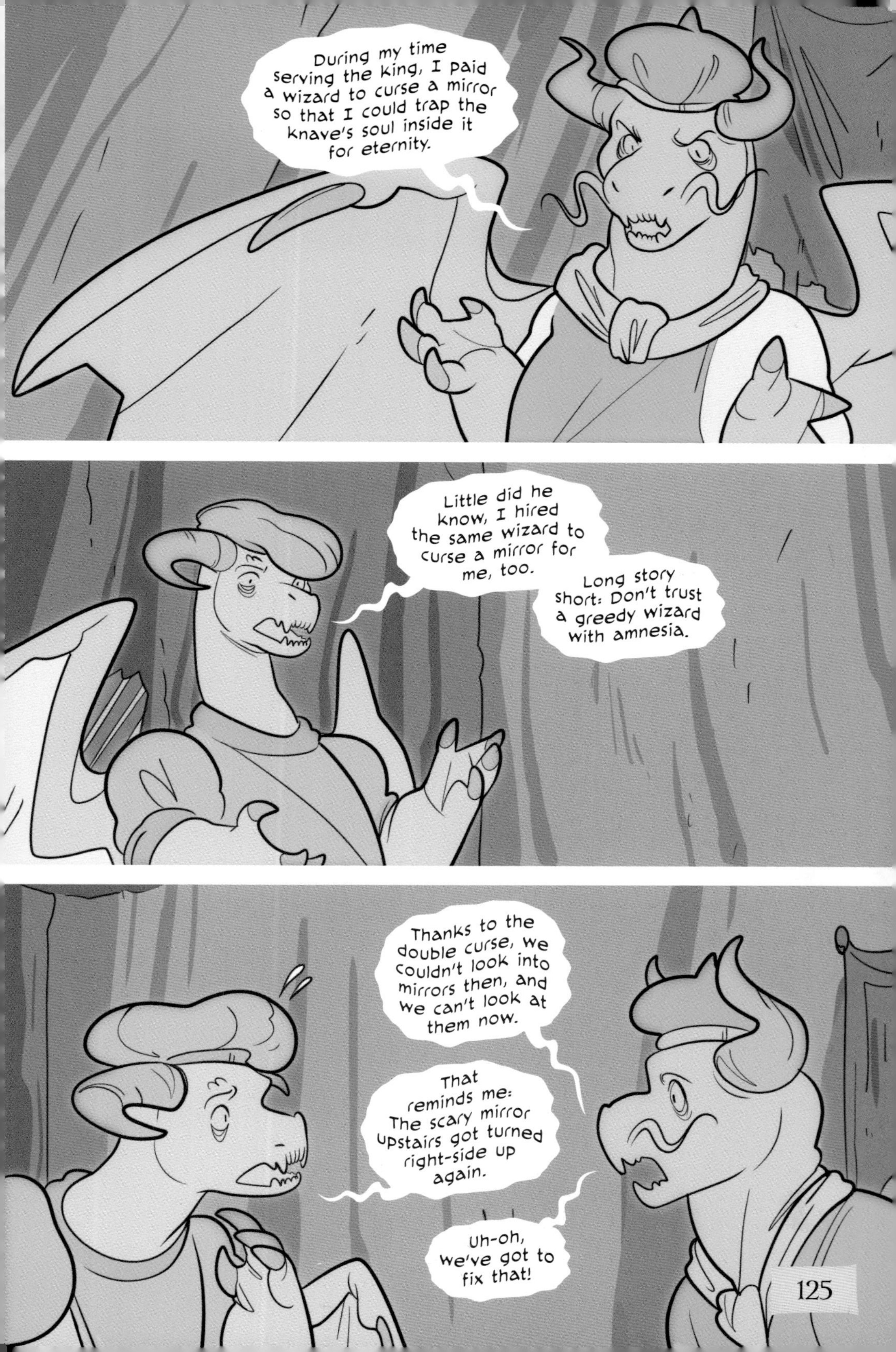
During my time serving the king, I paid a wizard to curse a mirror so that I could trap the knave's soul inside it for eternity.
Little did he know, I hired the same wizard to curse a mirror for me, too.
Long story short: Don't trust a greedy wizard with amnesia.
Thanks to the double curse, we couldn't look into mirrors then, and we can't look at them now.
That reminds me: The scary mirror upstairs got turned right-side up again.
Uh-oh, we've got to fix that!

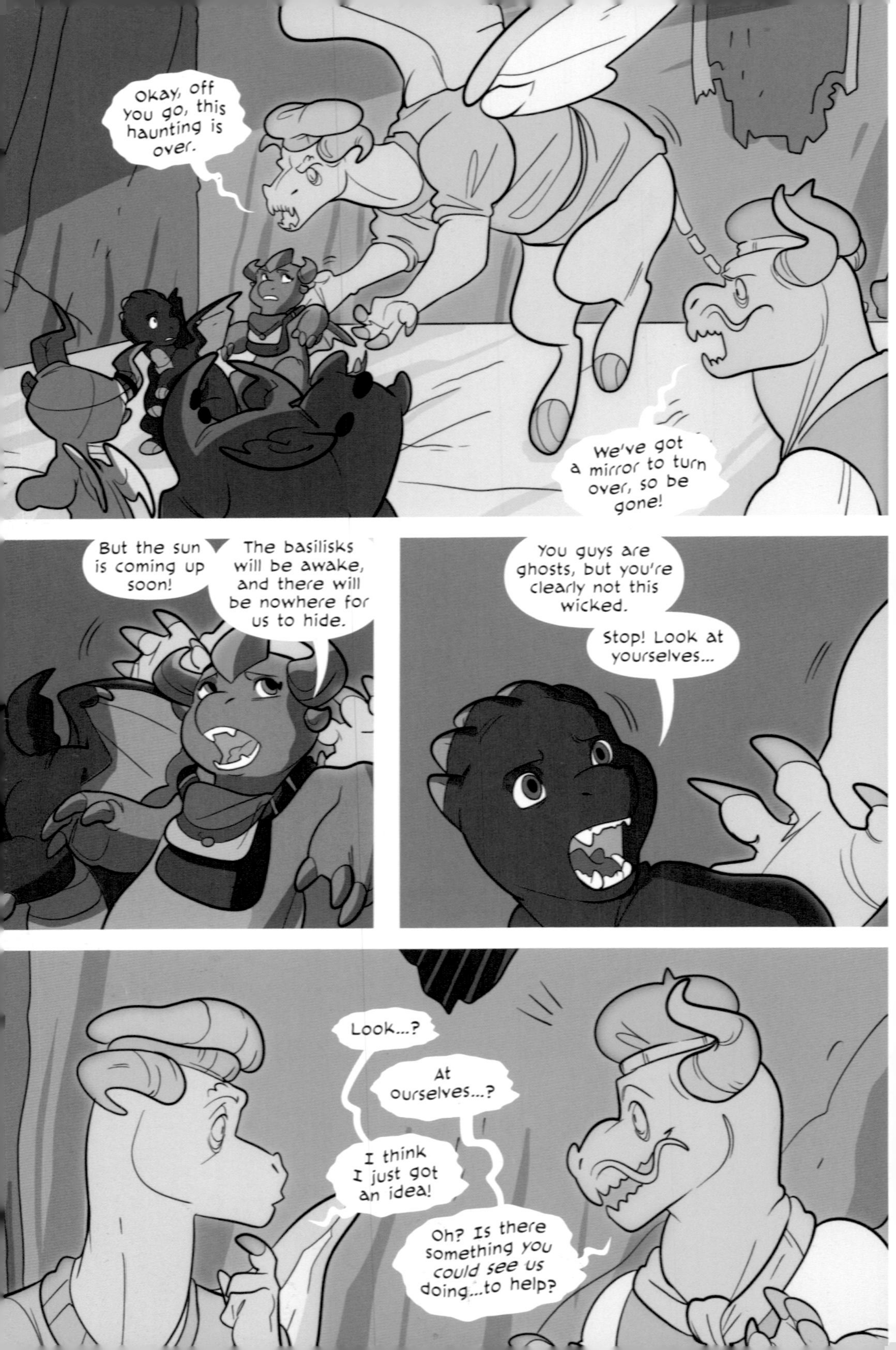
Okay, off you go, this haunting is over.
We've got a mirror to turn over, so be gone!
But the sun is coming up soon!
The basilisks will be awake, and there will be nowhere for us to hide.
You guys are ghosts, but you're clearly not this wicked.
Stop! Look at yourselves...
Look...?
At ourselves...?
I think I just got an idea!
Oh? Is there something you could see us doing...to help?

Chapter 10

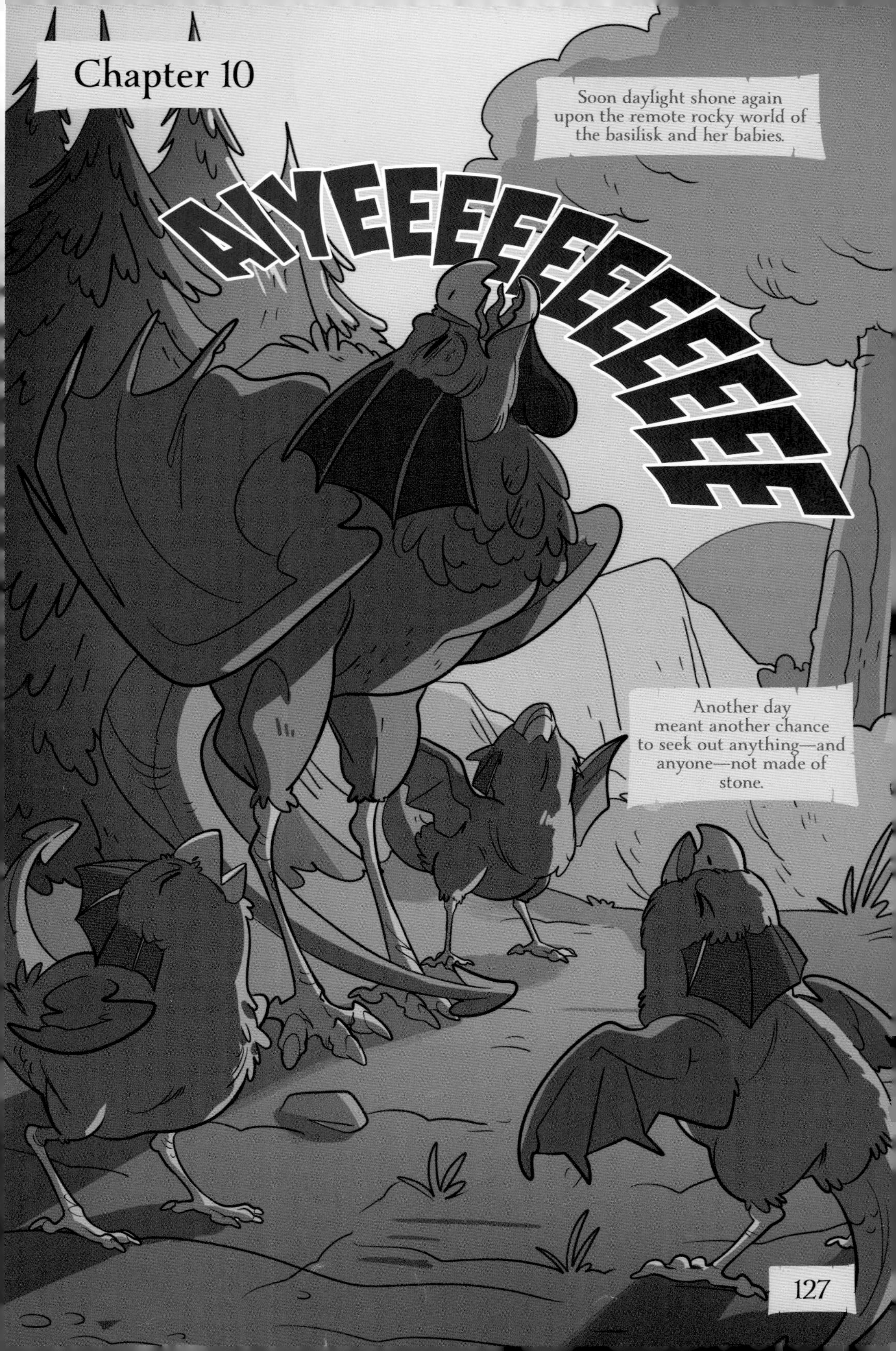
Soon daylight shone again upon the remote rocky world of the basilisk and her babies.
AIYEEEEEEEEEEEE
Another day meant another chance to seek out anything—and anyone—not made of stone.

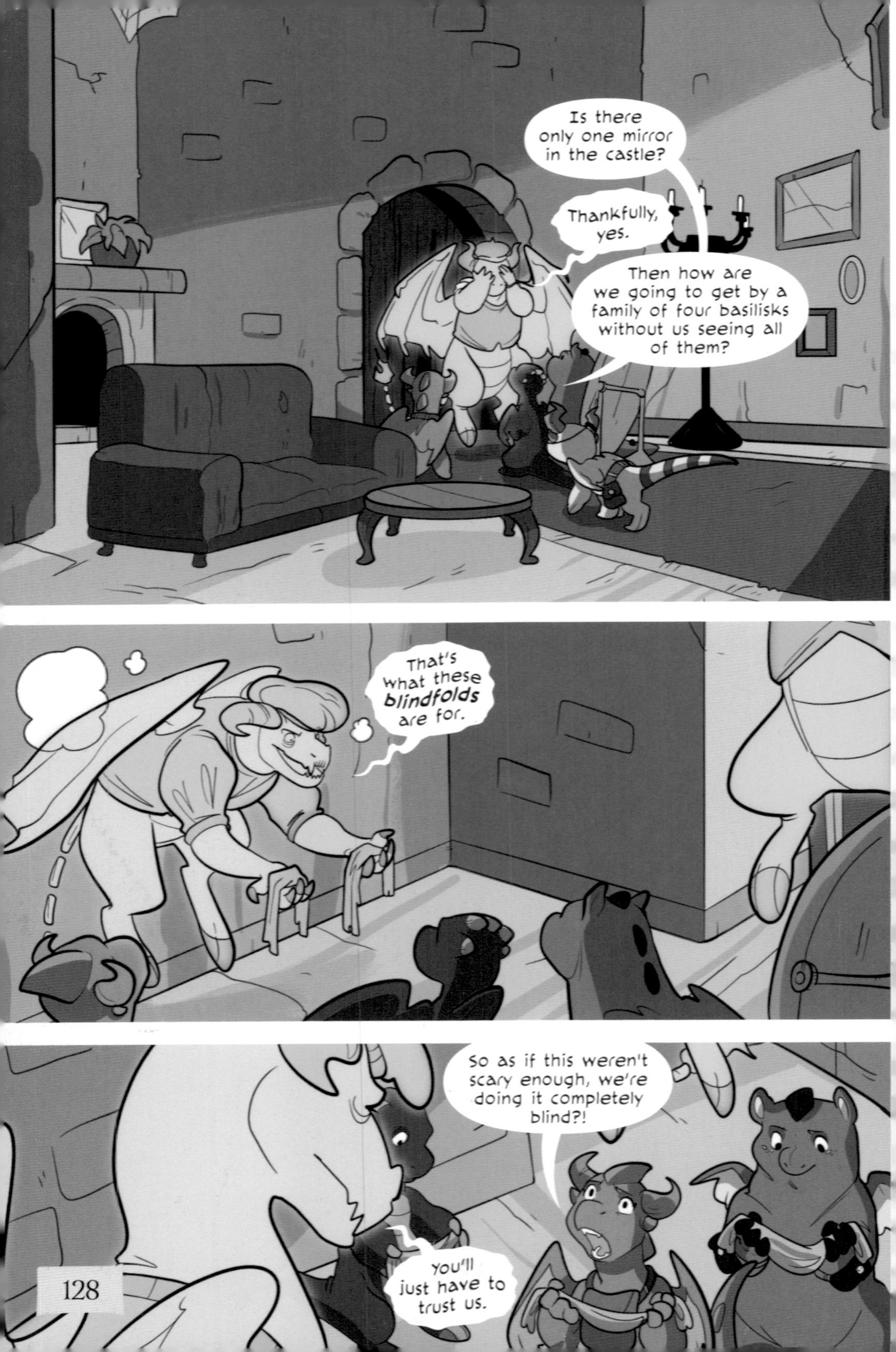
Is there only one mirror in the castle?
Thankfully, yes.
Then how are we going to get by a family of four basilisks without us seeing all of them?
That's what these *blindfolds* are for.
So as if this weren't scary enough, we're doing it completely blind?!
You'll just have to trust us.

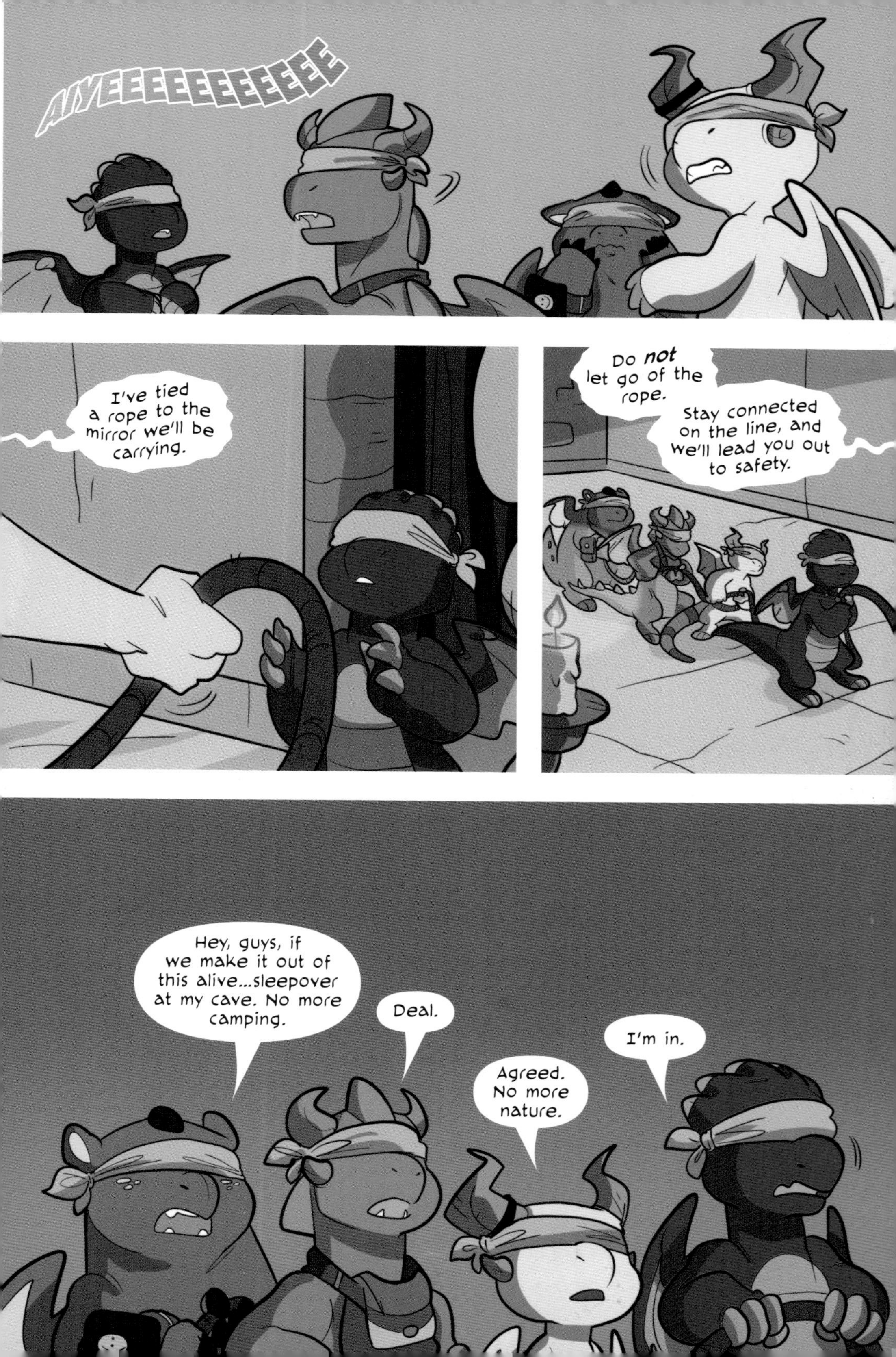
AIYEEEEEEEEEEE
I've tied a rope to the mirror we'll be carrying.
Do *not* let go of the rope.
Stay connected on the line, and we'll lead you out to safety.
Hey, guys, if we make it out of this alive...sleepover at my cave. No more camping.
Deal.
Agreed. No more nature.
I'm in.

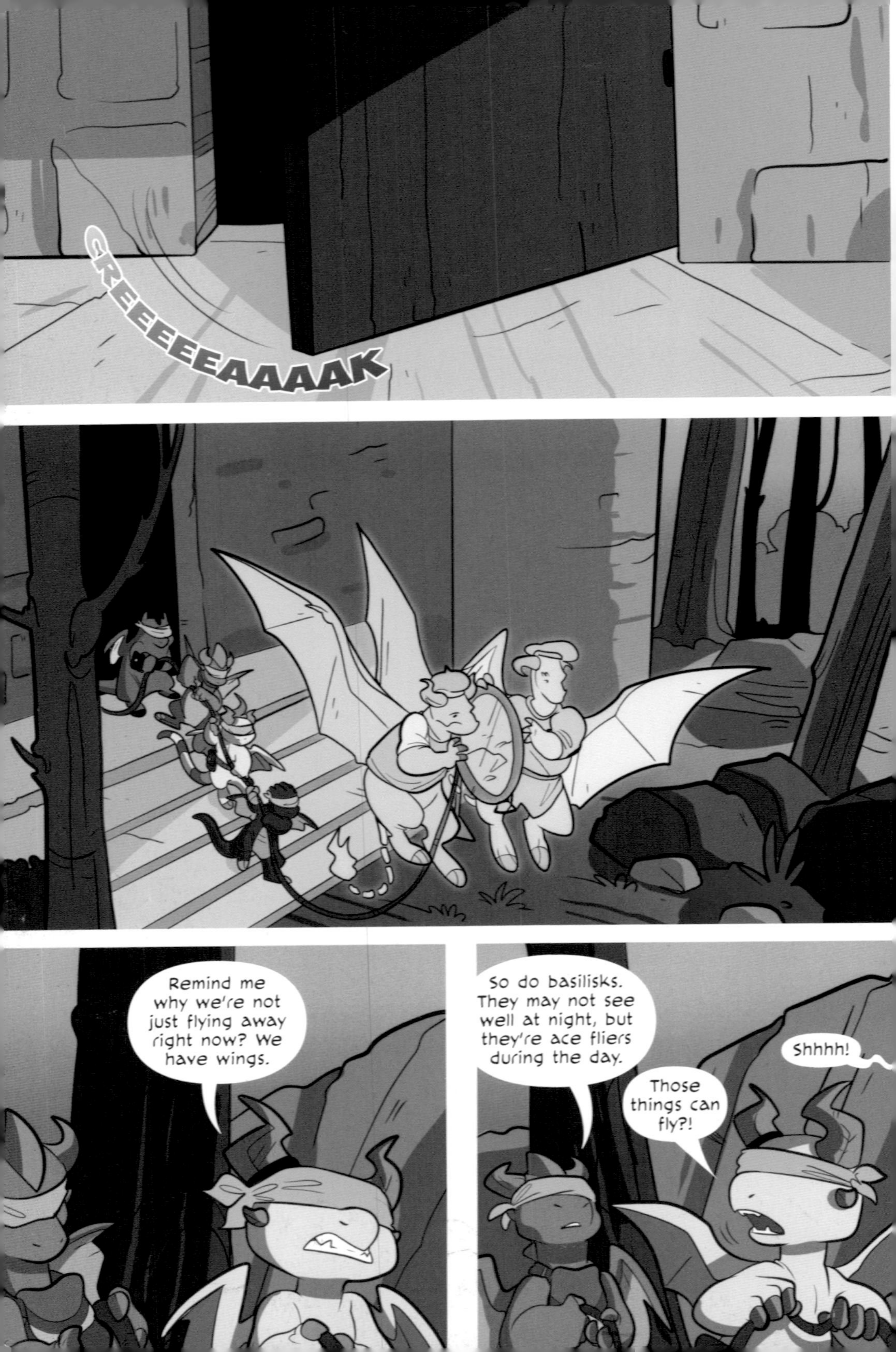
CREEEEEEAAAAAK
Remind me why we're not just flying away right now? We have wings.
So do basilisks. They may not see well at night, but they're ace fliers during the day.
Those things can fly?!
Shhhh!

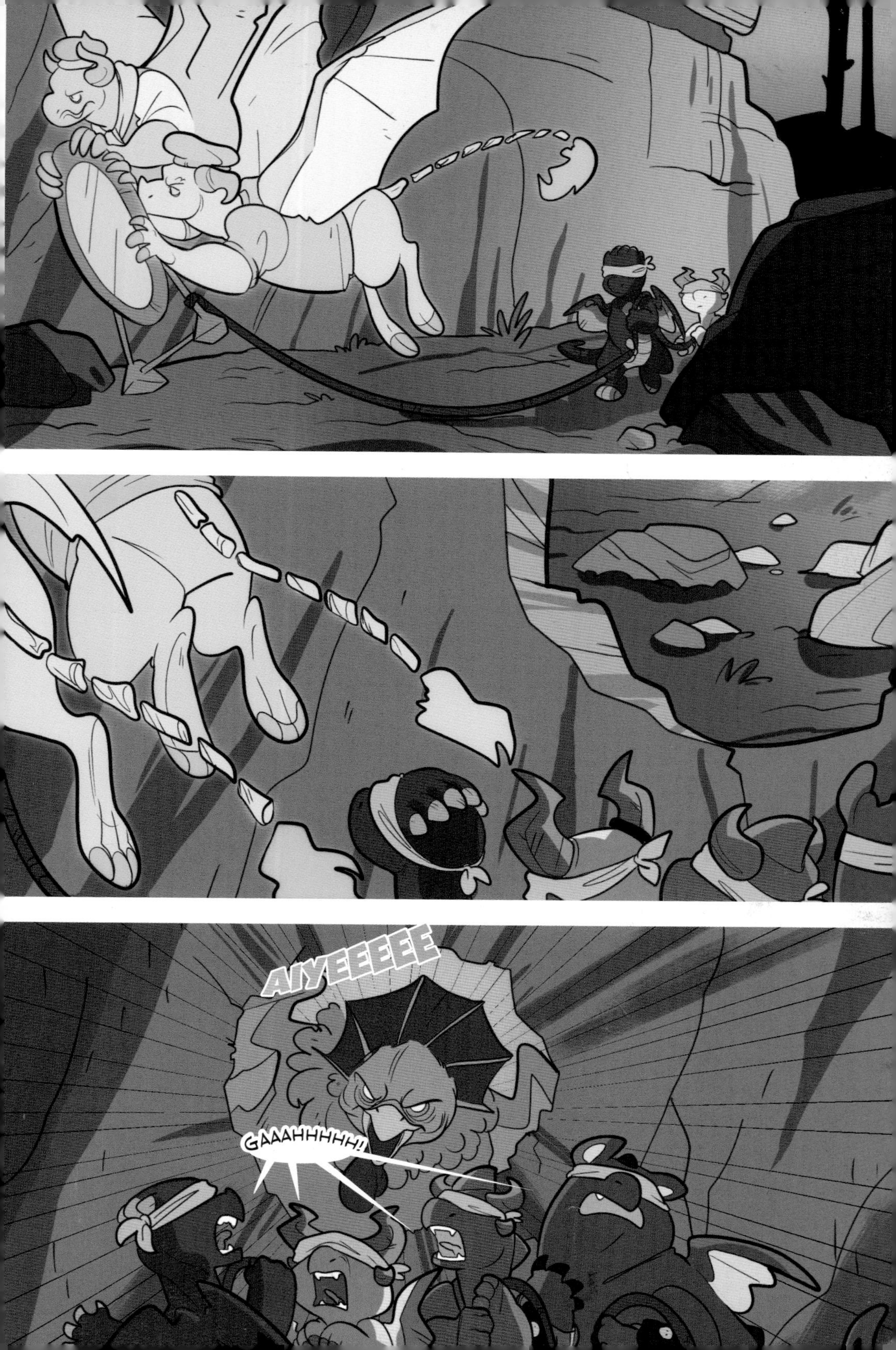
AIYEEEEE
GAAAHHHHH!

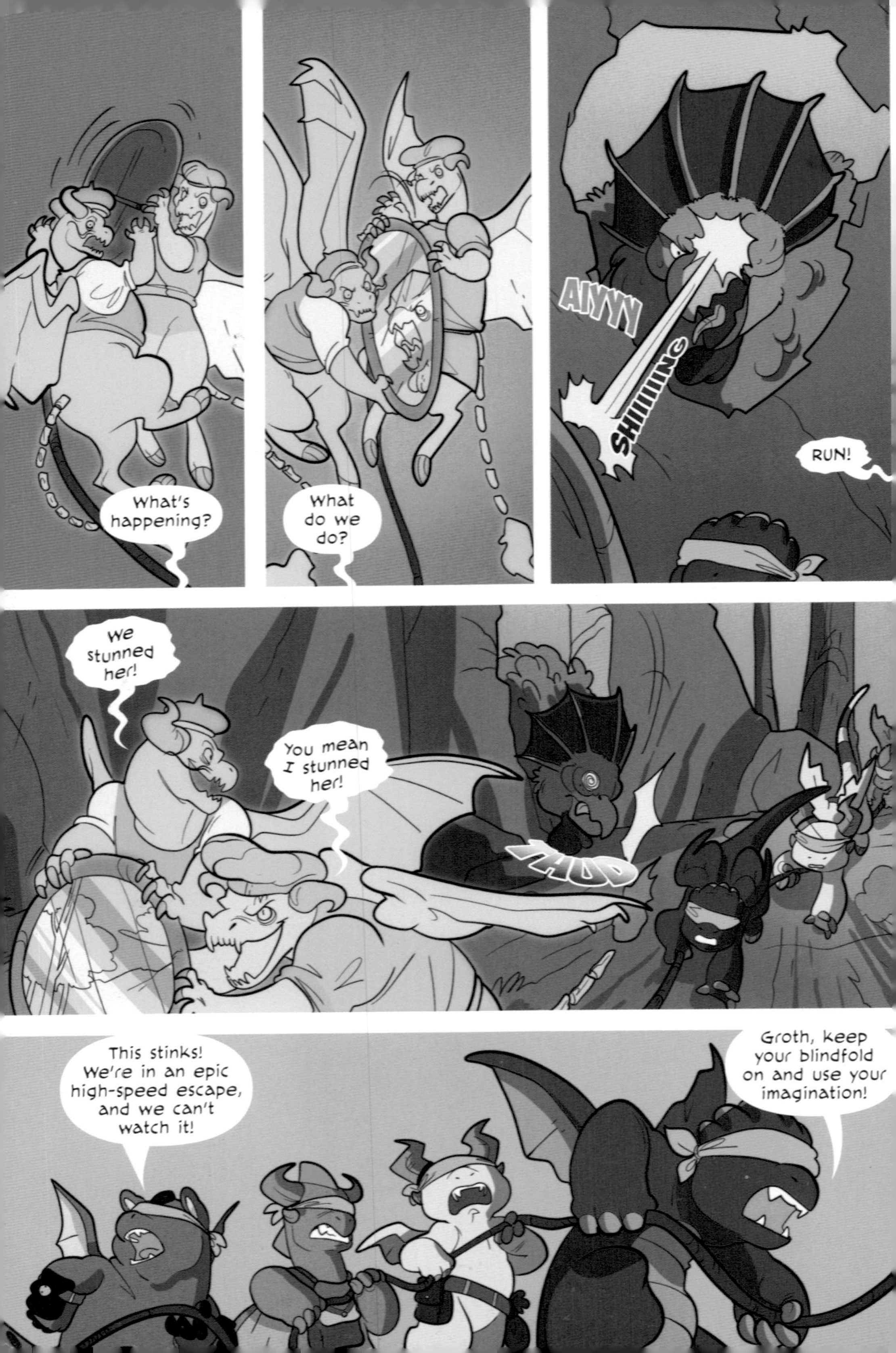
What's happening?
What do we do?
AIYYN
SHIIIIIIING
RUN!
We stunned her!
You mean I stunned her!
THUD
This stinks! We're in an epic high-speed escape, and we can't watch it!
Groth, keep your blindfold on and use your imagination!

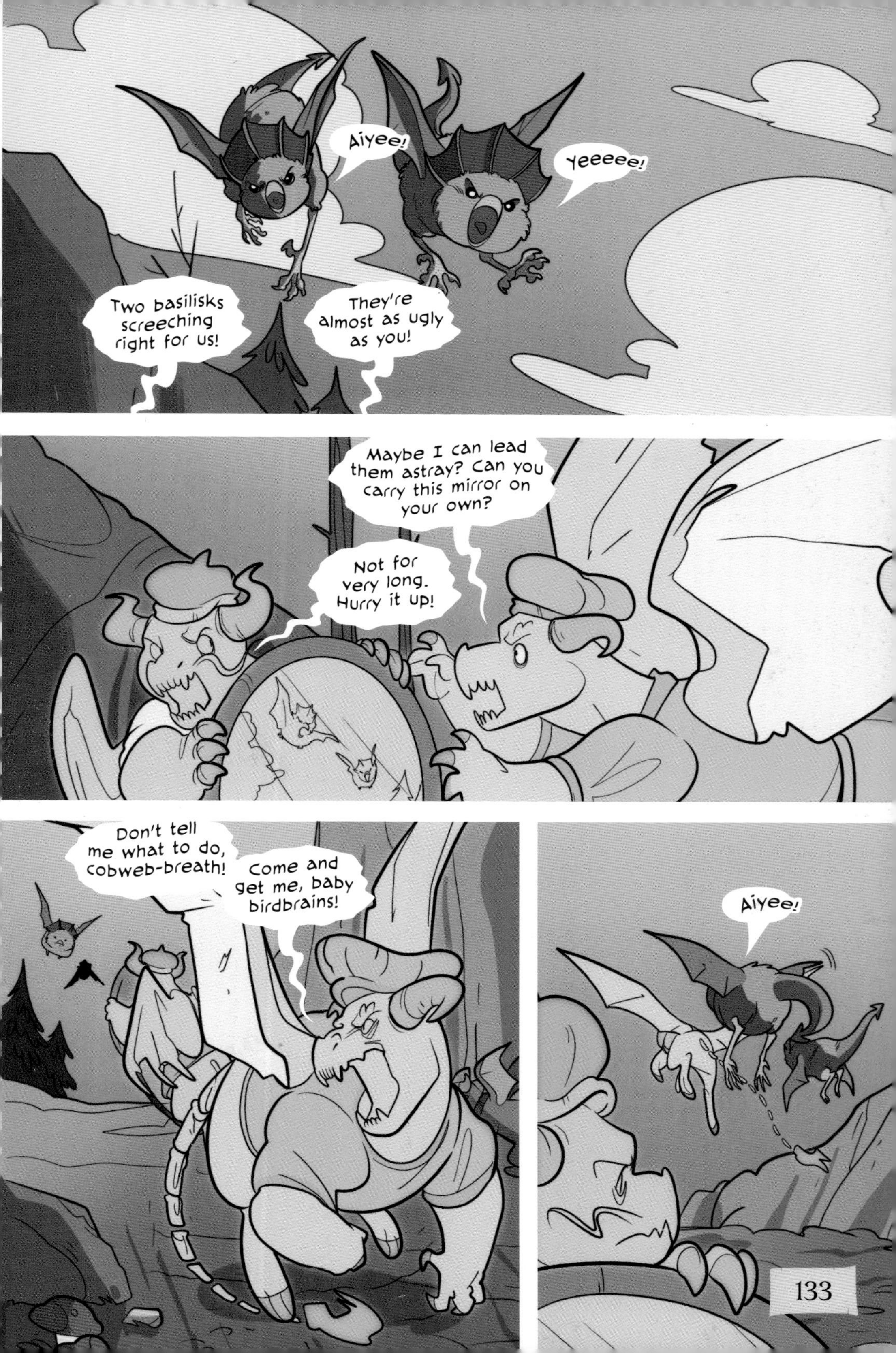
Aiyee!
Yeeeee!
Two basilisks screeching right for us!
They're almost as ugly as you!
Maybe I can lead them astray? Can you carry this mirror on your own?
Not for very long. Hurry it up!
Don't tell me what to do, cobweb-breath!
Come and get me, baby birdbrains!
Aiyee!

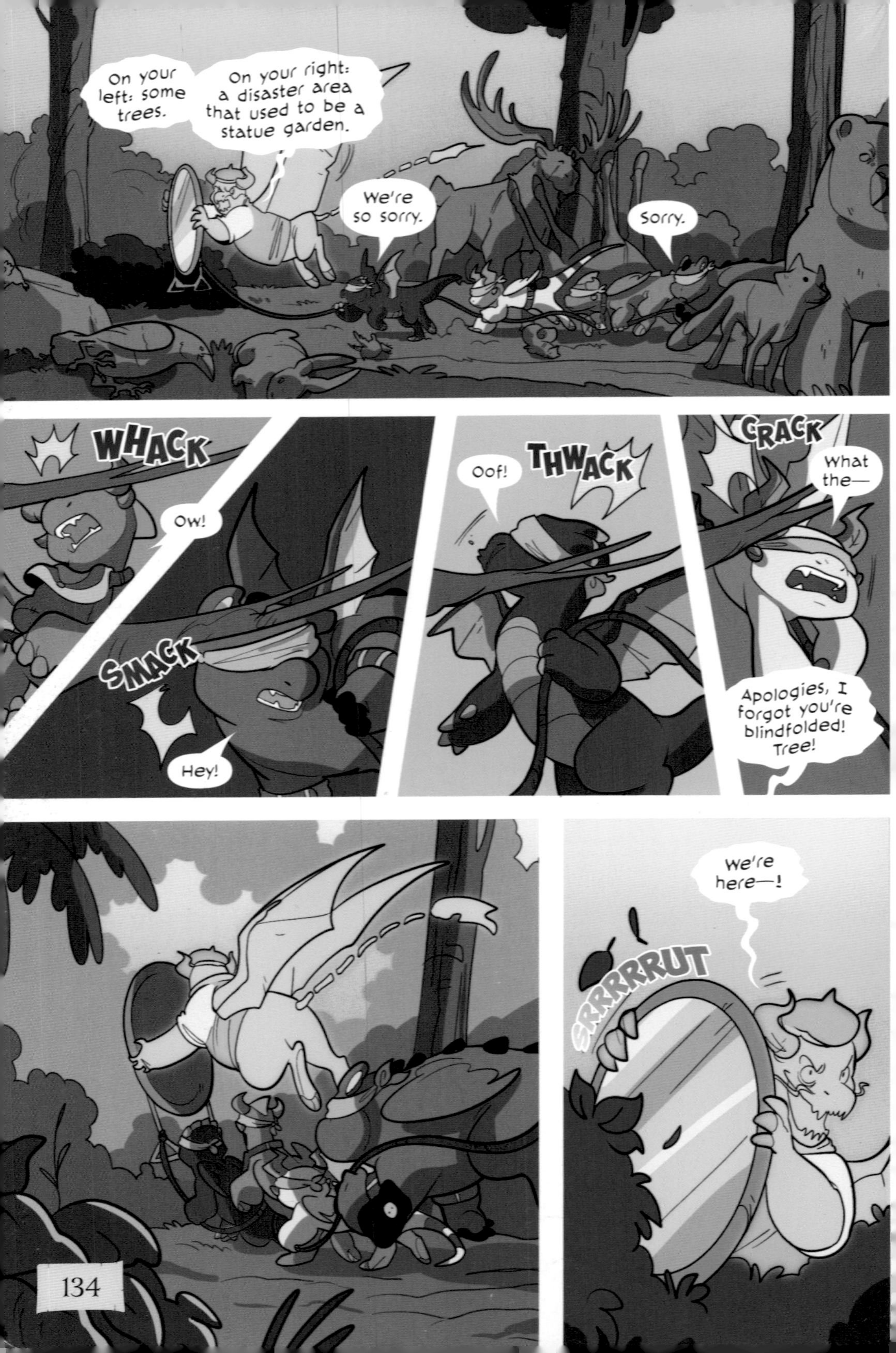
On your left: some trees.
On your right: a disaster area that used to be a statue garden.
We're so sorry.
Sorry.
WHACK
Ow!
SMACK
Hey!
Oof!
THWACK
CRACK
What the—
Apologies, I forgot you're blindfolded! Tree!
We're here—!
!
SRRRRRUT

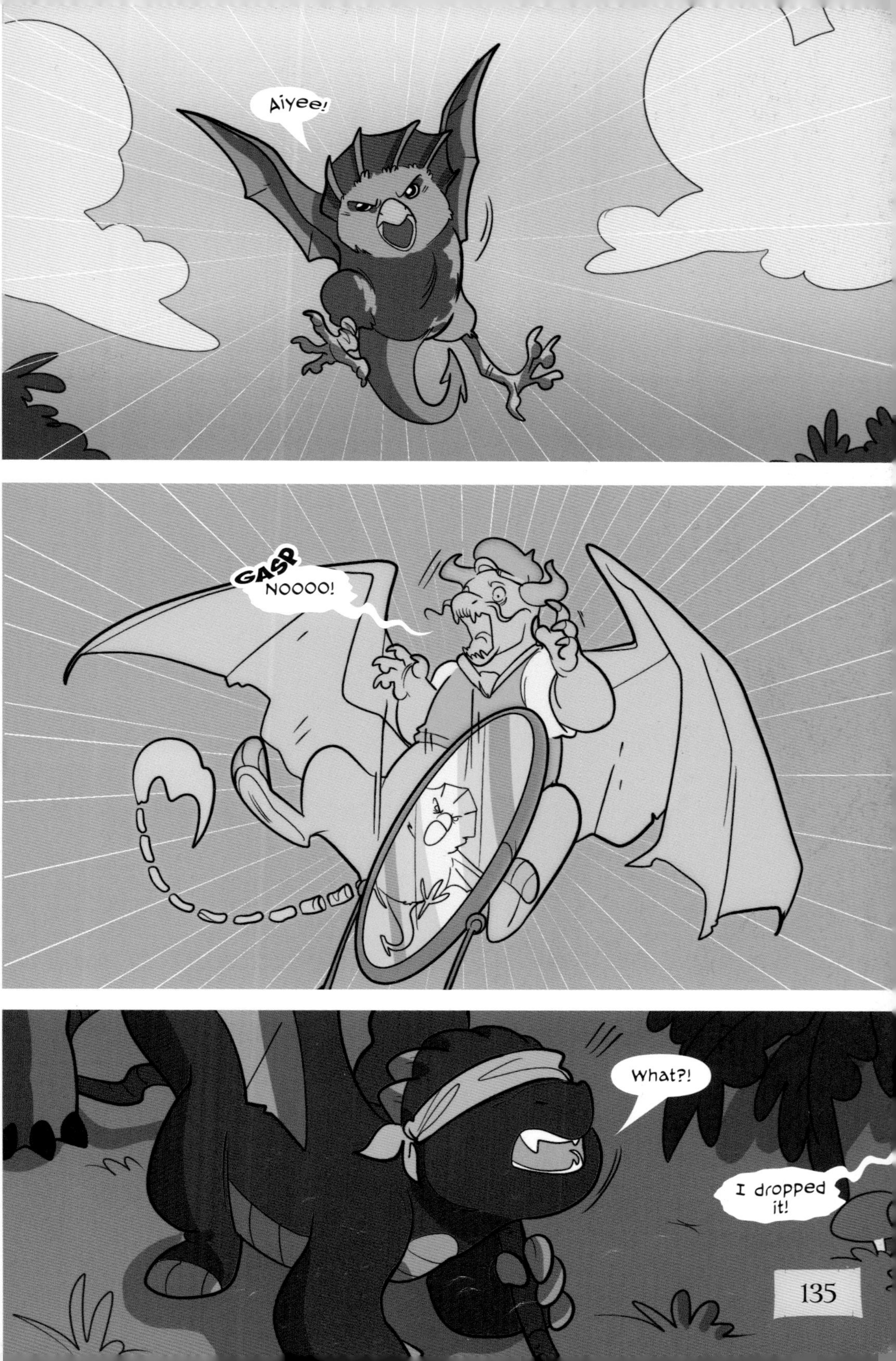
Aiyee!
GASP
NOOOO!
What?!
I dropped it!

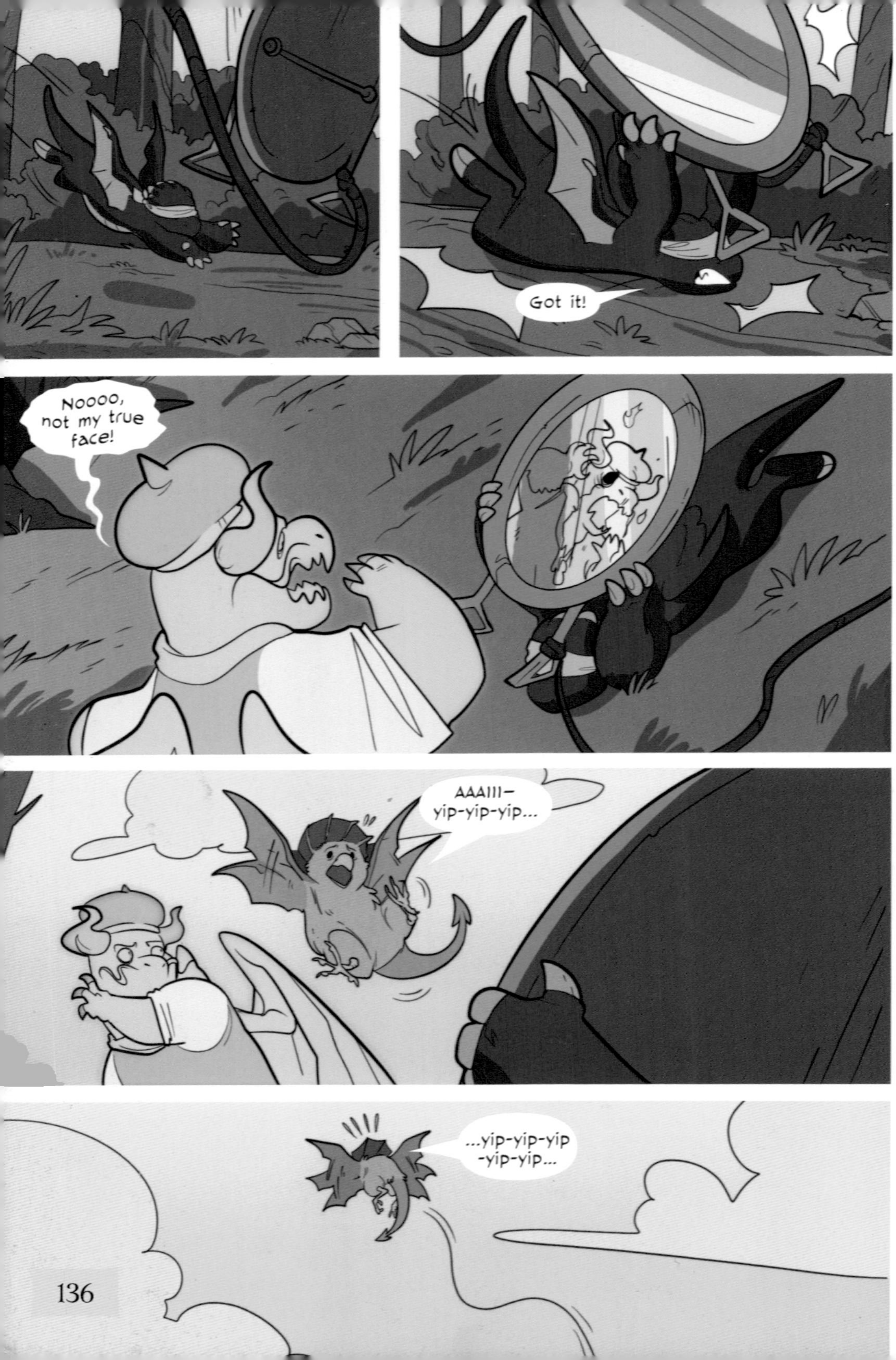
Got it!
Noooo, not my true face!
AAAIII— yip-yip-yip...
...yip-yip-yip -yip-yip...

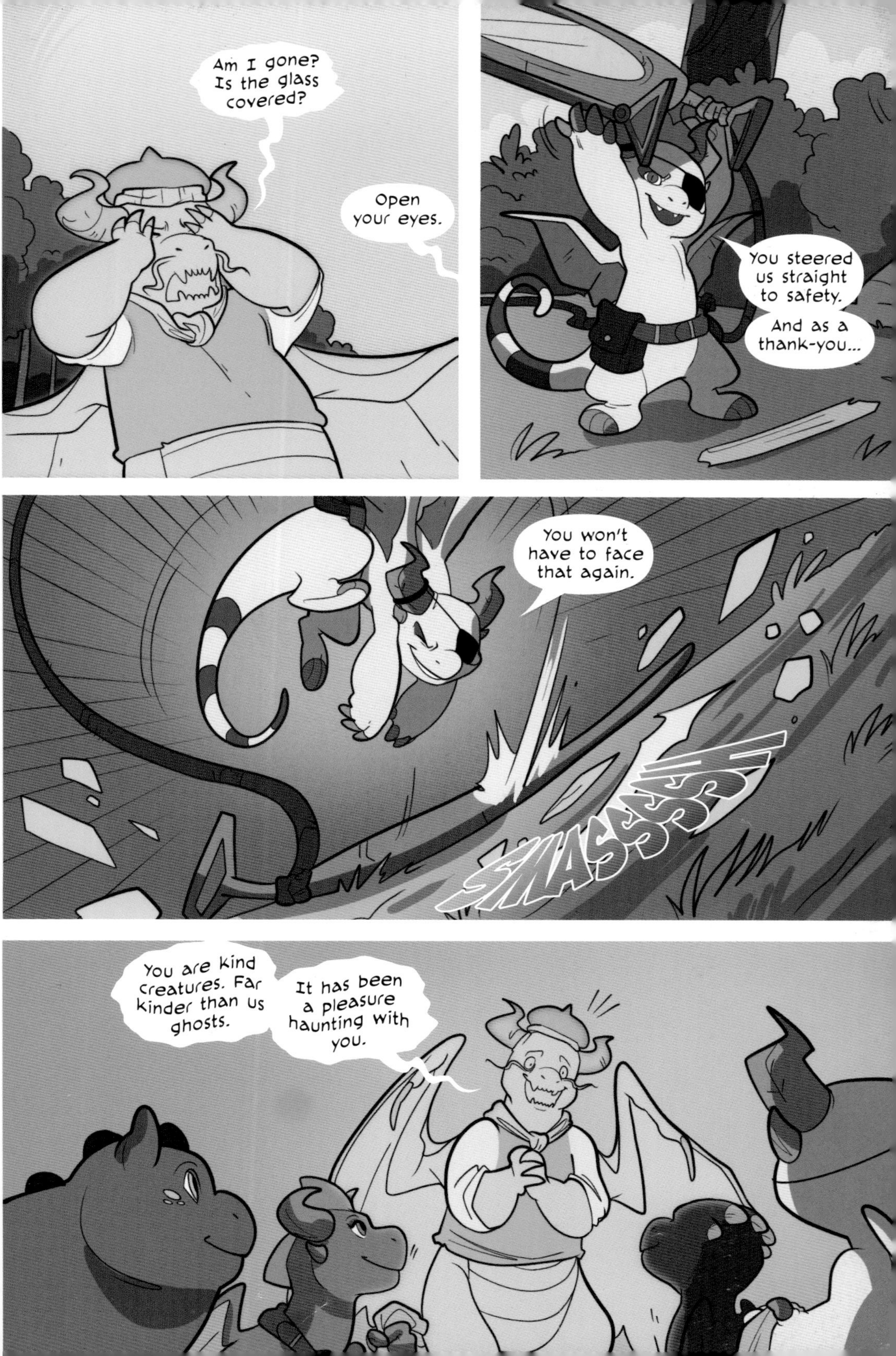
Am I gone? Is the glass covered?
Open your eyes.
You steered us straight to safety.
And as a thank-you...
You won't have to face that again.
SMASSSSH
You are kind creatures. Far kinder than us ghosts.
It has been a pleasure haunting with you.

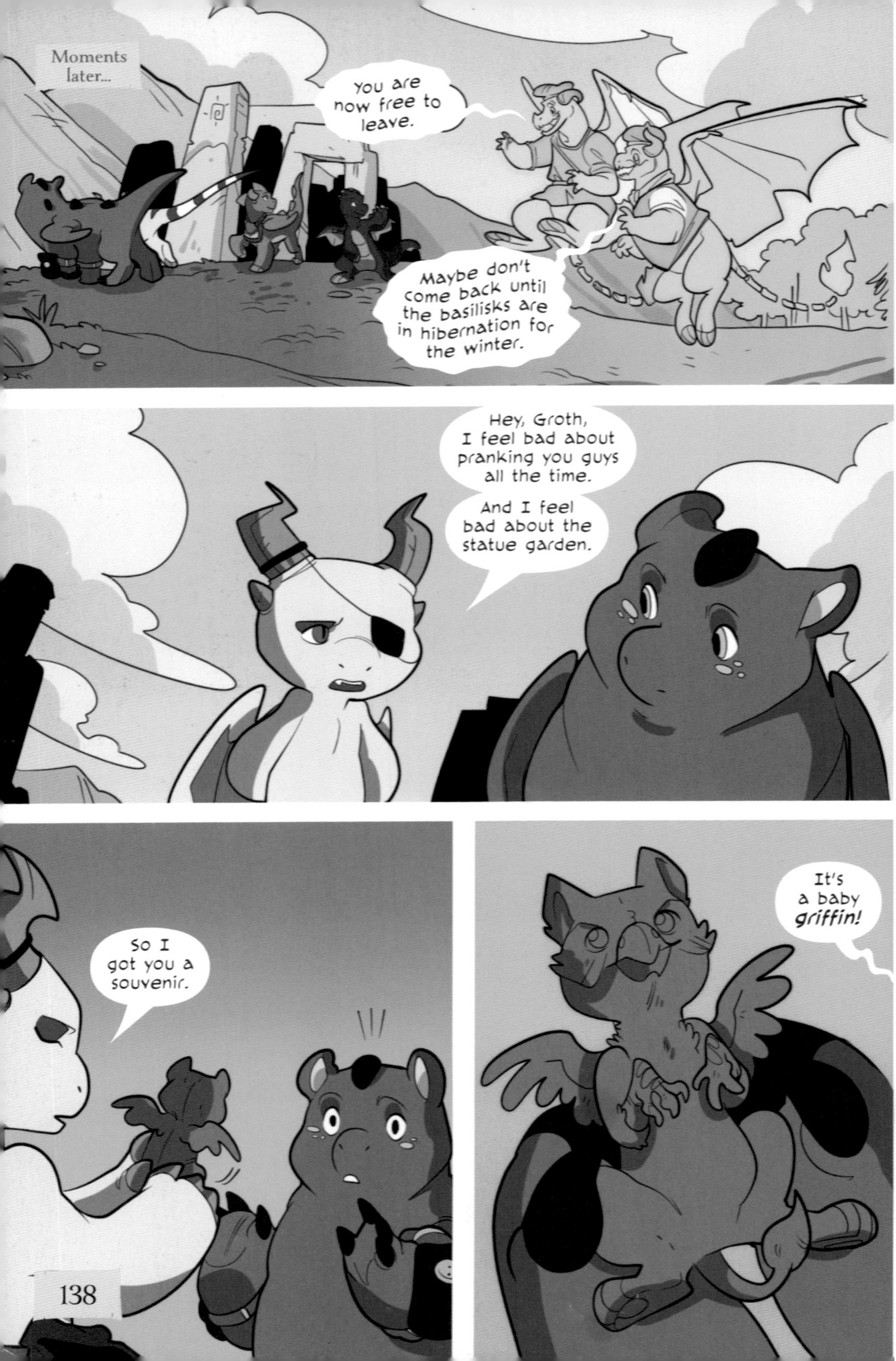
Moments later...
You are now free to leave.
Maybe don't come back until the basilisks are in hibernation for the winter.
Hey, Groth, I feel bad about pranking you guys all the time.
And I feel bad about the statue garden.
So I got you a souvenir.
It's a baby *griffin!*

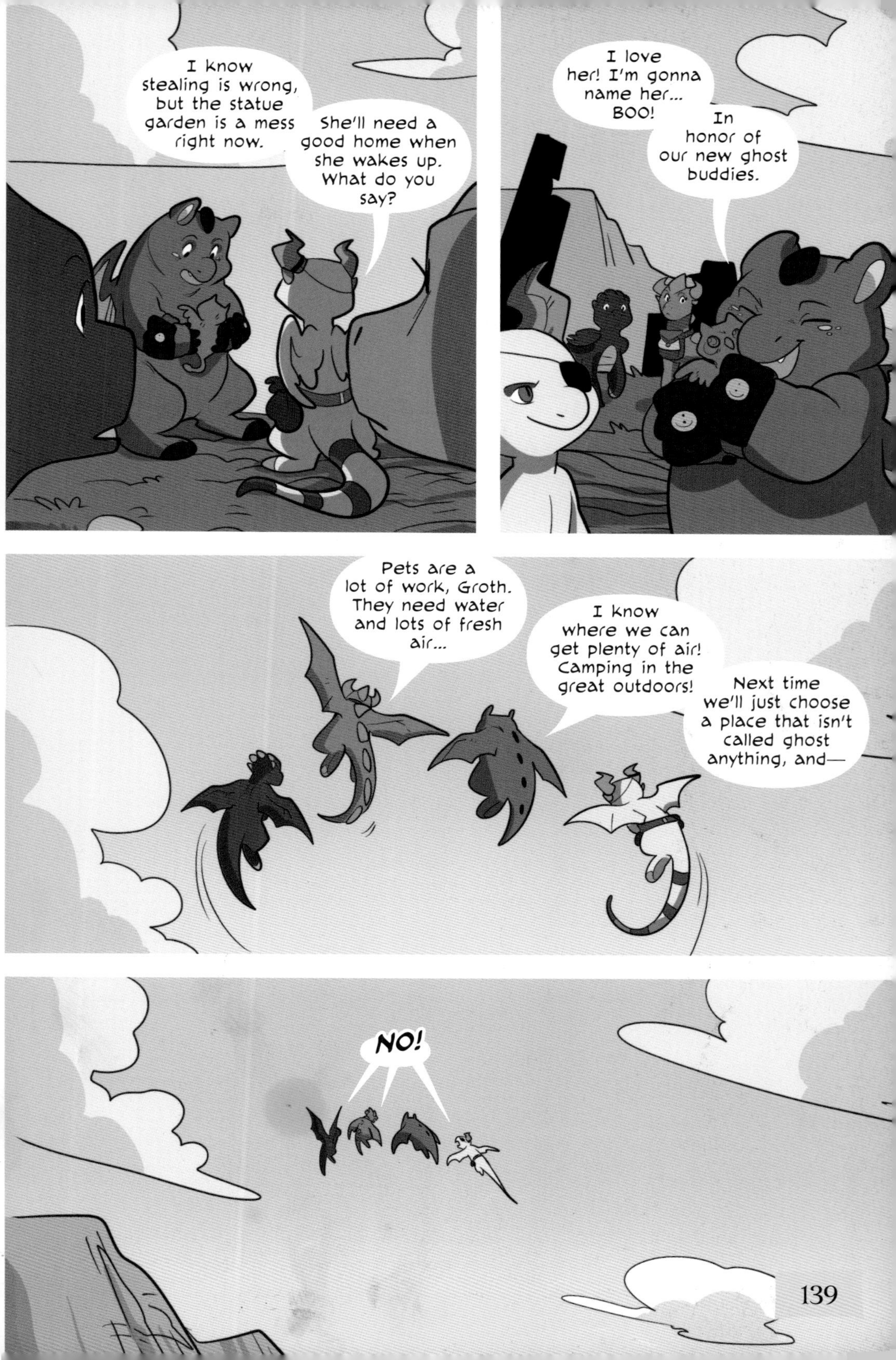
I know stealing is wrong, but the statue garden is a mess right now.
She'll need a good home when she wakes up. What do you say?
I love her! I'm gonna name her... BOO!
In honor of our new ghost buddies.
Pets are a lot of work, Groth. They need water and lots of fresh air...
I know where we can get plenty of air! Camping in the great outdoors!
Next time we'll just choose a place that isn't called ghost anything, and—
NO!

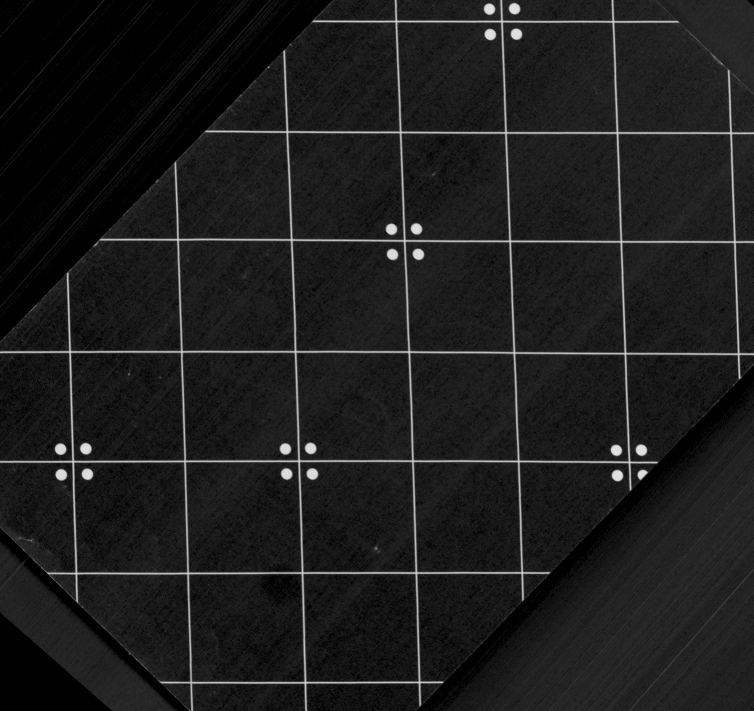

What's in store for Ruskin and his friends next? Find out in . . .

Graphic Novel
DRAGON KINGDOM
of Wrenly
INFERNO NEW YEAR

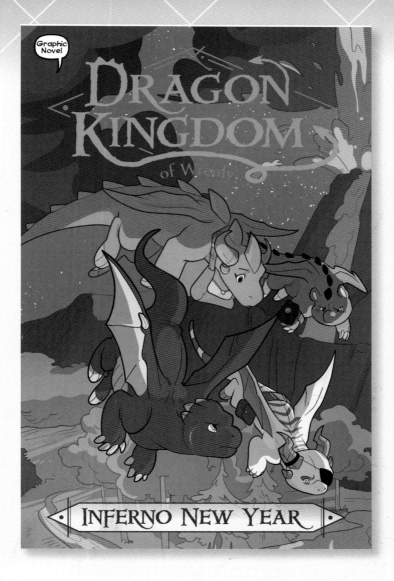

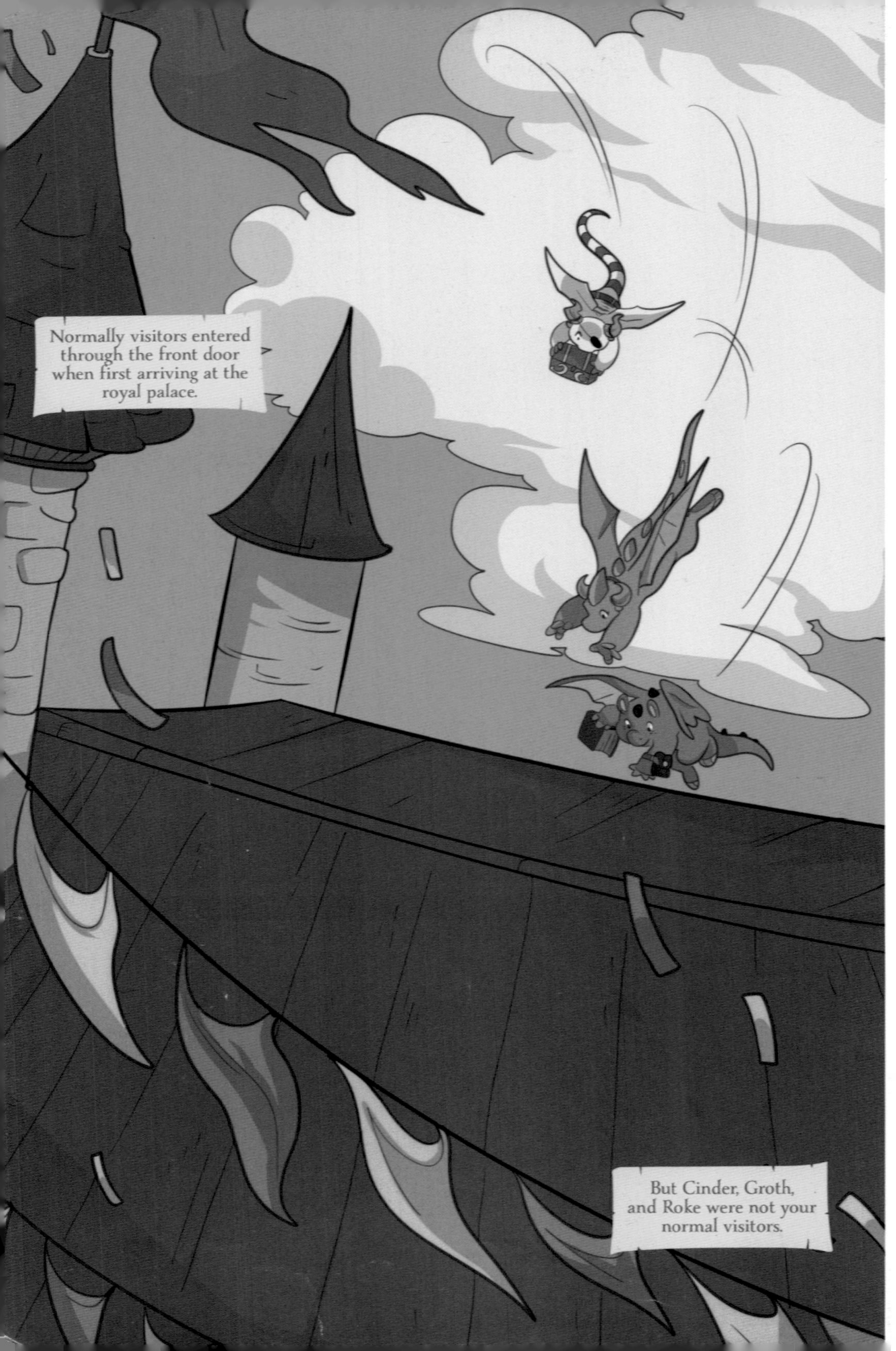
Normally visitors entered through the front door when first arriving at the royal palace.
But Cinder, Groth, and Roke were not your normal visitors.

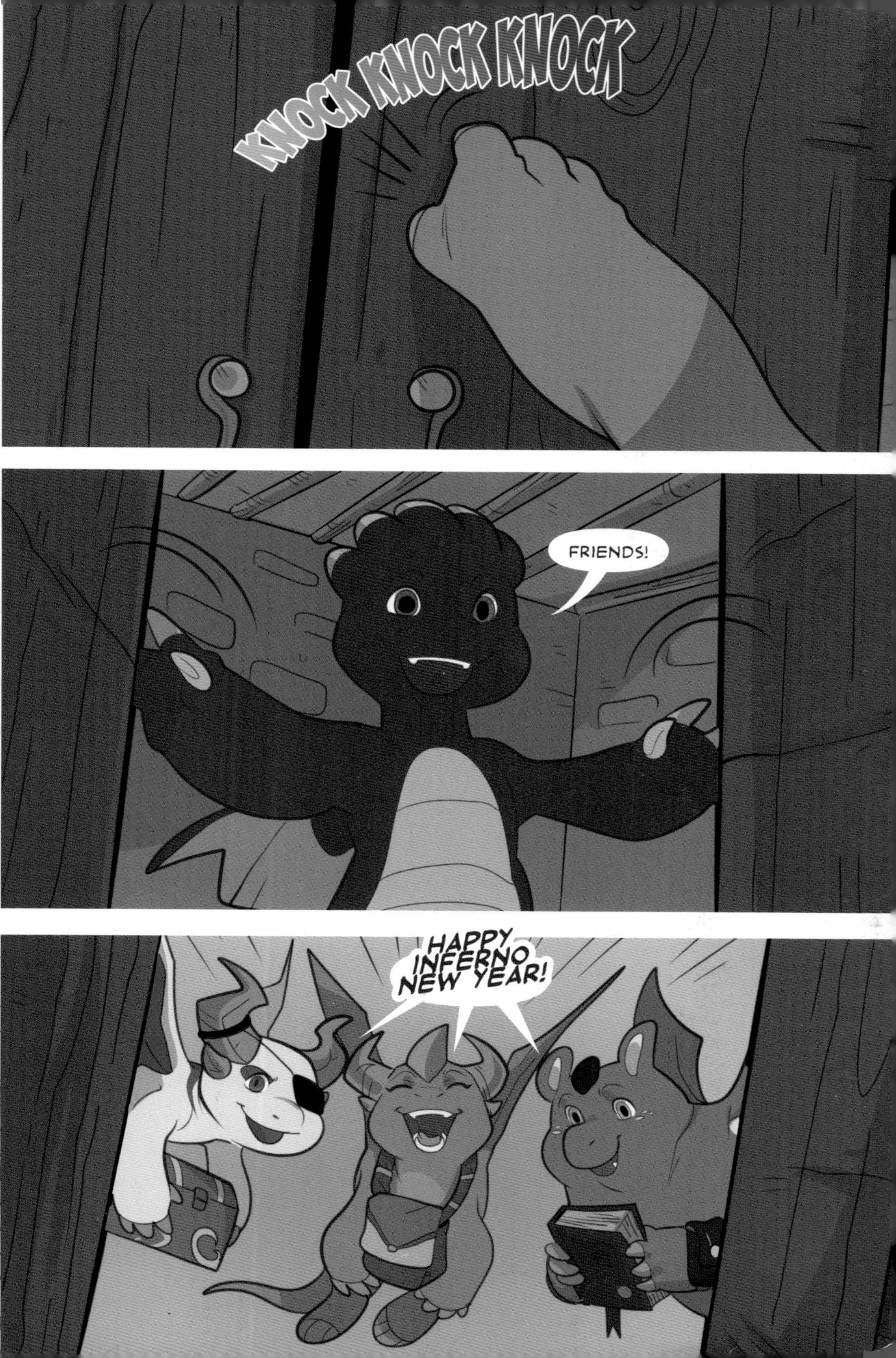
KNOCK KNOCK KNOCK
FRIENDS!
HAPPY INFERNO NEW YEAR!

5